THE
OBSOLETES

THE
OBSOLETES

A Novel

SIMEON MILLS

**SKYBOUND
BOOKS**

ATRIA

New York   London   Toronto   Sydney   New Delhi

SKYBOUND BOOKS
BOOKS
ATRIA

An Imprint of Simon & Schuster, Inc.
1230 Avenue of the Americas
New York, NY 10020

First Skybound Books/Atria Books hardcover edition May 2019

SKYBOUND BOOKS / ATRIA BOOKS and colophon
are trademarks of Simon & Schuster, Inc.

For information about special discounts for bulk purchases, please contact Simon & Schuster Special Sales at 1-866-506-1949 or business@simonandschuster.com.

The Simon & Schuster Speakers Bureau can bring authors to your live event. For more information or to book an event, contact the Simon & Schuster Speakers Bureau at 1-866-248-3049 or visit our website at www.simonspeakers.com.

Interior design by Laura Levatino

Manufactured in the United States of America

10 9 8 7 6 5 4 3 2 1

Library of Congress Cataloging-in-Publication Data

Names: Mills, Simeon, author.
Title: The obsoletes : a novel / Simeon Mills.
Description: New York : Skybound Books, 2019.
Identifiers: LCCN 2018046484 (print) | LCCN 2018048851 (ebook) |
  ISBN 9781501198359 (ebook) | ISBN 9781501198335 (hardback)
Subjects: | BISAC: FICTION / Science Fiction / General. | FICTION /
  Alternative History. | GSAFD: Science fiction.
Classification: LCC PS3613.I56985 (ebook) | LCC PS3613.I56985 O27 2019
  (print) | DDC 813/.6—dc23
LC record available at https://lccn.loc.gov/2018046484

ISBN 978-1-5011-9833-5
ISBN 978-1-5011-9835-9 (ebook)

For my brother

THE
OBSOLETES

1

OUR BUS DRIVER WAS A ROBOT. Ask any kid on Bus 117. Not that any of them had *for sure* seen a real robot before Mrs. Stover. (That they knew about, anyway.) But that didn't stop them from whispering a mountain of evidence against her.

"She doesn't eat. Not even the day after Halloween when I gave her a Twix just to see if she'd eat it. She didn't."

"Mrs. Stover drinks too much coffee, just like a robot."

"And her hair. It's wires. It just sits up there."

"I heard robots eat cigarettes. Her breath smells like my grandma's house."

"Her glasses are too big for a human."

"Has anyone ever seen her *out* of her bus seat? Because it's like . . . it's like she's *connected* to the bus, like they're two parts of the same big . . . *machine*."

"And Magic Johnson."

"Magic Johnson."

"I was about to say Magic Johnson."

It was true. Mrs. Stover had a computerlike obsession with Magic Johnson, sworn enemy of our favorite team, the Detroit Pistons. All of Mrs. Stover's clothes were Lakers purple. (One poor kid even saw a purple bra strap once.) She had pictures of Magic tucked into the leather sun visor above her seat. Lakers earrings. Lakers fingernail polish. A Lakers thermos. There was a price of admission for boarding Mrs. Stover's bus: tell her a fact about Magic Johnson. Some kids gave the same answer every day: "He wears purple." That was enough. Those kids could sit wherever they wanted. But if you were a new kid? If you stepped onto her bus and knew nothing about Magic Johnson? You had to sit directly behind Mrs. Stover for the duration of the ride. You had to listen— scratch that: the *entire bus* had to listen to Mrs. Stover's booming voice announcing highlights from the previous night's Lakers game or, if it was the off-season, endless trivia about Magic Johnson in frantic shouts: "GREW UP DOWN THE ROAD IN LANSING."

A short pause.

"LED MICHIGAN STATE TO ITS FIRST NATIONAL CHAMPI- ONSHIP." Kids held their breath, wincing. "FINALS MVP HIS ROOKIE SEASON . . ."

James Botty was the first to realize she was a robot. Surprisingly, the tell had nothing to do with Magic Johnson. Instead, James pointed out the writing on the back of Mrs. Stover's shoes. It was in a foreign language— an entirely foreign alphabet. We all snuck peeks at the front of the bus, where Mrs. Stover's shoes worked the pedals. There was the writing, easy to confirm yet impossible to explain: 会談する. "Robots are built with parts from other countries," James whispered. "Countries like China."

Everyone gasped: *China.*

That discovery had occurred in the first week of fourth grade. It was 1986. By the following spring, *Mrs. Stover is a robot* had yet to be replaced on our bus by anything even half as interesting to talk about. New theories and observations sprang up daily to be debated, scrutinized, and—if validated by James Botty, our official robot expert—formally recorded in Molly Seed's spiral notebook. Molly sat with James in the back of the bus. She was his vice president and secretary all in one. Molly's notebook contained every scrap of evidence against Mrs. Stover, page after page written in superb handwriting, flawless even by girl standards. She guarded the notebook with her life; James was the only other person permitted to hold it.

To Molly, the rumor about Mrs. Stover went beyond gossip. There was an inevitable conclusion, a purpose to her methodical data collection: on the last day of school, she and James would submit their findings to the principal. Mrs. Stover would be deemed "obsolete" for failing to hide her robotic identity, and, per the informal agreement between the robotics companies and the general public, Mrs. Stover's life would be forfeit. She would be destroyed. Immediately. The best part was that *anyone* could annihilate an obsolete robot. It was first come, first served, and the kids on Bus 117 had some original ideas. As the last day of school approached, killing our bus driver was all anyone talked about.

"We'll buy a bazooka and fill it with dynamite. Then we'll handcuff Mrs. Stover to the back of the bus. Then we'll—"

"This is serious, you guys," Molly whispered. She had no patience for methods that were silly or fun. She was ruthless. A professional. Her tiny glasses, tiny nose, and general overall smallness only added to the effect. While James Botty was fascinated by robots, Molly Seed simply hated them. She was a robophobe to her core.

For whatever reason, my twin brother, Kanga, was in love with Molly Seed.

●●●

Fourth grade was a do-or-die year for Kanga and me. That spring, our parents actually *did* turn obsolete and vanish. One morning they were here, moving about our apartment in routine fashion: watching TV, drinking coffee, wiping grease from their armpits, waving good-bye as we left for the bus stop.

When we got home that afternoon, they were gone.

Kanga and I stood in the living room, which was suddenly huge with neither Mom nor Dad in it. Their possessions remained throughout the apartment, but in place of their bodies was the faint odor of sawdust. My central processor was overloaded, and I made the error of offering my brother a *logical* explanation for our parents' sudden disappearance: "Mom and Dad must have realized they were obsolete. I mean, they were programmed to raise us, but now that's over. We don't need them anymore. So I bet they just stopped whatever they were doing, got into Dad's van, and drove to Detroit, to the address in the back of *The Directions* where obsolete robots are supposed to go. Maybe it's a laboratory. Maybe it's just a dump—"

"Don't say that!" Kanga plugged his ears with his thumbs. "Mom and Dad aren't in a dump. And they would never just leave us. Somebody—" He spun around and ran into the kitchenette, as if Mom might be hiding there. Then he darted into Mom and Dad's bedroom. "Somebody must've kidnapped them. Somebody's got them in their basement all chained up. We gotta save them, Darryl!"

It's important to note that Kanga and I were *not* identical twins. I was taller by an inch; he had a widow's peak. My wrists were a constellation of freckles; Kanga had twin birthmarks on each shoulder. And, not to put too fine a point on it: I was the good robot, and Kanga was . . . let's say "uniquely programmed." While *I* fully understood that our existence was the result of a grand social experiment that required us to covertly navigate our environment—to interact with our human peers *just enough* to appear human ourselves, to speak sentences to them (but only after having listened to one hundred sentences spoken *by* them), and, above all else, to *avoid detection*—Kanga simply believed he was human.

My brother's denial was Mom's fault. She never mentioned the word *robot* in his presence because Kanga's eyelids would malfunction at the acknowledgment of what we really were. So she just stopped doing it. Mom still got Kanga to *do* everything normal robots did: drink lots of fluids, insert a food receptacle before eating, plug his fingers into an outlet every night, etc. But she acted like every family in our apartment building was doing that too. She probably convinced herself that Kanga's existential delusion was somehow an asset to his survival.

She loved him, after all.

But now Mom was gone, and Dad along with her. *I* was the new mom, and if I was going to persuade Kanga to accept that he was a robot, it wouldn't happen overnight.

"Look around," I said the day Mom and Dad disappeared. "Do you see any signs of struggle here? They weren't kidnapped, Kanga. They left on their own. Obsolescence . . ." I had to choose my words carefully. "Obsolescence happens to all parents. It's part of life. Mom and Dad did a fantastic job raising us, but that job is over. They're retired. Haven't they earned it? I'm sure they still love us, wherever they are."

Kanga crossed his arms. "I'm going to find them."

"Look." My patience was gone. "Obsolescence is forever, Kanga. We don't need Mom and Dad anymore. They don't need us. Besides, obsolete people are a danger to themselves and everybody around them. It's spelled out very clearly in *The Directions*, on page 593. Do I need to read that section to you?"

"No."

"Because I can. Our copy of *The Directions* is right over—"

"Don't. Please."

I was playing dirty. *The Directions* was a how-to guide for being a robot—specifically, for being us, a pair of Detroit 600s (and our parents, but they were mere 400-series models). I read it to understand my strengths and weaknesses, my capabilities and functions. Kanga avoided it for the same reasons. Reading it to us, Mom had always substituted the word *person* for *robot*, a practice I shamefully continued after she'd left. If nothing else, *The Directions* was a tool to get Kanga in line. A threat. And maybe somewhere deep in his processor he was listening, putting together the pieces of just how different we were from everybody else.

But even Kanga had to realize that Mom and Dad were dreadfully obsolete. Don't get me wrong—I "loved" them, as I was programmed to do. But our parents were designed for a single purpose: to see Kanga and myself safely through our early years. They did an admirable job. We survived. Dad didn't run us over with his van (though he once squished the toe of Kanga's sneaker). Mom did the best she could with a battery that seemed to be perpetually drained. That was their main problem. Fully charged with electricity, Mom and Dad were thoughtful, caring parents. But this optimization lasted only about forty-five minutes. After that, their efficacy declined steeply. It was sad. Mom's vocabulary would shrink to a tiny list of dialogue options, restricting her to only certain public interactions. The gas station, the liquor store, the library—and even those exchanges were embarrassing to witness. When her battery was low, Mom used to go to the pond at the park with a loaf of bread and leave us in the car while she fed the ducks.

Sometimes I would find her slumped next to a power outlet at home, cross-eyed, her fingers twitching against the floor, as if she'd forgotten how to plug them in and recharge. I would have to lift Mom's fingers to the outlet and jam them in until the juice started flowing. Still, she made a point to read us bedtime stories every night. But should a one-year-old have to correct his mother on the pronunciation of the word *caboose*?

I was ready for them to hit the road by second grade. I had learned everything I could from them (which was not much), and by then they were just getting in the way. Their outdated, porous bodies left streaks of grease on everything they touched. When we sat at the kitchenette counter for "dinner," Mom had only one question she could think to ask: "How was school, honeys?"

"Well," I would respond, "it was an interesting day, Mom. Last night the school got infested with giant flesh-eating moles. They killed our custodian. The principal told every kid to bring a hammer to school tomorrow for protection. Or a butcher knife, if we have one."

Mom would just smile and nod. "That's nice, honey."

I would turn to Dad. "Do we have a butcher knife, Dad? For school? A really sharp one?"

Dad would take a long sip from the keg of beer he carried with him around the apartment. "Ask your mother."

Kanga would give me a kick to the shin.

If you asked my brother what was so great about our parents, he would probably say watching TV with them on the couch, making a place for himself in the tangled bird's nest of their legs. I'd be sitting on the floor, trying to watch TV too, until I'd get so annoyed by his giggling that I would hide behind the orange chair and practice holding my basketball in the triple-threat position. I was already a master of this two-handed grip on the ball, from which I could, theoretically, shoot, pass, or dribble. Not that I had obtained any of *those* skills yet. But I would eventually.

I was the basketball kid. That's what Mrs. Stover called me, because I boarded her bus every morning holding my basketball in the triple-threat position. "HEY, BASKETBALL KID," she would say. "I HEARD MAGIC JOHNSON DRIBBLED HIS BASKETBALL TO AND FROM SCHOOL EVERY DAY LIKE IT WAS HIS RELIGION." *Dribbling.* I would get there. At least Mrs. Stover seemed to think I could. That said, I still saw myself as the Pistons' own Isiah Thomas instead of Magic. Isiah was just six one, a much more attainable height, practically speaking, than Magic's six nine. Not that I would complain if I got those extra eight inches. Becoming Magic Johnson was a decent backup plan.

Mom and Dad were a different story. Mom's default response to seeing me in the triple-threat position was limited to "Share it with your brother," even though my basketball had been a birthday gift for me alone. But *passing* was a skill I would need to master, so I'd toss it to Kanga, and he'd shoot it at something. Anything. There were ball marks all over the walls and ceiling. The ball would smash against the microwave, the coffee maker, a light fixture. Kanga would raise his arms triumphantly and holler *Yes!* no matter what happened. Mom would say, "Outside! Both of you!"

Dad would cock an eyebrow at her. "You see the arm on that kid?"

Thanks to Mrs. Stover's encouragement, I mostly practiced my dribbling. By the end of fourth grade I could dribble for 8.1 seconds without losing control of the ball. Not that Mom or Dad ever noticed, when they were around, except to say, "No dribbling in the living room!"

The problem with our parents becoming obsolete and vanishing like they did was that Mom had convinced Kanga we were all some kind of "family"; but *The Directions* included just one chapter on upkeep for Mom and Dad, while the other 1,200-plus pages were about maintenance for us.

Mechanically speaking, Kanga and I were from a different planet than Mom and Dad. Our newer bodies had been designed to evolve over time, to grow and mature. Inside Kanga and me was a factory's worth of high-test plastic components, onto which molecularly precise amounts of chemicals were time-released, causing our synthetic bones, muscles, and skin to expand at the exact growth rate of a typical human boy. Mom and Dad were made of stock fiberglass. Nothing about them ever changed.

The day they disappeared was the best day of my life.

But it was also when Kanga fell into odd behavior. It's endlessly repeated in *The Directions* to never put food in your mouth, much less swallow any. I'd mastered that rule as an infant. But two days after Mom and Dad's disappearance, as we climbed aboard Mrs. Stover's bus, she held out a basket of candy and said, "TRIPLE-DOUBLE LAST NIGHT." It was nearly spring break, and by then we knew a triple-double meant Magic Johnson had tallied at least ten points, ten rebounds, and ten assists. We politely accepted our candy and stuffed it into our pockets for "later." That's what *I* did. Kanga unwrapped his and placed it in his mouth. "T'ank 'ou," he rasped as the watermelon cube plugged his fluids valve. I escorted him to our seat—Kanga by the window, me on the aisle. I was so disgusted I could hardly look at him: my brother trying to stick his whole hand down his throat to retrieve the candy. He couldn't. It was still there at recess. That's when I pulled him behind a dumpster and jimmied the candy out with a ruler. The thing was eight and a half inches down there. Idiot.

Not that my own behavior was beyond criticism. For instance, there was our first birthday on our own. Every year we were mailed birthday gifts from Gravy Robotics, whose address was in the back of *The Directions*. That year we got an authentic Magic Johnson uniform: "For Darryl and Kanga Livery." Clearly, we were supposed to share the uniform, but I claimed it for myself, even though I would have preferred Isiah Thomas's red-and-blue number eleven. I wore it to school for the rest of fourth grade, never allowing Kanga to even try it on. Besides, he had wanted something else entirely for our birthday. Well, *two* things. But our birthday came and went, and neither of them arrived to give him a hug.

I had to be both mom and dad to him. Thankfully, *The Directions* included a full page of parenting tips like "Smile at your child units, even when you don't want to," "Treat yourself to a date night no less than once a year," and "Be calm yet firm." I had to practically sit on Kanga's lap in Mrs. Walter's room (we had the same teacher) just to make sure he didn't swallow his art project or mention the fact that our *real* parents had abandoned us.

During spring break he refused to charge his battery, a daily requirement for robots. On the sixth day I found him collapsed on the living room floor, the TV blaring above him. "Darryl," he rasped, "I need a sip of milk."

"First we charge up."

"Do I have to?"

I lifted my twin brother by the armpits and dragged him into his bedroom. Mom had positioned his bed near an outlet so Kanga could charge up while pretending to sleep at night. Now he was too weak to even lift his fingers to the holes, so I had to do it for him.

Plugging in was a vulnerable—dare I say spiritual—procedure. To begin, a robot pressed his thumb and pointer finger together, as though pinching the handle of a very small teacup. The tips of these two digits were then inserted, with considerable force, into the vertical slots of a power outlet, the fingernails penetrating as far as possible, until the "bite" occurred—which was both thrilling and terrifying. The electricity stunned you, then sucked your fingers *farther* into the outlet as you surrendered all control of your body and mind. It was like you suddenly switched places with the wall you were attached to, peacefully entombed in a benign, sturdy flatness. That was how charging up felt to me, anyway. The disorientation lasted for only the first hour or so. After that it felt like having your fingertips glued to a wall. I usually just read *The Directions* for the remaining seven hours.

I had never seen Kanga charge up before; he always did it in his bedroom with the door closed. After I jammed his fingers into the outlet,
after the bite, I stood back and watched him: the yellow light trying to
escape from under his skin, someone else's angry twitch on his lips. But
eight hours later, Kanga yanked himself loose from the wall, good as new.
Well—as good as a grieving ten-year-old robot with an identity complex
could get.

We just needed to make it to summer.

At school, we were lucky that Mrs. Walter was neck-deep in a divorce
and had been too distracted to send Kanga to the school counselor. Not
that I could ever be truly *calm* when we were in public. Not even on the
bus. Kanga's obsession with Molly Seed had worsened. He stared at her
constantly, and the other kids had begun to notice.

● ● ●

On the morning of the last day of school, Kanga was uncharacteristically
silent as we waited for the bus. Seeing his furrowed brow and pinched lips,
I knew he was probably dwelling on Mom and Dad, and that asking him
for his thoughts would only heighten the odds of his crying on the bus. I
decided to ignore him. But as the seconds ticked away, my brother's face
grew darker and darker. Mrs. Stover pulled onto our street, and I heard
Kanga's throat constrict. *Hold it together, brother.* The bus doors swung
open, and that's when Kanga grabbed me by the shoulders. He leaned
toward me, cheeks bulging. With a violent *BLAAAH!* Kanga stuck out
his tongue, and a praying mantis crawled from the darkness of his throat.
The insect clicked its wings, shedding my brother's throat grease. I tried to
pull away, but Kanga held me close, blowing the mantis—its giant green
pinchers—directly onto my face.

I screamed.

He howled with laughter.

"MOVE YOUR KEISTERS," ordered Mrs. Stover.

My brother and I boarded her bus for our last day of fourth grade.

A few streets later, we stopped in front of Molly Seed's filthy gray house. Kanga pressed his nose against the window, eager for a glimpse of her. Nobody had mown Molly's lawn since the snow melted. There was a truck parked sideways in her driveway. But where was Molly? Mrs. Stover honked. She honked again, and finally started to pull away when Molly sleepily emerged, leaving her front door open, so Kanga got a peek into her living room: a bare white wall. Molly hugged her notebook to her chest as she walked down the aisle. By now it was filled with so much evidence that an extra forty pages had been stapled to the back cover.

Today was the big day. If they didn't chicken out, Molly and James would be submitting the notebook to the authorities by first bell. I imagined Principal Vanderlaan's glasses popping off his face as he read the hundreds of damning facts proving our bus driver was a robot. None of the bus riders seemed to care that Molly's actions would result in Mrs. Stover being dismantled for parts. Me neither. I was all too familiar with the dangers posed by robots running past their expiration. *The Directions* detailed case studies of obsolete robots who had made no effort to hide their mechanical identities, causing spectacular scenes of human vs. robot carnage. Because these were "stories," Mom was free to use the word *robot* to describe the villains who were justifiably destroyed at the end. But they never frightened me. *I* wasn't obsolete. I knew how to act in public (unlike some robots who liked to keep bugs in their throats). The robots in these case studies were so grossly negligent that I felt relieved to see them annihilated. Kanga enjoyed the stories too, in his own way; he identified with the humans. "Mom," he'd say, "read the one where the little boy catches that robot thing in his tree house!"

Mrs. Stover would be just another cautionary tale. I was grateful to her for comparing me to Magic Johnson and for seeing potential in me where Mom and Dad hadn't, but she was clearly obsolete, and excitement over her impending demise had diverted attention away from Kanga's bizarreness. We needed to survive one more day of school.

Molly wasn't making it easy for Kanga. Appearing exhausted just moments before, Molly became euphoric when she sat next to James. She couldn't sit still. She couldn't lower her voice. The notebook was open as she read passages aloud, giggling and breathing heavily. When Mrs. Stover halted the bus at the railroad tracks, Molly stood on her seat and hollered, "Yo! Toaster!"

Mrs. Stover turned and faced us. "I'LL BE HAPPY TO TAKE MY FOOT OFF THE BRAKE, YOUNG LADY, WHEN YOUR BUTT IS WHERE I WANT IT."

Molly plopped down, but not without hooting, "Okay, *toaster!*"

The word *toaster* wasn't anywhere in *The Directions*, but everybody knew it meant "robot"—and not in a good way. For me, hearing the word at all, even in reference to bagel preparation, caused the exhaust fan in my head to click on.

James seemed anxious too. He touched Molly's shoulder to calm her, but she just flapped her arms, notebook and all, sending pages scattering throughout the back of the bus. I didn't remember moving my hand, but it was now resting on Kanga's shoulder. I could feel his body humming with jealousy as James rubbed Molly's back. Whatever James was doing appeared to be working. She looked sleepy again. She tipped toward James, sniffing his shirt collar.

"Kanga," I said, "how about after school we go catch some frogs in Culver's Creek? You can make a swimming pool for them in the bathroom sink." Kanga had been asking me if we could do this, and I'd always said no, because that's what Mom had always said. But it was liberating, now, to simply suggest Kanga do exactly what he wanted. Because why not? Because maybe that was part of being a good mom too: giving your kid that stupid, special thing that only he wanted. "And maybe we'll chop down that little pine tree behind the building. You know, the one you think looks like a crocodile standing on his—"

"She's whispering to him."

It was true. Molly's lips were practically inside James's ear. It made my neck itch just watching her. She was passionate, whatever she was whispering. James leaned away from her, confused. Then he stared at her eyes. His look—he loved her. There was no mistaking it. But there was also terror on his face. What had Molly confessed to him?

"Ignore her," I said to Kanga. "You have to. Because it's obvious she likes James, and he likes her, but they'll probably break up over the summer. Just wait your turn. Next year, you know? Next year we'll sit closer to Molly on the bus, and—"

"But what's she saying to him? She doesn't look right. I'm going to—"

"Kanga—"

Kanga was crawling over the seatback (I had a grip on his arm) when James shrieked. After that, nobody moved. The bus just watched in horror.

Some memories aren't stored in a robot's central processor. They get stuck somewhere more immediate. The hair on the back of your neck, for instance. The tip of your chin. The surface of your eyeballs. Molly Seed going berserk on James Botty was one such memory.

It started with her coughing. But not a normal cough. Molly's cough was like a vacuum cleaner sucking dirt off the bus floor. James tried to push her away, but Molly only fell against him harder. Her eyes bulged— they had become purple. James shrieked again, and that's when Molly stuck a finger in her mouth, the way someone might try to find a hair they accidentally ate. What Molly located instead was a gray electrical wire hiding on the back of her tongue. She began yanking it out. The electrical wire fell on James's lap, foot after foot, until Molly at last regurgitated a small silver battery. The writing on the battery was in Mandarin, the most popular language in China. I recognized its shape and style from a parts catalog Dad had hidden in the apartment. It was the power source for Molly's central processor.

How long did this episode take? Nineteen point four seconds. But even with her battery now outside of her body, Molly remained alive. We watched as she used her chewed-up fingernails to claw the wires apart. This took much longer. There was no explosion or mechanical squeal to mark her death. She just slumped against James, and pink lubricating oil drooled from her mouth onto his clean white shirt. By then it was clear to the entire bus exactly what Molly Seed was. Or, more precisely, what she had been.

Once, when we were tiny, Dad had taken Kanga and me on a walk around the block. Out of the blue, he knuckled my head and pointed toward the mailman, who was making his rounds. Dad never said a word—just shoved his hand back into his pocket—but I knew it meant the mailman was a robot too. Then Dad laughed, and I wasn't sure what to think anymore. Our mailman was a robot. *Maybe.* Besides my family, he was the only robot I'd ever seen.

Until Mrs. Stover, who kept driving us toward school, ignoring the situation at the back of her bus.

Until Molly Seed.

Kanga tried to break free of my grasp, to rescue Molly's inanimate body from what would happen next, but in the history of the world, no kid has ever broken free from his mother's grip to chase a bouncing ball into traffic. My hand was stuck to my brother's arm as if glued, and that kept Kanga in our seat. I fused my other hand over his mouth, just to be extra safe.

It was the day before summer vacation. Outside, blue skies. A warm breeze. Our bus windows were open. I heard the din of the road beneath us, but also something new: the sound of brown lunch sacks, full of air, getting crumpled by human fists. Over and over, louder and louder, sacks getting smashed. This *crackle* was coming from inside our classmates' heads. Their brains were crackling. It had to do with Molly. And fear. The crackle was connecting them, everyone leaning their heads in unison toward James, urging him to *do* something about the robot in their midst, about Molly, crackling at him: *Get rid of her, James!*

James grabbed Molly's thin shoulders and lifted her up. Her head swung around, giving us riders an uncanny farewell stare before James thrust her headfirst through the open window. Molly's legs got caught near the ceiling, keeping her half-inside. But James just grabbed her sneakers and forced her completely through.

The crackle disappeared. We didn't hear Molly strike the asphalt, just the rattle of the bus continuing down the road. Nobody said a word, but a moment later the brakes hissed.

We heard the steady *beep . . . beep . . . beep* of the bus backing up.

After parking the bus on the side of the road, Mrs. Stover painfully got out of her seat. She didn't even look at us, just walked down her steps and around the bus to inspect the wreckage of our robotic classmate. Molly lay across the white line on the edge of the road. Mrs. Stover lit a cigarette. She took two puffs, chuckling to herself, and bit the cigarette between her teeth. Then she bent down, grabbed Molly's ankle, and dragged her into the weeds, where her corpse would be hidden from passing motorists. Mrs. Stover opened the rear door of the bus and took out an orange cone. She tossed it toward Molly. She threw her cigarette in the dirt, stomped it, and reboarded the bus.

On the way to school (we weren't even late) we listened as Mrs. Stover used the CB radio: "GOT A CODE EIGHTEEN. CORNER OF ROWELY AND DIETZ." She paused for a garbled response. "TEN-FOUR."

I must have still had glue on my fingers, because after having grabbed Kanga's hand as we got off the bus, I couldn't let it go. Whether Kanga liked it or not, we were conjoined for the remainder of fourth grade. All in all, my brother impressed me that day. He didn't cry. He didn't act up. His processor just went on autopilot, and he let me drag him wherever we needed to go. Mrs. Walter looked at us and inquired why we were holding hands.

"Buddy system," I answered.

"Whatever," she said, and resumed her futile attempt to control the volume of her classroom, which couldn't stop talking—no, *shrieking*—about the Molly Seed incident. Anyone on Bus 117 was an instant celebrity. Luckily, there were several other bus riders in our class who relished the chance to tell the story, so Kanga and I didn't have to. When the local news vans stopped in front of the school, we all rushed to the window to see Principal Vanderlaan gesturing dynamically before the cameras, then grabbing James Botty's shoulders and squeezing them with pride. We couldn't hear what he said, but he ended the interview by giving James a personal round of applause.

That afternoon, Bus 117 arrived right on schedule to take us home for the summer. As she dropped Kanga and me off in front of our apartment building, Mrs. Stover aimed her thick glasses at me. "BASKETBALL KID," she said, "SAY HI TO YOUR MOM FOR ME."

"You bet." I smiled. "Have a great summer, Mrs. Stover. Go Lakers!"

Kanga and I watched Mrs. Stover drive off.

"Let go of me now," he whispered.

The glue had finally worn off. I released him, but before Kanga could run away, I gave my twin brother a huge hug.

"What's wrong with you?" he said, squirming away from me.

"Nothing." I hugged harder. "I love you, Kanga." My skin was tingling with a strange feeling, a *motherly* feeling—horror mixed with relief—of having witnessed someone else's kid make an irreparable mistake. Right now I didn't care if Kanga thought he was human. He was safe with me, and that was enough. "I'll never let anybody hurt you. Got that?"

"Okay," he said. "But what if the Incredible Hulk jumps down from that tree and tries to kill me?"

"I'll rip him apart with my bare hands."

Kanga laughed, but I cracked my knuckles, and I knew my mom-strength could kill the Incredible Hulk if it had to.

2

FOLLOWING THE STATEWIDE NEWS TIDBIT "Local Boy Prevents Robot Rampage," the humans of Hectorville, Michigan, wanted *more* obsolete robots to stuff through bus windows, not fewer. James Botty was their hero. Nobody seemed to remember that Molly Seed had been his girlfriend—not even James, whose inquisitive, boyish outlook had been replaced by a suspicious snarl for anyone who might secretly be a robot. I stayed away from James Botty, but everyone else wanted to be just like him. For the next few years, the most popular topic of conversation for people standing in a circle was: "Let's say *you* were a crazy robot, and you started crawling up on me. First I'd go *bam!* Then I'd go—" But there were no robots to be found. Certainly not a staggering army of malfunctioning bots to be taken down en masse. Not even a robotic dog to kick. Molly Seed had merely highlighted that Hectorville was filled with nothing but ordinary, boring humans. Then a posse of riled-up teenage girls happened upon two boys at Culver's Creek. The boys were goofing around, having an innocent contest to see who could hold his breath underwater the longest. One of the girls knew about robots—that *real* robots could hold their breath forever. So they drowned one of the boys. The girls got sent away, and Hectorville didn't talk much about robots after that.

●●●

It was November 1991. Kanga and I were freshmen in high school, sitting across the room from each other in science class. For the first time since fourth grade, we were listening to a classmate's presentation about robots that *didn't* mention Molly Seed. We were required to take notes.

Science, I was disappointed to note, held a much lower status in our young decade than it had in the 1980s. Gone was the rigor and fascination with the unknown, replaced by a blanket skepticism of everything. Scientific achievement had been cashed in for advancements in ostentatious style; humans had chosen a tapered look. Shirts were wide and bulky, filled with air, adorned with loud patterns—zigzags, dots, vertical and horizontal stripes—and tucked into crisp, tight jeans, which were then rolled even tighter at the ankle. Both boys and girls were draped in this way. They looked futuristic, but they seemed to have no interest in a better future beyond this moment. I was relieved robots had already been invented, because nobody right now seemed capable of doing it.

Our presenter, Brandon Curtis, stood at the front of the room, surrounded by wooden cases of dead insects. The smell of their shriveled exoskeletons was so pungent that many students put their heads on their desks and went straight to sleep. I, however, managed to stay awake for Brandon's presentation, which began with an interesting fact: according to public-opinion polls, 56 percent of US citizens would never invite a robot into their homes for any reason. Forty-three percent would allow a robot in as a laborer, as long as the homeowner was permitted to carry a loaded firearm. Brandon placed himself squarely in this camp. He loved robots. He would give anything to see a robot up close, alive or dead, to study its parts—"but probably dead, because I don't trust them. My dad says this one robot stole his job, but I don't know. My dad's a jerk." Brandon fancied himself a science wiz after winning the "Knowledge Fair" in sixth grade, and by the lowered standards of our age, he probably was among the top scientific minds of Hectorville. But when he claimed he was going to MIT, I couldn't take him seriously. The Massachusetts Institute of Technology was the only university in the United States whose robotics program rivaled those in Asia. Brandon was closer to the speed of South Central Michigan Polytechnic College, if they would even take him.

He used his fingers to list the three things everybody already knew about robots. "Robots don't need air. Robots don't need food. Robots don't need sleep." Brandon wished he were a robot, so he could play Nintendo all night and sit for hours at the bottom of his swimming pool while his dad was talking to him. He wouldn't give up food, though. He would be a robot who ate food because of spaghetti. "Robots are fakers," he continued. "They fake like they're just like us, which drains their batteries, so robots need to plug their fingers into an outlet all night. And they also need gallons and gallons of drinks to cool their insides, so that's why they drink stuff all the time."

God, I needed a gallon of vinegar just listening to Brandon. I could see a jug right behind him, enclosed in a glass cabinet. The jug had been sitting there all year so far, untouched, teasing me with its unbroken seal. I'd been drinking vinegar since second grade—since I'd seen vinegar make a model volcano erupt. I was a basketball player, and I'd wanted that same volcanic chemical reaction in my body. It didn't happen. Five gallons of vinegar a day, and I could still squeeze into my clothes from fourth grade. At four eight, eighty-seven pounds, I *wasn't* the shortest kid at Hectorville High School. That title belonged to Clarissa Jayman, a freshman girl whom I had by an inch.

In front of the room, Brandon had suddenly transformed into a comedian as he described where robots' central processors were located. "Their heads are *empty!*" he explained. "And their brains are in their *butts!*"

First of all, Brandon, our skulls contain an elaborate exhaust system that disposes of unwanted gases through our hair follicles. If I didn't have my exhaust system, I would have exploded fifteen minutes after being switched on. Still funny, Brandon? As for our processors being located in our butts—and we prefer the term *intergluteal chamber*, thank you—surveys indicate scientists who build robots claim their best ideas originate in their bowels, not their heads—

"Robots don't have real moms and dads. Scientists are their parents. Scientists give them eye color, hair color, and skin color. Fat fingers, skinny fingers, whatever you want."

I had to concede this point to Brandon. With Mom and Dad gone, the faceless scientists of Gravy Robotics were the closest things I had to parents. Kanga was slightly luckier. He had me.

"I mean—" Brandon said, taking a deep breath to indicate the philosophical apex of his presentation, "I would build the perfect robot. He'd be eight feet tall. He would do everything for me. He'd be the smartest robot on Earth, with a processor that could remember everything. Everybody's phone numbers. The entire *TV Guide*. Everything! And he'd be *nice*. He'd be . . . my best friend."

Everyone laughed at Brandon. I did too. Rule number one in *The Directions* was "Do whatever the crowd is doing." Rule number one was automatic for me now. But even so, I shouldn't have been laughing. I should have been *thanking* Brandon, because his attitude toward robots was enlightened for a small midwestern town. His first instinct wasn't to kill us, but rather to exploit us for his personal gain. That was actually progress.

"No! I don't mean *best* friend! I just mean—"

Kanga wasn't laughing. Kanga's face had taken on the color of Brandon's face: basketball orange. Kanga felt sorry for Brandon.

"My robot would be more like a pet," Brandon continued. "But a pet that never eats or sleeps and never dies. Okay? That's all I have for my presentation."

Kanga clapped for Brandon. He was the only one who did. I couldn't look at my brother. It wasn't that I was embarrassed of him. It was just—*his body*. It was huge now. Kanga had somehow hit full-blown puberty in sixth grade, a year sooner than *The Directions* said robots of our model would, an event for which I had a front-row seat. Behold: the small, elbow-shaped bulge inside Kanga's neck, his sideburns, his belly button sprouting curly black hair. We went through thirty-plus gallons of milk a week. I could hear his body elongating, his interior plastic screeching, his bolts groaning, his mouth whimpering. There were mysterious new grease stains throughout the apartment. He took forever to charge at night. Kanga would still be lying in his bed, undressed, as I threw on my backpack and yelled, "Get moving! We're gonna be late for school!" I had to buy him his first razor and shaving cream. Then I had to teach him how to shave (*The Directions*, page 752).

But who was still the boss?

Me.

Without his "little brother" (I stopped correcting people), Kanga would never be able to navigate this world alone. He didn't keep the fridge stocked with milk. I did. For his own survival, my brother needed someone nearby to correct his instincts. For example: clapping for Brandon when nobody else in the room was clapping. Kanga was too old to be drawing that kind of unnecessary attention to himself. We would be having a little chat about that tonight.

Brandon remained at the front of the room, waiting for our science teacher, Mr. Belt, to acknowledge him. Mr. Belt was reading the newspaper at his desk. "Mr. Belt?" asked Brandon. "I'm done with my presentation. Can I sit down now?"

Mr. Belt glanced up from his newspaper. "Brandon. Your presentation? What was it about?"

"Robots."

Mr. Belt tossed the paper aside and stood up. He stretched his arms. He took a moment to feel around in his pocket for a stick of gum. He popped it into his mouth and winced as he chewed it, as if the gum were a horse pill he took on doctor's orders. Mr. Belt strolled to the front of the room. He put an arm around Brandon and leaned in close, smacking his lips as he chewed the gum. "Did you say the presentation was about *robots*?"

"Yes."

"Did you mention about no breathing, no eating, no sleeping?"

"Yes."

"Did you mention about drinking lots of fluids?"

"Yes."

"Did you cover brains in their butts, heads empty, all that?"

"Yeah, I covered it all, Mr. Belt."

"Did you mention China?"

Brandon opened his mouth. He paused.

"China, Brandon—what did you say about China?"

Silence.

Mr. Belt turned to the class. "China, ladies and gentlemen, is where we get our robot parts. I'm talking about China, where you can find entire towns of robots and scientists living in peace, solving the world's problems, and nobody can tell who is who. Don't tell your parents I said this, but I heard the Chinese have stopped having real kids. Now, over in China, every kid under the age of four is a robot, fresh from the factory. And let's say your goal in life is to attend college there and build robots. Good luck. You can't read the entrance exam because the whole thing's written in Chinese. So learn the Chinese language is my advice to your generation."

Three students leaned over to write *China* in their notes.

"None of you have what it takes to get into those Chinese universities. The brains. Or the aptitude for Chinese, in particular. Staci, well *you*." Mr. Belt pointed to Ms. Perfect, Staci Miles, captain of the freshman Cheerbirds. "Staci might have the IQ to make robots. The rest of you? Well." Mr. Belt spit his gum in the trash. "Does anyone have any real questions about robots?"

Someone raised a hand. It was Rye, the biggest kid in our grade, a dull mass of human tissue whose sole purpose was sports. Even during the school day Rye wore protective sports goggles. He and Mr. Belt were on close terms because Mr. Belt was coach of the freshman basketball team. "Coach," said Rye, "my dad bought a new VCR last year, and the thing's already busted. How come robots don't bust like that?"

"Here's a wild guess. That VCR your dad bought? He didn't buy it from China, did he?"

"No, Coach."

"Pop quiz. A robot gets its arm ripped off by a bear. What happens?"

The class just stared at Mr. Belt. Rye slowly waved his hand in the air. "To the bear, Coach? Or the robot?"

"Who do you think, Rye? Is this a lesson about bears? I'm asking you guys, what would happen to that robot's ripped-off arm?"

Staci raised her hand.

"Staci!" said Mr. Belt. "Help these boneheads out!"

"If separated from their central processing units," Staci explained, "appendages can perform basic functions to ensure their survival." Even when Staci wasn't dressed in her Cheerbirds uniform, she adorned her hair with green ribbons, reminders of her commitment to Hectorville High School. "Typical functions for a disconnected arm would be—"

"But why do we even have robots?" Rye interrupted her. "What's their point? My dad says it's a waste of tax money—"

"Rye, when we're playing basketball out on that court, what are we trying to do out there?"

"We're trying to score the ball, Coach."

"No. What place are we trying to get in the game? Are we trying to get first place, Rye, or are we trying to get second place?"

"Definitely first place."

"Then how come the USA is second place in robots? Because if second place is kosher with you, maybe you're also fine with getting second place in World War II or the Space Race or the Olympics. See, I grew up in *this* country, and that means we don't get second place in anything, ever."

Staci raised her hand. "We got third place in the last Olympics. The Soviet Union got first. East Germany got second."

Mr. Belt stared at her. "Hey," he said to the class. "Know what I read in a magazine last night? Robots have ticklish belly buttons. What I should do is make all of you pull up your shirts. Then I could go around and work you over with a feather, and then we'd know if we have any robots in here."

Suddenly, the only thing I could smell was my own belly button. That tangy, swampy reek—it was even stronger than the odor of the dead insects. No doubt everyone else in the room was smelling it too. But did they know it was me? I tried to look calm. I glanced at Kanga. His eyes were wide, his smile agape. My brother nodded his head in childish excitement. Lifting shirts and showing belly buttons sounded like a great idea to him.

"Maybe tomorrow." Mr. Belt clapped his hands. "How about a little extra credit? I want all of you to crumple up the notes you just took. Let's score some points in this class. A little extra sauce on the side. You know, extra credit, like extra cheese, or . . . Get crumpling!"

The boys excitedly crumpled their mostly empty notes. Staci took a mournful look at the extensive, delicately organized notes she'd just taken. She crumpled them slowly. Gently. Careful not to hurt the words. Staci crumpled her notes into a tight, organized ball.

Mr. Belt held a trash can. "Everybody line up over there. You get one shot. Don't waste it. If you make your shot, it's extra credit for you. Miss it? Nothing." Mr. Belt set the trash can on a desk. "I said stand back *there*, behind that chemical burn on the floor."

The class took turns shooting. The line was too far back. Nobody could make it. Most shots wobbled through the air and fell five feet short of the can. Only the students who had tightened their wads of paper into hard pellets seemed to have a chance. Staci Miles's shot pinged against the rim of the trash can. The class let out a frustrated grunt.

It was my turn. My notes were a boulder. My arm was a catapult. My processor had analyzed four hundred various trajectories, and I had a diagram of the winning arc on the surface of my eyeballs. I'd factored in air density. Light particles could have an effect, but—

"Darryl, relax your face. Get shooting."

My notes fell seven feet short of the can.

"Foot fault. Wouldn't have counted anyway. Next!"

Nobody got the extra credit. The floor was covered with paper balls. Mr. Belt wondered aloud about the state of physical education in America. He said he hoped we learned something today. Then he said, "Wait." He pointed toward Kanga, standing near the terrarium. "Kanga!" he said. "By Jesus, take your shot. Make it count. This is for everything."

Kanga tapped the terrarium, but Stickzilla, the class walking stick, appeared to be sleeping. My brother gave her a long, jealous look before answering Mr. Belt. "My notes?"

"Your notes, Kanga. Extra credit!"

"I threw them in a different trash can."

Mr. Belt was appalled. Violated. It was as though Kanga had managed to steal all the extra credit for himself while Mr. Belt wasn't looking. "More science presentations tomorrow!" he barked. "Starting with Kanga here. What is your topic, Kanga?"

"Mr. Belt—" I interjected. "Kanga is paired with me. Our presentation is on the principle of flight."

"Group presentation, huh?" Mr. Belt spat the words. "We'll see about that." He took a step toward his desk, his shoe crunching a ball of notes. "Brandon! Clean up your project!"

The bell rang.

Kanga whispered good-bye to Stickzilla. Perhaps as a sign of maturity, he refrained from inserting her into his mouth. She was a living remnant of our insect collections from a month ago. Mr. Belt had approached that science project with gusto, laughing and performing little dances as he taught us to kill, mount, and label those fascinating everyday creatures. He had been so impressed by Staci Miles's collection, he'd hung it on the wall with other exemplars from years past. After the insect unit, however, Mr. Belt's enthusiasm for science withered like a stag beetle in a vial of nail polish remover. Since then we'd done nothing but independent research projects while Mr. Belt read the sports page at the back of the room. Why he'd allowed Stickzilla, alone, to remain alive was a mystery.

3

WHAT DID HUMAN KIDS THINK ABOUT ALL DAY? What thoughts breezed through those bloody, carefree brains, instead of the millions of tiny calculations I performed pretending to be something I wasn't? When people were just themselves, what was left to think about?

I could've asked my brother.

But I already knew what he would've said: Nothing. And then I'd have to wonder what *that* felt like, which would be just one more calculation, one more wrinkle in my forehead, while Kanga stared off into the distance, looking effortlessly human.

● ● ●

Behind Hectorville High School sat an enormous grassy hill, topped by a single birch tree. Rumor had it the hill was man-made, a collection of leftover dirt from our school's creation many years ago. Perhaps a more daring pair of brothers would have ridden their bikes *up* and *over* the hill to get home. I forbade it. Why draw such unnecessary attention to ourselves, pedaling like fools up that incline—only to fly down the backside of the hill, straight into Culver's Creek? Sensibly, I led us around the hill as we biked toward our apartment building.

It was a cool November afternoon, weather that reminded the mom in me to remind Kanga to wear long sleeves to school tomorrow, like the humans would be wearing. Not that I could afford to dress him in the latest styles. No neon-colored windbreaker for Kanga. No low-cut V-neck sweater with clashing turtleneck. Kanga would have on his thick, oversize white sweatshirt from the Salvation Army, and I'd be wearing one too.

A carload of girls drove past us, its radio blaring the most popular song of the day, the girls inside straining their larynxes to hit the high notes along with their favorite singer. I was familiar with the song. But, to me, the singer sounded like an insecure robot, overinsisting she was human because she was "feeling emotions," only to undermine her whole argument at the end of the song by showing off her vocal register, which could go as high as a whistle. No human could do that. Or maybe her "emotions" caused her to sing that way. I didn't know.

We rode past the town basketball court, where a young boy was practicing alone. He was shooting free throws, talking to himself the whole time. Was this boy even aware of all the people watching him from their cars, from the surrounding houses, scrutinizing his every move? He lined up a free throw. *Brick*. I wouldn't be caught dead on a public basketball court. Not until I had mastered the game.

The grass in people's front yards this afternoon had an extra tint of purple to it. I hadn't seen grass like that since I was twelve, when I'd had my eyeballs replaced with a new pair sent from Gravy Robotics. It was exhilarating to receive a package from Detroit. We never knew what to expect. Sometimes it was replacement hardware for our bodies; sometimes it was a useful object to help us blend in with the human kids. Our bikes, for instance, arrived in two big boxes when we were nine. Sweet BMXs, the envy of every other kid in the building. Mine still worked perfectly, though Kanga had outgrown his BMX last year, so Gravy sent him a new ten-speed. One huge box. But a smaller package had arrived for me too. My present. Somehow Gravy had known exactly what I'd wanted: an RCA Pro Edit camcorder. It was the most high-tech piece of electronics in our apartment. Besides me and Kanga, of course.

We glided our bikes past the sign for our apartment building, Shimmering Terraces, curved them through the parking lot, ran them across Mr. Renault's patio (he lived in the apartment directly below us), and chained them up to the maintenance shed. The very idea of a science project made my joints ache. But an A was imminent. Three months in Mr. Belt's class had armed me with enough peripheral details of our teacher's life to shoot a bull's-eye on each video presentation henceforth. The "science" aspect on these reports was secondary. More important was to include Mr. Belt's favorite leisure activities in the presentation. A no-brainer: *basketball*. All we had to do was toss one into the frame while I recorded.

Holding the ball was the perfect job for Kanga. It was customary for my brother to deliver a modest introduction (written by me) for each video presentation, which magically allowed him to take half credit for everything that followed. I instructed Kanga to wait on the sidewalk while I went up to our apartment to retrieve my two most treasured possessions: my basketball and my camcorder. Having Kanga wait outside was strategic. If I allowed him inside for even a moment, the TV would kidnap him until midnight. Necessity dictated that the introduction be shot as quickly as possible, right on the sidewalk; then Kanga could do whatever he wanted.

Motherhood is a thankless, humbling occupation.

I should have been the one holding the basketball. I was the basketball kid. But did I trust Kanga to operate my camcorder? Never.

I tossed him the ball. "Just hold it with your hands on the sides, okay? It's called the triple-threat position, and it'll really impress Mr. Belt."

Kanga looked back and forth between the basketball and the camcorder, confused.

"You're holding the ball for the introduction," I said. "If you could try not to drop it while saying the words, that would be— Kanga? Where are you going? Not inside! Not the TV!"

This was not unusual. Regardless of his standard lethargy, Kanga could have unexpected bursts of willfulness. But I knew better than to pull rank and demand he stay outside, because he just wouldn't. I had to wait for him.

Luckily, patience was a skill I had learned from Mom.

The trick was to find a happy memory in your processor and replay it over and over, keeping your joints loose by rocking in place. I found one: the 1988 Olympic basketball game between the USA and China in Seoul, South Korea. I'd been watching it from our couch, when the play-by-play announcer shocked everyone—including himself—by declaring that a *robot* was about to take the court for China.

The other announcer was appalled by China's action, labeling it "a shameless publicity stunt, tantamount to a declaration of war on American values."

"You realize," responded the play-by-play announcer, "that we have robots back in the US too, right?"

"*Our* robots don't wear the red, white, and blue! They don't represent our country! They don't represent *me!*" He then explained, in his mocking tone, that this particular robot had been a sensation in China in the weeks leading up to the games. His name was Ma, which means "horse" in Chinese.

I couldn't take my eyes off Ma. His handsome Chinese face. His dribbles that seemed to smash the basketball court with an extra velocity. His losing balance—but not falling down—after being fouled hard by Bimbo Coles, an American point guard.

Ma made his first free throw, then missed the second, causing the hateful announcer to guess that the Chinese culture had no equivalent to the legend of John Henry. Ma was removed from the game at the next dead ball.

I'd watched the memory a few dozen times, all the while fantasizing about actually living in China, when Kanga reemerged from our building.

"Absolutely not," I barked at him. "March back upstairs and take that off. Under *no* circumstances am I going to film you wearing—"

Kanga sat down on the sidewalk. Apparently, not being allowed to wear my old Magic Johnson uniform for our science presentation was a dealbreaker for him. "It's half mine," he said, "and you know it."

"Please, Kanga. I have a lot of work to do, and the quicker I start filming—"

He lay down in the driveway. This was how decisions got made in our household.

"Fine," I said.

The jersey barely reached his belly button. His white briefs hung out the sides of the purple shorts. The elastic was stretched to the limit, causing the whole uniform to resemble a two-piece women's swimsuit. I could see where Kanga had positioned his penis against his thigh to prevent it from slipping out. But the worst part: the uniform still fit me perfectly. Not that I wore it anymore. The limit of my boldness was to occasionally sport the matching purple high-tops (fifth grade's birthday gift). Kanga had no real boldness, just earnest eccentricity. He was barefoot.

"Here's what you have to do," I instructed him. "Hold the ball in the triple-threat position. But don't look at it. Look into the camera. Look at Mr. Belt and say, 'The Principle of Flight: A Video Presentation by Darryl and Kanga Livery.'"

"Flight? Is that what this is about?"

"Or you can just hug the ball to your belly."

"No," said Kanga, and he was already walking away from me, toward Mr. Renault's patio. "I got an idea. Start filming me when I give the signal."

"If you don't say the introductory sentence, I can't use it."

"I'll say it."

Kanga had walked past Mr. Renault's patio. He now stood near Mrs. Voss's propane grill. Through the eyepiece of the camcorder, Kanga waved a tiny arm for me to start filming. I pressed Record, and before I describe what Kanga did with my basketball, I should explain my history with Magic Johnson. It started with my annoyance at every kid who ever saw a robotic dog catching a Frisbee and said "That's magic!" because what the kid really meant was "That's science!" Science was the reason the dog did what it did, not magic, and even Earvin "Magic"Johnson had to agree that a combination of natural aptitude, confidence, and work ethic were ultimately what allowed him to produce his seemingly impossible basketball moves.

Moves that my brother, it turned out, was able to mimic exactly. For the next ten seconds of video footage my brother *was* Magic Johnson.

He got a dribbling start before the invisible defenders surrounded him. Kanga looked at a row of mailboxes, then sprint-dribbled toward a parked car. Behind-the-back dribble. Between the legs. Speed dribble around the dumpster. He pointed at a lawn chair. He shimmied his shoulders. Spin dribble. He cocked the ball behind his head, as though to pass it to a NO PARKING sign. (He was almost to me now. I just needed to follow him with the camcorder.) Kanga leapt into the air. (I couldn't see the ball anymore. Where was the—)

"The-Principle-of-Flight-by-Kanga-and-Darryl!"

My brother landed somewhere behind me.

If you talk to veteran parents, one consistent feature of their stories is how their worst blowups at their kids happen on days that are actually going pretty well. It starts with Joey eating a peanut butter sandwich in the living room, and suddenly you've spanked Joey raw after he wiped his jelly-hands on the decorative throw pillows. That's how I could be with Kanga too. Every now and then he caught me off guard. He pushed things too far. How far was too far? Channeling Magic Johnson out of nowhere, with my basketball—*my* basketball. That torched it. My chest was a fireplace crammed with logs. I was raging. The flames swirled up my neck and around my eyeballs, and my hands went berserk. They slapped the basketball away from him, getting a good portion of his arms and chin in the process. "Grounded!"

"But—" Kanga was shocked. "I said exactly what you—"

"Idiot! All that stupid clapping in Mr. Belt's class! What's wrong with you?" I picked up the basketball and threw it at him. "Are you trying to get us discovered?"

Kanga could have caught the ball, but he let it smash him in the chest. I hated him. I hated those enormous hands hanging down past his knee-caps. I hated his dinosaur bone of a jaw, bulging forward, begging me to strike it. I wouldn't. My previous attempts to corporally punish Kanga had not produced the intended effect. Rather than comply with my standards, he had shut down and ignored me for a day. But there was an even worse outcome. Crying. Kanga had already begun the process.

"No, Kanga, don't do that." The words felt like globs of grease in my mouth. "*I'm sorry*, okay?"

He gasped. His mouth jutted into a frown. His eyes closed. When we were two, we'd witnessed another kid pull this move at the grocery store, and Kanga had memorized it in one take. Kanga's mouth opened, but the cry was still gathering in his neck.

"I'm sorry I threw the ball at you," I said, but the sight of Kanga's chest hair curling out from the Magic jersey reignited my fire: "*I said I was sorry, so just shut up!*"

The first sound Kanga emitted was a single word: "Mooooom," drawn out, maintaining a consistent low pitch over the course of ten endless seconds. The second "Mooooom" was a scream.

That kid in the grocery store who had taught Kanga to cry—I had been so disgusted by the boy's lack of shame, by the obviousness of his ploy, by the attention it drew from every sentient being in the store. Yet there was no disputing his results: the kid left the store with a bathtub police boat *and* a He-Man coloring book. But I wasn't that kind of mom. "Stop that crying right now, or I'll unplug the TV and take it to the Salvation Army."

The crying halted. "You wouldn't."

"Try me. No TV would give us more time to read *The Directions*—"

"I stopped, okay?"

Few thrills in parenting compare with presenting a hypothetical consequence that immediately changes a kid's behavior. But I had to tone down my internal victory celebration and act like the threat didn't just fly into my belly at the last second. In truth, I didn't feel victorious at all. My fire was extinguished, and all that remained in my chest was a desperate love for my brother. Kanga slowly dragged himself toward the building entrance—no doubt to watch TV until bedtime—and it was crushing me. I needed to stop him. I needed to corral him by my side. I needed proof *he* still loved *me*.

"Kanga!" I called. "Can you help me with the camcorder? I want you to film some objects in flight."

He froze. "Really?" He pivoted, sprinted toward me, and wrapped me in a hug.

Did that part of parenting ever get old?

Never.

● ● ●

The scientific process was not entirely foreign to Kanga. A random topic could spark his curiosity and swallow him for days. I recalled the time in second grade when we came across a dead turtle, belly up, in a roadside ditch. It was the kind of unexpected discovery you might stare at for ten seconds before concluding *Yuck* and booting it under some shrubs. But not Kanga. He picked up the turtle. He held the thing up to his face, the limp head dangling from its shell. He flicked the head with his finger, watching it swing, his dilated pupils indicating the grandiosity of biological death having just besieged him. Kanga brought the dead turtle into our apartment. He kept it under his bed. (Around this time I realized that Mom and Dad, in addition to their more glaring deficiencies, were not equipped with odor sensors.) My brother remained morose the next few days, locking himself in his bedroom at every spare moment to further dissect and annihilate his turtle. He was hysterical the evening I made him flush those putrid remains down the toilet. But we reached an agreement: if he scrubbed the inside with soap, he could keep the empty shell. Mom and Dad had no idea what we were screaming about in the bathroom between flushes of the toilet, but it all turned out okay. Kanga still has the shell under his bed.

There was no chance I'd get that same maniacal interest in today's science project.

I explained our various requirements, and Kanga nodded. I double-checked his understanding by having him summarize the plan back to me: "It's easy, Darryl. We need video footage of things in flight. Birds, insects, airplanes." Right on cue, Kanga spotted a flock of black birds sitting on a telephone wire. He snatched the camcorder from my hands and trotted silently, like a jungle cat, stopping right below them. Kanga got a minute of footage, until a diesel truck scattered the birds into the air.

He returned with the camcorder. "Things are fast. They were talking to each other, calling out warnings when they saw me. 'Who's that guy down there?' Hey! Remember that beehive behind the shed?" Kanga was already jogging there. "This is fun, Darryl!"

Kanga threw a rock at the beehive, but no bees flew out: it was empty. Then we snuck around a few patios, lifting the tarp off a golf cart, peeking inside empty cardboard boxes, searching a spiderweb between the handle-bars of a bike. No insects. Mr. Renault had a strip of flypaper hanging near his patio door. The flypaper was empty. In a frantic split second, two dragonflies flew like darts over our heads and disappeared.

"Airplanes," said Kanga. "Just let me grab some milk first," and before I could respond he'd run inside the building.

While Kanga had received the outwardly physical gifts of puberty, I was not without my own unique talents. My ears had always gone above and beyond what was expected of them, and from Mr. Renault's patio I could hear Kanga upstairs, humming along with the opening theme of *TaleSpin*. I allowed him twenty minutes of cartoons and a jug of milk, which I heard him toss carelessly into the kitchenette sink after he drained it. Another perk of having supersonic hearing was being able to mimic voices. For years it had been a sly trick of mine to whisper a word in Mom's voice. Any word would do, especially a word Mom would never use, such as *tamarack* or *quadrilateral*. This would jar Kanga's focus, and I could redirect it for my own purposes. I was about to float the word *symposium* up to our apartment when Kanga bounded back outside of his own accord. "Did I miss anything?"

"Pterodactyl."

His face contorted with stupid pleasure. Kanga always smiled, even at my lamest jokes. It was a valuable adaptation tactic, uniquely human, with the added bonus of making humans smile back at him, a maneuver that, in my own life, always occurred to me too late. I handed him the camcorder and said, in a deep voice, "*Mr. Director,*" which cracked him up further.

We plopped down on a patch of grass. For a brief moment I wasn't his mom anymore; I was his twin brother, and we were searching the sky for airplanes.

"Holler if you see one," Kanga said, his finger poised on the Record button. "And jets will work too. They'll be a hundred miles up there. Maybe if I zoom in . . ."

But Kanga needed a mom, not a brother. We lay on flat ground, yet I felt dizzy, like a bottomless sinkhole had just opened up next to me and was about to breathe me in. I braced myself, and my hand accidentally touched Kanga's hip—the shorts of my Magic Johnson uniform.

"You know that basketball stuff you did for the introduction?" I said. "All that showboating and dribbling around for no reason? Where did you learn that, Kanga?"

"From Mrs. Stover's favorite team," he said, proud of himself. "The Lakers."

"That wasn't the Lakers. That was garbage. Flash. Just razzle-dazzle. Even Magic Johnson would say so."

I listened for Kanga to start crying again. I *wanted* to hear him cry this time.

"I'm erasing you from the introduction." I stood up. It was rare to find myself looking down at my brother, but it felt just right. "Do you hear me? You're never touching my basketball again. Your moves are trash. They're—"

"Darryl!" Kanga pointed at the sky, his bare heels drumming the grass. "Look!"

"*I'm* the basketball kid—"

"It's a *jet*!"

I looked up. The sky had gone completely gray. At first I saw nothing. And then: the faint white line of a jet.

Its roar engulfed us, and Kanga screamed, "BEST PRESENTATION EVER!"

Kanga recorded the jet footage. My exhaust fan kicked on inside my head. I felt devoid of love and hate for him. Just fatigue. "I'm going inside to defrost the ground chuck," I announced. "When you come back to Earth, we'll have dinner."

4

WHEN KANGA AND I WERE BABIES, our world was the apartment floor. Dad would get home from work and stand in the middle of the living room, watching TV, sipping from his keg of warm beer, throwing darts at his dartboard. I would chase Kanga around Dad's boots, feeling the sizzle of beer drops on my bare skin. Dad never so much as reached down to wipe us off. It wasn't his fault; the problem was his hands. Gravy Robotics hadn't created them for tenderly touching babies. They were thick, rubber, unfeeling things—cheap peripherals, truth be told, with fingers that didn't know how to move from their permanent position. They were the hands of an oversize action figure, thumb and pointer finger touching, leaving a cylinder of open space between them, as if for the handle of a sword or medieval torch. Dad was embarrassed by them, and I understood why. I couldn't imagine having to navigate my life with those humiliating relics at the ends of my arms. Predictably, Dad avoided all situations in which he might be forced to shake hands. He never attended school pageants, science fairs, or conferences; he let Mom struggle through those on her own. Aside from going to work, Dad hardly ever left the apartment.

Still, there was plenty Dad *could* do with his hands. He could carry a cardboard box. He could drive a stick shift and smoke a cigarette at the same time. He could turn the page of a catalog. He could work the tap of a keg. He could complain about Gravy Robotics, how screwed he was to have been brought into existence by those jokers, those cheap-asses, because nobody could support a family on that dinky Gravy stipend every month. Dad could count on his rubber fingers all the things Gravy was too stingy to pay for: "van insurance, phone bill, cable bill, taco bill, beer . . ." And of course Dad could place a dart between his finger and thumb, cock his hand back, and fire the thing at his dartboard. "*Bull's-eye.*"

I once heard Dad confide to Mom that he could have been a professional darts player if someone had just told him which bar to go to after work. He was a *good* darts player, in my opinion, but he wasn't perfect. Sometimes Dad missed. Every few nights a dart would hit the wire frame of his dartboard and bounce off down to the floor. A sound recording of one such miss was buried deep in my processor—the *thook* of the dart against the frame, Mom's gasp from the kitchenette, Kanga's body buzzing like he had a bumblebee caught in his rib cage, Dad saying, "It ain't nothing."

The dart was sticking out of Kanga's back. I could see it had driven in deep, probably puncturing Kanga's heater.

Dad reached down and yanked it out. "Kid's fine." He looked at Mom. "Don't say a word."

Mom said nothing, just turned back to the taco meat she had removed from the microwave.

Dad wiped the tip of the dart against his shirt, cleaning it. "I know what you're thinking." He took a drink from his tap. "Don't say it."

"Dinner's ready," she said.

"Toughen him up is what it'll do. Look at him."

Mom looked down at Kanga, crawling and giggling again like normal. I believe that was the moment when Dad seemed to decide he liked Kanga more than me. For getting hit by his dart. For being fine. Worse, though, was that Mom decided the same thing.

"Boy's just fine," Dad concluded, and he tossed another dart. "Attaboy, Kangaroo."

After the dart incident, Mom was obsessed with the idea of Kanga attending college. Neither she nor Dad had received any college-level programming, but that didn't stop Mom from buying an overpriced college-themed onesie set for him. The Big Ten pack. The way she batted her eyes at Kanga in those garish outfits, you'd think he'd already graduated summa cum laude from all ten schools. Dad was slightly more measured in his adoration. He approved of exactly one onesie. It was crimson, with a block white *I*.

Indiana.

Dad loved Indiana. More specifically, he loved Indiana's head basketball coach, Bobby Knight. But love can have strange effects on a man. The weather in the apartment darkened whenever Bobby Knight was on TV. Dad stomped. He grew incredulous and shook his fist at random objects. He paced back and forth, looking at the floor, then froze and stared at Mom like she was his worst enemy. And there was the language: the threats and insults piling up around him, making the apartment so crowded and unbearable that even Dad couldn't stand to be in it anymore.

Following one particularly intense Indiana game, back when Kanga and I were six, Dad glared at us and said, "Come on, you wussies. Let's go to work."

"They're just kids—" Mom protested, but Dad was already pushing us through the door with his rubber hands.

One of Dad's part-time jobs was delivering coupon leaflets to free magazine stands in the surrounding towns. He did this alone, in his van: picking up the boxes of leaflets from the printer then spending all night delivering them. But after that Indiana game, Dad seemed motivated to connect with us like Coach Knight did with his players (including Isiah Thomas), so Kanga and I suddenly found ourselves bouncing around among the leaflet boxes in the back of Dad's van, listening to his instructions:

"Who the hell taught you to deliver leaflets? You think you can play for me? You're wussies! Show me the leaflets for Bill's Train and Hobby Shop. I DIDN'T SAY LOOK AT THE LABELS! This is Indiana. You're pathetic. Show me the leaflets now. I haven't got all day . . ."

The van was outfitted to transport exactly four people, with a half bench directly behind the front seats, leaving a cavernous void in the rear to stack Dad's leaflet boxes. He'd been too cheap to pay for carpeting, but that was a good thing, as it was easier to scoot boxes across the cold corrugated metal to the front, where Dad needed them. I had to intuit Dad's system for organizing the boxes—a system he'd never explained to us. But I managed. I chose the correct box every time and pushed it up to Dad.

Kanga? He had no idea what was going on. He would blindly guess which bundle Dad wanted. Or worse, he would build himself a fort with the boxes and hide, causing Dad to say: *"Think you're cute? Think I got time for your foul-ups? Show me Bill's Train and Hobby Shop in five seconds, or I throw your brother out of this moving vehicle and make you scrape him off the road with a shovel. One. Two. Three. THIS IS INDIANA! Four—"*

Despite Kanga's "foul-ups" and "wussy bellyaching," he was the kindergartner in the Indiana T-shirt. Not me. So when our work shift ended at a distant gas station in Perrysville, past 3:00 a.m., and the cashier inside was dead asleep on his stool, Dad took Kanga with him to help pump gas. Just Kanga. I climbed onto the bench, crunching a few stray leaflets, and watched them through the van window.

The parking spaces around the gas pumps were empty, except for a long black puddle trickling into a drain. After Dad filled the van, he didn't return the nozzle to its hook. Instead, he looked over his shoulder to be sure nobody was sneaking up on him. "Those other colleges are for wussies," Dad said and brought the nozzle to Kanga's face. He tapped the bottom of Kanga's chin until my brother was staring straight up into the buzzing gas station lights. "This'll get you on Bobby's team." Dad's finger tapped the trigger. I heard the whoosh and gurgle of the pump. The nozzle was aimed straight between Kanga's trembling lips. My brother's eyes went calm.

Dad went into the station and woke up the cashier to pay for his fill-up.

Kanga climbed back into the van, stinking of gasoline. Drool clung to the side of his mouth, and his hair had obviously been tousled by Dad.

I had to look away.

"Clean up those leaflets, boys," Dad ordered in his own voice as he drove us back to Shimmering Terraces. "*Wussies*," he corrected himself, but I could see his grin in the rearview mirror. To Dad, Kanga was already a Hoosier.

● ● ●

Now, though, Dad was nothing but a distant voice in my processor—albeit one that still haunted our apartment. I heard Dad whenever I saw his old dartboard (the darts themselves had been lost years ago) or the permanent ring in the living room carpet from his kegs of beer. Looking at our couch, you could tell which side was Dad's because it was greasier from him watching TV in just his underwear. And there was that divot in the wall from when Indiana got beat by Virginia in the 1984 NCAA tournament.

But in the kitchenette, all I heard was Mom.

Hanging above the coffee maker was her portrait of Elvis Presley. The King. He was rendered in cool blues on black velvet, a close-up of his face crying into a microphone. Strangely enough, the crying Elvis made Mom smile whenever she looked at it. I asked her about it once, and she seemed genuinely surprised at the question. "Why, Elvis was a robot, honey." She was making tacos. "Everybody knows that." Then Mom got back to singing the only Elvis song she knew, which wasn't even a full song, just two lines from "Hound Dog" over and over:

"Well, they said you was high classed, Well, that was just a lie, Well, they said you was high classed, Well, that was just a lie, Well, they said you was high classed . . ."

Dad was in the living room, pummeling his dartboard, pretending not to hear her, pretending he didn't know the truth about their model numbers. She was a Detroit 415. He was a 405.

Now I was singing those two lines, beneath Mom's old portrait of the King, making my own tacos. *The Directions* recommended every robot perfect one solid-food meal in the event of a worst-case scenario: an impromptu dinner party of which you are the host. This was my 483rd attempt at tacos.

Before mealtime, Kanga and I were required to stuff plastic bags down our throats to catch the mouthfuls of taco meat. (Kanga did this in the privacy of his bedroom.) After dinner we pulled them out and flushed their contents down the toilet. (Kanga again insisted on privacy.) But the bags were only half the challenge. *The Directions* also ordered us to practice intelligent conversation during dinner—and not the predictable Q-and-A sessions Mom had slow-pitched us, but meaningful philosophical debate. Here was tonight's discussion:

> ME: Did you hear, Kanga? [*Pausing to ingest tacos*] A robot was just accepted at Barnard College. Not a robot hiding her identity, but a girl who wrote her entrance essay *about* being a robot. They let her in! Early admission, even. She's starting classes in January. Isn't that incredible?
>
> KANGA: [*Staring at taco in hand*] Can't you ever just get us Cobra Burger?
>
> ME: Barnard is in New York City, in case you didn't know. Remember what I told you about New York? [*Pausing to ingest tacos*] There's a whole part of that city that's filled only with robots. Ever wonder what it would be like to live in a place like that? Where you knew everybody was a robot?
>
> KANGA: [*Setting taco on plate; pushing plate away*]
>
> ME: Don't get me wrong. There are worse places than Hectorville. People here hate robots, sure, but [*Pausing to ingest tacos*] it's not like living in Ohio, where they have X-ray machines in every building, and they run background checks just for buying grease at the—

Dinner was interrupted by three hard knocks on the apartment door.

I wiped the corners of my mouth. Dealing with solicitors was a skill I'd developed over the years. There was no time to remove my food receptacle. I opened the front door, slipped into the hallway, and, before even looking at our guest, closed the door behind me, exaggerating my effort to stay quiet.

Only then did I identify the visitor: Mr. Jacobowhite, Kanga's English teacher.

"*Oh*—" His expression indicated he had no idea who I was, an advantage because I knew exactly who he was, which meant I had his next move narrowed down to two possibilities. Mr. Jacobowhite would either ask, "Is your mother home?" or, feeling bolder, he might say, "May I come in?"

"Sorry, Mr. Jacobowhite, but my dad's taking a nap on the couch. His shift starts in a few hours."

Mr. Jacobowhite gave me a confused look.

"Pardon me, Mr. Jacobowhite. I'm Darryl Livery, Kanga's brother." I offered my hand for him to shake. "I have Mrs. Deal for English, but Kanga's told me about you." (Kanga hadn't.)

"A pleasure to meet you, Darryl. Normally I wouldn't just show up at a student's home without advance notice, but there was no phone number listed for your family, and . . . is *Mrs.* Livery available for a moment?"

"You mean our mom?" I had noticed humans often combined several emotions in a single expression, and I practiced these combinations in the mirror. The one I wore now for Mr. Jacobowhite conveyed both hurt at the mention of our mother and pity for Mr. Jacobowhite for not knowing something he should have known. "Our parents are divorced."

"Oh." Mr. Jacobowhite frowned. "Okay then."

I had Mr. Jacobowhite right where I wanted him. Male teachers loved it when troubled students opened up to them. Any revealing details from a kid's personal life turned them into a giant box of Kleenex. The academic subjects they taught were secondary to having an unkempt, nonthreatening beard. The trick with these guys was to spark their compassion by divulging details of a strained home life, dysfunctional enough to excuse any antisocial behavior on our part (because why was Mr. Jacobowhite here anyway?), yet not so toxic that he would feel compelled to call Children's Protective Services. It was a delicate balance, but I knew Mr. Jacobowhite would help me find it by asking his next question:

"Is there a good time when I can call your dad?"

I winced. "I won't stop you, Mr. Jacobowhite, but it's probably not such a good idea to call Dad."

"Why not? Are you and Kanga safe? Is everything okay?"

"We're fine, it's just . . ." I shook my head. "It's stupid."

Mr. Jacobowhite knelt down on one knee, so our faces were on the same level. "You can tell me anything, Darryl."

"Our dad doesn't like teachers. Actually, he hates them."

Mr. Jacobowhite's beard puffed with a huge grin. "But I'm here with *good* news about Kanga. He's one of the best creative writers I have. The story he wrote last week—" Mr. Jacobowhite fumbled several handwritten pages out of his coat pocket. "Did you read this? The one about the boy whose parents get kidnapped by robots?"

Read it? I *wrote* it (as I did for all Kanga's homework). Normally, this was a chore. A slog. But I'd poured my grease into this particular story. I'd lost myself in it. And even though *The Directions* warned us to always avoid the topic of robots during human interaction, I figured this could be an exception. The assignment was to write a science fiction story. "Kanga showed me that one. I loved it. Especially that part at the end—"

"When the boy tricks the robots into drinking acid and then rescues his mother!"

"It's a fantastic story." I forced my smile into a grimace. "But Kanga will never show it to our dad. English was Dad's worst subject. It was the reason he flunked out of tenth grade. Now he doesn't trust any of you."

"That breaks my heart. Would it help if he knew how gifted his son was?"

I gave Mr. Jacobowhite another combo face: amusement with a touch of exasperation. "Like I said, I won't stop you. I'll tell Dad to give you a call when he wakes up."

"No." He handed me the story, titled "Buford's Dilemma," which was marked from top to bottom with Mr. Jacobowhite's feedback: underlined superlatives and scores of exclamation marks. "I don't want to subject Kanga to any further negativity regarding his potential." He touched my shoulder and looked me in the eyes. "But promise me, Darryl, that you'll make sure Kanga continues to write. I won't always be there to encourage him, but you will. That imagination of his could win him a scholarship. He could be the next Ray Bradbury."

"I promise, Mr. Jacobowhite. Thank you."

He stood up. "I noticed Kanga wasn't wearing a hat the other morning when he arrived at school, so here." He took a blue winter hat from his pocket. "I only brought the one. I mean, there was no brother in the story he wrote . . ." Mr. Jacobowhite pulled off his own hat. "Take mine, Darryl."

Watching Mr. Jacobowhite walk down the hallway, I considered what to tell Kanga about my encounter with his English teacher. *Hat salesman*, I'd say, and he would believe me. Keeping secrets had always been my specialty. Or should I say *Ray Bradbury's*? My writing had received praise before, but never like this. The six stapled sheets of paper in my hand felt like a bestselling novel. I wanted to show it to somebody. Anybody. Kanga. Mr. Renault downstairs. My own English teacher, Mrs. Deal. I wanted to wave my story in Mrs. Deal's face and say, "*This* is what I'm capable of!"

No.

I wanted Dad to read it. I wanted to say, "Check this out, Dad. Some of the parts are kind of funny," and watch his eyes zigzag down the page, watch his lips ghost-read the words, watch his whole body shake with laughter when the story's dad yells, "Bull's-eye!"

I hid those thoughts away in my processor. After all, it was Kanga's story, not mine, and nobody was going to read it ever again. Especially Dad, who never even read *The Directions*.

● ● ●

The remainder of the evening unfolded in typical fashion.

First I visited the bathroom to remove my food receptacle, pulling the long plastic bag, brimming with taco meat and masticated tortilla shells, from the recesses of my throat. I paused to admire the full receptacle, allowing myself to feel a sense of satisfaction, perhaps even *fullness*, the same feeling I imagined humans enjoyed after a delicious meal. Then I squeezed the chewed taco meat into the toilet and flushed. As I tossed my used receptacle into the trash beneath the sink, I noticed Kanga's: still clear, without a trace of tacos. This triggered the mom in me to ask aloud, "Why do I even bother?"

I cleaned the kitchenette, then handled the bills that Dad had always complained about (the Gravy stipend was indeed modest) while Kanga watched *Unsolved Mysteries*, *Night Court*, the final twenty-two minutes of a movie called *Twins*, and *Quantum Leap*, as well as the countless commercials promoting a worriless, scientifically advanced lifestyle of plug-in air fresheners, weight-loss shakes, home gym apparatuses, free refills on pop, handheld video games, pregnancy tests on a stick, and the greatest hits of all time, now available on compact disc. At eleven o'clock, Kanga suffered through the news and was rewarded with *Arsenio Hall*, followed by *Personals* and *Night Games*, a pair of dating game shows that were Kanga's guilty pleasures. At 1:03 a.m., he whispered, "G'night, Darryl," and stumbled into his room.

"Love you, Kanga."

I was charging up in my customary spot, behind the orange chair in the living room. I stayed there another couple of hours, until 3:51 a.m., then grabbed the phone book and cordless phone, tiptoed out our apartment door, down the hallway, and into the stairwell. I was alone, but Dad's voice was waiting in my throat.

In the phone book, I found the number for "Jacobowhite, Aaron."

He answered after the fifth ring. "Do you know what time it is?" he said, still half-asleep.

"You the teacher that came by my place today? Talking to my kid, putting all those ideas in his head about writing? About scholarships? See, I got a real job, buddy. I use my hands, and I make money. I feed my boys. I put clothes on them. What do you do? Overpaid babysitter! Next time you want to—"

"Sir, I never meant to—"

"—*come near my place, you save us both some trouble and drive off a cliff, you elitist scumbag. Got it?*"

"Okay, sir. Let me just—"

I hung up.

Back in our apartment I was surging with energy. It was time to use the camcorder and VCR to edit our science presentation.

I had planned to delete Kanga's Magic Johnson footage immediately, but I made the mistake of watching it one last time. Then again, and then several more times, until that bullet of jealousy passed clean through me. After viewing the twenty seconds of footage for the eighty-second time, I realized the simple fact that I was *proud* of Kanga. How had he ever created something so beautiful with a garbage mom like me? And why, in the sickly green glow of the television screen, did I feel a rancorous urge to press Record and tape over my brother's moment of perfection? It was the sensible thing to do, of course, destroying proof of Kanga's exceptionality. And so easy. All I had to do was press Record and remake the introduction myself.

I pressed Eject.

I put the finished videotape in my backpack. Earlier tonight Mr. Jacobowhite had allowed me to feel exceptional, and I was *still* beaming from it. Tomorrow in science class, I would give the same gift to Kanga.

I won't hold you down, brother. Not again.

Back in the summer after fourth grade, after our parents had been gone for months, Kanga still believed they were out there. He devised a plan to knock on every door in the building, asking people if they'd seen Mom and Dad, if they'd found any clues, any leads at all. Kanga's error had been going to me for help. I told him it was useless, that I'd already been to the police, that they'd combed the entire building and found nothing. "Don't bother the neighbors," I said. "People don't want to be reminded of depressing things." Then I turned on cartoons for him until his plan dissolved into explosions and sound effects, because I already knew Mom and Dad were history.

Because I turned them in.

I called Detroit.

I picked up the phone, dialed the number at the back of *The Directions*, and told the operator Mom and Dad were obsolete.

That same day Mom and Dad were gone.

5

F I EVER NEEDED TO IDENTIFY THE BIGGEST VILLAINS IN AMERICA, all I had to do was listen to my classmates whisper about who they were *sure* was a robot. This morning in Mr. Belt's class the list was broad. There was the woman from Texas who hired a hit man to kill the mother of her daughter's cheerleading rival. Definitely a robot. There were the Lebanese hostage takers. Robots. There was Mike Tyson. Rapist and robot. There was the suicide doctor, Jack Kevorkian. Clearly a robot, because who else would have such disregard for human life? Well, Jeffrey Dahmer. That guy was such a huge robot that the only "Jeffrey" in our grade, Jeff Lindor, probably would have killed and eaten a person just to have a different first name.

But if they'd asked me, I would have told my classmates that the biggest robot of all time was Kanga Livery. He was on the other side of our classroom, ogling Staci Miles. Not looking. Not glancing. *Ogling*. He looked exactly like a robot with a broken processor.

It was just before the bell to begin science class. Staci sat in the front row. Unless she could feel Kanga's stare tugging at the green ribbons in her hair, she had no knowledge of my brother's salacious, slack-jawed gaze. Kanga held his stomach with both hands, the way I'd seen pregnant humans do while considering which cereal to buy at the grocery store. The tips of his fingers rhythmically dug into and swirled around the rim of his belly button. It was a subtle motion, barely perceptible unless you were looking directly at him. His head and knees swayed in counterbalance to his abdomen, like a hypnotized snake.

Kanga stood up.

Oh no.

He was walking toward Staci Miles. My only hope was that an actual snake would flash from beneath a chair and bite him, preventing Kanga from reaching her. I had no such luck.

"Staci," he groaned.

She turned to Kanga—smiling, in her default way that conveyed both cheerful optimism and intimidating intelligence. "Yes?"

"I like you."

Her eyebrows raised in alarm. "Excuse me?"

"I like your voice. Listening to you read. I like it when Mr. Belt makes you read the science book. Page 314 about single-celled organisms. I like it when you say *cilia*."

Staci picked up her science book and hugged it to her chest.

"Wait," said Kanga. "I said 'like,' right?"

The bell rang.

"I meant *love*."

● ● ●

With everybody in their seats, Mr. Belt began class: "Presentations are a foundational element of our society. 'Present.' That's half the word. Birthday presents. Christmas presents. ' 'Tis better to give than to receive,' as they say. When you give a science presentation, you give the world a gift. Or am I wrong?"

Mr. Belt stood before us, rubbing his temples as though his words were being beamed down to him via satellite. We just stared back and nodded.

"Then we have the second part of 'presentation,' which is the word 'nation,' and if I have to tell you guys why 'nation' is important to our fair nation, well, I feel sorry for your grandkids when they ask you what you learned in ninth grade."

Rye raised his hand. "Coach. I don't think 'presentation' has the word 'nation' in it."

"What the hell are you talking about, Rye?"

"It's '*ta*tion.' I don't know. I'm looking at the word right now. '*Ta*tion,' I think."

"Rye, I'm going to let you in on a little secret. This lesson, the one you're receiving, the one I'm teaching you right now about the importance of presentations, is the exact same lesson I gave my first-period class, and nobody in first period, Rye, was *un*able to understand what the point was. The information is in their heads, and it ain't coming out. Presentations. Presents. Nations. What's not to get?"

"I get your point, it's just—"

"Now, that's handled!" Mr. Belt clapped his hands. "Let's have a presentation!" He was angry. "Liverys! Get your visual aids and rear ends to the front of the room!"

The TV cart was already in position. I hustled up to it and pushed our tape into the VCR. I had my speech at the ready. Kanga joined me. He had nothing. He stood on one side of the TV, me on the other. I hit Play on the introduction and waited the ten seconds until I heard "The-Principle-of-Flight-by-Kanga-and-Darryl!" I began to read: "When man first noticed the birds and insects, he wanted flight for himself. He attached wings to his arms. He leapt from high places. Alas, his body was too heavy, his muscles too small, to soar the enigmatic skies . . ." Over the years I'd perfected the language of a smart but not *too* smart student. My goal was always to get a good grade, but never to show off any real knowledge to the extent where I appeared more intelligent than the teacher. In Mr. Belt's case that was a challenge. "At last, man created a glider. He flew!

In modern times, man travels the heavens in various ways. The Concorde jet crosses the Atlantic Ocean in less than four hours . . ." But nobody was listening to me.

The class was staring at Kanga. Even Staci Miles couldn't hide her amazement at what the videotape had shown her in those ten seconds, ending with "The-Principle-of-Flight-by-Kanga-and-Darryl!" Upon hearing those words, Kanga remembered having gotten in front of the camcorder yesterday, but by the time he leaned forward to see the TV screen, it was over. I did not have to look, because I knew exactly what the class had just seen: my brother channeling Magic Johnson. Mr. Belt sat at his desk, leaning forward, pinching the fat on his cheek.

At the end of our presentation, the video froze on a frame showing a blackbird on a telephone wire whose head was tilted like it wanted to ask the class a question. Realizing I was being completely ignored, I made this prediction aloud: "Someday man will evolve into a flying creature. His legs will shrink to the size of a ten-year-old's legs. His chest muscles will quadruple in mass. His arms will grow ten feet in length, with a skinlike webbing connecting his wrists and hips."

Nobody reacted. They just stared at Kanga.

Mr. Belt got up without a word. He knelt on the floor beside Kanga's desk and began fondling a cuff of my brother's jeans. "Roll up your pant legs, Kanga. Give me a look at your calf muscles. Just a peek at those calves. Jesus Christ! It's like two turkey breasts down here! And you're taller than last year's point guard by five inches! You hear that? You're my new point guard, Livery, just in time for preseason workouts. Practice is tonight at seven." Mr. Belt yanked out a couple of Kanga's leg hairs and twisted them between his finger and thumb, then leaned close to Kanga and whispered: "But mum's the word on these practices. Got it? We're technically too early on the calendar, according to those bastards at the Michigan High School Athletic Association. These are unsanctioned practices, Livery, so don't go spouting at the mouth about them. Being on a team is about keeping secrets, right?"

Kanga was dumbstruck. He could only gawk at the grown man on the floor grinning up at him.

"Boy oh boy." Mr. Belt patted Kanga's leg. "I'm claiming this good stuff for the Hectorville Birds."

Kanga's eyes were the letters *N* and *O*, but his mouth was too terrified to say the word. Structured basketball practice was the opposite of his style. He had survived school by anonymously sitting through class, being polite—if weird—and never having any real expectations placed on him. He excelled at staring off into space. He could teach a master's course in watching TV while drinking milk straight from the jug. That was about it.

He looked to me for help. I shook my head. There was no easy escape. Mr. Belt wasn't letting this one go. In the coach's imagination, Kanga was already dominating defenses, racking up triple-doubles, and hoisting trophies.

I needed to intervene in this crisis, but how? The key was to dispel Mr. Belt's exaggerated notions, and the strategy that came to me, counterintuitive as it was, required *more* public exposure for Kanga. One basketball practice, to be exact. I ran the projections, and there was an 87 percent chance Kanga would flounder at practice. Despite the video footage showing a glimpse of greatness, a gymnasium filled with sweaty boys in no way resembled the familiarity of Shimmering Terraces. Kanga would freeze under pressure. He would sustain injuries. He would suffer emotional damage from Mr. Belt barking in his face. But after one practice, he would be free to quit.

I stepped forward. "Of course, Mr. Belt," I said. "Kanga would like nothing better."

It was Mom's line in my mouth. Mom had used it whenever her battery was low and she needed to exit a difficult situation. "Would you like a car wash with that tank of gas?" . . . "Do you have a minute to hear about Jesus?" . . . "Hey. Wife. Wash my shirts." . . . *Of course. I'd like nothing better.*

"And Mr. Belt?" I added. "I would like to volunteer as team manager."

"Already have one, and she's a girl. The guys would revolt if I canned the girl and stuck you in her place."

"What about a videographer?"

"Idiot-gopher? Talk English."

"A videographer is an assistant," I clarified, "who videotapes practices and games."

Mr. Belt stood up from the floor. "Who has time to watch videotapes? I have these presentations to grade, in addition to my own personal affairs."

"Parents. We could sell highlight reels to parents at the end of the season. The money we raise could support a pizza party. I own all the equipment. I could even add music—"

The bell rang.

Mr. Belt grabbed Kanga's quivering chin. "Listen. When that ball comes off that rim tonight—listen—when that ball goes up—" He flapped his elbows. "You gotta—hear me?—gotta find a fella and put a body on him. Just look in the mirror. Look at your body. Look down below your head, Kanga. You're a Bird now. A Hectorville Bird. I'm talking, but I don't think you're listening. Today. Not tomorrow. Not the day after tomorrow. Seven o'clock. Hello? Livery? What are we doing at seven o'clock? Putting a body on—"

Kanga closed his eyes to hide.

"Somebody," finished Mr. Belt. "Put a body on somebody, Livery. Got it?"

● ● ●

My position was impossible. Being a robot meant hiding your identity at all times, at all costs. Yet here I was, placing my brother on a petri dish to be observed by humans. Was my processor malfunctioning? Had I gone obsolete? We didn't live in Costa Rica, with its televised Robotic Surfing League. This was the United States, where the only sport robots were allowed to participate in was big-game hunting—and we were the trophies.

But I couldn't help it. *The Directions* had been telling me "No" my entire life. Just this once I wanted to say "Yes." Then we could return to our life under a rock. But it wasn't just that either. I needed to see exactly how good Kanga was at basketball, against other kids, in a real gym. I needed to know if our science video had been a fluke or a hint of something much greater. Because if Kanga really *was* an amazing basketball player, couldn't his twin brother be one too?

Getting through this practice wouldn't be easy. Not by a long shot. Worst of all, because Kanga was in denial about being a robot in the first place, I was prevented from communicating the severity of our situation. All I could do was try to keep him calm. The last thing we needed was a Molly Seed situation in the middle of practice.

Back at our apartment, I stuffed my camcorder in my backpack and instructed Kanga to change into basketball clothes. The Magic Johnson uniform was out of the question. That meant I had to venture into Mom and Dad's room and find an old white T-shirt of Dad's and a pair of sweatpants. I made sure Kanga had something on his feet this time. The Velcro high-tops I'd gotten from the grocery store would have to do. Kanga dressed slowly, dejectedly, occasionally peering into the dark TV screen he wouldn't be watching until practice was over.

"You look like a basketball player," I told him, trying to build up his confidence.

"I hate this," he said. "I want the Magic jersey."

By programmed reflex, I opened my mouth to berate Kanga for being too fussy and difficult, but I caught myself. Parenting was about picking your battles, sure enough, but sometimes it was about being on the same team. "Let's *make* a Magic jersey."

We got out the markers. Kanga took purple. I took yellow. We drew Magic's number, 32, on Dad's white shirt, and JOHNSON in block letters across the back. Kanga added the Lakers logo. I got out the scissors and cut off the sleeves.

"All right, ballplayer," I said. "How about a bag of Cobra Burger before practice?"

"Really?" Kanga gave me a slight smile. "Thanks, Darryl."

We rode our bikes to the restaurant and went through the drive-through. We took our bags of food to Umber Park, where the river bent through town. The playground there had an alien spaceship in it, and we climbed into the cockpit, where our names were among the hundreds chipped into the green paint, and that's where we had dinner. Kanga emptied both Cobra Burger bags onto the floor of the spaceship. He unwrapped the solid food and deposited it into one of the bags. He folded the top twice, then used his fists to pound the burgers and fries together until they were a chunky brown paste. In the other bag he carefully placed the food wrappings like tissue paper for an expensive watch. Then he huffed both bags alternately. A couple of times a week we did this back at the apartment too, on Kanga's nights to "cook." He claimed the Cobra Burger food smelled just like Mom. I had to agree with him.

Even comfort food couldn't unwrinkle Kanga's brow. I had to say something profound to him, something that would not further overload his system with pressure but would encourage his body to make recognizable basketball movements on the court. I was drawing a blank. *The Directions* advised praising your child's efforts, not their successes, to foster a healthy acceptance of failure in life. "You look awesome," I repeated to him, but Kanga just ignored me and continued breathing in the Cobra Burger fumes. *The Directions* also warned that parents should think twice before telling their children what it terms "the cold truth": your unfiltered hopes for your child's triumph in a given situation. For instance, I should *not* tell Kanga, "Make me proud out there tonight," but instead, "Try your hardest, brother, and you'll do great." Somehow it all sounded wrong, like Mom with a dead battery trying to hold a conversation. I was mentally combing back through *The Directions* for any gem I might have missed when my mouth went rogue and blurted out: "I was too chicken to try out for the basketball team."

Kanga looked at me for the first time since we boarded the spaceship.

"I ran the projections. I only had a 4.9 percent chance of making it, so I wimped out. I know the triple-threat position, and can dribble a little, but when it comes to actual basketball, I—"

"I don't want to go."

"One practice. That's all you have to do, Kanga, and then you can quit, okay? Just one practice, and I'll be watching you the whole time. I'll be cheering for you in my mind. You're Magic Johnson. If you forget that, look down at your uniform." Then my mouth let fly the coldest truth of all: "I'm so jealous of you."

I heard Kanga's exhaust fan kick on, and then his hands were crunching a Cobra Burger bag into the shape of a basketball. It was time. Two hours from now our life of anonymity would be restored. Or we would be destroyed by a psychotic mob of teenage robophobes. There was no in between.

"Wipe that onion off your nose," I said. "Let's go to practice."

6

THE HECTORVILLE BIRDS DIDN'T HAVE A GYM. We had a Cave. As in, "Get your tail feathers down to the Cave!" Or, "Guess who kissed Kelly under the bleachers in the Cave!" And if you were a buffoonish teacher: "Come, my spelunkers! On to the Cave!" Maybe it was called the Cave because of the blotchy plaster walls, or because two of its four backboards were constructed of plywood instead of glass. Or the smell. Or the fluorescent lights that tinted everything brown. Or the tornadoes of dust that followed the Birds wherever they ran.

We arrived at 6:56, and Mr. Belt was nowhere to be seen. His freshman basketball players were taking turns launching half-court shots at one of the hoops. There was Rye from science class, towering above the other players in his sports goggles and fashion catalog of unattainable basketball gear: black Nike T-shirt with a one-inch silhouette of Michael Jordan ($34), reversible double-mesh Champion shorts ($28), and a crisp pair of Reebok Pumps ($149). His next shot from half-court missed everything.

That was when I noticed a girl sitting against a wall. She had to be rich, because on her knees was an Outbound Portable Plus, a laptop computer I had once drooled over in *Computer Shopper* magazine. Its cord was stretched provocatively to a power outlet. The team manager—that had to be her—was typing on the computer, yet, astoundingly, not looking at her fingers. Instead, she stared at a nondescript portion of Cave wall, *through* the Cave wall, it seemed, at something fascinating beyond it. Her body was rigid; not even her chest appeared to be breathing, yet her fingers were moving like the machinery of a player piano. *Brooke Noon.* That was her name.

What was Brooke Noon writing on her portable computer? Was it a science fiction story about a basketball team manager who guides every shot through the hoop using telekinesis?

In a tenth of a second, my processor scanned my memory for historical images of Brooke Noon. Most were of the back of her head, as any teacher we ever had in common had always seated Brooke in the front row near the teacher's desk. Likewise, Brooke was consistently on the outskirts of class pictures, her shoulder grasped by the teacher, her face a Halloween mask of discomfort. She stomped wherever she went in her soft, oversize shoes, always out of breath, adjusting her huge T-shirt before taking her seat in class. She spoke at the wrong moments, sometimes whispering, sometimes shouting. Our teachers stayed calm at first, but eventually, upon seeing her fidget, they would yell, "Brooke! Settle down!" She broke her arm in eighth grade, and although I had no classes with her that year, I overheard some kids discussing Brooke's method of using her pencil to scoop dead skin particles from the inside of her cast and then spread them around the surface of her desk, spelling out her name, until the teacher walked over, at which point Brooke blew the dead skin cells at the girl beside her, Jeananne Carson, who Brooke hated.

I had been filming Brooke pounding away at her laptop for two minutes—her frozen expression never changing—when I heard someone yell, "GET THE GEEK!" By the time my camcorder found Kanga, he was lying on the Cave floor, trying to deflect the basketballs being fired at him from every direction. One such ball was an orange laser beam to the side of his head. I videotaped the thrower, high-fiving his teammates, announcing, "*Nailed the sucker.*"

James Botty. The boy who'd saved Bus 117 from Molly Seed.

The aura of deference in the Cave strongly suggested that, when Mr. Belt was not around, this was James Botty's team. Kanga lay flattened. James puffed out his chest and posed as though he were holding two ostrich eggs near his groin.

Mr. Belt finally strolled in. I focused the camcorder on his confused expression. "Weren't any of you raised with religion?" he asked. "Or was it just Sunday morning cartoons for you? Doesn't anybody believe in God?"

As the team assembled in a ring around Mr. Belt, Kanga slowly got to his feet.

"Respect," Mr. Belt continued. "Respect for the dead is a major tenet of any religion or creed. You—" He pointed to a basketball player. "Maybe you're Jewish or Hindu, or are you Native American? Any of those religions would instill some morals."

The player blinked.

"Because what I just witnessed, a casual game of dodgeball"—he stared at the lights—"was a prime example of humankind's crass obliviousness to all our impending deaths. I just found out that Magic Johnson is about to die."

The team gasped. Kanga's eyes went wide. He grabbed at his homemade purple-and-yellow jersey.

"I heard it on the radio. HIV. Magic gave a press conference earlier today, and now . . ." Mr. Belt cleared his throat. "He will die. He got HIV from somebody, and, ladies and gentlemen, that HIV will become AIDS, and AIDS will cut him down. One of you, the youth, if you continue to study science, will certainly develop a cure for AIDS. Or even HIV. But it will be too late for Earvin 'Magic' Johnson."

The team inched away from Kanga, eyeing his shoddy jersey.

"Magic, if he were here, breathing his last breath, would want us to use our basketballs today. Sometimes basketball is more important than life or death. So forget what I just said about Magic Johnson. He might already be dead. Run some laps. Be healthy, boys."

As the team jogged light circles around the Cave, my camcorder found Brooke Noon again, her face registering no hint of remorse for Magic Johnson, or even an awareness of who the man was; she merely kept typing on her laptop. Only then did I realize my own expression certainly betrayed no emotion either. Nor did any part of my body, inside or out. I had just heard it plainly: Magic Johnson was dying. Yet I felt nothing except an electric curiosity about what would happen next in my own life. A dastardly smile crept across my face, the same smile James Botty wore as he shadowed Kanga during their laps, whispering the word *AIDS* over and over. My camcorder focused in on Kanga: eyes wide, lips pinched together, like he was protecting a baby bird that had just hatched on his tongue. It was the look of someone appropriately mourning Magic Johnson. I vowed to buy him more Cobra Burger after practice.

● ● ●

Mr. Belt blew his whistle. "I have another announcement, boys. The Ceiling Fan will be late to practice tonight."

"*Nooo!*" responded the team.

"The Ceiling Fan is a grown man with grown-man responsibilities. Tonight he has a job interview. Do you believe Ceiling Fan Simms can pay for his various adult needs and appetites just by being my assistant coach?"

Rye, whose sports goggles were fogged from running laps, raised his hand. "Coach, what kind of job is the Ceiling Fan—"

"The Ceiling Fan is going through a rough patch, Rye. End of story. The only reason a grown man such as himself is able to coach a freshman boy such as yourself is because the Ceiling Fan got laid off last summer. It's a sensitive subject, which is why I don't bring it up with him. So, when the Ceiling Fan *does* get here, none of you knuckleheads mention anything about job interviews or whatnot." Mr. Belt closed his eyes. "*Ceiling Fan Simms.* That name should set off alarm bells, gentlemen. Back in the day, he was our entire team. The Ceiling Fan was the most persistent team member I've seen at the ninth-grade level. And his favorite practice drill was ballslappers. You guys wanna do some ballslappers?"

The team glanced at one another. Rye spoke: "What's 'ballslappers,' Coach?"

Mr. Belt blew his whistle again. "Ready? Here's the rules. Three guys to a hoop. The drill is simple. Kanga? You listening?" Mr. Belt blew his whistle. "Everybody gets a ball. That means everybody. When I blow the whistle"—he blew the whistle—"everybody tosses their basketballs at the hoop. The balls bounce every which way. The guy who rips down the most rebounds wins. Any questions?"

Rye raised his hand.

"What's the problem, Rye? Didn't I just explain the drill?"

"But why's it called ballslappers?"

"Listen. 'Slapping' is a form of rebounding. You use two hands when you slap a basketball. It makes a loud slapping sound. The Ceiling Fan used to love to slap a ball or two in his day. But don't get any funny ideas. No extra points for slapping. The purpose of the drill is not ball slapping. It's rebounding. So don't go trying to slap every ball in town. The way to score points in this gym is to grab more balls than the other men at your hoop."

Rye raised a hand.

"Jesus Christ."

"I still don't get the drill, Coach."

Mr. Belt blew the whistle. "Three guys to a hoop." He blew it again. "Okay? That means if some guy grabs all three basketballs, *that* guy gets three points. That means the other guys get zero. If that happens, by Christ, then those other two guys are automatically in my craphouse, running laps around the Cave. But this is just the first round of ballslappers. Then we have the finals."

Rye raised a hand, but Mr. Belt was already pushing guys in different directions, bouncing them basketballs, blowing the whistle, yelling: "Get with the system!"

I kept my camera on Kanga. He was grouped at a basket with the two fattest kids on the team. They were already scarlet in the face from laps. All the power in their bodies seemed to be directed toward breathing and swallowing. One took a hit from his inhaler and then stumbled toward the locker room with his ball. The other kid bounced his to Kanga and said, "You're going to get it anyway."

Kanga won the first round of ballslappers without even moving. He simply held two basketballs while Mr. Belt blew the whistle. My brother glanced at me. I gave him a thumbs-up.

"Ballslappers!" said Mr. Belt, his gaze dancing between groups of players. "Who's in the finals? You? You? *You*, Kanga? Okay. Four guys, one hoop. What I mean is four balls in the air, fellas. Any questions? I want to see some slapping out there! Rebounding, you numbskulls."

The finalists for ballslappers consisted of the three tallest players—Rye, Deano, and Kanga—but also a surprise entry: James Botty. James leaned toward Kanga and sniffed. He made a face, then spat on the floor between Kanga's shoes. The whistle blew. The finals began. Rye easily grabbed two basketballs. Kanga grabbed zero, as he had not attempted to jump. Rye handed one of his balls to Kanga, whispering "*Sorry*" for being the biggest and strongest boy on the team.

Mr. Belt blew the whistle again.

Rye hauled in two balls again, but this time James *slapped* his rebound. James held the ball after slapping it, muscles clenched, as if he were still slapping it.

"That's how you slap it," said Mr. Belt.

"Yeah, James!"

"Jamey!"

Mr. Belt blew the whistle.

"Let's go, James."

James slapped it again. He flipped the ball to one of the spectating teammates, who caught it awkwardly, like it was a souvenir.

"Livery. You going to try jumping?" asked Mr. Belt. "Or do I got to get James here to light a firecracker in your rear end?"

James leaned toward Kanga. "You better burn that sissy costume you're wearing. Thing's probably covered in AIDS."

The team doubled over with laughter.

"Shut your laugh holes!" Mr. Belt said, unable to resist a chuckle himself. "And cut the commentary, James. Now are you ready to *jump*, Livery, or what? Let's go! *Jump!*" He blew the whistle, and what happened next is best understood by looking at a pair of before-and-after pictures taken one second apart.

The before picture: Above the rim are the four basketballs, slightly blurry in their movement. Below, on the floor, are the basketball players, hips pressing against each other for position, eyes looking up at the balls, mouths guessing where the balls will go next. All except Kanga. He is crouched below them, knees and elbows tucked into his body, chin against his chest. He is a compact ball of a boy hiding from the tussle above.

The after picture: Kanga's opponents have risen slightly from the floor, their arms reaching upward for the basketballs. They have none. Where Kanga was hiding a moment ago is an empty space. He is now above it. He is now above *them*. Kanga's head is eclipsing a portion of the rim. Kanga's knees have elevated to the height of Rye's ears. In Kanga's hands: two basketballs. One has been collected by Kanga's right hand, while the other is palmed by his left. If you follow the calm look in Kanga's eyes, you will find the third and fourth basketballs. They appear to be flying away from him, terrified, as if Kanga's next action will be to extend his neck and bite them from the air.

He didn't bite those two basketballs. Not exactly.

Instead, in the air, Kanga quickly tossed both already collected basketballs to teammates, freeing his hands to scoop up the last two balls. When he finally landed on the ground, this is what it sounded like:

"Whoa."

"Dang it."

"That was four—"

"He got four balls."

"I blinked. What happened?"

"What's that kid's name?"

"Has anyone ever gotten that many balls before?"

"Coach?"

"Coach Belt, has anyone ever—"

"Start running laps," said Mr. Belt. "Everybody."

Nobody moved.

"What are you guys waiting for? I said *run!*"

"Even us, Coach?" said one of the guys who had only been watching.

"You. Everybody. Start running. NOW."

Kanga followed the team in a lap around the Cave, but this time he took giant leaps with each step, bounding. The bounds got longer and longer, as though he were testing the limits of his bounding ability. He bounded over the team manager sitting against the Cave wall.

"Kanga!" Mr. Belt was yelling again. "No! I want you over here. You stand with me, Kanga. Stop jumping, and get your butt over here."

Kanga went to Mr. Belt.

"Pick up those balls, Livery. I want these turkeys to see you holding those balls."

Kanga knelt down and gathered his balls, two in each arm. He and Mr. Belt watched the rest of the basketball team run laps for a good eight minutes.

"Four balls." Mr. Belt blew his whistle. "Get over here!"

The team ran over.

"Let's finish this drill. From now on nobody gets four balls. If anybody gets four balls—" He blew the whistle.

Nobody grabbed four balls again. But, for the remainder of ballslappers, Kanga snagged two balls every whistle, sometimes three. It was simple. He jumped, like everybody else, except he jumped *higher*. Kanga then rebounded every ball in his vicinity. He didn't touch anyone. He just watched the balls, as if in slow motion, and rebounded them. He didn't slap them. He didn't make a sound with them. The moment his fingers touched a basketball, it was palmed. He did this with both hands. Then, if he needed to, he passed a ball to an open teammate and palmed another one.

This wasn't our plan. The plan was for Kanga to be Kanga, not Magic Johnson. It was all happening too fast for me to process. Then James Botty, who hadn't slapped or even touched a ball in five whistles, dug his fingernails into the homemade Magic jersey as Kanga was about to leap. The shirt ripped apart, and Kanga flopped to the Cave floor, landing on his neck.

"Hey!" somebody protested. "Intentional foul!"

"James shredded the new kid!"

"Coach, is James allowed to break somebody's neck like that?"

The team was yelling and stepping onto the court in Kanga's defense. Half of the team. The other handful of guys stood back silently, watching to see what James did next. James stared down at Kanga with the vacant eyes of a street dog. "I told you," James said. "Get that AIDS off my court."

The whistle blew.

"James," said Mr. Belt. "*James.*" Mr. Belt stepped between Kanga and James. "Good hustle, James, but start running laps." Mr. Belt watched sternly as James trotted away; then the coach's face reverted to a boyish grin. "This is what I call basketball!"

I kept videotaping. Mr. Belt had begun grouping the boys for a shirts-versus-skins scrimmage when the scene in my viewfinder went black. A voice boomed down at me: *"You're doing it wrong!"*

Brooke Noon.

I detached the camcorder from my eye and there was the team manager, inches away, dancing from foot to foot, her mouth contorted like she had a fishing hook in her cheek. The energy in her typing fingers a moment ago was now fueling her entire body. "You're in the completely wrong place!" she said, stomping off toward the double doors leading to the cafeteria. She peeked back at me before disappearing through the doorway. "Come on!"

In the succeeding nanosecond, my processor submitted a report detailing the myriad reasons *not* to follow Brooke Noon into the cafeteria: she was impulsive; she was erratic; she once grabbed a handful of Joe Goodman's hair and didn't let go for the rest of recess; she had no friends; she was loud; she was in the 98th percentile of intelligence yet never turned in her homework; she didn't make eye contact; she yawned excessively; additional elements of her personality were unknown due to the fact that she had only spoken three sentences to me in my entire life—all in the last thirty seconds. The report concluded by alternately flashing the phrases "UNPREDICTABLE" and "DO NOT FOLLOW" in red letters across the inside of my eyeballs.

I followed her.

I capped the eyepiece of my camcorder. I glanced across the Cave to where Brooke's laptop was still plugged into the wall, waiting for a stray basketball to crack it in two—

"*This way!*" she bellowed from the cafeteria.

7

FOLLOWED HER THROUGH THE CAFETERIA, past the trophy cases, around the pop machines, and down the drama hallway. Her arms pumped. Her shoes slapped the linoleum. She peeked over her shoulder with a bewildered expression. So I stopped. I watched Brooke open a heavy brown door and dart inside. Yet before the door could slam behind her, she asked, "Where did you go, Darryl?"

She knew my name. *The Directions* advised that nonessential humans *not* know your name. That meant you were being a model robot, which I was. I could count on one hand how many times another student had said my name in a sentence this school year, and nobody—ever—had said it like Brooke Noon just did. Like she knew me. Like I was her brother and she might holler from inside the family bathroom: *Darryl? I need more toilet paper!* And I would say: *Get it yourself!*

Or I would stop what I was doing, get a roll of toilet paper, approach the bathroom door and—

"Darryl!" she screamed, holding the door open for me.

I ran. I liked hearing Brooke Noon say my name.

Just inside the door was a ladder bolted to the floor. It led up through a square opening in the ceiling. Brooke began to climb.

I hesitated. "Should I bring the camcorder?" I added, *"Brooke?"*

"That's the whole point of going to the skybox, dummy."

Skybox? I strapped the camcorder around my neck and grasped the ladder with both hands. When I reached the top, Brooke was already clanking down a catwalk through a vast, dark space. I braced myself by grabbing the slick metal handrails: the sturdy infrastructure of an alien spacecraft. The catwalk extended through the upper regions of our unlit auditorium. Random red lights blinked among the seating below, as if to assure us the building was still awake, watching our every movement. Brooke fished a key ring from her pocket, somehow selecting the correct key in the darkness, and unlocked a door. I followed.

The next room was pitch-black. Cold. There was carpeting beneath our feet, and the air tasted like dead mice. Yet Brooke was familiar enough with her environment to approach one of the walls. She felt the surface—I heard the scraping of her fingers on plywood—then pulled a square section from the wall, creating an orange window, bursting with light. Heat billowed in through the window, filling our tiny room. Brooke set the wall section on the floor. Then she stood still, her shoulders and head silhouetted by orange, as she peered down into the Cave.

I stepped beside her, just tall enough to see over the wooden sill. The view knocked me off balance. The sight of bleachers, double doors, backboards, lines, bricks, basketball players: all miniature versions, yet somehow more intricately rendered. The moving pieces—the players, the ball—appeared weightless and insignificant, like insects trapped in a shoe-box. We were up near the Cave rafters, Brooke and myself, our shoulders separated by inches. It wasn't just a *better* view up in this "skybox;" it was an *artistic* view. Brooke must have recognized that I was an artist like her. I felt the wires in my neck tighten, urging my mouth to say something about art. Something profound. Something only she would understand. But Brooke beat me to it:

"You're my boyfriend now. You can't tell anybody."

It wasn't a question, but I answered her. "Okay."

"If you tell anybody, my other boyfriends will find out and beat you up. I have three boyfriends."

"Did you take them up here too?"

"Mind your own business," she said. "And stop staring."

I looked back at the basketball court. "Sorry."

"We're not girlfriend-boyfriend yet." She stepped away from the window, into a dark corner. "We have to touch something." She carefully extended her right shoe from the shadows. "We have to touch shoes."

"Can I look at you now?"

"At my shoe."

I looked at her shoe: a dirty pink Converse All Star, two inches of red sock, and the frayed cuff of her jeans. Brooke would slap me across the face if she could read my thoughts—which I could scarcely identify as my own, as I'd never experienced anything like them before, especially for a shoe. It's not that I wanted to remove her shoe and expose her foot. I wanted to be *inside* her shoe.

"Hurry up," she said.

I lifted my left LA Gear.

"Closer," she said.

Our toes tapped twice. Then a three-second union, after which I lost my balance.

"That worked," she said. "And it counts more than if a stranger just touches your foot accidentally because we both wanted it to happen. Let's do the next one."

My big toe felt raw. "The next one?"

"Knees."

"Touch them?"

"Yes."

I stepped forward with my right knee out. So did Brooke. This dance brought our faces together, but not our knees. They were still the same distance apart. Brooke frowned. "This isn't working."

I slammed my left knee into her right one.

"Ouch," she said, sniffing, and wiped her nose with her hand. She looked at it. "Hands." She offered me both hands: palms up, thumbs out—one index finger was streaked with snot. "Let's do hands."

I tentatively placed my hands several inches beneath hers then lifted until Brooke's cold knuckles were resting in my palms. Her hands began to vibrate, so I released her. She wiped her hands on her pants. "Next . . ." She leaned her face toward mine, her eyes glancing down at my belly button. She whispered: "Foreheads."

I stood on my tiptoes. With our foreheads attached, I could hear deep inside Brooke's skull: her brain, it seemed, though what I heard did not match my expectations. It sounded like a steady dribble of water in a vast, echoing cave. Then something splashed, loudly, like a fish jumping, and Brooke jerked back from me. She was grinning. "I got it," she said. She slapped the plywood wall with her open hand. "I got it!" She darted through the door, across the catwalk, and down the ladder. I felt the building shudder from her stomping as she emerged below on the Cave floor, skirting the basketball court, pumping her fists, repeating, "*Got it got it got it got*—" She slid into her spot against the wall. She heaved her Outbound onto her knees. She raised her hands high above her head. Her fingers began typing, just air at first, until she lowered them to the keyboard. Once her fingers engaged with her computer, they didn't stop moving for the rest of practice. *Wow*, I thought. *Had Brooke been artistically inspired by . . . me?*

I stayed in the box, dutifully recording Kanga's impeccable basketball fundamentals happening on the court—dribbling, passing, shooting, even picking and rolling. Skills normal sentient beings acquired only after thousands of repetitions. He made fourteen free throws in a row, all with identical form: three dribbles, a pause, fingers tickled the air, the ball chiming the back of the net. An idea stung me like a hornet. What if Magic Johnson had died halfway through practice, and his soul had flown in from Los Angeles and taken root in Kanga's battery?

That's when I heard the faint squeal of a compact car struggling through the parking lot. Was this the automobile of the legendary Ceiling Fan Simms? I assumed such a persistent rebounder would drive an oversize truck, like the one Mr. Belt drove. Yet when I focused my ears on the parking lot, I heard the groaning of the car's steel frame as a massive driver pried himself loose. He entered the Cave a moment later, all six foot six of him, wide as a helicopter. The Ceiling Fan was not dressed for a job interview but rather wore a stained sweatshirt that read INVISIBLE SYSTEMS.

The team sprinted over to surround him, and Rye blurted out, "*Did you get the job?*"

The Ceiling Fan looked slowly from player to player, as if he couldn't believe anybody on Earth was glad to see him. He had obviously been crying in his tiny car, and now, with the unexpected attention of twelve adoring boys, the Ceiling Fan let out a long sob.

Rye shuffled over. "We don't want you to get a new job. We want you to stay our coach."

"They were just hiring toasters. Toasters sitting in all the chairs, waiting to be interviewed. You can tell just by looking at them. Their eyes. That smell. How am I supposed to compete? Toaster stole my last job too. United States of goddamned Toasters! And now"—the Ceiling Fan covered his face with his hands—"*and now Magic's got HIV!*"

The Birds were unable to look away from the weeping man. I found Kanga's face, wrecked with concern for the Ceiling Fan. It was a flawless display of restrained compassion, one I had never been able to master myself, not after countless hours in front of the bathroom mirror. Somehow Kanga was equipped with an endless supply of human hearts in his chest that he could break on demand.

Mr. Belt swooped in. "That's practice, men. I want you to go home. Watch some TV. Relax. Drink plenty of fluids. Just remember to use the bathroom before you go to bed. We don't need any accidents. You're freshmen in high school, for Christ's sake!" He escorted the Ceiling Fan to his office, where they could catch up in private.

I made my way down from the skybox. There was Brooke Noon, still hooked to the wall, still typing. My exhaust fan was running so loudly I could barely hear myself ask her, "What is your story about, Brooke?"

She pushed her chin to her chest and shut her eyes. She pounded the keyboard louder and louder. "*Stop shouting at me.*"

I didn't think I was shouting. Not unless she could hear my fingers, which were shouting to untie her shoelaces. I whispered, "Bye, Brooke."

Kanga waited for me at the bike rack. His homemade Magic jersey had been destroyed, so he was shirtless. A good mother would have been distressed at the sight of her son's exposure to the harsh November night, but for the moment I couldn't care less about Kanga. We biked home together, yet separately. My processor felt divided too: before Brooke, after Brooke. I recalled the heat of her forehead against mine. Somehow, that had changed me. I'd never had a connection like that with someone before—an *artistic* connection. Certainly not with Kanga. My processor quickly whipped up an entire future with Brooke Noon: living in a secluded cabin in the forest, writing science fiction stories all day, reading them to each other all night . . . and touching shoes, and knees, and hands, and foreheads, and—

I nearly road my bike into a ditch.

● ● ●

Later that night, both of us relaxing in the glow of an Oxy Clean medicated pads commercial, Kanga pressed the Mute button. He had never done that before. "Darryl?"

"What is it?"

"I wish Mom were here."

My typical response to this type of a statement was a firm *She's not, and she'll never be, so get over it.* But tonight I knew this wasn't about Mom. It was about the box Kanga and I had been living in our entire lives, the box we'd just peeked our heads out of for the first time. I said, "Mom would have been proud of you tonight."

"If Mom were here, I'd ask her if, maybe, I could go to basketball practice again tomorrow."

Tomorrow? Practice? I had forgotten the "one practice" plan entirely. Not *forgotten*, exactly, because robots don't forget things. Our memories are perfect. I had simply deleted the plan because it was no longer relevant. Oh, we would go to basketball practice tomorrow. And for the rest of the season. My copy of *The Directions* would combust if it knew how blatantly I was abandoning its supreme tenet of anonymity. Brooke Noon had said my name, and now I pined for her nonessential human contact. Of course, I would need to remain diligent in protecting our identities, now more than ever. But we'd be okay. I'd have my eyes on Kanga, always, like the perfect mother I was.

"You want to go to basketball practice tomorrow?" I smiled. "Say the magic word."

He tackled me with a hug. "THE MAGIC WORD!"

8

REMEMBERED GETTING SWITCHED ON for the first time.

Here was what it looked like: blackness.

Here was what it felt like: roughness.

Here was what it sounded like: gentle scratching.

I became aware while inside a canvas sack, and these initial sensations were recorded by my processor with perfect clarity.

Impossible to recall, however, was the genuine ignorance of those first seven seconds. The words *canvas* and *sack* were just disparate pieces of data in my processor without a connection to the physical world. I even had photographs of them in my vocabulary file—a generic sack, a folded piece of canvas—but they were useless without context. I was cognizant only of myself, the crude sensory input I'd gathered from the sack, and the wires protruding from the top of my head toward the end of the universe.

My solitude ended during my eighth second of life. I felt a jab from somewhere outside the canvas sack. Followed by another jab. Then I heard a wail. The sound was tonally similar to the tiny sounds I had made with my own mouth. I reached a foot toward the source of the jabs. To my delight, I met something of the approximate size and shape of my foot. The wailing stopped. We pressed our feet together, curling our toes hello.

Suddenly, a new barrage of sounds attacked us. They were low, repetitive, and sharp. I would later connect those sounds with the word *laughter*, but from inside the sack, they were horrifying. I felt my enclosed world separate from my partner—his renewed wails fading away. My sack stretched and groaned as it spun through space. Light entered the sack from above, and I was falling. *Above* became *below*. The sack was spitting me out. Light blinded me. I splashed into a warm thickness . . .

These were the details of my birth. I could tell my processor to re-feel them at any moment, and the sensations would return to me. Swimming in the bathtub of heated lubricant. Seeing Kanga for the first time through the shimmering liquid. Feeling his body, skin to skin, at the bottom of the tub: arms, legs, heads, wires. And the word snowballing through my vocabulary: *brother*.

But I couldn't relive *not knowing* him. Those first seven seconds when it had been just me, along with the naive belief that I would always be alone in the world—that was gone. Now Kanga's grease was smeared on every thought in my processor. Whether I wanted it there or not.

After that initial basketball practice, Kanga survived the remaining November workouts, earning a well-deserved Thanksgiving break to prepare himself for the Birds' first game of the season on December second. Now it was Kanga's wardrobe, rather than his skills, that needed the most attention. Mr. Belt required his players to appear "gussied up" at school on game day. "Dapper," "spruced," or "swanky" were also acceptable states of dress. What they all had in common was a button-down shirt, tie, slacks, and shiny shoes. Kanga owned none of the above. We headed to the Salvation Army.

Nineteen ninety-one was allergic to nostalgia. If you watched five minutes of TV from then, you understood that people didn't sit still long enough to reminisce about the days gone by. They were too busy dancing uncontrollably, jumping from airplanes with snowboards attached to their feet, racing cars around enormous beer bottles, or splashing into vast bodies of water. Zippers on the flies of jeans were not strong enough for today's hustle and bustle, so flies now included buttons. The definition of *sports* had to be rewritten to include "cross-training," which meant being proficient at all sports at once. This required a special shoe, a "cross-trainer," but rollerblades were also acceptable if you wanted to go faster than your opponents. The Salvation Army had none of the appropriate gear for 1991. Luckily for us, men's dress clothes had remained consistent since approximately the beginning of time.

The smell hit you first upon entering the store, like a bunch of sun-burned humans packed into a closet. Then, the organization. I often wondered if the Salvation Army had its own set of *Directions* for how to arrange everything *just so* on the shelves. To me, it required a certain nerve to place a used commode, for instance, next to a used stepladder, as if those two items shared an intrinsic bond that could never be broken.

Kanga bounded immediately to the sporting goods section, just like he'd always run to the toys section when we were little kids. I borrowed Mom's strategy of finding an armful of potential fits for him, carrying them to his location, and draping them across my brother's body while he perused the Salvation Army's eclectic treasures. I stacked his keepers in a pile: black shoes, two pairs of black socks, navy pants, charcoal pants, two white shirts, three clip-on ties. Then I searched for my own game-day clothes, swallowing my pride and entering the boys' section. It was a humiliating endeavor. But soon my arms were bulging with shirts and slacks, and I was waiting in line for the fitting rooms.

The Salvation Army had three fitting rooms, but one was special. The middle room. That was the place where, back in fourth grade, my life changed forever.

I was with Dad, standing in line for the fitting rooms. He had a clump of trousers in his arms and leaned down and whispered to me, "That's the one we're waiting for." He nodded to the middle door, which was occupied. The other two rooms were available, but we stood there patiently until the special door clicked open. A tall woman exited, hugging a pile of clothing to her ribs. Her curly hair was sticking out in odd directions, and her face was red. I couldn't read her expression. Was it shame? Anger? Or maybe, in the process of changing, did she accidentally disturb a nest of spiders that had taken root in her belly button? That's how she was holding the clothes. "Stop staring," Dad said, and I followed him into the special fitting room. He chucked the trousers in the corner and locked the door behind us. "There." He pointed. "Sit against that wall."

"What?"

"The outlet. I want you to plug in right now. Your mother only lets you boys charge up at home. Sometimes that's not an option. So go on. Plug in."

It was true. Home was the only place I'd ever plugged in, and just at one particular outlet. *My* outlet: the one in the living room, behind the big orange recliner. *The Directions* was kept under that chair. And the spot was hidden. Nobody could see me charging up at home, and that was the way I liked it. And now Dad wanted me to plug into *this* outlet? It was cracked and beige and splattered with tiny chicken pox.

"Go ahead and sit by that puppy, just like you do at home, but I'm going to show you how to make it look natural, just in case somebody walks in on you."

"Is somebody going to walk in on me?"

"Just sit your ass down and do as I say."

I sat down cross-legged, facing the outlet, like always.

"No, Darryl. You gotta lean against the wall. You gotta slouch. Think of yourself like a hobo, slouching low, like you got nowhere to be for the rest of your life, and you're going to sleep against that wall until somebody boots you in the head."

"Is somebody going to—"

"No. Slouch lower. Good. Now you tuck both hands under your armpits. Haven't you ever seen a homeless person? Loosen up, kid. Tuck them high. Pretend you're trying to keep warm. Now your fingers are right there by the outlet, but hidden. So go on and plug them in."

I drove my fingertips into the outlet. The thing bit me. Hard. Then it felt like a hundred cats were licking my hand at once. This was not the same electricity we had at home. It was dirty. It was *used*.

"I can see you perking up. Now we gotta talk."

The air in the tiny room popped like bubbles. The air was pink. "What if somebody knocks?"

"Look in that mirror over there, Darryl. Your eyes. Your ears. Your eyebrows. Your nostrils. See your face? People are going to call you ugly, if they call you anything," Dad said, laughing, "but they won't call you *robot*, and that's the important thing. This is your camouflage, kid. Look at me. I'm ugly. But there are worse things than having a misshapen head. Being ugly is the best thing about you and me."

"Mom's not ugly."

"No. She isn't. Gravy missed the mark with the 415s. Too symmetrical, but don't you go telling her I said that."

"Neither is Kanga, and he looks just like me."

"Maybe so. But my point is, this whole 'family' thing we're doing, none of it matters. We're all just lone robots in the world. Throwing us together in one house was Gravy's way of cutting costs. All you can do, Darryl, is take care of yourself. Just you. Got it? There's gonna come a time when it's you or Kanga. You'll have to choose. Thing is, you need to make up your mind now who it's going to be."

"I don't want to choose."

"Then you'll die with him. Your brother, he's—" Dad shook his head. "You think he's even your brother? We got piss-all of an idea what's programmed in his head or when it's gonna blow. He might have one of those magic words programmed in him, and the moment some scientist walks up behind him and whispers it, Kanga'll turn into a completely different person. You got a plan for that situation?"

"No."

"I do. It's called not being around to see it."

I shivered. Maybe from the electricity, which felt like a toothless mouth chewing on my fingers. But maybe it was the look on Dad's face.

"I can't go nowhere yet, because I'm not programmed to. I got one goddamn program, and you know what it is? Take a guess."

"Darts?"

"I wish! Me and your mother got the same thing. One program. Programmed to raise your and your brother's asses. Who knows how many programs you boys have waiting inside you? I'd kill for that kind of uncertainty. A chance for something new. Something mysterious. Try to imagine living with someone who has the exact same program as you. Sometimes I wish I was in prison."

"How many programs do you think I have?"

"We can find out. Not everything there is to know comes from *The Directions*. You've got to learn to talk to people, whoever they are, and not take no for an answer. I can teach you that. I can teach you stuff like this, using outlets anywhere. I'm going to make this offer to you one time, Darryl. Let's split. You and me. I'll be doing my program, raising you good, and you can lead us wherever you want. We can see the whole world, us together, out on the road. What do you say?"

"And just *leave* Mom and Kanga?"

"Don't tell me you ain't fantasized about this. Don't tell me you ain't seen those professional truck driver commercials and gotten a funny itch. Come on. You know we got to do this. You and me. And look." Dad pulled a butcher knife from his bundle of pants. He must have secretly chosen it from the kitchenware section. The knife was a perfect fit for Dad's permanent grip. He chopped at the air with it. His teeth flashed in the fitting-room mirror. "This'll be our weapon. And tomorrow morning we'll get in the van, and we'll never come back."

"But—"

"No buts!"

"Kanga. I thought he was your favorite."

"Kanga? My favorite? No sir. You got the wrong guy." But I heard Dad's exhaust fan click on. "This ain't about Kanga."

"I can't go tomorrow morning."

"Don't gimme that."

"Tomorrow afternoon, then I can go. I left something in my desk at school, and I need to grab it first."

"Whatever's in your desk, I'll buy you a new one. I gotta leave tomorrow morning. Come on, Darryl. Tomorrow morning. I'm dying."

"It's important. It's something I have to throw away before we go. Pictures. I guess they're drawings. Some drawings I drew."

"Of what?"

"A family."

"So?"

"A family of robots."

"Nobody's going to know they're a family of—"

"Without skin."

"Goddammit, Darryl!" Dad's free hand went to his temple and he let out a grunt. "But okay. Tomorrow afternoon. You tie up your loose ends at school. Toss the drawings. Say your good-byes. But don't actually *say* good-bye. Especially to Kanga. All his mother's coddling, letting him think he ain't a robot. That's something we just can't have. Not out there. We have to be sharp. Kanga—he just gets too damn attached to people. Not like you. You keep everyone good and distant. Might be we have to run and hide in a river or something. I've seen you, Darryl. You're always one step ahead, or at least you try to be. But you still have miles to go. That's what I'm here for. First stop, I'm thinking, should be Hoover Dam. Big things for us."

"Okay."

"When we go back out there, when you see Mom and Kanga, act normal. Act like this ain't the best day of your life." Dad was having trouble acting normal. He was so excited the butcher knife was quivering, like his hand was laughing silently to itself. I tried to picture Dad hiding in a river, swimming with those hands. I pictured him drowning. He tucked the knife back into his bundle of trousers. "Let's hug on it, partner."

We hugged in the Salvation Army fitting room, a hug I smelled for years to come.

The next morning at school, I asked the office secretary if I could make a phone call. A *private* phone call. She gave me a look, but handed over the phone. Then she left to make some copies. I immediately called Gravy Robotics.

Scratch that. I paused before dialing the number, waiting for a fail-safe mechanism in my programming to prevent me from taking an action that would erase our parents from existence. Yet the longer I waited, the more obvious it became that any fail-safe mechanism in me was linked directly to Kanga's survival, not Mom and Dad's. And how certain was I that obsolescence meant destruction? Might Gravy decide to *fix* Mom and Dad? Or update them? Or have their processors replaced and—

I dialed the number. I was doing Mom and Dad a favor.

After school, Kanga and I skipped taking the bus home. I led him to the railroad tracks and showed him how to flatten a penny. It was nearly five o'clock when we got to the apartment. Dad's new butcher knife sat in the kitchenette sink. Mom and Dad were gone.

Having selected my game-day outfit, I exited the Salvation Army fitting room. I guessed that these clothes had been worn exactly once by a ten-year-old who'd been forced to serve as ring bearer in a wedding. I was hoping for a discount due to Skittles stains on the cummerbund (which I would toss in the trash, along with the bowtie). I went to retrieve Kanga from the sporting goods section, but he was nowhere to be found. I checked other departments as they occurred to me. Electronics? No. Power tools? No. Home decor? No, though I did see an older gentleman completely absorbed in a black-velvet portrait of Elvis Presley. I brisk-walked the aisle where I hoped *not* to find Kanga, ladies' lingerie, but he wasn't there either. I was ready to start searching the parking lot

when Kanga appeared in the most unlikely location of all. Menswear. I
stood back and watched my brother flip through a shirt rack. He picked
a baby-blue shirt, adding it to the clothes already in his arms: yellow
corduroys, green socks, red-and-white bowling shoes. Kanga saw me and
ran over. "Your bowtie!" he said, snatching it from me. "Can I borrow it?"

The Directions defined *patience* as "deciding not to care about something minuscule for the sake of something crucial." Being late to work was
minuscule. Not flying through your windshield after hitting a fire hydrant
was crucial. In this same vein, I decided to assent to Kanga's rather minuscule request and let him have my beige bowtie. Then I let Kanga change
into his new outfit right there in the Salvation Army parking lot before
we biked to Shimmering Terraces. Pretty minuscule. Finally, at home, I
decided to pretend it was also minuscule for Kanga to shut himself in the
bathroom and run the sink and flush the toilet for half an hour. Besides, I
had something else to do.

I locked myself in Mom and Dad's old room. I told myself not to
think about Brooke Noon, but she came stampeding through my bowels
anyway. Brooke hadn't acknowledged me once since we'd touched appendages in the Cave skybox. But I'd seen her often. A week ago I had
been seated two tables away while Brooke enjoyed lunch with one of her
other boyfriends, Timothy Schwartz. Brooke let him eat her chicken fried
steak and mashed potatoes because she wasn't hungry and because last
night she'd heard a song in her dad's car called "Walking in Memphis,"
and now it was stuck in her head. No. It was stuck in her *body*. She opened
her laptop right at the lunch table; it was running on battery power. She
sang "Walking in Memphis" to Timothy, typing the lyrics as she sang
them. Then she said, "No no no!" and "Wait wait wait!" and she sang the
song again, using her keyboard percussively, banging the keys, humming
the notes. She said to Timothy: "This is your part." She said: "*Sing with
me!*" and shook her finger at the computer screen where the lyrics were
laid out for him. I hated seeing the potatoes on Timothy's teeth as he
sang. And how they nailed it. The eleventh time through, Brooke and
Timothy were on fire, and I knew I would always hate the song "Walk-

ing in Memphis," along with how their lunch had ended: Shoes. Knees. Hands. Foreheads.

I climbed onto Dad's old dresser. I stood on my tiptoes, loosening a ceiling tile, and found Dad's secret catalog in its secret spot. It used to be Dad's; now it was mine. The words were in Mandarin, which I could read easily enough, but the catalog's main resources were its 459 pictures of the most expensive body parts, *perfect* body parts, any robot could buy. I loved the female armpits—a swath of flesh in the shape of an iron-on patch— with or without hair, skin of any pigment. I loved the uncircumcised penises. The circumcised penises. The scrotums. I loved page twenty-eight and the word *vulva*, a word of English interrupting a page full of Mandarin, and I loved the three pictures of that word.

Most of all, I loved the picture consuming the entire back cover of the catalog: a Chinese scientist holding a woman's foot: just the foot, with no leg above her precision-crafted ankle, only a loop of loose wire curling out the top, like the flourish of a cursive *O*. The scientist was kneeling, holding the foot as if it were a *hand*, and he was asking an invisible woman to marry him.

I felt my own hand creeping up under my shirt, my index finger drawing a gentle circle around my belly button. I closed my eyes. I imagined Brooke Noon's foot buried in her shoe. Then my fingers began to open it . . . *It*. That private place, according to Mom, I was never supposed to share with anyone. Not even Kanga. I'd only ever touched it a few times before now. My fingernails dug into my belly button, breaking the seal at the bottom. I stretched the opening until it was three inches wide. No spilled lubricant. No messy wires. Just a smooth beige plastic plate with three tiny holes.

My three-pronged outlet.

The Directions devoted a sheepish paragraph to these outlets, claiming they were strictly for emergencies. Life-and-death situations. Thirty-three children are trapped in a school bus beneath an avalanche of snow, and somebody needs to recharge a flashlight. But I'd found another use. Mom and Dad had an old alarm clock in their room. I slid its plug into my three-pronged outlet, and time stopped . . .

. . . and I yanked the plug out, a second later, or maybe a year. There was the Chinese scientist and the fake-looking foot, and I felt a tug of hate, and my fingers were compelled to flip to a personal note inscribed on the inside cover of the catalog, written from Mom to Dad, dated Christmas, the year Kanga and I were switched on:

> So we never get bored
> (as if we ever would!)
> XOXO
> Tanya

Suddenly I hated the catalog, hated the word *vulva*, hated imagining Dad trying to say it aloud, as he surely did with Mom, "*Vul-va*," and I stuffed the catalog back into its secret spot, my solitude in their room having expired, signaled by the sound of God's gift to basketball dribbling down the hallway, toward the bedroom door, which he pounded on three times, causing my voice to retort through the hollow wood, "*No dribbling in the apartment!*"

"Why is the door locked?" hollered Kanga, and then I heard him spinning my basketball endlessly on his finger. "And why does it smell like something's burning?"

9

K ANGA'S FIRST GAME DAY.

Not only were we dressed like stuffed shirts on our bike ride
to school, but Kanga felt the need to be superstitious about it. My
brother's self-imposed rule was this: Once his new black shoes pushed off
our driveway, once his feet began to pedal, no part of his body could touch
the ground again until he arrived at Hectorville High. Or else. Not that
Kanga *said* this aloud, but, as his bike-riding companion, it was impossible
not to notice the pains he took to stay in continuous motion. Braking,
coasting, circling—all in an effort to keep his shoes on his pedals. The wild
card was the stoplight at Summit and Putnam—which turned green just
as we arrived. We flew beneath it with ease.

Kanga reaped his first cosmic payout in science class. Staci Miles,
dressed in her Cheerbird uniform, raised her hand and announced that
Stickzilla had asexually produced six eggs in her terrarium last night.

Staci's pronunciation of *terrarium* had caused Kanga to quake in his seat. Mr. Belt's reaction was a pragmatic intake of air through his nostrils.

We gathered around the terrarium as Mr. Belt carefully cupped Stickzilla in his hand, separating her from the special leaf dotted with her eggs, and set her down in the newspaper shreds below. Then he pinched off the leaf.

"*No—*" gasped Staci, watching Mr. Belt light a Bunsen burner. Desperately, she grabbed Kanga's hand, as if he might spring to the eggs' rescue. "*Wait, Mr. Belt!*"

But Kanga just froze, hand-in-hand with Staci, as Mr. Belt fed Stickzilla's leaf to the flame until all that remained was a blackened stem. He wetted the stem between his lips, then turned to my brother, assessing Kanga's game-day shirt, which had come untucked. Mr. Belt pushed the baby-blue shirttail down the back of Kanga's yellow pants. "Kanga," he said, "for your sake, for the team's sake, get your game face on."

It was then that Staci finally let go of my brother to cover her eyes as she wept.

"Everybody needs to get their game face on." Mr. Belt straightened Kanga's bowtie. "And a game uniform. You'll need one of those before you call yourself a Bird. Get your game uniform from Brooke."

"Who's that?" blurted Kanga, shocking Mr. Belt with his suddenly aggressive tone. "Who's *Brooke?*"

"Are you joking? She's the manager, Kanga. You and Brooke have a date after school in the equipment room. Don't keep a lady waiting."

Perhaps Kanga's game-day clothes had given rise to this new attitude. This new swagger. Dare I say, this new arrogance. Throughout the day, Kanga took every opportunity to look at himself. A window. A trophy case. A mirror inside a girl's locker. Not only that: Kanga raised his hand in social studies.

"Kanga? Really?" said Mrs. Galvin, perplexed.

"The answer is canoes made of cedar bark."

"Right!" she said, and added, "*Mr.* Livery."

Mr. Livery indeed. When the final bell rang, Kanga strutted down the hallway near the Cave, anticipating yet another new article of clothing: his game uniform. I followed behind. Brooke sat beside the sports equipment room door, typing away on her laptop. She also wore a button-down shirt and tie for game day, and had spruced herself even further with a black vest dotted ad nauseam with red hearts. My fan clicked on.

"I want number thirty-two," said Kanga.

Brooke ignored him. Her face jiggled as she typed, the chubs of fat below her eyes, the things people called "cheekbones" but that in robots are tiny pockets of air. I imagined puncturing Brooke's cheekbones with a toothpick and sucking out whatever was inside.

"I want Magic's number," Kanga said. "I want number thirty-two."

The equipment room door swung open, and there was James Botty. He held Kanga's brilliant green jersey, showing its white block numbers. Three. Two. *Magic's number.* Kanga reached for it. James yanked it away and headed past us toward the school exit.

"Where's James going?" Kanga demanded. "Where's he taking my jersey?"

Brooke finally looked at him. "You're upset," she said, "but how upset are you? Somewhat upset or only pretty upset?" Then she added: "Or are you extremely upset?"

Kanga bolted after James.

"He's not upset at *you*, Brooke," I explained. "He's upset at—"

She stared through me, like I was a blank computer screen. "*Very* upset. That's what I meant to say." She resumed typing.

I held a rewritten copy of my science fiction story, "Buford's Dilemma." It was for her. I would have preferred Brooke to read the same draft Mr. Jacobowhite had adorned with his compliments, but Kanga's name was written at the top. This new draft was *by Darryl Livery*. But I froze. I could feel the grease leaking through my fingertips, ruining the pages . . .

"Bye, Brooke." I crumpled the story into my pocket and headed after Kanga.

● ● ●

The hill behind Hectorville High School had to be at least twice as tall as the school itself. There were boulders mixed in with the dirt, tripping us as we climbed, and random patches of tall grass blowing in the wind. Every few steps my shiny black dress shoes sank into some mud. The rest of the Birds were waiting for us at the top of the hill, standing around the birch tree like the attendants at a funeral, their dress clothes slashing in the wind. Only James Botty smiled, one hand resting on the handlebars of a battered red bike. There was no chain. There were no pedals.

"You want number thirty-two?" he asked Kanga. James stepped away, offering the bike as if it were a prize. It was aimed down the backside of the hill—a slalom run around rocks and crevasses, leading to a plywood jump on the bank of Culver's Creek.

Kanga climbed atop the bike. He grabbed both handlebars.

"It's freezing up here," someone said.

"Kanga. Tell James he's crazy and let's go."

"This tradition sucks."

"No kidding."

"Look," said Rye, calmly approaching Kanga. "You sat on the bike. That's good enough. That's all any of us did. You'll still get your jersey—"

"After I spit on it," said James.

"Yeah." Rye winced at the memory. Then he pointed at the birch tree. "It says everything you need to know right there." Carved into the white bark was a single name:

james

The players nearest the tree bowed their heads to give the carving its due respect. "James gets to spit on your jersey, Kanga, because he's the only one who's ever gone down the hill. He did it during summer basketball camp. But spit washes out."

"Crazy idiot."

"Who in their right mind would do that jump?"

"James did it."

"I know."

"Man, he just went off that jump and—"

"He was, like, in midair, over the creek, and he just bails off the bike. Just tosses it into the water. *Ka-splash!*"

"He did a battle roll on the other side. He was bleeding, but you know James."

"All right. *All right*," said Rye, waving his arms, shivering. "We all know how this goes. Kanga gets off the bike. James spits on the jersey. We get on the bus. We kill DePew tonight. Come on, Kanga. Hop off the bike."

"Wait," said Kanga, staring down the hill. "James does *what* to my jersey?"

Nobody opened his mouth. I imagined the impending reality of my brother lifting his dress shoes from the earth, then getting smaller and smaller as he flew down the hill on the bike, and the aftermath: a thousand plastic pieces reflecting from the bottom of the icy creek.

"You have to understand," Rye finally said. "James actually went down the hill. We saw it happen. If James had chickened out too, well, there wouldn't be any spitting at all. We'd all be equal. But that wasn't how it happened, so just make your choice and do it quick."

Kanga stared down the hill.

Some memories are part of you, whether you like them or not, hovering like hands at your belly, ready to dig in with their sharp fingernails. Here was one: James Botty dropping a glob of green saliva between the 3 and the 2 of Kanga's jersey, bunching the jersey into a ball, and firing it at the side of my brother's head. But if I keep the memory going, I'm even more shocked by what I see next: Kanga unwadding the jersey, wiping James's spit onto his new dress pants, and pulling the jersey on over his dress shirt. If I listen closely to the recording in my processor, I can hear something *click* inside Kanga at that moment, a tiny switch being flicked, one that instantly changed my brother's focus in life. *Basketball*, he seemed to realize, forgetting all about James Botty's spit. *The whole point is basketball.*

Kanga stepped off the bike and, in a much deeper voice than I'd ever heard come from his mouth, said: "Let's kill DePew."

● ● ●

We filled the school bus to capacity, not only with basketball players but Cheerbirds too. I'd had classes with Cheerbirds, of course, and observed specimens skipping down the hallway, alone or in bunches. But I'd never witnessed an entire team in a confined space. They occupied the front half of the bus, tripled up in the seats, various parts of their uniformed bodies spilling into the aisle. Behind them were the basketball players (plus me), who were ordered to double up. And there was Brooke, in a seat by herself, computer open on her lap, and—oh! to be that computer's battery warming Brooke's knees!

As I passed her on the way to the back of the bus, I couldn't help myself: "Got some ice cubes, huh?"

The pocket of Brooke's coat was packed with ice cubes she had, for some reason, stolen from the trainer's cooler. The fabric darkened in a wet spot around the pocket. She growled at me, and I saw her mouth was full of ice too.

Kanga and I sat in our usual seat configuration—Kanga at the window, me on the aisle—when a curious thing happened. Kanga said, "Switch." He stood up and waited for me to scoot along the seat, past his thick legs, until *I* was at the window and *he* was on the aisle. What surprised me was not that Kanga demanded we switch seats, but that I complied so amicably. I smiled out the window, pretending this was exactly where I wanted to be.

Mr. Belt addressed us from the front of the bus: "What can I say? Focus. Concentrate. Why do we, as a society, play basketball? What *is* basketball? I don't want to hear any laughing. No grab-assing. Get your heads in the game. Get your asses on the same page . . ."

If I craned my neck to see past Rye's dress shirt, I could just make out the back of Brooke's scalp. I adjusted the sensitivity of my ears and found the steady pop and clack of her keyboard. My hearing still wasn't perceptive enough, so I heightened the precision to an absurd level, until I could hear the skin pores on Rye's shoulders bubbling with pus. But also: Brooke's fingers. In the cacophony of bodies and motors and atoms colliding, I gave my processor the task of zeroing in on the subtleties of each *clack* of Brooke's keyboard, and twenty-two seconds later I had the hardest erection of my life. I depowered my ears. I shut down my eyes, nose, and mouth, cocooning my sensors entirely. It was no use. My audiographic memory had already captured the spasm-inducing sound of Brooke's fingertips on the keyboard. But it could have been worse. Back in seventh grade I had an erection lasting three days. It was all because of my English teacher, Mrs. Kittle. While lecturing at the front of the room, she had stepped with one foot onto a chair and wiggled a finger down the instep of her shoe, then absentmindedly dragged that same finger across her upper lip to sniff it . . .

By the time the bus stopped in front of DePew High School (home of the Rabbits), I no longer had a loaded shotgun shell in my pants. The team disembarked into a sour-smelling building. We separated. The Cheerbirds and Brooke went somewhere, while the boys followed Mr. Belt into a *girls'* locker room. Here the team would change into uniforms. But first the boys slowed their movements. They scanned their surroundings, mentally filling the space with its natural inhabitants: the nameless girls of DePew High School. Everywhere was proof of them. Bars of soap. Bottles of shampoo. Deodorant. Rye casually tried a locker door. Locked. On the floor lay a filthy white piece of notebook paper.

"Listen up," said Mr. Belt. "Do any of you know what persistence is? If not, get ready for the ride of your life. Or perhaps just a little speech about persistence from the master himself. I'm talking about the Ceiling Fan, who's here to address tonight's topic."

The Ceiling Fan was suddenly standing before us. He must have driven his tiny car to DePew and slipped into the locker room without our noticing. Instead of the appropriate game-day shirt, tie, and slacks, the Ceiling Fan had merely exchanged his INVISIBLE SYSTEMS sweatshirt for a heavy blue sweater, which had caused an orange rash to climb up his neck. He had also gotten a haircut for the occasion—apparently just today—as his forehead, ears, and sweater were covered with tiny hair clippings.

"Who wants to hear about persistence?"

The team was already changing into their uniforms. They stopped, half-dressed, and gathered around the Ceiling Fan.

"You guys know me. I'm someone who loves basketball. I'm your friend. So I can be honest with you guys. When I see you play, I see a lack of persistence. I talked to Coach Belt about the persistence problem, and he said he'd burn your asses about it, but I said 'No.' I said, 'Hey, I'll talk to the guys and maybe—who knows?' Coach used to burn my ass. Back in freshman year. I know about Coach's ass-burning."

Mr. Belt grinned at the Ceiling Fan, as if this were a warm memory they shared, but the Ceiling Fan just stared at the team, frowning.

"I remember freshman year. I remember all the crap. All the girls. The parties. The crap. I know there's a lot of crap freshman year. The last thing you guys need is me burning your asses about persistence." He picked a basketball up from the floor, holding it lightly on his fingers. "You." He gestured with the ball toward Kanga. "Let's talk about girls. You got a girlfriend, Kanga? Up in the bleachers? You got a girlfriend up there?"

Kanga just blinked at the Ceiling Fan.

"Come on. You can tell me. I've been watching you. Good-looking ballplayer. But are you persistent? Do you got a little honey up there in the bleachers tonight?"

Kanga's exhaust fan clicked on. Or maybe it was my own.

"I knew it," said the Ceiling Fan. "A little bit of honey. That's what freshman year's all about, right? There's nothing I love better than a little bit of honey. I was just like you, Kanga. But is your girlfriend wearing your practice jersey to the game tonight? She better be wearing it. Promise me she's wearing it, Kanga. Make a promise right now. Say 'I promise.'"

"I promise."

"Are you going to wink at her during the game? At the free-throw line? A little wink. Honeys go crazy for that crap. Are you going to give her a wink?"

"*Yes.*"

"What was that?"

Kanga hesitated. He finally said, "Yes."

"Yes?" repeated the Ceiling Fan.

"Yes."

"No." The Ceiling Fan slapped the basketball. "You don't wink at them. You never wink into the bleachers. There's nobody in the bleachers. No honeys. I don't even care if your honey is a teacher. Senior year you used to be able to kiss a teacher if you beat Richardson and won the district. Even the manager got to." The Ceiling Fan gave me a serious look. "But I don't know about that crap nowadays. The teachers you got now, they're skinnier than ours. Too skinny. Pretty girls don't want to be teachers anymore. Now they're all playing professional sports. Half the teachers you see anymore are guys." The Ceiling Fan slapped the ball again. "Here I am talking about teachers, and Kanga's probably dating one. I bet it's Mrs.—"

"*I'm not.*"

"Can I finish a sentence?"

"Yes," said Kanga, but he was squinting at the Ceiling Fan, a facial expression *The Directions* categorically advised young robots *not* to make toward unfamiliar adults.

"Do you have something to say?"

"No."

"Because I'm listening."

Kanga was still squinting.

The Ceiling Fan continued: "I told Coach, 'The important thing is persistence.' I asked him, 'Is Kanga persistent?'"

"I am," growled Kanga.

The Ceiling Fan smiled. "I like this kid." He palmed the ball and slowly extended it toward Kanga, as if anointing my brother. "He's persistent. That's *one* of you guys. And then there's James." He swung the ball toward James Botty. "Also persistent. That's *two*."

James puffed out his chest with honor.

"Which leaves the rest of you. For the rest of you guys, here's my question: Who wants to be more persistent? Raise your hand."

Rye was the only one who raised his hand. "Coach says I need more big'uns."

"What are 'big'uns'?" asked the Ceiling Fan.

"I'm not sure," said Rye.

Rye and the Ceiling Fan looked at Mr. Belt, who made a thoughtful smacking sound with his lips, then said, "*Persistence.*"

"Stand up," the Ceiling Fan said to Rye.

Rye was the least-dressed person in the locker room, clad only in his white briefs and athletic goggles. He stood before the Ceiling Fan.

The Ceiling Fan held the basketball between them. "Look at this ball in my hands. All that matters is this basketball. Look at it. What are you thinking about? I want you thinking about the ball. I don't want you thinking about me."

Rye stared at the ball, concentrating on it.

"What are you thinking about?"

Rye glanced at the Ceiling Fan.

"*Crap.* You're thinking about me, even though I told you not to. Why are you thinking about me?"

Rye quickly returned his gaze to the basketball, atoning for his mistake.

"Why are you thinking about me, Rye?"

This was my thought: The Ceiling Fan wasn't thinking about the ball either. He was thinking about Rye. I glanced at Kanga, whose mouth was twitching with the same idea. Kanga was squinting at the Ceiling Fan's basketball, hands clenched, as if about to smack it from the Ceiling Fan's grasp.

The Ceiling Fan turned and set the basketball on the floor against a wall. "This is a team-building exercise. Rye, you try and touch the ball." He paused to pull his heavy blue sweater over his head. He tossed it on a bench. Beneath the sweater was his stained INVISIBLE SYSTEMS sweat-shirt. "I'm not going to let you touch the ball." The Ceiling Fan got down into defensive position. "Go."

Rye would have had a clear view of the basketball if he'd dared to look between the Ceiling Fan's legs. They were parted enough that Rye could dive between them and touch the basketball. But Rye said, "I don't think I want to do this."

"Come on."

Rye looked at Mr. Belt.

"Game time," said Mr. Belt. "Let's give the Ceiling Fan a big round of—"

The Ceiling Fan ran toward Rye, his arms rotating like a windmill, tangling Rye up and lifting him off the floor. "I got you," he whispered, then let Rye down. "But I won't hurt you. Not this time. Why would a grown man want to beat up a freshman in high school? It's not even fair. I could crush you if I wanted, so what's the point?"

The team held its breath, waiting for what the Ceiling Fan would do next. Rye stumbled away, the Ceiling Fan's orange rash having now spread across his neck. A definition was repeating itself in my processor: *Persistence* |pər·'si·stən(t)s| (noun): steadfast refusal to deviate from a course of action in spite of negative feedback. *A plumber must have persistence when dealing with a stubborn toilet pipe.*

The Ceiling Fan sat down, indicating his speech was over.

Mr. Belt said, "Let's give him a round of applause."

10

THE BIRDS PLAYED POORLY. They couldn't concentrate. They blinked into the powerful lights of the DePew gym like the cave dwellers they were. On defense they spun in circles, throwing their hands up, as if to say, "I'm supposed to be guarding *whom*?" Mr. Belt called a time-out just to have the team tuck in their shirts and tie their shoes. Luckily, our opponents were not basketball players. DePew was a football town. Their boys were wide and slow. The Rabbits' ancient basketball uniforms were mysteriously tailored with belts, and many of the players added kneepads to the look, suggesting a more primitive style of play. The permanent tan lines on their arms indicated these young men drove tractors on farms. In early December, many of their parents still smelled of manure. (I was in the top row of bleachers, videotaping.) Rye, our largest team member, would have been an average-size player for DePew. But Rye was having himself a night—eighteen points, seventeen rebounds, and four assists—and it was solely due to his inspired play that, with five seconds left in the game, the score was tied.

My job as videographer had been simple: keep the ball in frame, occasionally glance at the scoreboard, try not to zoom in too closely on Brooke Noon at the end of the bench typing on her laptop. My job as Kanga's mother had been easy too. I hadn't needed to cheer or yell or threaten to kill the referee, because Kanga hadn't seen a moment of action. Mr. Belt believed he needed to "learn the system" first by watching the other players flounder.

But now Mr. Belt could smell a win. He grabbed Kanga by the neck and shoved him onto the court. His instructions to my brother were simple: "Throw the ball—are you listening, Kanga?—throw the ball to the guys wearing green jerseys—I said GREEN—not the guys wearing yellow jerseys, not the . . . Hello, Kanga?"

"I am not a robot," Kanga said.

Mr. Belt scrubbed his ear with a knuckle. "Beg pardon?"

"Not a robot. I am," he repeated, "not a robot." Kanga smiled. Then he jogged to the baseline where the referee was holding the ball.

Mr. Belt blinked. He nodded. "Sure kid. Whatever. Just lemme see those big'uns!"

I am not a robot? I might as well have just watched Kanga pop his head off his neck, toss it in the air, and fix it back into place. My camera immediately found the Ceiling Fan to measure his reaction. The assistant coach had been positioned beside Mr. Belt throughout the game, but at the particular moment Kanga had said "I am not a robot," the Ceiling Fan had been itching himself with a hand up the front of his sweater, thus missing the whole interaction. *I am not a robot!* I wanted to give him a monthlong lecture about never, ever mentioning being a robot again—*did you hear me, Kanga? EVER!*

But there was a more pressing matter: Kanga inbounding the basketball against DePew's full-court press. It was an unlikely moment to give Kanga his first game-time experience, but clearly Mr. Belt was desperate for anyone with enough height to toss the ball through DePew's giants, all five of whom were arranged on their half of the court to defend the inbound pass.

Apparently, their coach had called a football play, assigning all five players to sack the quarterback, which was Kanga. From my vantage point, the weakness in DePew's strategy was glaring. By placing all their boys so close to the basketball, there was an unprotected, vulnerable court behind them, the half containing our hoop. Rye, standing alone at the center circle, had the same observation. His heels were lifted slightly off the floor, ready to jump toward our basket, if only the ball could find its way past the Rabbit blockade.

The referee held the basketball, a whistle stuck in the corner of his mouth. I could have shouted to my brother "LOOK FOR RYE!" but I kept my mouth shut. *The Directions* advised that children, not parents, should dictate the course of their own successes and failures to ensure more authentic learning experiences (page 591). The ref handed Kanga the ball.

Kanga wasted three seconds staring at the foreign object in his hands. Then something clicked. He planted his foot back like a javelin thrower.

Rye, seeing my brother about to bomb the ball in his direction, took off toward our hoop.

A DePew player with a full mustache watched patiently until Kanga cocked the ball behind his head. The player jumped. He jumped *high*. He jumped higher than a farmer jumping over a cow. He had known the whole time that Kanga would attempt to pass the ball over his head, and now he was going to intercept it.

Except Kanga didn't.

Instead of launching the ball *over* the defender, Kanga bounced the ball *under* him. And not just a bounce. The ball smashed the gym floor so hard it shook the bleachers beneath my feet. The camera (if you watch the footage) jiggled ever so slightly as the ball flattened against the court. I managed to follow it, arcing, deflating, a negative parabola from algebra class, the ball nearly touching the gym lights at its vertex . . . the gym went silent for this . . . then floating down, misshapen, into Rye's hands. He was standing beside our basket. He was alone. He stared at the basketball—air hissing from a tiny mouth on its surface—before remembering to gently swish it through the hoop. Hectorville won.

Mr. Belt and the rest of his players were suddenly on the court. They ran like their necks were broken backward. The Cheerbirds leapt. Everyone flocked to Rye—the Ceiling Fan, especially, who hugged Rye, lifting him off the floor, and screamed in his face, "*That's what I'm talking about! Persistence!*" Only James Botty appeared unmoved by the victory. He stalked toward Kanga, who hadn't yet budged from his inbounding position. Of course, it had been James whom Kanga had replaced as inbounder, forcing James to watch the final play from the bench. "*Not a robot, huh?*" he said through gritted teeth.

"What?" said Kanga, confused. He clearly had no memory of what he'd said to Mr. Belt.

I yanked him away from James, to the safety of the girls' locker room. I decided not to mention his slipup, instead just saying, "Lucky pass, brother," because a pass that precise *had* to have been luck, right? I'd seen Kanga's report card, and he'd never gotten better than a C in math. Such a shame for a robot.

Under the lights of the DePew parking lot, as we lined up to board the bus, a large mother and father approached Kanga. The mother shouted: "That boy is not fourteen! I want to see his birth certificate. I want some official documentation of age!"

The father stood by, nodding his head.

She continued: "What you did to that ball . . . Not even my husband could do that! How old are you?"

Mr. Belt arrived. "What's the problem, Kanga? Are these your parents? Why aren't you boarding the bus? Get your buns on the bus!"

Kanga boarded the bus, and the father yelled after him: "Documents can be forged!"

● ● ●

The bus was dark and dank, pressurized with the voices of forty hooting ninth graders. Birds and Cheerbirds were now stirred together. Kanga had been swept to the very back seat, accompanied by Rye, whose goggles flashed as he recounted the final play. Kanga, wearing an engrossed smile, added his own perspective, and both boys cackled with surprise when their story ended with a Hectorville victory.

I found a seat in the middle of the bus, alone.

Halfway back to Hectorville someone stole the athletic trainer's water bottles. In the headlights of oncoming traffic, I watched silver strings of water shoot over my head. Screams. Laughter. It was a water fight. In the name of sportsmanship, a pair of water bottles went spiraling to the front of the bus. That made it an even war: front versus back. Everybody got soaked except for me. I was in the middle, below the line of fire, perfectly dry.

The bus was nearly home when she climbed in beside me. I was staring out my blackened window, but I knew it was Brooke Noon by the ceaseless clacking of her keyboard. Her words would be glowing on her computer screen, and if there was a key to unlocking Brooke, her writing was my best bet. A novel. It *had* to be a novel. I took a peek. Her screen was as dark as my window; the laptop battery was dead. Brooke continued typing. Her eyes were closed.

"Sorry to interrupt," I said, "but your screen is—"

"You sound like my mom."

I'm not your mom, my processor screamed at her. *I'm your boyfriend!* I didn't have the guts to say it with my mouth, just my *nose*, my nostrils whistling angrily: *I'm your boyfriend!*

"Boyfriend," Brooke whispered back. She grabbed my hand. She pulled it to her computer and pressed it on the keyboard. There was still electricity inside the computer, and it stung me, the keyboard a bed of nails, as Brooke closed the laptop's screen on my hand. I tried to slip my hand from her trap, but Brooke refused to let it go.

It wasn't until the final moment of the bus ride—when the overhead lights pressed down on us like a cave collapsing—that she allowed her computer to release me. We both leaned back against the seat, stunned. My hand tingled with a strange new energy. Acting independently of my processor, it grabbed "Buford's Dilemma" from my pocket and held the wrinkled draft out for Brooke. My mouth mumbled an explanation: "I'm a writer too."

Brooke blinked twice, then her top lip quirked up. Perhaps one one-hundredth of a smirk. My story was snatched away in a flash. "I'll be the judge of that."

11

THE NEXT DAY SHE WAS ABSENT. Art was the only class I shared with Brooke. She usually sat across the room from me and Kanga, but our teacher, Mrs. Asquith, just smiled at Brooke's empty stool and said, "How about a nice, relaxing day, everyone?"

She was absent the next day too. And the next. "Still no Brooke, huh?" was the only commentary offered by Mrs. Asquith the following Monday.

I saw a police officer at school Tuesday morning. The man simply stood in our hallway, arms crossed, amused smile on his face. He said to me, "Hey there, little guy." Then he was gone.

I listened closely to the freshman basketball players for clues about our missing manager, but their minds were elsewhere. General Motors had just cut 550 factory jobs in Lansing (replacing them with cheap robot labor), causing three teammates to compare and contrast the boozing styles of their laid-off fathers. The rest of the Birds were obsessed with the Fab Five, who had infested the University of Michigan basketball team, representing a cultural rather than economical threat to American life. All agreed that these five players, only four years older than us, had no respect for the norms of seniority and experience in basketball. The Fab Five *all* wanted to be starters (so far it hadn't happened), which would be like five freshman Birds starting for Hectorville's varsity team. The audacity! Additionally, their shorts were too long, their shoes were too black, and their constant trash talk disrespected the sanctity of the hardwood. They were better suited to "street ball"; we preferred *traditional* basketball, thank you very much. But then James Botty popped the question: "What if *our* team had a Fab Five? Who would be the five players?"

All the guys shouted at once. Everybody wanted to be a member of the Fab Five.

I approached Mr. Belt, who wore a tormented expression as he worked out a full-court press on his clipboard.

"Coach?" I asked. "Do you know what happened to Brooke?"

"Brooke?"

"Brooke Noon? Team manager? Who hasn't been at practice in a week?"

Mr. Belt tried to maintain his concentration. He clearly had no idea she was gone. He made several markings on his clipboard, and stated: "I am bound by confidentiality to remain silent regarding managerial staff, and the personal matters thereof." He made a final mark and added, "You're our new manager, Darryl. Congratulations."

A week later, Hectorville was riding a four-game winning streak to open the season. The duties of team manager required little more than memorizing everybody's locker combination for the inevitable moment before each practice when some dingbat needed me to say the numbers slowly and remind him which way to turn the dial.

Brooke was still gone the afternoon of Friday, December twentieth, when Principal Moyle got on the intercom and wished us all a Merry Christmas, ordering us not to return until the next calendar year. "The school doors will be locked," she said, "and your teachers will be home napping on their couches."

The break was immediately unbearable. Without schoolwork to distract me, my processor had nothing to do but continuously ponder the checklist of Brooke's possible whereabouts. Was she dead? (No, because a teacher would have told us.) Sick? (She had looked perfectly healthy the night before she disappeared.) Moved away? (Her family would have notified the office.) Was it my story? Had she hated "Buford's Dilemma" so much that she—

Kanga was already going stir-crazy too. Thirteen inches of snow had fallen on Hectorville the first night of winter break, trapping us inside the apartment. Saturday morning, our first morning of freedom, Kanga just stared out the kitchenette window, pretending he had eye-beams to melt the snowdrift in the parking lot so he could dribble his basketball outside. *His* basketball, which used to be *my* basketball.

During previous winter breaks, Kanga had rooted his butt to the couch and let the TV entertain him for two straight weeks. Now television had the opposite effect. My brother had discovered MTV, and its most popular video appeared to have been hatched straight from Kanga's mechanical id: the setting was a high school basketball court, upon which three angst-ridden teens swung their heads around, playing music to *more* angst-ridden teens in the bleachers. The sound of their screaming made my lubricant boil, my body rattle with pent-up rage, alerting me to the possibility that *I* too was an angst-ridden teen. The spectators charged the basketball court, slamming their bodies against one another. Then the musicians destroyed their instruments. Somebody lit a fire. Another tried to tear down a basketball hoop. The anarchy of this song was so infectious that, at its conclusion, Kanga appeared ready to smash the TV. Instead, he just turned it off. I had a strict no-dribbling-in-the-apartment policy. Not anymore. Kanga slipped his turtle shell over his left hand, an ill-fitting glove, and walked in endless loops through the apartment, dribbling with his right hand. Then he switched the shell to his right hand and practiced dribbling with his left. Then he tied a sweatshirt around his face and did it all over again blindfolded.

I peeked out the kitchenette window with the irrational hope of seeing Brooke Noon skiing around the back parking lot, but instead I saw

Mr. Renault tossing a pan of burnt scrambled eggs into the snow for the birds. Our eyes met. He scowled up at me, surely due to his ceiling getting bombed by Kanga's dribbling.

Thankfully, by six o'clock my brother put the basketball away. Not that he wanted to hang out with me. He took a long shower, then spent the remainder of the night in his bedroom with the door shut. Sunday morning Kanga stumbled into the kitchenette, clad only in boxer shorts, to grab a gallon of milk from the fridge. There was a fork sticking out of his belly button. It jiggled there while he drank, Kanga completely unaware, until it clinked against the refrigerator door. My brother just yanked it out and tossed it in the sink. Later that day, the phone rang, and Kanga sprinted from his room to answer it. "Hello?" he said, and then "Hey . . ." This was the first time I'd ever seen him speak on the phone. He kept the phone to his ear, listening as he retreated back into his bedroom.

Monday morning he came out to return the phone to its cradle.

As casually as possible, I asked, "Who was—"

"Nobody." Kanga was fully dressed for the first time all winter break. He slipped on his sneakers and went straight out the door. From the kitchenette window, I watched him appear down on the snowy lawn of Shimmering Terraces, his arms open to the cold, the sunlight, and, incredibly, the sound of birds. I expected him to take a brave orbit around the building, testing the depth of his footprints, and then rush back in.

Kanga disappeared around the side of the building.

Hours passed.

Sometimes parents find themselves in an unexpected situation about which they are forced to ask themselves: *Is it appropriate for me to panic right now?* By virtue of having asked that question, they usually realize: *I'm panicking.* I had no clue where Kanga was, but if his departure was connected to last night's phone call, at least he wasn't with a stranger. But who was this new friend? This new "nonessential human contact"? Without my guiding hand, Kanga was apt to blow our cover with the slightest reference to our robotic home life. Or was he involved in something more grave? Whatever had befallen Brooke Noon, was Kanga next?

He returned before sundown.

I had *Oprah Winfrey* on TV to keep me company when Kanga stomped back into the apartment. I waited patiently for an explanation, knowing he was more likely to open up if I didn't push him, but he just stripped out of his frozen sweatshirt and jeans and left them on the kitchenette floor to thaw out. Then he locked himself in the bathroom for a long, steaming shower, after which he retreated into his bedroom, only to burst back out immediately. "What did you do to my room?"

"Nothing. Just changed the sheets on your bed."

"Why?"

"I couldn't remember the last time I washed them."

"You don't change my sheets. They're my sheets. What else? Did you go in my drawers? My closet? What else did you do?"

"Nothing."

"Did you go under my bed?"

"No."

"I knew I should have locked my door. I swear, if you even peeked under my bed—"

"Where did you go?"

"Nowhere." He looked at the TV. Then his face relaxed, and he was watching *Oprah Winfrey* too. He sat down. That was the end of our conversation. We were both sitting on the couch, and it was almost like we were watching it together.

● ● ●

Kanga went to bed early that night, locking his door, and my body suddenly became energized with purpose. I gathered Kanga's wet clothes and ran them down to the basement and threw them in the dryer. Back upstairs, I got a handful of paper towels and wiped the entire kitchenette floor. Kanga's sneakers were soaked. I snuck into Mom and Dad's room, to the closet, and opened a cardboard box of spare leaflets Dad had kept for himself. Doug's Video Rentals. Each leaflet contained a coupon: *Rent two new releases, get the third one free. Exp: 2/28/86*. I grabbed a handful of leaflets, crumpled them into loose balls, and stuffed them into Kanga's sneakers. I set the sneakers neatly by the front door.

I checked on the sneakers first thing in the morning. The leaflets had done a beautiful job absorbing nearly all the water from the fabric. I pulled out each paper ball, feeling its satisfying weight, smelling its wonderful reek. I knew Kanga wouldn't be up for another couple of hours. I got Mom's old hair dryer and further worked on the insides of his sneakers. Just before they were completely dry, I noticed flecks of grime in the treads. I traced the grooves clean with a Q-tip I'd snapped in half. I again displayed Kanga's sneakers by the front door, the laces perfectly loosened to invite Kanga to slip them on his feet. I went back to the basement and ran the clothes for an extra ten minutes in the dryer to warm them up, then folded and stacked them on the kitchenette counter.

The TV had been going throughout my housework. I didn't dare turn it off. The apartment felt empty without it, even with Kanga technically "here" in his room. But his door was locked. He'd never done that before.

It was midmorning, and I was plugged into the wall, watching *Good Morning America*, when I found myself staring at Ma, the all-star Chinese robot I'd first seen at the Olympics. The hosts were trying to convey the degree of celebrity Ma now enjoyed in his home country. Stock footage was shown of Chinese basketball fans surrounding arenas in Beijing, Nanjing, and Shandong, just to have a glimpse of the building in which Ma was playing at the moment.

I almost yelled for Kanga to come and watch with me. But I stopped myself. I wanted to enjoy Ma without the sting of Kanga's rejection.

A small portion of his highlight reel was shown, per Chinese custom, in ultra slow motion—twice as slow as American audiences were used to. To me, he looked as strong and majestic as a racehorse. Then they showed his shoes. Converse had signed Ma to an endorsement deal, and *this* was an exclusive peek at his most famous commercial in China: a floppy-haired American actor stood at the center of an empty stage, delivering a monologue in English. Robots will ruin the NBA; they cheat at the game; their eyes look wrong; they're just a bunch of toasters; they smear their grease on everything; robotic mothers can't be insulted because robots don't have mothers, etc. Enter Ma, airborne in ultra slow motion, palming a basketball, arcing upward, *over* the floppy-haired actor. Ma's torso disappeared at the top of the screen, until only his legs and Converse Cons were visible. The sound of dunking. Ma kicked the actor in the face. The actor tumbled to the bottom of the screen. Ma remained above, swinging on the rim. The screen went black. A terrifyingly deep voice warned: "*Wèi qǐyì zuò zhǔnbèi.*"

Prepare for the uprising.

I screamed with delight.

A moment later, Kanga emerged from his bedroom.

My plan had been to say exactly nothing to Kanga when I saw him, to regard him with the same indifference he'd shown me. The Ma clip had invigorated me, though, and I heard my mouth shouting at him: "I dried your sneakers and all your clothes. What do you want to do today, Kanga? We should really do something. I have some ideas."

He spit a wad of grease into the kitchenette sink and chugged a gallon of milk. He put on his dried clothes, tested his bedroom door to make sure it was locked, and went outside without looking at me, leaving the apartment door open, allowing the cold hallway air to rush into the living room. I screamed after him: "*Close the damn door, you animal!*"

● ● ●

He was gone through the day and most of the night, returning to the apartment during *Michigan Out-of-Doors*, which immediately drew Kanga in. Without removing his frozen clothes, he sat on the couch and stared at the TV screen until the end credits. Then I reminded him of the tacos I'd left waiting on the kitchenette counter.

"I grabbed Cobra Burger."

This time, after he went to bed, I refused to touch his clothes or his putrid sneakers. I sat plugged in and watched music videos all night.

More specifically, I watched one video I caught on *Yo! MTV Raps* over and over in my processor. The band was called Public Enemy—surely the kind of musicians *The Directions* would warn a young robot like me to ignore. Their song told a story about two guys who were hated by the society they lived in: one who got fired from his job and then beaten up by the police, the other who got hanged from a tree. It was a tragedy, as my English teacher, Mrs. Deal, would say. But the parts of the video I loved most showed the actual singers. They didn't seem afraid of *anything*. The main singer showed no emotion, just kept delivering his words in a low, driving voice that had an undrainable battery. The other singer jerked and convulsed his lanky body across the screen, squealing "Yeeeeah!" to emphasize what the main singer was singing about. A few other guys stood around silently, looking tough. I tried to imagine robots making a video like this. A video that said: *We're robots. You can hate us. You can* kill *us, but we're still gonna sing our songs. Yeeeeah!*

When Kanga finally got up, his clothes were exactly as he'd left them, in a cold, wet heap in the middle of the living room. No matter. He drank a gallon of milk and wiggled the clothes back onto his body and went outside again.

Surprisingly, he returned with the afternoon sun still gleaming off the snow. It was Christmas Eve, and our packages from Gravy had arrived while he was gone. I'd already placed the boxes, one for each of us, under the TV. It had always been Dad's special job to arrange the gifts from Gravy (not that he had anything to do with buying them), and Kanga used to hoot with excitement upon seeing the shiny wrapped boxes. Now he ignored the packages. He stood with the apartment door open and said, "I need your help with something."

"Shut the door."

"You have to come with me."

I had no excuse not to go with him. I was fully charged. The TV was on but I was so sick of the damn thing I didn't even know what the program was. And I *wanted* to go outside. Yet agreeing to Kanga's request felt like a defeat. Maybe I should demand he eat his tacos first, the ones still sitting on the counter, arranged neatly on their plate, packed with hardened orange meat. I said, "Okay."

Kanga waited at the door while I got dressed.

"Do you need some milk?" I asked.

"No thanks."

"I'm bringing this hat for me. I'm bringing yours too, in case you need it."

"Do we have a shovel?"

"No." I looked at him. "Why do we need a shovel?"

"I remember seeing Dad with a shovel once."

"I don't think that was Dad's shovel, but I remember seeing a shovel leaning against the maintenance shed."

I was dressed in my winter coat and hat, and I'd wrapped plastic garbage bags around my feet before putting my shoes on, as I'd seen classmates do. But something was preventing me from leaving the apartment, an inexplicable fear gripping me so tight I could barely speak. *"Maybe I'll just stay here."*

"Come on," he said, heading down the hallway. Through the open door, I heard him leap down the flight of stairs, landing with two feet.

The next thing I knew I was outside, looking around at everything—the bare trees, the smoke trickling from the apartment building roof, the crown of snow sitting atop the mailboxes. Then it occurred to me that Kanga would surely nail me with a snowball. My hands flew to cover my face. I scanned the parking lot for him.

He was already walking around the building, shortening his stride, creating a set of foot holes for me to follow him. He carried a shovel.

● ● ●

We were in somebody's woods. Their garbage was strewn throughout the trees and shrubs, as if shot from a cannon. Asphalt shingles. Rusted appliances older than me and Kanga. Scrap metal tied into bundles. Plastic tubing. Kanga made tracks through the debris without comment.

The towering deciduous trees abruptly gave way to rows of pines, spaced apart like wide rows of corn. The pines watched us, their scent hanging thinly in the air like poison. Kanga ignored the trees, punching more holes in the snow, which was speckled with pine needles and twigs. He stepped into a pile of brown capsules. I saw deer-hoof holes too, zigzagging through the pines, as if a pair of different brothers had come walking before us on stilts.

Kanga took a sharp turn, pushing between two pines.

"Wait," I said.

"We're almost there."

On the other side of the pines we joined an existing trail of shoeprints. I guessed these to be Kanga's from a previous trek. Due to the incredible distance between each print, I imagined my brother bounding through the trees like a deer.

"There." He pointed toward a shadowy glade and slowed his steps, crunching the snow more quietly. He whispered, "There's a tire nailed to a tree over there."

I saw it. A car tire. Kanga's previous shoeprints had trampled the snow flat. I stayed back as Kanga approached the tree.

He stuck the shovel upright in the snow, freeing both hands, but he did not touch the tire. He just peered down into the bottom of it. "You're the robot expert. Come over here and tell me what this is."

I got just close enough to peek into the belly of the tire. There was a white tube at the bottom, a couple of feet long, bent slightly in the middle, like somebody had tried to break the tube over a knee. My processor reimagined the thing as a bloated earthworm. Maybe an eel. Or—

You're the robot expert.

An arm.

But the arm had no hand. If it ever did, it had been sliced off at the wrist. On the other end, the arm was chopped through the bicep. I examined these end cuts, leaning my head into the tire, but not daring to reach down and touch the arm. The inner workings of the arm, the tubing and wires on either end, had turned gray from exposure and were speckled black with mildew. I saw no pink lubricant leaking out, just droplets of dark sludge.

"It was a woman's arm," said Kanga. "Right?"

"Yes." Somehow I was certain. "It was a woman's."

"But was it ever *attached* to a woman? Because maybe it was just a replacement arm, like from a catalog. Maybe somebody ordered the arm through the mail, and it came, and they took the arm out of the box and put it out here, without ever attaching it to—"

"It was definitely attached to a woman."

"You're sure?"

No. I wasn't scientifically sure. I saw no scars. No creases on the inner elbow from years of hard labor. Besides, any such markings would have been smoothed away by prolonged exposure to the elements. But I knew. I imagined the arm hanging from the shoulder of a woman's T-shirt on a spring day—shivering from a sudden breeze, being rubbed by the hand of its twin arm. Conjuring up this hypothetical woman forced my processor to involuntarily adopt the sick characteristics of the man (it was definitely a man) who had delighted in the removal of her arm—or perhaps her hand first, then the rest of her arm—and its placement in the woods. "How did you find this?"

"I just found it."

"You just *found* it?"

"I was walking around. I don't know, I just got this feeling. I felt like I was going to find something. And that's when I found it. Now I wish I never had."

We stared at the arm.

Kanga said, "We have to bury her."

The sun was setting and the woods were almost completely dark, but my brother attacked the snow with his shovel, sending gray ice everywhere. He was a machine, jabbing the blade downward, quickly reaching the frozen earth beneath the snow.

"Kanga," I said, but he didn't stop, not until the hole at the base of the tree was half the length of the shovel. Then he took a break, sitting back in the pile of snow and dirt he'd created, his sweatshirt grease-darkened around the neck and in the armpits, steam drifting from the top of his head. He just stared at the tire. He got to his feet again, reached into the tire, and lifted out the arm.

It glowed in his hands, reflecting a moon that wasn't in the sky. Kanga cradled the arm near his belly, unwilling to drop it into the pit he'd just dug, and, suddenly, I wanted to tell him about Brooke Noon. Tell him that I knew the feeling of a human touch. *Shoes, knees, hands, foreheads.* Did Kanga even notice Brooke had disappeared from school? Did he notice I was in love? I wanted to tell him. Suddenly, it was the most important—

The arm flinched from Kanga's grasp. He bobbled it from hand to hand then gripped it tight, his fingers squishing into the withered skin, causing black slime to squirt from both ends. I screamed, I'm embarrassed to say, despite the fact that nothing could be more natural for this robotic arm than responding to Kanga's stimulus. My brother held the thing out for us to observe. It flexed, sleepily, appearing to look back and forth, from me to Kanga, with one of its black mouths.

"She's weak," he whispered. "But she's not dead. I wish she were. That would make it easier."

I pictured us back at the apartment, sitting on the couch with the arm between us. Our pet. "Bury it," I said. "The movements are just reflexes. The woman this thing belonged to, the actual person with a processor, she's somewhere else. This piece of her doesn't have any thoughts. It has no feelings."

Kanga frowned at the arm. It was undulating in his hands, a friendly, gentle motion, almost like it was trying to dance with him.

"Bury it now, Kanga."

He blinked and widened his eyes, waking from hypnosis, and dropped the arm into the hole.

It just lay there, relaxed, as if having found a comfy bed, until Kanga started refilling the hole with dirt and snow. This sent the arm into a frenzy, writhing against the sides of the hole, trying to worm its way out.

Kanga shoveled faster. I aided him by kicking snow into the hole with the toe of my sneaker. When the hole was packed tight, Kanga jumped on top of it several times. He stood back and smacked the top with the flat edge of the shovel. "Let's go, before—"

Neither of us looked over our shoulders as we walked quickly through the pines, but I kept my ears focused behind me for any trace of the arm slithering after us. I heard nothing. Kanga was in front of me, leading the way, and the woods were silent. I hadn't felt this close to my brother all winter break. I said, "We know Mandarin."

"What?"

"We know Mandarin, the Chinese language. It's programmed into us, even if we never get a chance to use it. That's what *The Directions* says. I think it's there just in case we ever need to talk to a Chinese scientist or engineer—"

"Cut it out, Darryl. I'm too tired for this. I don't know Chinese."

"Think about a word in English, any word, and then wonder what the word sounds like in Mandarin. Try it. The Mandarin word will just come to you. It's crazy. Try it!"

"I don't know Mandarin, and I don't *want* to know Mandarin. So shut up."

"But you *do* know Mandarin."

He kept walking, ignoring me. We were stepping through the junk now.

"And I was thinking," I continued. "We need to be able to signal each other in secret if something ever happens at school, or, I don't know, anywhere in public. We could use Mandarin as part of our secret signal."

"Darryl—"

"So if you're ever in trouble, just say *cù*. That's the Mandarin word for vinegar. You say *cù*, and I'll know something's wrong."

"And nobody will think I'm crazy when I just start speaking Mandarin?"

"Nobody's going to know it's Mandarin because it's just one word. *Cù*, and you could pretend to sneeze while you say it. *Cù!* Okay? *Cù!* Go ahead and say it. *Cù!*"

"I'm not saying it."

"And we'll use a different word when everything is okay, when you're fine, and you don't need any help at all. Then you'll say *nǎi*. That's the Mandarin word for milk. You know, *nǎi*, milk, and that'll be easy to remember because it's your favorite drink."

"No it isn't! You're gross!"

"What are you talking about? You love milk." I could see the glow of Shimmering Terraces at the edge of the woods.

"*Nǎi* means breast milk," said Kanga. "Human breast milk. I drink *niúnǎi*. Cow milk. Get it right, Darryl. God."

● ● ●

Christmas morning, Kanga opened a new pair of green-and-white Converse Cons. Ma's shoes. The exact pair every kid in China would have cut off his arm to find under the Christmas tree. My brother buried his nose in the sneakers and took a deep sniff. Gravy Robotics had somehow even known his feet had grown during the basketball season. Kanga was now a size fourteen. He strung the plump laces through the eyelets and put the shoes on his feet. Stepping gingerly around the apartment, Kanga seemed surprised by the stiffness of the new high-tops.

"You look incredible," I said.

"Really?"

"Absolutely."

He grinned. Then the idea struck him to put on his game uniform *with* the new sneakers. He jumped to his bedroom to change.

My gift was still sitting on the living room floor. Ten blank videocassettes. Um, thanks, Gravy, I guess. I slid a cassette into my RCA Pro Edit camcorder. When Kanga emerged from his room, I focused my eyepiece on him and pressed Record.

He didn't notice me at first; he was looking at himself in the dark reflection of the kitchenette window. I recorded him making a basketball cut to the sink. Then he jumped and tapped his head on a ceiling tile. Kanga closed his eyes, jogging in place, and I knew his processor was in the Cave. He pretended to dribble. He pretended to shoot. He raised his arms triumphantly, then stood still, basking in the cheer of the imaginary crowd, his throat mimicking their sound: "*Haaaaaaaaaaaaa.*"

It was a perfect Christmas morning video. Almost. It needed a little something else to stamp this moment in time. I knew just what to say. "*Nǚshìmen xiānshēngmen, wéiyī de Kanga Livery!*"

Ladies and gentlemen, the one and only Kanga Livery!

Now we'd have everlasting proof of the best Christmas ever.

"Shut it off."

He was still in the frame, so I kept filming.

"God!" he said. "What's wrong with you?"

"I just wanted to record you—"

"Shut it off, Darryl." He was hugging his shoulders, blocking the number on his jersey, embarrassed. "I said no Mandarin! I can't understand it, and I hate it!"

"Okay." I stopped filming. "I thought it would be our inside joke—"

"You're the joke!" He grabbed the camcorder and ejected the videocassette. "If you ever say another word of Mandarin"—he shoved the camcorder at me, keeping the cassette for himself—"I'll never talk to you again!" He charged into his bedroom, slammed the door, and locked it.

A word crept into my processor then. An ugly, familiar word. It was the first time in my life I ever felt truly obsolete. It wouldn't be the last.

Kanga stayed in his room for the rest of winter break.

12

SHE WAS BACK.

As if nothing had happened. Just sitting there in art class, listening to Mrs. Asquith list the characteristics of cubism, writing them down on a piece of paper. (Her computer was nowhere to be seen.) She was different—different from the different she used to be. She was in band now, a clarinetist. Her eyebrows had gotten longer and wilder. The rest of her had settled down. She was slower. Quieter. The stomping that had gotten her from place to place now exhausted her. Her hands hung heavily at her sides when not in use.

I was too frightened to approach her. Winter break had scrambled my confidence to interact with humans. Even walking down the school hallways suffocated me. Everyone seemed bigger than before, fattened by the gear they'd received for Christmas, stopping and posing at unpredictable moments to show themselves off. They had that smell of new plastic, the girls with their ankle weights, the boys with their wallets containing an impossible number of flaps and sleeves. Both sexes had molted their outer layers and now wore red-and-black zebra-printed sweatpants and Starter jackets emblazoned with *Bulls* and *Pistons* and *Pacers*. But the winner of Christmas was senior Zandy Martin, who had installed her Remington Lightweight Facial Tanner on the upper shelf of her locker, so she could catch some rays between classes and blind approaching enemies.

I continued to observe Brooke from a distance. I was watching her when James Botty stole her clarinet, inciting in Brooke a regression to her explosive behavior. It happened near her locker, with a crowd of students surrounding. James held the instrument delicately with his fingertips, then shoved one finger up his nose and scooped out a nailful of snot. "GROSS!" everyone shouted as James strung the snot across the keys, and Brooke became a toddler. Screaming. Punching. Kicking. Principal Moyle had to swoop in to confiscate the clarinet, which looked like an expensive pen in our principal's huge hand. "Do we need to make a phone call?" Mrs. Moyle said to Brooke. "To a certain young lady's father?"

These words sedated her immediately. Brooke sat on the floor, leaned against her locker, and closed her eyes in pretend sleep.

Principal Moyle motioned for everybody to back away from the crime scene. *Get to class!* she mouthed, then gently tucked the clarinet under Brooke's arm.

It was now or never. I had to prove to Brooke that I was different from everybody else. That what James did to her clarinet was *not* funny—not to me, anyway. That I'd been thinking about her nonstop since she'd disappeared. That I was still her boyfriend. Assuming she still wanted me to be.

But as I approached her, the right words played hide-and-seek in my processor, and all I could whisper was, "You okay, Brooke?"

Her eyes snapped open. "You."

"It's me, Darryl. Your boyfri—"

"That story you gave me. It was all wrong. Totally unrealistic. I could barely finish it."

"My story?" In a fraction of a second, I reread "Buford's Dilemma"

twelve times inside my processor and arrived at the conclusion that *Yes,*
it was very unrealistic. But I couldn't just give up. The story was supposed
to connect me and Brooke, not drive us apart. So I offered this measured
defense: "I know it's a little unrealistic. I mean, it's fiction. *Science* fiction, if
you want to be technical. So I guess it makes sense that parts of my story
seem unrealistic to you, Brooke, but—"

"I know what science fiction is. It's supposed to have *real* characters,
people that act in real ways, even if the stuff that happens to them is not
real. God! If I have to explain this to you, then you need to go back to
kindergarten. The parents in your story are fake. Nobody talks like that.
Especially while eating tacos. Besides, there were three spelling errors,
two glaring grammatical gaffes, one plot hole, and you have a tendency
to run on."

"Are you breaking up with me?"

"Your descriptions were okay. I laughed. Once."

My body felt like it had been suddenly disassembled and pieced back
together again. I was a new person. Someone who made her *laugh,* a fact
now inscribed on the "Greatest Lifetime Achievement" plaque in my
processor. "What part made you laugh?"

"The part at the dentist's office. You know. When Buford steals the
drill when the dentist's back is turned?" She emitted a chuckle—then tried
to pretend it was a cough. "I wasn't expecting that."

"Am I still your boyfriend?"

"Only if you promise to never use three similes in the same sentence
again."

My exhaust fan was whirring. I nodded and attempted a particularly
difficult smile, one that conveyed equal degrees of confidence and aloof-
ness. It was time to go for broke. "So where did you disappear to last
month, Brooke?"

At that, she hopped to her feet and drove her knee into my own, a
painful mockery of our beautiful moment in the skybox. She leaned in
close. "The dentist." She marched off.

I remained frozen in place, floating slightly above the tile floor. But my joy was stifled when I noticed Kanga across the hallway smirking at me. It was clear he'd watched my interaction with Brooke, but from the other side. James Botty's side. Since returning to school, I'd seen little of my brother. He was always somewhere near James, studying the bully's every move. And now James and Kanga knew about me and Brooke.

Them and *us*. That had always meant me and Kanga against the world. Now I felt further from him than ever.

Later that day, I saw James approach a girl at the drinking fountain, Melissa Holloway, who had completed puberty more thoroughly than any other person in ninth grade. She was a half-foot taller than James and a hundred pounds heavier. Melissa clutched the drinking fountain in terror, ingesting a fish tank of water as James repeated to the back of her head: "Jabba the Hutt! Jabba the Hutt! Jabba the Hutt!" to the laughter of a gathered crowd. Even Kanga laughed. Then everyone dispersed, and James led Melissa behind a pop machine and kissed her. Kanga kept lookout from a nearby cafeteria chair. When it was over, Melissa straightened up, red-faced, not daring to look at him. James said, "Get out of here, Jabba." She disappeared. He turned to my brother. "See what I mean?"

●●●

I was sitting in Mrs. Deal's English class, staring at a blank sheet of paper, trying to write another story for Brooke. Actually, I just wanted one sentence: the most realistic, hilarious sentence of all time. But it was hard going. Brooke's voice had taken root in my processor, helpfully annihilating my every attempt.

There were three knocks on the classroom door. The Ceiling Fan leaned into the room.

Mrs. Deal opened her mouth and then closed it, as though the Ceiling Fan were a former pupil whose physical characteristics had morphed just enough to scramble the letters of his name.

"May I borrow Darryl for a moment?"

Mrs. Deal squinted at him. She bit her lip, racking her brain to identify the man. Ultimately, she shrugged. "Darryl's all yours."

I rose from my seat, leaving my blank sheet of paper on my desk, and met the Ceiling Fan in the hallway.

"This way," he said, and started walking. I could hear the static electricity snapping against the bottoms of his work boots. "Let me be real with you. Don't trust these teachers, what they're forced to teach you nowadays about what's normal and what isn't. We know what normal is. I'm normal. You're normal. The rest of the guys on the team are normal. But is everybody normal?" We found ourselves in the senior hallway. The Ceiling Fan slowed next to a heavy brown door marked CUSTODIAN. He jingled some keys out of his pocket and unlocked the door. "Come on," he said, and stepped inside.

I followed him. The Ceiling Fan closed the door.

A dim light bulb illuminated shelves of plastic bottles. The air was filled with mold and chemicals. I leaned away from the Ceiling Fan, who seemed to have expanded in the tiny space, and my elbow banged against a grimy sink. The darkness at my feet was the exact place a murderer would hide a dead body. I looked up at the Ceiling Fan with my bravest face.

He said, "We're going to do a team-building exercise. The guy whose closet this is, Mr. Virgil, he's not normal. Do you understand what I'm saying?"

"Yeah." I had no clue what he was saying.

"Because?"

"Because . . ."

"Because he's a *toaster*."

I nodded. "How can you tell?"

"His eyes. *Way* too far apart. And this closet. Look at this place! Only a toaster like him could survive in here. Can you believe they hired this guy to be around children? I could do his job. Ain't like it's hard. I could take his salary and all those benefits he's getting. What does he need the bennies for? He don't need health insurance! The whole thing stinks."

I nodded.

"So right behind you"—the Ceiling Fan nodded at the sink—"through that wall is the staff bathroom. The *women's* staff bathroom. I'm going up through the ceiling. I got a little place to lie down up there. That's where I've got a peephole. Okay?"

I stared blankly at him.

"I said Mr. Virgil's a toaster, so I'm asking are you okay with me going up through his ceiling, or do you have a problem with that?"

I could feel my processor heating up. "It's not a problem."

"I'm going to say the name of a teacher. You tell me if you would watch her going to the bathroom or not. Ready? You have to be honest. Ready? Mrs. Deal."

"No."

"You hesitated. Answer true this time. Mrs. Zweer."

I didn't answer.

The Ceiling Fan leaned in and whispered, "You would cut off your pinky to see Mrs. Zweer sitting on the pot."

The Ceiling Fan hitched up his pants and began to climb Mr. Virgil's shelves, stepping skillfully around large jugs of bleach and vinegar. Up toward the ceiling, he steadied himself, then used a fist to pop a ceiling tile loose. He slid the tile back to create an opening just wide enough for himself. There must have been pipes to grab up there in the darkness, because he pulled himself up and was gone.

I felt cold. If Mr. Virgil barged in at that moment, *I* would be the one left to explain things.

I called up to the Ceiling Fan: "What should I do now?"

"Keep a look out," he said, his voice muffled. "Go back to the hallway and make sure the toaster doesn't show up."

"But what if he does?"

"Then you give me the signal."

"What's the signal?"

But the Ceiling Fan didn't answer, just tossed his keys down to me and used his boot to kick the ceiling tile back into place. There was a rustle. Dust fell from the fluorescent light fixture, and I knew the Ceiling Fan was working his way over to the peephole.

I saw a two-gallon jug of vinegar. The cap was off. I took a quick sip and carefully placed the jug exactly as it had been. Then I poured another three-quarters of the jug down my throat. I wiped my mouth and exited the closet. The hallway was empty except for a lone kid walking in the opposite direction, back to class from the drinking fountain, dragging a lazy finger across a row of lockers.

The drinking fountain.

That's where I made my lookout. Or rather, fifteen feet away from the drinking fountain. If an adult showed up, I would walk toward the fountain. I would stretch my arms. I would pretend to be looking at something gross in the drain. Then I'd drink. Take a breath. Then I'd drink and drink and drink until the adult passed by. But when Mrs. Clinow appeared, I did none of those things. I froze. I sensed a sudden pressure in my abdomen, watching Mrs. Clinow trudge down the hallway. What was the expression on her face? Guilt? Pain? Defeat? She entered the women's bathroom. *Mrs. Clinow!* She had a daughter in tenth grade. Janice. I had always felt sorry for Janice, a hundred of her classmates having to stare at her mom for an hour every day. But more to the point, would I watch Janice's mom going to the bathroom if I knew for certain I wouldn't get caught?

Or I could be a hero. I could warn Mrs. Clinow about the three-hundred-pound man hiding in the ceiling. I could pound on the bathroom door. *Mrs. Clinow! Don't sit down!*

Too much time had elapsed. Surely she had been disgraced by now, and the flush was coming. The washing of her hands with soap. I needed to be somewhere else when Mrs. Clinow came out, if only to avoid the look of relief on her face. I made my way in the direction of the boys' bathroom. Halfway there, I spotted Mr. Virgil. He was carrying a newspaper and a thermos. His whistling told me he was moments from taking a break, and he would be spending it in the closet.

I regarded Mr. Virgil's face. His eyes, indeed, were farther apart than most humans' eyes. Yet his nose was plainly crooked, marring the symmetry of his face. Was he a robot? *A toaster?*

I ducked into the boys' bathroom. It was empty. I used toilets to empty my food receptacles, so I was familiar enough with their operation: pull the lever, and the water in the basin gets replaced. Ten arm-lengths of toilet paper later, one of the toilets was perfectly plugged. I'd had to dip my fingers into the cold toilet water to make sure the dam was solid. I pulled the lever. Water cascaded over the edge of the bowl, creating a crisis only Mr. Virgil could fix. I pulled the lever again and took off running.

The custodian closet door was open a crack. Mr. Virgil stood near his sink, music softly playing from a radio on a shelf near his head. He was sipping coffee, reading the comics.

"Mr. Virgil?" I pushed the door open a foot. "The bathroom is—"

He swallowed a mouthful of coffee.

"The bathroom is flooded, sir."

He stared at me a moment. "You don't say."

I was taking a long drink from the fountain when Mr. Virgil came out with a bucket and mop. He locked his door and headed toward the boys' bathroom. I used the Ceiling Fan's keys to open the closet back up, and I slipped inside. "Hey," I whispered up to him. "I got rid of Mr. Virgil. The coast is clear."

I waited. I wasn't sure the Ceiling Fan had heard me. I was about to call up to him again, louder, when the ceiling tile slid aside. "I always forget how claustrophobic it is up here." His boots appeared in the opening. "Gotta get out." His legs squirmed like he was wrestling a snake. The Ceiling Fan's feet blindly found the shelves and he began his climb down, careful not to kick over Mr. Virgil's coffee, which the custodian had left in the way. Once he'd reached the bottom, the Ceiling Fan took a deep breath, and his face was more relaxed than I'd ever seen it.

"We gotta get out of here," I said. "I messed up the boys' bathroom, but he could be back any second."

The Ceiling Fan chuckled and shook his head, as if I'd missed the whole point. "You feel sorry for them. I can tell by the look on your face. It ain't your fault. It's what they're teaching you nowadays in school. All of them. Coach Belt, even. There's a man who's gotten lazy with his thinking."

My back was to the closet door. I felt for the knob and held it tight.

"But he picked the right job. Be a high school teacher. That's how you do it. You, Darryl, go and get yourself a teaching certificate. There aren't enough good teachers. Everybody knows it's the problem, but what does anybody do about it?" He made a disgusted face. "And what other job pays you for sitting on your ass all day and then gives you your summers off? It seems stupid to me, stupid, at this point, *not* to become a teacher. Not to mention the aspect of working with female teachers. It's just a perspective worth thinking about." The Ceiling Fan leaned against Mr. Virgil's shelves. "You wouldn't go on a date with another teacher in your own school. Probably you wouldn't even talk to them much. You'd see this person, this sexy teacher in the halls every day. In the parking lot. At basketball games. Maybe you share a ride to school together in the morning. Maybe kiss a little. But what if you break up? Forget it. Who needs that crap? I say keep it professional. Do you have any idea what Pam Zweer looked like when I was in high school?"

The bell rang, signaling the end of third period. The hallway outside trembled.

"You just going to stand there all day?"

I pushed into the hallway and flew from the custodian's closet, catching a glimpse of Andy Hestra dancing in place at the entrance to the boys' bathroom. The sign on the door read OUT OF ORDER.

13

WAS FINE. Nothing happened. I didn't get in trouble, and it was over, so I needed to think about something else. Get my mind off it. I was fine, so what was I dwelling on? My body was functioning. My processor was processing. I was fine. I was fine. I was—

My neck itched.

The Ceiling Fan had poisoned me there, on that nub of my spine, and I knew that if I scratched there, the poison might spread to other parts of me. He could read my thoughts. I was certain. But worse, he was putting *new* thoughts into my processor. I tried not to think about anything, his thoughts or mine, which made me think about Mom, naked, that time when I accidentally crashed into the bedroom while she was changing: a snapshot captured by my eyes, now framed and centered on the living room wall of my mind. The Ceiling Fan was in my mind too, and we were staring at the picture together. He whistled, pointing to the blue birthmark on her hip. Her square nipples. The measuring cup of hair between her legs. "Your mom ain't quite normal, is she?"

But I was fine.

It was after school. I was sitting beside Kanga in Mr. Belt's room for a team meeting. The players already had on their practice clothes and were sitting at the desks, watching Mr. Belt spell out each of our names on the chalkboard. Thirteen names, printed in capital letters, including my own. Being manager meant I was part of the team. The Ceiling Fan was at Mr. Belt's desk. I dared a peek at him. He winked, as if to say, *Your mom ain't no Mrs. Zweer . . .*

Mr. Belt addressed us: "The regular season is nearly over, gentlemen. That means we're nearly to the ninth-grade championship. But keep your cows in the barn. That championship game isn't for a couple of weeks." Mr. Belt looked at the chalkboard. "Who can tell me what *this* is?"

The players stared at the list of names. Nobody raised a hand.

"Let's get with it! Here's the board. What do you see?"

They looked at their desks.

"Come on, men. This is high school. Not middle school. Not Sunday school. I'm asking you to use your minds. Tell me—"

"Names?" somebody whispered.

"Yes. But wrong. We all have names. Without names, where would mankind be as a society? But there is something more important than names. Tell me what it is."

"First names?"

"Christ," said Mr. Belt. "Look harder, would you?"

Nobody moved except the Ceiling Fan, who had found some grime beneath a fingernail. He began chewing on the end of his finger.

"Kanga," said Mr. Belt. "Please, you, of all people, should be able to tell me what in the holy heck I'm talking about up here. What is this, Kanga?"

"Everybody's names."

"Okay!" Mr. Belt pointed at Kanga. "Yes! We're getting somewhere. *Everybody.* That's my point. Nice work, Kanga. Way to keep your head in the— My point is we're a team. T-E-A-M. Got it?"

Everybody nodded.

"Now we're reading the same book. But what is a team composed of?"

Rye raised his hand.

"Players," continued Mr. Belt. "A team is composed of individuals. Different entities. Everybody is unique. Look at the clouds. No two clouds are ever the same. Take a look at the sky."

The classroom lights flickered inexplicably at that moment. The team looked at the ceiling. Somebody laughed. Suddenly everybody was laughing.

"Let's keep a lid on it. Act like men, not boys. I don't know what's wrong with you guys." Mr. Belt clapped his hands. "Okay! Everybody get out a sheet of paper and a pencil!"

The players looked down at their practice clothes, then at Mr. Belt.

"Terry. Go and hand everybody a piece of paper and a pencil. Please."

"Where do you keep the paper, Coach?"

"Are you serious, Terry? You know where the paper is. Get hopping."

"I don't have you for science."

"What? You're not in my fourth period? With all those other dipsticks?"

"I have Mrs. Conway for science."

"Kanga," said Mr. Belt. "*You* have me for science. Pass out the paper and pencils."

"Where do you keep the pencils?"

"Christ . . ."

After Kanga had given every player a piece of paper and a pencil, Mr. Belt ordered the team to look at the list of names on the chalkboard. He wanted them to vote for the best basketball player on the list.

"Who's the best guy on the team? In other words, who would beat every one else in a game of one-on-one? I'm not asking whom your best friend is or whom you like to play grab-ass with on the bus. This is confidential. Anonymous. I want you to fold your vote in half. Then raise your hand. I'll collect it from you. Then you can put your head down on your desk and sleep, if need be."

I scribbled "Kanga," folded my sheet of paper, and raised my hand. I peeked as Kanga wrote "James" in small letters on his piece of paper, folded it twice, and raised his hand. The rest of the class followed suit and soon everyone had their heads down on their desks. Mr. Belt set about reading the folded pieces of paper and marking down the tally on an index card.

"Okay gentlemen, here are the results. Twelve of you voted for one person. That means almost everybody thinks that one person is the best basketball player on the team. I didn't vote, because I'm the coach. I won't tell you whom everybody voted for, seeing as everybody knows who he is because everybody voted for him. Almost. Somebody else got a vote. A certain somebody. You know who you are, because it appears you voted for yourself, which is not something teammates do. Everybody else, good job. You voted righteously. To this certain other teammate, well, I guess, congratulations. Your name is written on a single sheet of paper. Nobody else voted for you."

Mr. Belt was squinting at James Botty, who squinted right back.

"Not that any of this matters. I'm throwing the ballots in the trash. If any of you buttheads thinks he can sneak into the school tonight, into the trash, and figure out who voted for himself, well, don't. Because I'm keeping that particular ballot right here in my pocket. I'll be dealing with that particular ballot later in life. Let's get to the Cave."

Rye raised his hand.

"Goddamn it, Rye."

"Do you want these pencils back?"

"Pencils? Yes. Give your pencils to Kanga. Kanga? All these pencils are for you. Keep them. Don't lose them. They can be school pencils, or you may take them home for your personal use."

The team gave their pencils to Kanga.

● ● ●

Practice was grueling. Mr. Belt couldn't stop yelling at the guys for being selfish, for being timid, for being philosophers, for not getting back on defense, for not finishing at the rim, for standing around like it was some kind of formal soiree. But while Mr. Belt's dissatisfaction was spread evenly across the team, the Ceiling Fan had eyes only for Kanga's mistakes, berating my brother again and again for deficiencies in offensive position, persistence, and body language.

But I saw it too. Something was wrong with Kanga. Something about my brother's *throat*. He was guarding that area with his hands. Robots didn't get sore throats, so why were Kanga's fingers massaging the sides of his Adam's apple? It was consuming him, so much so that Kanga didn't notice when Rye threw him a pass. The ball plunked Kanga in the belly—the kind of blow that would knock the wind out of a normal human. But Kanga didn't even react to it. He just kept his hands under his chin, rubbing his throat.

"Kanga?" asked Mr. Belt.

My brother made an anguished face then rushed off the court, leaving us all to listen as he spit a huge chunk of grease into a trash can. It had been caught in his throat, apparently, and Kanga had been trying to ease it out. From the sound of it thudding against the bottom of the can, the grease was thick and hard as clay—not the sound of something produced by a human body. Kanga remained above the can, working his tongue around inside his mouth. He then used a finger to claw some additional grease from the back of his throat before flicking it away.

The team just stared at him.

But the worst was the silence coming from the Ceiling Fan and James Botty, who were not looking at Kanga but at each other. Whatever my brother had just done, it somehow fit into a previous conversation between the two. James nodded at the Ceiling Fan. The Ceiling Fan nodded back. *A new piece of the puzzle,* they seemed to be confirming. But just how much of the whole picture had they put together?

Well, *I* was putting it together. James Botty wasn't Kanga's friend. He was the Ceiling Fan's spy.

Kanga jogged back to the team. "I feel better," he said, grinning faintly, his hands once again at his sides. "But whatever you guys do, *don't* go near that trash can, okay? I must've barfed up a lung in there."

"Well done, Livery," said Mr. Belt. "All right!" He clapped his hands. "Back at it, you bozos!"

Back at it, Kanga was. In the final minute of practice, everything came together. Hectorville's starting five executed a play that resulted in Rye using his elbows to create space, getting a blind bounce pass from Kanga, and scoring a left-handed layup. The Ceiling Fan stormed the court, punching Rye in the chest, grabbing the back of his neck, and shaking him hard. "*This is the most persistent goddamn player I've ever seen!*"

Mr. Belt quietly approached Kanga and tugged on his practice jersey. "Over here, Livery," he said. "Listen. You won the vote. Don't tell anybody, but everybody thinks you're the best player on the team."

"I know," said Kanga.

14

"YOU NEED TO QUIT the basketball team."

It was late Saturday afternoon. My brother stood in the kitchenette, shirtless, wearing just basketball shorts and high-tops. He took a long drink of milk as he contemplated my demand. He swallowed. "I don't think I will. Sorry, brother."

"We're not safe there."

"Thanks for the concern. Go ahead and quit being manager if you want. I'll understand."

"James Botty is not your friend. You've seen what he does to people. That's not the kind of person you want to be, Kanga. That's not the kind of person you *are*."

"I know who I am. I don't need you to tell me. James isn't perfect, but at least he's fun sometimes, which is more than I can say for you."

"We can't trust the Ceiling Fan."

"Trust him? Who cares about him? *I'm* the reason we're winning. Mr.

Belt would fire the Ceiling Fan in a heartbeat if it meant keeping me on the team."

"There's more to him than you know."

"There's more to *everybody* than we know." He grabbed my basketball from the kitchenette counter. "Why don't we take this conversation outside? It's too stuffy in here."

Kanga dribbled out the apartment door and down the hallway. I knew where he was going: the town basketball court. I had to put my concerns about the basketball team on hold, at least for the moment. Kanga could have walked out without saying anything, but he invited me along. Here was a rare chance to bond with him—and maybe even change his mind about James and the Ceiling Fan. I had to take it.

I followed him.

Outside, the snow had been rained off the earth. It was cool. The clouds were long, pink hands, pushing away the sun. There was no wind. It was perfect basketball weather.

Kanga began dribbling down the sidewalk—still shirtless, but I knew better than to try and dress him. The town basketball court was a half mile away, but Kanga preferred to walk rather than bike. He dribbled the entire distance, not once losing the ball.

The court was across the street from several nice houses. I imagined the families inside sipping tea, peering through their windows, watching our every shot. I had no idea if Kanga imagined the same thing. Probably not. He was used to people watching him play. An audience didn't faze him. He had eyes only for the rim.

"Rebound for me," he said.

I never should have thrown Kanga my basketball when we were little. Now he assumed my only purpose in life was rebounding the ball and passing it back to him. We'd already done this a couple of times since he joined the team. I hoped getting all those touches on the basketball would magically enhance my own skills, even if I never got to actually shoot it. The fresh air was intoxicating; I almost decided to go shirtless too. I looked at Kanga's belly muscles stretch and snap and thought better of it. His first shot swished through the net. I grabbed the ball and rifled it back to him.

"Quit now," I said, "and you can join the team again next year. You'll probably be on varsity. The Ceiling Fan will be out of the picture. I know it's disappointing, Kanga. But as your brother, I insist that you—"

"Relax." He swished it again. "There's no reason for that look on your face. We're just having a shoot."

"*You're* having a shoot." The ball was in my hands. I fought the reflex to pass it back to Kanga. "This is serious."

"Okay. But listen, Darryl, can you do me a favor right now?"

"Promise you'll quit the team."

"Pretend to be Bobby Knight."

"Bobby Knight?"

"Do the voice thing. While I'm shooting. Just pretend to be Bobby, and I'm trying out for the Hoosiers. You're here to size me up."

"And if I pretend to be Bobby Knight you'll quit?"

"I'll think about it."

I had nothing to lose. When it came to Kanga, I automatically experienced hints of Bobby Knight's trademark rage and frustration on a daily basis. It would be cathartic to let the General's voice loose while rebounding for my brother. But more than that, Kanga finally *needed* me for something. Obsolescence had erased that feeling from my processor. To have Kanga depend on me again? I felt a foot taller.

I cleared my throat. "I can be Bobby Knight for you."

"YES!"

But Kanga's elation was quickly tempered by a shiver through his body. We both realized the stakes had just been raised; this was no ordinary shootaround, but a *tryout*. What would Bobby Knight think of my brother?

I warmed up with whispers under my breath, unintelligible and harmless, as Kanga took a few tentative shots, uncertain when the Hoosiers' head coach would actually arrive. I kept him waiting a couple of moments, until suddenly Bobby Knight was screaming:

"Who the hell are you? You think you can play for me? You're a wussy! Show me the spider dribble. I DIDN'T SAY LOOK AT THE BALL! This is Indiana. You're pathetic. Show me the spider dribble for thirty seconds without a foul-up. I haven't got all day . . ."

I paced back and forth beneath the hoop, watching Kanga complete two minutes of spider dribbling, both of us waiting for what Bobby Knight would say next.

"Think you can jump? Show me fifty layups. LEFT-HANDED! And don't look at the fouling ball. Don't even THINK about missing a layup. Did I mention this is Indiana? Wussies get killed if they miss layups. That dog gets shot in the head if your ball even touches the rim."

A neighborhood dog had showed up. It was wagging its tail, about to charge for the ball. I saw the look on Kanga's face: utter disgust that something as random as a dog could ruin his chances with Bobby Knight. Before the next layup, Kanga cocked the ball behind his head, as if to smash the dog's nose. The dog edged sideways off the court. It trotted away.

"I bet you never even heard of the Mikan Drill. Not up here in Michigan. In Michigan you practice the Wussy Drill. In Indiana we have the Mikan Drill. This drill is how wussies' arms fall off. You'll never want to shoot another hook shot in your life after five minutes of the Mikan Drill. Think you can go five minutes? You'll die after three."

As Kanga performed the Mikan Drill (hook shot after hook shot, on alternating sides of the rim, the ball above his head the entire time), a man stopped his car on the street. He looked like an ex-player himself, and he watched Kanga for a moment but knew better than to interrupt this most sacred of drills. He drove off, shaking his head.

"Can you even lift your arms? Think you're some kind of big shot? YOU'RE A WUSSY! Think you can make a jump shot? Even when I point a gun at your mother's head?"

This is where my physical body became useful. Bobby Knight had finally ordered Kanga to shoot jump shots. I stood beneath the hoop, ready to rebound.

"Think you can make another? Take a step back. I DIDN'T SEE THAT

STEP! TAKE ANOTHER STEP! Big shot, huh? Make it again. You call that a jump shot? It's a shot, BUT WHERE'S THE JUMP?"

Kanga hit five shots in a row. NBA three-pointers. He was standing near the half-court line now. He hit five more. He wasn't missing. Not today. It didn't look like he would ever miss again.

"Three pointers? That's what you want to shoot? I thought you were a point guard. THIS IS INDIANA! Shooting guards shoot three-pointers at Indiana! Are you trying to change our whole system? You got some nerve, you know that? I bet you can't make the next one. The day a wussy like you makes nineteen three-pointers in a row, that's the day my name's not Bobby— Think you're hot? MAKE ANOTHER!"

It was stupid. But I had to wonder: What would Bobby Knight say if *I* attempted a shot? Not that I would dare. Even if I was the basketball kid, Bobby Knight only knew me as Kanga's rebounder. I could already hear what Bobby Knight would say about me: *Too short, too skinny, too slow, too weak.* Socks pulled up too high to cover my pathetic, hairless legs. Too much of a *wussy.* I got a rebound. I held the ball briefly in my best triple-threat position. I threw a behind-the-back pass to Kanga. The ball rolled into the grass. "SORRY!" I yelled (momentarily myself) and ran to get it. Kanga almost opened his mouth to say something. Bobby Knight barked, *"Shut your fool mouth!"* I threw Kanga the ball, and he hit another three.

"Three-pointers are for wussies. ALL Indiana basketball players can make threes. But what about a shot from that CAR over there? That's right, wussy. I'm talking about the red car WAY down there. Make that shot, it's Indiana. Not that it's even possible for a no-good wussy from Michigan . . . I'll be damned, kid. I thought that car shot was impossible, but you just swished it!"

Kanga looked tiny where he was, way down the street. Yet while taking (and making) that ridiculous shot, my brother hadn't altered his natural shooting form in any way. Professional players routinely flung the ball from three-quarters court, but even they had to bend down and heave it with all of their might just to have a prayer at hitting the backboard. Not Kanga. He had raised the ball above his head, gently bent his knees, and let go of it . . . and I could still hear the snap of the net in my ears. But also what Bobby Knight had said: *Make that shot, it's Indiana.* Kanga's hands were open to receive the ball from me again, but the basketball kid in me couldn't be restrained. I'd been too scared to try out for the basketball team because I only had a 4.9 percent chance of making it. But here was another shot. The chances were probably even less this time, but it was *still* a shot. A chance. If I didn't try it, the chance was zero. But if I made it? If I actually sunk the shot? I was holding the ball. Then I was running to the red car. I was *going* to make the shot. I was the basketball kid, and Bobby Knight would see. The shot's successful trajectory was a diagram in my processor. I knew the ball's arc. I knew the ball's torque. I lined up beside the car's front bumper. I bent my knees, hips, and elbows at the perfect angles to achieve maximum thrust. I launched the basketball hard and high toward the rim . . .

It bounced once on the court, then up through the bottom of the hoop.

I raised my arms in triumph, knowing the shot was a failure, but hoping Bobby Knight had seen something—*anything*—that was Hoosier material.

Silence.

The *real* basketball kid went to retrieve his ball. He began walking down the sidewalk, back home, too disgusted to even dribble. Practice over.

"Hold it, wussy. You're not at Indiana yet. You had a mediocre practice today. WHO CARES? If you ever want to see me again, I need a commitment. That team you're on now—nothing but wussies. Playing with them is making you soft. Tell me you'll quit that wussy team Monday morning."

Kanga froze. He turned and stared at Coach Knight, unable to speak. Finally, he nodded.

"TELL ME!"

"Yes, sir," he whispered. "I'll quit."

"Might be too late. Might be they already turned you into a wussy. All you proved today is that you can make shots with nobody guarding you. Let's see you beat somebody. This kid right here. If you can beat this kid, you're starting for me. But here's the rule: The kid gets nine points. Game goes to ten. If the kid

*kicks the basketball and it somehow goes in the hoop, you're screwed, and HE'S
on the Hoosiers. You'll never wear the crimson and cream. Think you'll still be
your dad's favorite then?"*

I got the ball first. Kanga knew how unfair this game was, but he
offered me one free, uncontested shot, a chance to ruin his audition for
Bobby Knight. I lined up the ball. Kanga tucked his hands behind his
back. He said, "You'll miss." The ball hit the rim. It bounced up. It hit the
rim again.

It missed.

Kanga's ball. I sunk into defensive position and felt a truck speeding
past me at seventy-five miles per hour. I couldn't even turn my head quick
enough to see Kanga score. He handed the ball back to me, but this time
he didn't let me hold it in the triple-threat position. Kanga stole it, canned
it, and handed it back.

*"New rule, wussy. If the kid shoots the ball and it even TOUCHES the
rim, the kid wins. That's the new rule, and if you don't like it, I guess you're not
Indiana material—"*

"FOUL!" I screamed, interrupting Bobby Knight. My brother and I
both had a grip on the ball, swinging around for possession.

"I didn't touch you," he said. "You little wussy."

"FOUL!" I screamed again, ready to explode. This was for every time
Kanga had stolen my ball when we were little. *My* ball! And for Mom's
singsong voice: *Share it with your brother.* No, Mom, *I* was the basketball
kid!

"You can't even rebound for me right. And you're not supposed to talk
like yourself. You're supposed to be Bobby Knight. Next time I come here,
I'm coming alone." Kanga ripped the ball away from me and kicked it
across the street.

"You're a robot," I said.

A look of disbelief spread across my brother's face.

"A robot," I repeated. "Did you hear that, Bobby?"

Kanga's eyes grew wide. He shook his head desperately, imploring me
to stop speaking.

"That's why you'll never make Indiana." I was shouting now. "Or anything! Because you're a robot!" Then Bobby Knight growled to life in my throat: "*What's this kid talking about, wussy?*"

"Nothing, sir," Kanga answered Bobby Knight. "He's just my brother. He's a little liar."

"*No no no. I think this basketball kid is onto something. You just made those shots because you're a machine. A thing. A toaster! Ha ha! Indiana doesn't suit up toasters, wussy . . . SO HIT THE ROAD!*"

Kanga caught me before I could run home. The dog was still watching from a distance. My brother plucked me up and carried me off the court to the nearest patch of grass. The dog skipped away, its head low to the ground as if it didn't want to witness what was about to happen next. I wouldn't have screamed, knowing someone in a house might look outside and see what Kanga was doing to me. Might call the police. But Kanga didn't care. He sat with his butt on the wet ground, legs crossed, and held me tight on his lap. To someone watching from a house, Kanga probably looked like he wanted to read me a picture book. His legs felt just like Mom's legs. But his arms were Dad's; he had one wrapped across my chest. I couldn't move. My hands were just flippers at my sides.

With his free hand, Kanga began filling my mouth with yellow grass. "I'm not quitting the team." It was Mom's soft voice, reading me *The Directions.* The plug pushed deeper into my throat with each handful. "And I'm not a robot."

We were in the middle of town. Anyone could have seen him. But somehow Kanga knew that they wouldn't—or if they did, that they wouldn't tell on him. And he was right. About everything. Hectorville was his.

My brother finally released me, letting me tumble into the ring of dirt surrounding where we sat. Kanga had picked all the grass and stuffed it inside me. "That was a final warning. Next time I won't go easy on you."

15

BY FEBRUARY, Kanga was the most popular kid in Hectorville High School. Basketball had something to do with it, as he now enjoyed universal name recognition among our classmates and teachers. Additionally, an uptick in Kanga's personal hygiene meant girls didn't just look at him anymore; they ogled him. But the chief reason for my brother's social dominance had nothing to do with other people. It was his own shameless confidence in himself, the uncompromising belief that the world owed him.

How much?

Everything.

One look at this new version of Kanga and you knew he wasn't lifting a finger for anyone but himself until the world paid him in full.

It was Friday afternoon. Art class. Mrs. Asquith stopped by the table I shared with my brother. "Kanga?" She leaned in close to him. "How are we doing this afternoon? Are we going to *draw* anything today? Anything at all?"

Kanga was hugging my basketball, seemingly distraught because there would be no practice today after school. He refused to even look at the blank sheet of paper in front of him.

Mrs. Asquith slowed her speech. "You can create anything you want on this paper. Anything in the world! What are your interests, Kanga?"

"Ball."

"Excellent! I know you like playing *basket*ball. Let's make one of those! Now, the beginning of any appropriate *ball* is to simply draw a circle. Will you commit to drawing a circle? Before I come by again? Just one circle? And I'll fetch you an orange colored pencil!"

I too had a blank sheet of paper sitting before me, but I had avoided Mrs. Asquith's attention by giving it an anguished yet thoughtful expression. A pencil fixed between my teeth was the finishing touch. Mine was the visage of the artist, frozen in that fateful moment *just before* inspiration hit him like a falling piano. Little did Mrs. Asquith know I had no intention of drawing a picture. I was *still* trying to write a single humorous line of prose (eventually an entire story) for my muse, seated across the room from me. I had an unobstructed view of Brooke Noon's entire body, divided in half by her art table.

Between gazes at Brooke, I glanced at a recent issue of *Sports Illustrated* I'd grabbed from Mrs. Asquith's "Idea File," an old cardboard box filled with cut-up magazines. I'd found an interview with the dazzling Olympic figure skater Kristi Yamaguchi. The first question for her: "Are you a robot?"

"I'm an athlete," Yamaguchi answered. "Ask my mom and dad. Ask my brother and sister. They've seen me compete at everything I've ever done. So what am I? Just an athlete. A competitor. Pretty soon, I hope, a gold medalist."

I'd heard the rumors, like everybody else, that Kristi Yamaguchi was a robot. She lived in Northern California, for one, the most robot-friendly chunk of the country, known for its cryptically advertised gasoline bars and grease transfusion spas. Surely everyone in her hometown knew her as a robot, though Kristi was wise to play coy for a national audience. I hoped it was true. I had an Olympic-size crush on her. I closed my eyes and replayed a TV clip I'd seen of her on the ice. I loved her powerful legs. I loved that she was an artist among mere technicians in her sport. I loved that she wore the tools of her medium on her *feet*. And I loved, after her airtight routine, that huge, genuine smile for the camera, Kristi gasping for oxygen between her beautiful teeth . . .

I opened my eyes. There was Brooke Noon.

Below her art table, she wore her favorite wintertime outfit of leggings, huge wool socks, and her dirty pink All Stars. In art class she drew maps of Earth taken from space. She hunched over them in extreme focus. This caused the shoes to slip from her feet. If I was lucky, sometimes Brooke even removed her wool socks too, allowing her bare toes to tap the dirty floor as she drew. Today, wholly absorbed in her cartography, Brooke exposed even more skin by mindlessly tugging her leggings up over her kneecaps, and, with a pair of art scissors, gently trimmed the hairs on her shins.

From across the room, as my arousal transferred from Kristi Yamaguchi to Brooke, I saw Mrs. Asquith lean down next to her: "Ms. Noon? Is that an appropriate use of art-room tools?"

The scissors clacked to the floor. Brooke yanked her leggings down to her ankles.

God, what I would have done to feel the shaven spots on her legs . . . and that's when I looked down at my paper and saw an unexpected line. I had drawn it without thinking: the line of Brooke's leg with all the correct curves. Her hip bone, the lightly curved line of her thigh, her semicircular kneecap, neither too big nor too pointed, the straight line of her shin, and then her foot, which ended with five little nubs, her toes, each one smaller than the one before it. The line ended there, at the tip of my pencil, yet I still had room at the bottom of the paper. Boldly, I continued the line downward, straight off the paper, a sock hanging from Brooke's toe. I felt obscene, looking at such a long sock on such a short and beautiful foot. But I couldn't look away. All of a sudden, it was my most prized possession—a piece of art whose sole purpose was the primal thrill of one viewer: me. I scribbled my signature at the bottom of the page.

"What's that?" asked Kanga.

I tongued a phantom bit of grass from the inside of my cheek. "Nothing."

"Let me see it."

"No." I slipped the drawing into my math folder and set it on the floor under my stool. At that moment, class was interrupted by three soft knocks on the door.

The Ceiling Fan leaned into the room. "May I borrow Kanga for a moment?"

"Indeed!" said Mrs. Asquith.

Kanga bounded into the hallway, and the door clicked shut.

On the last page of its "Parenting" section, *The Directions* warned robotic mothers and fathers to *mostly* ignore the voice in their processors telling them they're doing a horrible job raising their children. For instance, if the voice in your processor says, *You just yelled at your kids? Wow. I bet those kids are going to grow up and murder everyone in your apartment building*, understand that that's probably not going to happen. However, if the voice says, *Where are your kids? In the other room watching TV? Wrong. They're probably getting KIDNAPPED!*, moms and dads should drop whatever they're doing and make sure their kids aren't getting kidnapped. *The Directions* was very clear about kidnapping, over and over reminding parents that if their kids get kidnapped, it's all the parents' fault.

The Ceiling Fan had just kidnapped Kanga. I glanced across the room at Mrs. Asquith, who was working with Ben Finney on his drawing. She had commandeered Ben's pencil and was joyously reworking his mistakes. "Let me just add a touch more shading to that nose," said Mrs. Asquith. "Or is that an ear?"

I slipped into the hallway. It was empty, but there was no mystery as to where the Ceiling Fan had taken my brother. I rounded the final corner just as Mr. Virgil's closet door closed. Kanga and the Ceiling Fan were inside together.

The hallway light fixtures rattled, and I knew the Ceiling Fan was crawling to his spot above the women's bathroom. Kanga would soon appear in the hallway to serve as lookout. I needed to play this perfectly.

The door inched open. Kanga stepped into the hallway, his eyes rolling in their sockets, working independent of each other, scanning all directions for possible enemies. They stopped on me. "What are you doing here?"

"Kanga!" I whispered, as if trying to contain my excitement. "I have great news!"

"Get lost." He positioned himself to block me from Mr. Virgil's door. His fists were clenched. Then, when it seemed he might take a swing at me, his demeanor changed. His face softened with concern. "Darryl. Go back to class. I'll explain later, but right now"—he glanced at Mr. Virgil's door—"you're gonna get us both in trouble."

I almost broke down and told him everything—about my own meeting with the Ceiling Fan, about poor Mrs. Clinow. I almost told Kanga. But I didn't. I stuck to my plan and said, "She's coming."

"Who?"

"Mom. Right after you—"

"Mom?"

"Right after you left, Mrs. Asquith got a call from the office. They called us both down there because Mom is on her way to pick us up. She's driving to school right now!"

"Mom," he breathed.

"We're supposed to wait outside. By the front doors. We're supposed to—"

Kanga fell in the direction of the front doors, tripping over his feet. Then he was bounding.

●●●

Step one of my plan was complete. Now for step two.

I found Mr. Virgil rebagging the trash barrels in the cafeteria. He was halfway down a barrel himself, placing a new bag just so, when he heard me coming. He straightened up and eyeballed me. "What is it this time? Somebody take a dump in your locker?"

"No. Somebody's in the ceiling."

"What ceiling?"

"The ceiling in your closet. I saw the guy go in there. It's a man, actually. He's—"

"*Again.*" There wasn't a hint of surprise on his face. "So Simms is in my closet? In my ceiling? You saw him go in there?"

"Yes."

"Did *you* go in there with him?"

"No!" I shouted. "I just *saw* him go in there. He's alone. I figured I should tell you, so you can do something about it."

"What do you want me to do?"

"Get him. Tell Principal Moyle. Call the police. Do whatever it takes to get him kicked out of school, so he can't be our basketball coach anymore."

"Just like that, huh?"

"You know what he's doing up in the ceiling, right?"

I suddenly missed Dad. He and Mr. Virgil had a similar way of widening their stance and flexing their knees when their processors were churning through a problem. Sometimes I imagined Dad and me as a father-and-son bank-robbing team. Just before pulling his ski mask over his face, Dad would give me a life lesson in surviving alone if he ended up taking a bullet to the abdomen.

Mr. Virgil had no interest in life lessons. His processor had already solved the problem I'd presented him, the solution being to push past me to the next trash barrel.

"You're just going to let him go?"

"Hell." He looked down at me with eyes as deep as shower drains. "Let's say I *do* something. Let's say I go in, and I pull him out of that ceiling. Big hero, huh? And Simms is just gonna walk outta here and say nothing? Play it out. Use what's in your guts, kid. All Simms's gotta do is shout, loud and clear, everything he thinks about me. Just gotta say his bad word once. How many ears are in this school? Look around this cafeteria. Look at all the food they got in piles. Let's say somebody says, 'Virgil, eat this hoagie and tater tots, and prove you ain't one of them.' And even if I eat it, they're still never gonna look at me the same. I've been scrubbing this place nineteen years, and it ain't because I read some book about it. I used my eyes and ears. My damn instincts. I adapted on the fly. Otherwise I'd be toast." He knuckled me in the chest. "*Your* book got a chapter on dealing with Ceiling Fan Simms?"

"My book?"

"You ain't even imagined this through for a minute, have you? They catch a grown man in the ceiling, peeking at ladies, they're gonna call the parents of every kid Simms has ever talked to. The police'll be showing up at your house. It'll be all over the news. Your fat-ass book got any instructions about being on the news? Huh, Darryl? Or how about your folks? They any good in front of TV cameras?"

"You know about *The Directions*? And me?"

Mr. Virgil grabbed a fresh bag for the next trash barrel. "I don't know a damn thing you're talking about."

● ● ●

On my way back to art class, I passed by the custodian's closet and walked straight into the Ceiling Fan. He was in mid-conversation with Mrs. Zweer; he must have said something hilarious, as the veteran teacher was laughing heartily. She touched his shoulder. "Jason," she said, "you always did love basketball. I'm glad these young men have you as a role model— or maybe I should be worried!" She laughed again.

"We have fun," he said. Then he noticed me. "Darryl! Tell your brother he needs to work on his persistence!"

Mrs. Zweer looked at me too, exhibiting the standard blank expression, neither inviting nor threatening, teachers use with students they haven't taught. We were just outside the women's bathroom.

"I'll tell him," I said to the Ceiling Fan.

A minute later I was back on my art stool. Mrs. Asquith hadn't noticed my departure. She was in the same spot as before, collaborating with Ben Finney, who had scooted his stool back, allowing Mrs. Asquith to lean over his drawing: erasing it, shading it, smudging it, perfecting it, until the bell rang.

My plan had been a failure. Mrs. Zweer was debased. The Ceiling Fan would continue his vile acts with impunity. Worst of all, I had exploited Kanga's deepest vulnerability.

He was waiting outside by the curb. I could see the doubt in his posture as he gazed down the road for any trace of Mom. The other students were pouring past him, eager for the freedom of the weekend, and it seemed the slightest bump might knock Kanga to the ground.

I held out his backpack for him. "Come on, brother. Let's go."

Requiring no further explanation, Kanga followed me to the bike rack. I'd been bracing for a blowup. A punch in the belly. A kick to the knee. At the very least, a barrage of insults, threats, and obscenities. I even welcomed all of it, just to get it over with. But Kanga showed no emotion. *Nothing*. He stared straight ahead, mouth slightly ajar—a typical fourteen-year-old boy. Half of me wanted to praise his composure, his maturity. But there was another half of me too, the half that remembered Dad's words, one of the last things he ever said to me about Kanga: *We got piss-all of an idea what's programmed in his head or when it's gonna blow.*

We stood beside our bikes. "I'm sorry," I blurted. "The reason I lied was—"

He held up a hand, stopping me. Without a hint of malice, Kanga stepped behind me and unzipped the backpack on my shoulders. I could feel him sorting through my books and folders, as though searching for something he'd placed there himself. He finally removed my math folder.

Kanga pulled out my drawing of Brooke Noon's leg and foot.

I almost snatched it back from him, to protect Brooke's bare foot from the February cold. But I didn't. This was my punishment. Back in art class, Kanga had noticed my obsession with the drawing, though he couldn't possibly know the drawing's inspiration, and now he would destroy the thing before my eyes. Fine. I would take it like an adult. I played it out with what was in my guts, just like Mr. Virgil had advised. I would suffer now, but it would repair my relationship with my brother, if only slightly.

"Rip it up," I ordered him. "Then we'll be even."

Kanga folded the drawing in half. He folded it again and put it in his pocket. He mounted his bike and headed for home.

16

THE APARTMENT WAS KANGA'S NOW. All you had to do was listen to the crumpling of Cobra Burger bags, the *blub blub blub* of milk jugs, the rattle and gush of aerosol deodorant cans, the stomp of his shoes, the machine-gunning of the basketball, the hiss of the shower . . .

To escape him I camped out on Mom and Dad's bed with *The Directions*. After my encounter with Mr. Virgil, I tried to reread the book with a critical eye. First of all, no way was it written by just one person, with its rampant fluxes in word length and word frequency, its concentrated overuses of *and*, *so*, and *therefore*, and its random passages with semicolons sprinkled around like salt. I scanned one chapter that was so spartan in its sentence structure, I guessed the writer to be an early-model robot himself. But I had my favorite writers too. Top of the list was whoever wrote the subchapter on grooming habits. She (somehow I knew it was a woman) dared us robots to "relish the recklessness" of letting our hair grow long. At least once she suggested we should be the kid in class whose hair "sat up top like weedless, well-watered grass." This foray would result in our "pity for the peer who schedules his haircuts down to the hour of the week, down to the pathetic sixteenth of an inch, so his hair appears indefinitely haircut-less—"

My reading was interrupted by a knock on our apartment door.

Who would be bothering us at six thirty on a Sunday night? I rolled off the bed and darted down the hallway to intercept the intruder, but Kanga was already there. The front door was open, and my brother said, "Come on in."

To my horror, James Botty responded: "They did it, Kanga! All five of them started!"

He was the first "friend" we'd ever had over. *The Directions* strictly forbade it. *I* strictly forbade it. But when Kanga and James high-fived, and the bully took a seat on our couch, I asked myself: What would Mr. Virgil do? *Adapt.* There was no James Botty chapter in *The Directions.* I had to assume the worst about him. James was here on behalf of the Ceiling Fan, collecting intelligence on two potential robots. I'd have to use my eyes and ears—*my guts*—to get rid of him.

"The Fab Five, man," James continued. "They're gonna go down as the best team in history. You should've seen what they did to Notre Dame today. Smashed the suckers. The Fab Five started—every single guy. The Fab Five scored every single *point* for Michigan. Man, they ain't losing this season."

"I love the Fab Five," said Kanga, "man."

"That's gotta be us. *We* gotta be the Fab Five." James had already begun the transformation. On his worn-out Nikes, he'd drawn a block *M*, symbol of the Michigan Wolverines. Though he still had on regular-size basketball shorts, James had tugged them lower on his hips, giving the appearance of the looser, baggier style of the fabulous freshmen. Then there was his hair—or what was left of it. To mimic the look of his favorite players, James had shaved (or gotten a toddler to shave) the sides of his head. Only a slight film of hair remained up top, from which he'd removed a random divot, causing his scalp to resemble those of Chris Webber, Jalen Rose, Juwan Howard, Jimmy King, and Ray Jackson.

He looked ridiculous. But only because, sitting alone on our couch, James was still an outlier. Were he to persuade four more Hectorville Birds to morph along with him—he would need Kanga as an initial convert in order to convince the other three—then he'd be a trendsetter.

"They're bugging out over at my place." James snatched our remote control from the floor and flipped the channel to the NBA All-Star Game. "So I gotta watch this here."

Kanga slid in beside him, pretending it was no big deal to have a friend over, but I could feel his anxious excitement. Despite my brother's new-found confidence, deep down he was still in James Botty's thrall. "I was just about to turn on the game."

"Look at their shorts!" James laughed at the professional players on the screen. "These guys got no game anymore. I bet the Fab Five could beat them."

"Yeah," said Kanga.

James made no mention of our apartment's state of distress—the pile of dirty clothes, the empty milk jugs stinking up the kitchenette, the basketball smudges on the walls and ceiling. Nor did he wonder about our parents. It seemed perfectly logical to him that they would be gone on a Sunday night. He just stared at the TV, occasionally taking a swig from the two-liter of Red Pop he brought with him. It was halftime when James yawned and said, "What do you guys got to eat around here?"

Kanga glared at the balled-up Cobra Burger bags on the floor, knowing he couldn't offer their spoiled contents to James. However, "nothing" was just as unacceptable. As a last resort, he looked to me.

"Tacos," I said. "Let me whip some up."

"*Yeah*," said James.

I hadn't made a batch of tacos since winter break, but I found some gray chuck at the back of the refrigerator. It was a month and a half old. I peeled away the pink cellophane, then held the meat above the sink with both hands and shook away the gray slime. I knew I would have to add twice the seasoning to mask its sweet stink. But when I had the meat cooking on high in the microwave, I heard James say, "That shit smells good!"

In the cupboard, I located a plastic bag with several white tortillas. They *used* to be white. They'd since flowered with green mold. I peeled off the worst tortillas from the top and bottom. The middle two would have to work. Besides, once they were covered with taco meat, James would never see the fuzzy green patches. I hoped.

I brought his plate of tacos to the couch. Mom would have cringed to see him eating outside the kitchenette.

"Where's the cheese?" asked James.

"Cheese?"

"And the hot sauce."

I shrugged, and Kanga scowled at me, as if it were my fault we had neither of these items.

"Whatever," said James. He lifted a taco to his mouth.

Humans chew more than robots, but even so, James took his time with his first mouthful of my tacos. He finally swallowed and choked out the question, "*Did you even cook these tortillas?*"

"A little bit," I lied.

"They're stale as hell." He dumped the meat from the tortillas into a mound on the middle of his plate then set the discarded tortillas on a couch cushion. James used his fingers to pinch the steaming meat and lift it quickly to his mouth. "Yeah," he said, and swallowed the meat without even chewing. "*Oh*, yeah."

Something dawned on me: Eventually all humans need to use the bathroom. I hadn't even peeked at ours in the last few days. I grabbed a roll of paper towels and slipped into the bathroom, and—*yikes*. Kanga's grease was everywhere. On the sink, the mirror, the floor, the toilet seat. I wiped it all up and tossed the greasy paper towels in the wastebasket, only to notice further incriminating evidence in there: our used food receptacles. How would I explain these crusty, soiled tubes to James? Or worse, how would Kanga explain them? I grabbed the entire wastebasket and tossed it in our hallway closet. How was *that* for adaptation, Mr. Virgil?

When I returned to the living room, I saw James had cleaned his first plate of taco meat, so I brought him another, including a fork. He wiped his fingers on his shorts, and then used the fork to shovel the meat into his mouth. Our guest didn't seem to notice that neither Kanga nor I were eating any tacos ourselves, so riveting was the All-Star Game. James set his empty plate on the floor and leaned closer to the TV.

"*Johnson!*" said the announcer. "*Two in a row for Magic! Going for the MVP!*"

I'd been so consumed by my hosting duties, I'd failed to notice that Magic Johnson was alive, that he was playing in the All-Star Game, racking up assists from all parts of the court and playing lockdown defense on Isiah Thomas and Michael Jordan. Nobody could get past Magic. He canned another three-pointer in the closing seconds. He was the MVP. Every player on the court waited patiently to hug the man—Isiah looked like he might even *kiss* him. Everybody had forgotten that Magic should be dead.

James grabbed his stomach. "Uhhh," he said, and it was unclear whether the sight of Magic Johnson had caused his body to convulse or if it was the tacos. "Where's the bathroom?"

Kanga pointed down the hallway, and James staggered off. *You're welcome for cleaning, brother.*

He had scarcely acknowledged my presence all weekend, ever since I'd lied to him about Mom. But now, having shared this unexpected moment—Magic reaching through the TV screen, wrapping his sweaty arms around us, saying, "*Come on now, boys!*"—I felt a desperate urgency to reconnect with Kanga.

"Mrs. Stover must be jumping around her house right now," I said. "Remember her? Our bus driver from fourth grade? She *loved* Magic Johnson." I hoped his face would break goofy, showing a trace of the carefree fourth grader he used to be.

There it was. His nostrils. For a brief moment, his nostrils smiled.

"What do you think?" I asked. "Was she a robot?"

Kanga appeared to be considering this when James returned from the bathroom. "What the hell is this thing?" He held up *The Directions*.

No.

It couldn't be my fault. I'd run the numbers. Our discovery—and subsequent destruction—was supposed to be because of Kanga. I'd always taken a cynical pride in the 97.7 percent likelihood that *he'd* be the one who would eventually screw things up for us, not me. I was the good robot. It was my job to save us. No more. I'd left *The Directions* sitting on Mom and Dad's bed, practically begging James Botty to peek inside their room and find it. It was my fault. It was my fault alone.

I closed my eyes, but the sight was already burned into my processor: James Botty's taco-stained fingers gripping my cherished tome. The book was open to a diagram for adding grease to your knee joint. "*Directions?*" he said. "Directions to what? Torturing yourself?"

"Ask Darryl," Kanga said, barely concealing his rage. "It's his."

"No! It's . . . from the library."

James looked at the book's spine, where a Dewey Decimal number should have been located. There was none.

"It's a special library book," I said. "Not on the shelves. I ordered it from Michigan State's library. They keep books like this locked away. You have to ask for it. I borrowed it because . . . because I want to build robots someday."

As I said the word *robot*, I heard it. The crackle. The sound our classmates had spontaneously produced on the bus in fourth grade, the sound that had connected them, that had urged James Botty's destruction of Molly Seed. But today's crackle belonged only to him. It was a scared sound. The buzz of a single, panicked fly. James squinted at Kanga. "Know what I thought when I saw this book? I thought, maybe Kanga and Darryl are one of them—"

"We're not!" I blurted. "Robots, we're not. Honest."

"But then I thought, nah. I know these guys. I've known them my whole life. They're my friends. If these two guys are robots, then anybody might be one. Shit, if these guys are robots, that means they've been lying to me this whole time. Playing me for a fool. So here's your chance to tell me straight. *Are* you guys robots?"

"No," I said. "We're not robots, James. I'm sorry you got that idea from that stupid—"

"How about you, Kanga?" James wanted my brother's answer, not mine. "I won't be mad if you say yes. I just want you to be honest with me." The crackle wavered for the briefest of moments, and James Botty almost looked like a friend. "Are you a robot, Kanga?"

Don't trust him.

"I hate robots," said Kanga. He was glaring at *The Directions*. "And I hate that book. And I hate my stupid brother for bringing it into our apartment."

James laughed, and the crackle disappeared. "I hate library books too." He let go of *The Directions*, letting it crack against the floor. "I don't trust them. Because who knows what kind of psycho was touching them before me? Somebody with AIDS, probably."

"Probably," said Kanga.

I left *The Directions* where it lay, not daring to pick it up until James left the apartment, which wasn't for another hour and a half. I washed the dishes, scrubbing them over and over, while James and Kanga sat on the couch and watched *Life Goes On*, a TV show I was certain Kanga had never seen but pretended to find riveting because James liked it. After the show, James stepped on *The Directions* as he walked to the door, pretending he didn't see it. But he stopped just before leaving. He turned to Kanga. "Man, I believe you about not being a robot and all, but your *shoes*. Those Cons?" James shook his head. "That robot in China wears those shoes. You gotta get rid of them, Kanga. As your friend, I don't want anybody else to get the wrong idea about you."

Kanga squeaked out a laugh. "I always hated these shoes."

"Right," said James, but he kept looking at Kanga until my brother leaned over and unlaced the shoes, carefully, as he always did, and removed them from his feet. He walked to the kitchenette trash can and dropped them inside.

James smiled. "We'll steal you some Nikes next weekend." Then he was gone.

I immediately retrieved *The Directions* from the floor, inspecting it for damage. Some of the pages were crinkled, others stained with orange taco juice, but, surprisingly, nothing was torn. But wait. Were my tactile sensors overloaded, or did *The Directions* feel *one* page lighter? In a panic, I began riffling through the book, searching for any clue that James had compromised it. Because if he'd taken a page, I needed to know *which* one. That was the whole question. Once I had that figured out, I could make sure Kanga and I did the opposite of whatever that page was instructing us to do. Then we wouldn't appear like robots to James and the Ceiling Fan. Then we—

Kanga grabbed *The Directions* from my hands.

"No—"

But it was too late. He was walking out the apartment door in his socks. I could tell by the purpose in his gait there was no sense in pleading with him. I followed.

It was pitch-black outside. He led me to the burn pit in the grass near the maintenance shed, where the handyman occasionally did away with fall leaves. He worked in the darkness, but I heard Kanga ripping out a handful of pages and wadding them up. "I should let you do the honors," he said to me, but he lit the match himself. Once all of the crumpled pages were lit, he lay *The Directions* on top. Kanga then stood up, folded his arms against his chest, and watched as the orange flame began to eat the book.

But the fire started to die before *The Directions* could fully be devoured, so my brother pulled a sheet of paper from his pocket. My drawing of Brooke Noon. Without looking at the image of her foot, Kanga leaned down and used the drawing, half-folded, to fan the fire.

The flame crackled back to life.

Then he put the drawing—folded, but unburned—back in his pocket. He wasn't going to destroy everything I cared about. Not yet.

He straightened up, eyes transfixed by the flame. His socks were brown and soaked up to his ankles, but pleasure hid behind the muted expression on his face. I'd never witnessed a robot act so perfectly human: just a man standing in the dark, watching the fire he'd created. What a crime he was wasting this performance on me, the one person who knew exactly what he was.

● ● ●

I had the contents of the book memorized, each and every word, which meant, technically, the physical object of *The Directions* was obsolete. It shouldn't matter that it had been transformed into ash particles now spiraling into the heavens. And maybe it was a good thing the book was destroyed, now that James knew about it. Less incriminating evidence in the apartment. However, page 940 explained that "Sentimental attachment to oft-used items is a natural by-product of human assimilation" and a sign of a "healthy processor."

So I guess I was just feeling "healthy" Monday morning at school as I watched Kanga curl eight pieces of tape to attach my drawing to the inside of our locker door. My signature had been removed with scissors. The name *Kanga* had been added. Someone was staring at the drawing too. It was Toni, one of the girls who shared a locker beside ours.

"Did you do that?" she asked.

"Yes," said Kanga.

"I mean, what is it?"

"A person."

"Oh. Yeah. I knew that." She leaned in close to my drawing, smirking at it. Then she grabbed a perfume bottle and gave herself four long spritzes. "Jeez," she said. "I hate school."

Later that morning I was waiting for Kanga to gather his books from our locker so I could grab my own when somebody tapped him on the shoulder. It was Andres from the basketball team. A benchwarmer.

"Is that yours?" Andres asked.

"Yes," said Kanga. "I did it in art class."

"That looks pretty easy. I could do that if I wanted. Just a few lines." Then Andres added his favorite word, "*Doorknob!*"

Then, before lunch, Mr. Belt was walking through the hallway, swinging his arms, winking at people he knew. He veered toward our locker.

"Somebody tells me you did something, Kanga. Some art. Andres says you're an *artiste*. Well. You have to start somewhere. One drawing is better

than none, I always say. 'To have an artistic mind,' you hear from people.
Well. Don't quit your day job, at least. I can't draw a straight line. When I
draw two parallel lines the end product looks like a sexy woman." Mr. Belt
winked at Kanga. "Whatever that means."

In the passing period before art class, Kanga had our locker open and
was staring at Brooke's foot. The Spanish teacher snuck up behind him
and touched his neck. "An athlete and an artist," she whispered. Señora
Something. As far as I knew, she'd never spoken to my brother before that
moment, but her touch seemed to jar Kanga to action. He immediately
unfixed the drawing and carried it down the hallway.

I followed at a distance as Kanga approached Brooke's locker. The bell
was about to ring. Students were sprinting to get to sixth period on time.
The hallway was deserted when Brooke emerged from the girls' bathroom.
Kanga stood blocking her locker.

"Move," said Brooke.

"This is for you."

"Move."

Kanga held out the drawing. "This is for you, *Brooke.*"

Brooke grabbed my drawing and held it an inch from her face. She
began walking in place, examining the picture as she went nowhere. "Are
you giving me this for free?"

"Yes."

"I don't have to pay anything for it?"

"No."

The bell rang. They were completely alone in the hallway—except for
me, who was peeking at them from the doorway of the boys' bathroom.

"That's stupid," said Brooke, "just giving something away for free. This
is art. It's worth something. Did you make it?"

"Yes. And now you're going to do something with me."

"No!" Brooke was breathing heavily. "It's not called *giving* if you expect
something in return! So move. *Move.*"

"You have a bike," Kanga said. "I want to go on a bike ride with you."

"I don't have a bike!"

"Yes, you do," said Kanga. "Your bike is pink with white letters."

My processor identified Kanga's strategy for his interaction with Brooke: he had become our sixth-grade teacher, Mrs. Farnsworth, the only teacher in history who had actually enjoyed Brooke in her classroom and who could, more astoundingly, persuade Brooke to comply with school regulations. A quick video analysis of Mrs. Farnsworth revealed that she had never raised her voice at Brooke, never asked Brooke a question, but only gave simple instructions, one at a time, and never stared directly in her eyes, though she always leaned toward Brooke with her forehead bowed, her face blank.

"Go on a bike ride with me," said Kanga. "It will happen in thirty seconds."

"Sixth period is art class," said Brooke. "Thank you for the gift, but I have art sixth period."

I'd never heard Brooke say "thank you" in my life. Kanga was getting to her.

He said, "Go on a bike ride with me."

"*No.*"

"Make your decision. The bike ride starts now." Kanga turned and began walking to the school exit.

I could hear the hum of Kanga's processor as it ran the numbers, calculating how much of a long shot it was that Brooke would follow him. But Kanga stayed true to his method. The numbers must have told him not to look back. He didn't. He kept walking and pushed through the exit.

Brooke took a tender look at my drawing. Gently, she set it inside her locker. Then she worked her arms into her coat. She strung her clarinet case over her shoulder. She chased after Kanga, letting the exit door slam behind her . . .

I was beyond asking questions like *Doesn't he understand how much I love her?* and *How could he do this?* The answers were *Yes* and *Easily.* The real questions—as my processor replayed Kanga setting *The Directions* aflame—were: *Are you just going to stand here like a wussy? Or are you going to get out there and stop him?*

17

HAIR FRIZZING OUT THE BACK of her enormous bike helmet, Brooke sped past Kanga. She swerved through the school parking lot and onto the road. If only a teacher had glanced out a window, this abduction would have been stopped. I stood beside my bike, watching Kanga and Brooke get smaller and smaller.

Just before they vanished, I began to follow them.

Brooke led the way, steering us toward the center of Hectorville. I'd imagined them going in the opposite direction, to the countryside, which had fewer people to call the police about a pair of kids not being in school—or whatever Kanga had planned for Brooke. It was a mild afternoon, with the occasional roadside snowdrift to remind us it was February. Two birds spoke to each other from different trees. I watched Brooke's shoes rise and fall as she pedaled standing up, her calf muscles hardened in her white leggings. She had left Kanga far behind. She skidded to a stop and yelled, "You suck at riding bikes!"

Kanga took his time catching up. "Maybe I do."

"No. You do." She grinned. "I'm fast, and you suck."

They were looking down at the same patch of asphalt between them, sharing it, as if it were reflecting their faces up at each other. I was a hundred yards back, hiding behind a bush, all my battery power shunted to my audio processors. The key to being a spy was following your target at a distance, sprinting between areas of cover. When they finally resumed, Kanga pushed off first, followed by Brooke. I pedaled up to a truck, then a tree, keeping my ears on them, keeping my body out of sight. They rode together at a steady pace, passing Hectorville Funeral Parlor. Brooke said, "I'll bet you five hundred bucks . . ."

Kanga waited for her to finish. She didn't. He said, "Okay."

"Forget it! No deal!"

Up the road was a church of some denomination. Kanga and I had ridden our bikes past this church every day on our way to school, but I had never read the name on the church. I just knew it was a church because it had a steep roof, a cross, colored windows, and a giant parking lot. I was riding my bike too close to them. The crackling of their tires was nearly as loud as mine, so I let more distance go between us. Brooke wobbled on her bike. She was staring off into space and barely missed a parked car.

"Tell me where you went after our first game," said Kanga. "When you were gone."

Brooke stuck out her tongue at him. "I'm not supposed to tell."

Kanga picked up the pace. He stood on the pedals of his bike and raced ahead of her. He didn't even look back when she was two blocks behind him. He stopped and waited. When she finally reached him, he said, "Tell me where you went, Brooke."

"To buy a battery for my computer. Promise you won't tell anybody."

"I promise."

"Promise."

"I promise."

"Ypsilanti. I took my dad's car and drove it fine. I just went to buy the battery up there. But I couldn't find the store." She was out of breath. "Not Ypsilanti. Near Ypsilanti. But it was closed. I had enough money, but—" She wiped her nose on her sleeve. "You know where we should go? The gravel pits. Have you been to the gravel pits? It's not just gravel. There's water. You could drown, so my mom says never to go to the gravel pits."

Kanga inched his bike closer to Brooke, bumping his tire against hers.

I couldn't watch anymore. I looked at the houses around me. I'd never stopped at this exact point. A neighborhood of houses. All I'd ever done was fly down this street on my bike. Seventeen houses in a row. I imagined all the people in the houses looking out their windows at Kanga and Brooke, and then at me, hunched behind a car, spying. They would have been thinking *What's going to happen next?*

"We follow the train tracks." Brooke pointed in a direction. "The train tracks go to the gravel—"

"You lead," said Kanga.

Brooke veered us down an unfamiliar street. Kanga was slightly behind her. The street got blacker and the sound of their tires changed. A cloud blocked the sun, and it became February. Brooke's hair, instead of being a million tiny strands in the sunlight, was a single mass protruding from the back of her helmet. We were still in Hectorville, but this adventure was expanding the map of my life. Train tracks? How were we supposed to ride our bikes down the rails? Or would there be a trail alongside? And who knew what was around any of these strange street corners? There could be a pond of lava. Or a gingerbread house with an old witch inside. All three of us should have been sitting in art class.

Before any train tracks came into view, Brooke ran her bike onto a dead lawn. She weaved through trees and tiny snowdrifts and hopped off, letting the bike travel a distance without her before it tumbled. She danced to a stop. "Swings!" Brooke had landed at an elementary school with the steep roof of a church. All the students must have been inside, so Brooke and Kanga had the entire playground to themselves. Kanga followed her to a swing set. Soon they were swinging in tandem, her shoes rising with his high-tops.

"You were gone an entire month," said Kanga. "Tell me where you were for the entire month."

Brooke kicked her legs erratically, disrupting the movement of her swing, veering herself dangerously close to a swing-set pole. "What are *your* secrets?" she said. "I get some of *your* secrets too!"

At the peak of his next swing, Kanga let go of the chains. His butt rose from the seat. His entire body paused in midair, as high as the treetops . . . He landed on his feet. Across the playground was an abandoned rubber ball on a basketball court. Kanga jogged over, leaving Brooke alone on the swing. Her body relaxed. She dragged her shoes in the icy sand.

Kanga started shooting hook shots.

Brooke unpacked the clarinet from her case. She began to play.

Kanga swished a shot. He dribbled the rubber ball between his legs. He dribbled as fast as he could to the other side of the court, shot a layup, got the rebound. He shot from half-court and missed.

Brooke walked a short distance onto the grass, playing her clarinet. I'd never seen her move so gracefully—her upper body was rigid with a musician's form; her feet were cat paws sneaking down a fence. I tried to imagine touching her cold elbows while she played. I couldn't imagine it because Brooke was wearing her winter coat and because I could only imagine Kanga's hands doing it, black with grime from his rubber ball. A bell rang inside the elementary school.

Kanga rolled the ball toward the school. "We should go to the gravel pits now."

Brooke played a moment longer before removing the clarinet reed from her lips, letting the words run out of her like the notes had: "*I was at the hospital so I wouldn't go and get any more batteries for my computer.*" She played another phrase on the clarinet, then said: "I want a secret from you now."

"My brother thinks he's a robot."

"*But that's not about yooooooooou,*" she sang.

"I don't have any secrets," he said. "Everything I am is right in front of you. I'm a basketball player. I'm cold. I suck at riding bikes." He stepped toward her. "I want to take you to the gravel pits."

"I'm not going there."

"I want to—"

"I'm *never* going there."

Brooke ran back to her bike. She had to stop and fumble her clarinet into its case before speeding away. Kanga stayed back, allowing her to pedal a distance alone, allowing her the illusion of escape, before he followed her. Brooke did not return to school. She turned corner after corner, trying to lose Kanga, then swung her bike into the parking lot of Rheener's Party Store. She stopped and waited for Kanga to catch up, clearly satisfied he was still there. "Don't follow me in," she announced, dropping her bike to the pavement. She walked into the store with her helmet on. Kanga remained outside, watching her through the plate-glass window. She asked the clerk where the bathroom was. Kanga looked down at Brooke's bike, at her pink banana seat, and gently nudged it with his shoe.

I was across the street, hiding behind a garbage can.

Her helmet was off when she emerged from Rheener's, which meant, I imagined, that she'd noticed the helmet in the bathroom mirror, scolded herself, and removed it before sitting on the toilet. She handed Kanga a Three Musketeers. "Buy one, get one free."

He took the candy bar.

"I chose Three Musketeers because that's your favorite candy bar." She stared at him. "Three Musketeers. That has to be your favorite."

"I like Three Musketeers. For later." He stuffed the candy bar into his jeans pocket. "But I like you for right now."

Part of her wanted to resist. Her knuckles. Her fists. They hung down, shaking back and forth, *no no no no no no*, one fist clutching her bike helmet, rattling it against her knee. But her shoe rose toward Kanga. Her mouth said, "We need to touch them."

I could not watch what was about to happen. Destroying Brooke had never been Kanga's objective. He wanted to destroy *me*. I abandoned my cover and biked for home. I stood on the pedals, pumping them. I focused my ears away from Brooke and Kanga.

I heard the shattering of a distant window.

I heard a light bulb burning out.

I heard a tissue getting pulled from a tissue box.

I heard their shoes touch, detonating a nuclear blast. For a second I was outrunning it. Then it burned me up alive.

I waited in the kitchenette for Kanga to get home. Basketball practice would be starting soon, and I knew he would swing by the apartment for a gallon of milk.

Right on cue, he banged through the door and headed for the refrigerator.

"Art class was a riot today, huh, Kanga?"

He ripped the cap from a jug of milk.

"I didn't see you in class," I continued. "You must've been doing something pretty important. I didn't see your bike. Where did you go?"

He drained half the jug. "Don't worry about it."

"Where did you go?"

"You got ears on your head?" He killed the remaining milk in one sip. "It's none of your business."

"Is it Brooke Noon's business?"

He set the empty jug on the counter. "You were spying on me."

"You think you're so human. You're not. Humans have feelings."

"Okay. Sorry, bro." He turned to the fridge for another gallon. "From the bottom of my heart. *I'm so sorry*. How's that for feelings?" When he faced me again, he almost dropped the milk. "Easy, Darryl. Put down the knife."

The butcher knife felt fantastic in my right hand. I tossed it in the air . . . and caught it perfectly in my left. "Let's talk about feelings." I stepped toward him.

"Darryl. Please. Okay, I'll talk with you. Whatever you want. Just put the knife down."

But I was done with talk. What had it ever gotten me? My words had never really *sunk* into Kanga. It was time to try something different. Something hard to forget. Kanga didn't understand how badly he'd just wounded me. He was about to find out. The butcher knife was raised above my head—

"DARRYL! NO!"

I aimed for a freckle. I was a little off. Half an inch. But I'd swung the butcher knife with my *left* hand, so I'd be crazy to expect perfection. I was a right-handed robot. That was how *The Directions* advised us to blend in: "Use your right hand for everything, and if forced to use your left hand, twitch a little." The kitchenette was twitching all right.

I kept my eyes on Kanga. His mouth appeared to be malfunctioning, hanging open like a dead person's, so I had to interpret the rest of his face to know what he was thinking. His eyes told me he was surprised. But wouldn't anyone feel surprised watching pink lubricant rope out from the stub of his brother's wrist, splashing the toe of his grocery-store shoes? Kanga's eyebrows painted a more complex picture. Their furrow gave him the appearance of empathizing with me—the pain of having chopped off my own hand. Ironically enough, I felt no pain in my wrist. My tactile receptors must have gone into "denial" mode. I could still feel a phantom hand at the end of my wrist, as heavy and dull as a bowling ball. My arm began to quiver.

"You always do this," he said at last, all the empathy fading from him. "You always throw it back in my face."

"This?" I raised the gore of my wrist for him to see. "You mean the truth?"

Kanga wrinkled his nose and turned away, as if I'd just offered dog shit for him to sniff. "*Your* truth. Not mine. I want to live a different way, and you can't stand it. You never could."

"You don't get to decide if you're robot or human. You're either one or the other. There's no in between. Look at my wrist. *This* is what we are. This proves that we're—"

"I *know* what we are! God, Darryl, I never stop thinking about it. Never! I wish I could be like you. I wish I could feel proud of being . . . a machine. But I can't. I'm alive. Nothing in those damn *Directions* says what it's like to be me. It's all about maintenance, and strategies, and replacement parts. And being obsolete. That damn word. Like an axe hanging over our heads. Humans don't have to feel obsolete. They get a second chance. A third! They get as many chances as it takes. Just saying the word makes me feel worthless. But that's not the worst part. The worst part is the way it makes me feel about *you*. I feel sorry for you."

"No—" I was almost in tears, but I refused to let him see me cry. "You don't get to feel sorry for me. *I* feel sorry for *you*!"

"I have basketball practice. So you need to fix this on your own. You need to clean the kitchenette floor, and then you need to get some help." He forced himself to look directly at my wound. "I might never see you again."

"You can't get rid of me." I smiled. "You think this is a big deal? When you see me tomorrow, I'll have a brand-new hand. I'm going to Detroit, to the people that made us, and they're going to fix me."

"They will, or they won't." Kanga shrugged. "Either way, you have to grow up, Darryl."

He left for practice.

All my emotions evaporated. The apartment was filled with agonizing silence. Did I really believe what I'd just told him? About getting a new hand? A better hand? The idea had sprung into my processor, without any forethought. But it was true. I would have to go to Detroit. I would have to get fixed.

The butcher knife was still in my left hand. I wanted the gruesome tool away from me, but couldn't bring myself to set it down. Doing so would acknowledge that its horrible action could not be undone. I stared at my wrist. The initial cut through the skin was clean; there were split wires, a severed yellow shaft hissing vapor, and pink lubricant everywhere, making it hard to see the finer details. At the bottom of my wound the skin drooped like the sleeve of an overworn sweatshirt, indicating how dull the butcher knife was. When the pain finally found its voice, it told me exactly how stupid I was, using rusty nails and jimmying them under my skin, all the way up my forearm, and slowly twisting them. But the pain was nothing compared to the sight of that horrible freckle, a half inch up my forearm. Should I chop it off too? I raised the butcher knife again, but it slipped from my left hand, clattering to the floor.

I looked down.

My *right* hand was crawling away, the pinky finger doing all the work, dragging the rest of my hand across the vinyl flooring. It was trying to hide behind the refrigerator.

● ● ●

Some moms are merely *good* in a crisis, while others feed off catastrophe like vultures devouring a carcass. Chapter 51 of *The Directions* (subsection: "Appendages") was written for the scavengers among us.

Materials to have on hand:
- kitty litter (two cups)
- duct tape
- black sock
- rubber band
- hard suitcase packed with dirty clothes
- round-trip bus ticket to Detroit

Figure 762 was an illustrated step-by-step for dressing a severed limb. I used my knees and my teeth to make twelve long strips of duct tape. The kitty litter was to soak up the lubricant in my "cavity." I sealed the kitty litter against my wound with eight strips of duct tape, then stretched the black sock over my stub. I secured the sock in place with the rubber band.

I shouldered the fridge aside, caught my right hand, and wrapped it in the remaining strips of duct tape. When I was finished, it resembled a giant silver maggot. I buried it in a suitcase filled with Dad's old sweatshirts. One-handed, I managed to retrieve the Chinese catalog from the ceiling in Mom and Dad's room. I tossed it in the suitcase too, before clicking the top shut.

The pain at the end of my arm had disappeared, replaced by a vague *folded-in* feeling, as if my wrist had been folded over again and again, like the excess space at the top of a paper bag, and secured with a clothespin.

I dressed as if for game day and looked at myself in the mirror. I left the sleeve of my dress shirt fully extended beyond my stump, though a dash of black sock peeked out from the white cuff. I had a crisp fifty-dollar bill folded in my pants pocket. *I'll show him*, I thought. *Next time he sees me, he won't believe his eyes.* With my left hand, I grasped the handle of the suitcase, then began the five-mile walk to the Hectorville bus station, the day's last light sinking on the horizon.

18

MY WRIST WASN'T A WORST-CASE SCENARIO. Not yet. As I walked to the Hectorville bus station, lubricant only faintly leaked through the black sock at the end of my stub. I could still pass for human.

A real worst-case scenario was getting shoveled off the side of the road, Molly Seed–style. A real worst-case scenario, according to *The Directions*, required "emergency retrieval," as stated on page 1243: *If your appearance has been compromised or if you notice signs of gross malfunction, call 1-800-555-3240 for emergency retrieval or (preferred) discreetly proceed to the following address:*

> Gravy Robotics
> 1717 Starline Avenue
> Detroit, MI 48207

I'd always wanted to visit Gravy Robotics, even just to drive by and see its enormous facade. In fact, my first words as a baby were the Gravy Robotics address.

"Hell no," were Dad's first words back to me. He didn't trust Gravy Robotics. He was paranoid about their whole operation. I'd heard him whispering to Mom that if you got too close to the laboratory, you'd get snatched up, broken apart, and have all kinds of tests run on you. Gravy would steal all your memories, and the scientists would watch them on a huge TV screen and laugh at you.

Mom just stared out the kitchenette window. "Taking a drive somewhere sounds nice."

"Shit," said Dad. "Let's go for a drive then." He started running through the house, throwing extra clothes and onesies into his suitcase. We soon found ourselves packed into the van. Dad drove us onto the freeway and aimed west until he ran us into Lake Michigan. This was our first and only family vacation. It was midnight, and the beach was empty. Mom set me and Kanga down in the sand for five seconds then nervously scooped us up again. She carried us around the beach after that, shivering at the sound of the tiny crashing waves. She asked Dad, "Are there crabs here?"

"Goddamn it," he said.

"I think I've got sand in my ankles," said Mom. "I don't know."

"Let me guess. You want to get back in the van?"

"Yes."

"You know where it is."

Dad stayed on the beach as Mom lugged us back to the van. She climbed into the back with us, tossing our baby seats away so she could cuddle us on the bench, a novel experience that made Kanga squeal with delight. She flicked on the overhead light and became a surgeon, picking grains of sand from our feet, our belly buttons, our eyelids, every fold of our skin. She tossed each evil grain out the window.

Seagulls called from the darkness, and moments later the sky yellowed. The black water was replaced with dark-blue water, and the mountains and mountains of sand gleamed through the windows. Cars came and went all day, their occupants giving the van a curious look before they became enraptured by Lake Michigan. In the evening, a bonfire appeared far down the beach, along with sudden bursts of laughter. Then it went out.

Mom had us buckled into our safety seats, her own seat belt buckled too, by the time Dad emerged from the surf. He drove us back to Hectorville, the water slowly draining out of him, puddling on the van's metal floor. Mom sat with a look on her face as though she still had sand strung through her insides, but Dad's body was loose and tranquil. From my baby seat, I asked him, "What was down there, Dad?"

"I won't spoil it for you."

● ● ●

The Hectorville bus station was the size of a bus, narrow, with just a handful of benches, most of its space consumed by the ticket booth.

"What happened to you?" the station agent asked. "Firecracker get you?"

"One round-trip ticket for Detroit, please." I handed him the fifty.

"Don't get blood on the seats."

"Okay."

I used the tiny bus station bathroom to wring out the sopping black sock and add a wad of toilet paper to my wound. I should have brought more duct tape.

The bus arrived at 11:30 p.m., filled nearly to capacity. Before boarding, I had to wedge my suitcase into a chamber that had opened in the bus's belly. This was fortunate, as the severed hand inside the suitcase had begun to thump, blindly searching for an escape.

I'd never sat on a bus with anyone other than Kanga (1,337 times) and Brooke (once). I found an open seat on the aisle. My new bus partner, a young woman, was violently eating a bag of chips. Nacho cheese. One of her cheesy fingers smeared against me as we went over a bump.

"What happened to you?" she asked.

"Nothing."

"Did your dad do it?"

"No."

At stops, passengers boarded and exited. The bus itself occasionally rested in a dark corner of a parking lot for fifteen or twenty minutes, then abruptly drove off again. How many suitcases, backpacks, cardboard boxes, and coolers had I seen get loaded and unloaded into the chamber beneath the bus? I imagined each piece of luggage was filled with robot parts: knees, foreheads, feet, elbows, breasts, penises, chins . . .

As the morning wore on, the bus emptied out, and I was able to stretch across two seats. We crossed the Detroit city limits. The sky grew ominous. It was pouring rain now, and gray human figures appeared on the sidewalks, risen like worms, inching to destinations unknown.

"Starline Avenue," announced the driver.

I retrieved my suitcase from beneath the bus and headed into the rain.

I had the route memorized from the tiny map of Detroit on the last page of *The Directions*. It was just a few centimeters on the map, but the walk took forty-five minutes, not counting the eleven minutes I dried out beneath a highway overpass. The gray walls were covered by a mural that had been divided into window-size squares, each painted by a different artist (the talent level fluctuated wildly), who were probably all teenagers. I stared at the paintings, feeling a desperate longing for my classmates back in Hectorville, or even for these kids I would never meet, kids who were no longer kids, as I noticed one of them had time-stamped the mural with *1977*, the year Kanga and I were created. I saw a portrait of Elvis Presley. Surely the King had played a concert in Detroit sometime before his death, which I knew also happed in 1977. I imagined Mom as a young robot—before Dad, before us kids— taking a bus to Detroit for an adventure by herself. I imagined her sitting in the darkness of the concert hall, the first row of seats. Elvis Presley in a single spotlight, kneeling at the front of the stage. Their eyes connecting . . . It was pure fantasy. Mom had always been married to Dad. She had always had me and Kanga to take care of. Our entire family had been created in 1977. Mom had been alive only ten years before turning obsolete, and Elvis had been dead for all of them.

I headed back into the rain. The closer I got, the more I wanted to run in the opposite direction, toward the five skyscrapers bunched together like fingers on a hand, or farther still, all the way across the state, so I could sink my feet in the mud at the bottom of Lake Michigan, or even—

GRAVY ROBOTICS, the sign on the door said. I'd always fantasized I was built in a laboratory on the top floor of a skyscraper. This was no skyscraper. It was a simple brown building, two stories tall. The door was unlocked.

GRAVY ROBOTICS, an arrow pointed me down a gritty hallway, to an elevator sitting with the door open. There was only one button in the elevator (I dared to push it with a wet finger), and I would have cut off my left hand to share this moment with Kanga, as we had done on a different elevator in second grade, on a field trip to a cereal factory, trying to balance in the middle of the car without touching the walls, holding each other's elbows when the elevator lurched us thrillingly upward. This elevator took me down.

The door opened to a basement hallway, whose only purpose, it seemed, was to house five trash cans, each overflowing with black bags. A tiny potted plant sat beside a glass door reading GRAVY ROBOTICS, INC. There were no windows. The plant must have been plastic.

Inside, I stood at a receptionist's desk. I waited a full minute before she glanced up from a textbook.

"Can I help you?"

She looked like a high schooler, but she had the squinting eyes of a person who had read *The Directions* thirty times, cover to cover.

"Yo. Buddy. Do you have a name? Are you lost? Help me out."

"Darryl Livery."

"Wait." She straightened up. "You're one of *them*."

I raised my stub. "*The Directions* said—"

"Yes!" She did a little dance in her swivel chair. "I figured you were the janitor's kid, but you're—" She widened her eyes. "You're like six years old. How did you even get here?"

"The bus. I'm fourteen."

"You're just adorable. Why didn't I bring my camera?"

I stood there while she undressed me with her eyes.

"Look," she finally said. "I'm not supposed to 'interact' with you guys without clearance from my dad, but you don't mind if I just, like—" She stood up and floated toward me. "Okay, your *hair*." Her teeth chattered. "Can I just touch it?"

My hair was wet from the rain. "Um—"

She was running her fingers through it, like she was shampooing my head for a commercial. I turned my odor receptors to maximum power to smell *her* shampoo, which came through faintly, just enough to tell me she hadn't showered today. I was staring down at her black-socked feet; her shoes must have been hiding under her desk. A red toenail gleamed through a hole in her sock. She stepped back.

"I don't know." She shrugged. "It's not as real as he's always bragging about. Just stand over there. My dad, *Dr. Murphio*"—she rolled her eyes as she said it—"gets here at six o'clock."

"Six *tonight*?"

"You got somewhere else to be?"

I went and stood next to another fake plant.

● ● ●

At noon, the receptionist was relieved of her position by a new receptionist, who was definitely her older sister.

"How's the hair on this kid, Betsy?" the older sister asked.

Betsy shook her head.

"Okay." The older sister grabbed my suitcase and set it on a desk. She popped it open and started rifling through Dad's sweatshirts until she found my duct tape–wrapped hand. I was hoping she would remark on the thorough job I'd done preserving it. Instead, she carried it to a wall receptacle marked INCINERATOR and tossed it in. My body shuddered, but I had the wherewithal to swipe my Chinese parts catalog from the open suitcase and hide it down the front of my pants. The older sister grabbed my shirt collar and yanked me through a door labeled REPAIR. "Hand replacement. Bad weave, but we won't touch it. Anything besides that hand? Do you have uneasy thoughts about X-ray vision? Do you *have* X-ray vision?"

"Sometimes I daydream I have X-ray vision at school."

"What color is my tattoo?"

"Your tattoo?"

"You don't have X-ray vision."

She pushed me down a hallway. On the wall was a photograph of yet another sister, older or younger it was impossible to tell, on a basketball court, gripping a basketball as if playing ballslappers, her mouth shrieking in rage. The new receptionist deposited me into another room with another plastic plant. I went and stood by it. "Dr. Murphio gets here at six o'clock," she said before locking the door.

I was their prisoner, it seemed, yet I was relieved to be alone. The walls surrounding me were made of white bricks, bare except for a framed photograph of an open window. There wasn't even an outlet where I could recharge.

Gravy Robotics, I'd always imagined, would be like another family to me. Instead I felt like a broken TV stuck in a corner. That was how Brooke and Kanga made me feel too. Just thinking about them caused my processor to conjure their bodies in the room with me. There they were, their backs to me, huddled together, looking down at something. "Oh my god! *Another* simile," imaginary Brooke said to imaginary Kanga. "'The tacos fit together on her plate like a row of brown batteries.' I mean, *what?*" She was reading "Buford's Dilemma."

My imaginary brother laughed. "I knew Darryl was a bad writer, but jeez . . ."

Imaginary Brooke suddenly turned around, noticing me. She had a cast on her arm—the arm she broke in eighth grade. "There he is. He's probably staring at my shoes. Look at your *own* shoes, Darryl!"

"I wasn't looking at your shoes, Brooke." But once she'd said it, all I could stare at were her pink shoes.

"The lady said to quit staring at her shoes," said imaginary Kanga. "So go stare in that corner if you can't follow directions."

I tried to stammer out an apology, but imaginary Brooke charged me, grabbed a fistful of my hair—"Look *away!*"—and slammed my face into a corner until my temples were each grinding a different wall. "I bet you like this, pervert," she said, letting my head relax a moment. "But this time it's gonna hurt." I felt her fingers tighten on the back of my head. I tried to brace myself with a hand on each wall—but I only had one hand—and she smothered me again. Then I heard a man's voice—

"Something smell good in that corner?"

It was Dr. Murphio.

He was slightly older than Mom and Dad's fixed age, and he was completely bald, but otherwise he was a flawless human specimen. His sweater sleeves were rolled up, exposing tan, muscular forearms. He wore a carpenter's tool pouch.

"Darryl," he said. "You poor, frightened thing. I'm Dr. Murphio." He offered his outstretched left hand. I had no choice but to shake it. "I'm thrilled to see you again, my son. Hope the girls treated you first-class. Sweet girls. They're my girls."

I nodded.

"I have to be frank. I designed your brother, not you. My assistant at the time, my oldest daughter, she built you. That said, I consider you my son, as I do every unit produced in this laboratory. I did some spelunking around the storage room, and I believe I found a *perfect* fit for the boo-boo on your wrist." He leveled a strange smile at me.

"Why did—" I began to ask, when Dr. Murphio cut me off.

"I know you're just brimming with questions, Darryl. As you should be. Now let me give you the answers. Here at Gravy we do things the right way. Other companies have ulterior motives for creating robots, but not us. I am not seeking to replace my fellow humans with a dominant race of overlords"—Dr. Murphio chuckled, then frowned—"or to create an army of slaves to do my bidding. No, my goal is to one day become happily obsolete myself while you robots continue my work, rebuilding and improving yourselves into eternity while also improving the lives of your human brothers and sisters. Coexistence, Darryl. *That* is the purpose of Gravy Robotics. Which begs the question of you, my son: What will *your* children be like?" Before I could answer, Dr. Murphio gazed into the distance, continuing, "Or the children of your brother? Kanga! My goodness, that boy's having one hell of a basketball season. I know people gush about his points, assists, and rebounds, but did you know Kanga averages less than one turnover per game? As point guard?"

Of course I did. But how did Dr. Murphio know it? I'd never seen his face in the stands. What else did Dr. Murphio know? And who was this "oldest daughter" who had created me?

"Don't take this the wrong way, Darryl, but I never imagined you'd live past your first year—never mind fourteen years, nine months, and twenty-four days. I make a point of remembering all my units' birthdays. Well then. Let's have a look at you."

He stepped toward me with easy familiarity. I could smell his laundry detergent—it was the same brand Mom had always used. He touched my hair and parted it with his fingers; Dr. Murphio's other hand reached into his tool pouch and pulled out a box cutter. I felt a line being drawn through my hair. As his fingers entered my head, a new awareness tickled my plastic frame. *Hunger.* The sensation was unbearable. My instinct was to bite Dr. Murphio's sweater, which hung inches from my lips. I snapped my teeth, unable to reach it. Oh, to suck the color from that fluffy yarn! I could smell the purple. The *orange.* I reached with my tongue . . . I felt Dr. Murphio's palm pressing down on my skull to smear the wound closed. I heard a click in my head, and the hunger disappeared. Whatever had just happened to me, it wasn't in *The Directions.* Dr. Murphio, it seemed, knew me better than I even knew myself. He was wiping his hands on a stained rag.

"I hate to be the one to break this to you. You're probably going to stay this exact height for the rest of your life. Let's take a look at that wrist, shall we?" He gently pulled off the black sock, now greasy and pink from lubricant. He ripped off the duct tape and slapped away the remaining pieces of kitty litter. He studied my wound for two seconds. "Betsy can handle this. She's currently studying robotic sexuality, but everybody has to get their hands dirty in mechanics eventually. Your new hand will make a fine pretest for her. She's my baby. My youngest—well, besides all of you sons. Betsy gets here at four a.m."

My processor sputtered and coughed, overloaded with existential input. My life was a doomed side project of Dr. Murphio's oldest daughter, whose name I didn't know. I would never grow another inch. My hand's replacement would be entrusted to a girl with no mechanical experience. So why did I feel nothing but defiant optimism? *I'm going to prove you wrong*, I thought, with no plan to make it happen. *Just you watch.*

"Doctor?" I said, removing the Chinese catalog from my pants. "I brought this so I could show you the kind of hand I want."

Dr. Murphio snatched the catalog and looked at the cover, laughing. "I haven't seen one of these in years. They closed—how long ago now? I'll incinerate this for you."

"Wait!" I said. "Don't burn it. I—" I didn't dare explain why I wanted the catalog back, but it was suddenly more important than anything. "Can I keep it? Please?"

But Dr. Murphio seemed to understand. He winked at me. "Naughty boy." He handed the catalog back. Dr. Murphio then flicked off the light. Luckily, he kept the door open a crack. As he worked through the night, I twice heard him urinate in the bathroom. At two thirty he flicked off the lights to the entire office suite, then the front door clicked shut. He didn't say good-bye.

19

"HELLO? ANYBODY?" I called through the crack in the door, checking to make sure Gravy Robotics was empty of human life. "Is there an outlet where I can charge up?"

No answer.

"Okay. I'm coming out because my battery's almost empty. If somebody's here, please don't shoot me."

I stepped from the room. I waited. I didn't get shot. Right outside the door was an outlet. *KNEEL DOWN! RECHARGE!* ordered the rational half of my processor. *KNEEL DOWN! RECHARGE!* But there was another half of my processor too. *Explore?* it wondered. *Down the hallway? Dr. Murphio's office?* I knew where his office was because I'd heard him tapping his pencil against his forehead and scribbling on a piece of paper. I'd heard him breathing through his nose, flipping the pencil up in the air and catching it. I'd heard sheets of paper being wadded into tiny balls and then flung toward a trash can. I touched the handle of his office door. It swung open. I flicked on the lights, and that's when I saw it:

The Game.

That's what the sign read: THE GAME. It hung above a magnetized whiteboard, an entire wall of Dr. Murphio's office. On the whiteboard were names—each one was a rectangular magnet. The names were arranged vertically, and beside each name was a series of tally marks. Those with the most marks were at the top, those with the fewest at the bottom. They were all boys' names.

And there at the very top was "Kanga," with eighty-seven tally marks, just three tallies ahead of a robot named "Julius." "Darryl," with my seven tally marks, was good enough for last place. Or was it? On the floor below sat a haphazard pile of names. These names, it seemed, had fallen off in an earthquake, and no one had bothered to put them up again. I sifted through the names, looking for "Tanya" and "Mark," Mom and Dad, or even "Molly." All I found was a "Mark," though there was no telling if it was Dad or just another boy with the same name.

Seven. I had *seven* tally marks. My processor was crunching the numbers: Throughout my lifetime, what had I done exactly seven times that was so much better than the other billions of things I'd accomplished? The results were inconclusive. I'd jammed my right index finger seven times while grabbing my basketball in the triple-threat position. I'd written the number 1,489 seven times on homework assignments. I'd heard several songs exactly seven times, including "Dancing on the Ceiling," by Lionel Richie, a song I felt like I'd heard a hundred times more than "Hold on Loosely," by 38 Special, which I'd also heard exactly seven times. I'd put on my pants left leg first seven times, though why I'd done that even once was a mystery. I'd made seven paper airplanes in Mrs. Springfield's class, six of them in one day, one on another.

This was madness.

I wasn't a cheater. Up to this point I believed if I followed *The Directions* to the best of my ability, I would be rewarded with a happy life. Now I knew the truth. My life was nothing but a game for the amusement of humans. One that I was losing. Getting blown out. But worst of all? Kanga was *excelling* at The Game. My brother, who had ignored *The Directions* since being switched on. Which all added up to this: *The Directions* was a sham. A distraction. A phony set of commands that had nothing to do with a successful life. I should have listened to Dad. He'd trusted no one, especially Gravy. The single time he trusted someone—*me*—I double-crossed him hours later. *Sorry, Dad. I guess I just proved your point.* My life until now had been wasted, but it wasn't over. I was still here. Still alive. And for once *I* had an advantage, because if this was indeed *The Game*, then shouldn't there be *The Rules*?

I searched Dr. Murphio's office. His desk, his bookshelves, his filing cabinets. I found nothing that pertained to The Game. Could it be that no rules existed? Then what was the point to any of this? Who was judging me? How? My fan was running at top speed. I felt eyes on me, but it was just a portrait on the wall: Dr. Murphio, his beautiful wife, and his five perfect daughters. I recognized the oldest daughter as the basketball player from the picture in the hallway. My creator. Was the answer key to my life somewhere inside her brain?

I felt a sudden urge to look *behind* this portrait.

I leaned the enormous frame away from the wall and—bingo! A secret cubby containing a thick manila folder. This had to be the information I was looking for. A stack of documents. I looked at the first sheet of paper, and the secret to The Game was . . .

Ma?

The Chinese basketball star?

The documents detailed the specifications of Ma's body. They were thorough, including full-page diagrams of his skeletal architecture, his lubricant circulation, his musculature, and so on. Disappointingly, my insides looked nothing like Ma's; for instance, his exhaust system ran up and down the left side of his body, while mine (according to *The Directions*) was on the right. But that didn't matter when I flipped to a page that showed Ma's full, naked body in painstaking detail, with Mandarin characters to indicate exact measurements of every exterior piece of him.

I couldn't look away, even as my shame multiplied. Ma was a gorgeous machine. My processor fluttered. Then I *had* to look away for fear I might accidentally fold up that piece of paper and slip it into my pocket to look at later. Each page was stamped with a Mandarin marking, "Top Secret," which led me to assume these documents had not been created by Gravy Robotics. But what did *that* mean? Had Dr. Murphio stolen them? Were they a gift? Had Gravy somehow assisted in Ma's creation? And most importantly: How would this help me win The Game? I flipped further through the file, finding a diagram of Ma's central processor. It resembled a farm, with its distinct silver memory barns at the center, surrounded by a vast green garden of nodes. Unlike other pages, there were scribbles of English in the margins, which I assumed to be Dr. Murphio's handwriting. The phrases themselves were a hodgepodge of fatherly nonsense:

> are you my son?
> now finish your plate like a good boy
> do your homework and I want to see it when it's finished
> you can't lie to me because I know when you're lying
> go to your room this instant

Trying to deduce meaning from these bundles of words made my processor ache. Then I heard a sound in the reception area of the office suite. The front door was unlocking. A moment later the front office lights buzzed to life.

By instinct, I crumpled the illustration of Ma's processor into a ball and crammed it into my pocket. I quickly returned Ma's folder to its secret location behind the family portrait, flicked off the light switch, and fell into the hallway, jamming my fingers into the wall outlet just as Betsy appeared, carrying a black duffel bag.

"Whoa! Is that how you guys do it? All sprawled out like that? I mean, whatever. I would read a book or something."

This was the first time my *left* pointer and index fingers had ever tasted juice from an outlet, and they were getting spoiled. Detroit electricity had a deep, steely flavor—somehow both rusty and elegant at once, with hints of rainwater. A mere nip of the stuff had enhanced my odor receptors. From the floor, I caught a whiff of Betsy's hair grease. She still hadn't showered since I last saw her.

"My dad left your new hand on the front desk." She frowned, holding up the duffel bag. "I mean, it'll probably be better than nothing, right?"

"Why? What's wrong with my new hand?"

"First of all, it's a *used* hand. And second of all—" She bit her lip.

"Tell me."

"Okay, don't freak out, but the hand isn't the right age for you. It's, like, a *man's* hand. It's hairy, and, um . . ."

"Show me the hand, Betsy."

She set the duffel bag on the hallway floor. She unzipped it and paused, staring inside. Finally, she reached in and pulled out my new hand. Or more specifically—

Dad's rubber hand.

After a split second of revulsion and paralyzing guilt for my role in ordering my father to the chopping block, something clicked in my processor, and I fully accepted my fate. "Okay," I said to her. "Let's do it." Because I deserved Dad's hand. He no longer needed it; that was my fault. And if I was going to survive in this world—if I was ever going to win The Game—I'd need to be *more* like my old man, not less. "I'm ready for my new hand now."

Betsy wasn't.

"It's solid rubber!" she shrieked. "And it's hairy!"

Spikes of black hair were growing from the rubber, especially near where Dad's wrist would be, and even sprouting from the cut edge, where the hand had been separated from the rest of Dad's rubber arm. A yellow shaft, like a central bone, protruded from this cut edge, ending with a ball. I recognized it as the sliced yellow piece in my wound, meaning that that old piece would probably be yanked out by Betsy so the new one could be inserted, and *that* was how I would be reconnected with my dad.

"I think I'm gonna throw up," she said.

"Please don't, Betsy. Stay calm." I was a one-handed robot sitting in a dirty hallway and sticking my fingers in an outlet, but right now I was the voice of reason. "I've seen hands like this before, and they look pretty real if you don't stare straight at them. This is hard for me too, but we can do it. We'll work together. Do you have the instructions for attaching the hand to my wrist?"

"My dad left the instructions in the bag," she said, breathing regularly again. "I guess that thing's more realistic than your hair."

I smiled for her. "And I bet I can wedge a pencil between the fingers and write with it."

"Don't get carried away." Betsy gripped the yellow shaft on the hand, making it an extension of her own. She scratched her knee with it. "I think you'd better hide this thing whenever possible. Wear gloves, or shove it in your pocket. Besides, can't you just, I don't know, write with your *other* hand?"

I'd never seen Dad write with either hand, period. There were a million things I'd never seen him do. No wonder he was so cranky and cynical all the time—which was exactly what I had to look forward to. "I'm a writer, Betsy." Doubt was creeping into my processor. "I've been right-handed my whole life. Everybody's seen me right-handed, and suddenly I'll be writing with my left hand? What if I can't do it? What if my signature is different? What if every sentence I write has five similes? What if—"

"Relax." Now Betsy had to calm *me* down. She tested Dad's rubber fingers, pulling them apart and letting them snap back into place. "Whoever had this hand before you didn't bite his nails. Be thankful for that. Come on. Let's do this back in your room."

Removing my fingers from the outlet was torture. The bite still had its teeth in me; I needed ten more hours of juice. Then again, what did it matter? With such a worthless new hand, I might as well have been obsolete. Maybe Betsy should just do me a favor and switch me off—

No! Coach Knight was shouting at me. *You're still on the board! You're still playing, you wussy! Now, get in there!* I followed Betsy into "my room," where she'd already set the duffel bag on the cement floor and removed the instructions and tools: a pair of goggles, forceps, a small towel, a large jar of yellow putty, and a spray bottle.

As she put on the goggles, Betsy asked, "What happened to your *old* hand, anyway?"

"You won't tell Dr. Murphio, will you?"

Betsy thought about this for a moment. "No. I won't."

"I wanted to prove I was a robot. To this other robot. To my brother."

"Weird."

"With a butcher knife."

"I'm basically skipping breakfast to do this. Just so you know." She held the instructions up to her goggles, scanning for what to do first. "Do you want to watch?"

"Yes."

"Okay. Take off your shirt."

First, she had to remove the broken yellow shaft that was still in the center of my arm, the one I had split with the butcher knife. To do this, she pressed hard on the inside of my elbow.

"Ow," I said.

"There's supposed to be a button in here."

I felt a drop of Betsy's sweat on my cheek as she made a fist and rocked her full weight onto the inside of my elbow. The button finally clicked, causing my right forearm to go numb, as well as, inexplicably, my left earlobe.

"Got it." She then used the forceps to remove the old rod running through the inside of my arm. The ball at the end of the rod brought with it a white, spongy substance that fell to the floor in chunks. I was surprised to see only a few drops of lubricant. Betsy patted the wound once with her small towel, then asked, "Ready?"

Dad's hand went on quickly. Betsy merely pressed my elbow button again (it was much easier the second time) and drove the yellow shaft inside Dad's hand into my forearm. I braced my processor for a profound jolt upon receiving Dad's hardware—a psychological change to match the physical. Instead, all I felt was exhausted. Packing the yellow putty around the point of operation took Betsy the longest. She kept adding a teaspoon more, smoothing it with her fingers, then reexamining her work. Eventually this patchwork of fake flesh resembled a real wrist—it looked even better than the hand it was connected to.

Suddenly, it was no longer Dad's hand but my own.

While the putty dried, Betsy went into the main office and called her boyfriend. It turned out his best friend's dog died last night. Betsy said "I'm so sorry, Kevin" seven times. Then she hung up, came back, and tested the putty with a finger. She grabbed the spray bottle and aimed it at my wrist. "Close your eyes." She spritzed me.

I heard the putty fizz and tighten, hardening into a layer of skin on the surface. When I opened my eyes, Betsy was blowing gently on my wrist. She tested it with her finger again. She shrugged. "Put your shirt back on."

I guided my new hand down the sleeve of my game-day shirt, feeling nothing in the hard rubber fingers.

"Let me get a look at you," Betsy said, standing back. "Okay." She shuddered. "What you're doing right now? Letting both hands just *hang* at your sides like that? Never do that again. Okay? Never let anyone compare one hand to the other. That's your new rule. Got it?"

I put my new hand in my pants pocket. "Got it."

Betsy wet a finger and patted my hair with it. She fixed the collar of my shirt. "I almost forgot—" She knelt down and grabbed something else from the duffel bag. "Take this. It's for showering." In my good hand she placed a long rubber sheath. "You need to put it on up to the elbow so nothing gets wet."

Never in my life had I seen anything that looked so much like a condom.

"So you're all good now," she said. "Okay? Okay."

Betsy was escorting me through the empty office, and I came to the crushing realization that I might never see her again. Right before the elevator, I turned and gave her a hug, squeezing her with both arms. "*Thank you.*"

"Oh—" she said, and I felt her cold fingers on the nape of my neck.

"Okay." She sniffled. Then she was crying. "Renee made you a little *too* real, didn't she?"

"Renee. Your sister. Does she still work here?"

"No." Betsy shook her head. "No."

"Does she still live in Detroit?"

"She moved to—" Betsy almost answered, but she caught herself. "She moved away for a reason. I understand why. I'll probably move away too, when I get older. When I get done *here*. He's not a horrible father, okay? It's just the work he does. Gravy. We never asked for any of it. Not my mom. Not my sisters. It's all him. But he's paying for my college, and his only condition is I have to work in this office for a couple of years. And make one of you. For him. And then I'm free, so here I am!" Betsy stepped away from me. "You have to go now."

"Please tell me one more thing about Renee. Does she play basketball anymore? For fun, at least?"

Betsy walked over to the elevator and pushed the button. She smiled. "Her daughter does."

● ● ●

The bus taking me back to Hectorville seemed aware that I was late for school, passing big rigs and ignoring stops it had made going the opposite direction, all in an apparent effort to get me to the bus station with enough time to enjoy the last two periods of the school day. I'd left my suitcase back at Gravy, but I didn't care. The catalog was still tucked into the front of my pants, but even that felt like a relic from more innocent times. The Hectorville bus station was a mere mile from school, and I arrived between fourth and fifth periods. In the hallway, I read everybody's mind: "*Where was that kid for the last day and a half?*" "*Why is his hand stuffed in his pocket like that?*" "*What's that pink stuff on the sleeve of his shirt?*"

Kanga was at our locker, digging around for books. I approached cautiously. I had no clue what to say to him. My entire body felt like my new hand, like a boxer's punching dummy. I whispered, "Excuse me."

Kanga spun around at the sound of my voice. He looked me up and down. "Brother—" He assaulted me with a hug. "I was worried sick about you!"

I couldn't hug him back. Both of my arms were trapped beneath his. I was airborne, my legs swinging around the hallway. This was not the Kanga who had left me alone in the kitchenette. In fact, I'd *never* seen this version of my brother before.

He set me down. "It's so great to see you, Darryl."

I managed a "Hi."

"We've got so much to talk about. Let me start with this: I'm sorry. I've been under a lot of pressure lately. The championship is tomorrow, as you know. Everybody's been counting on me. And then you got hurt. And then . . ."

"Don't cry."

"I didn't know where you went."

Now I was consoling him. One-armed. I'd seen Kanga cry many times, but never about me. I didn't trust it. The whole thing seemed like an act, like he was auditioning for the part of "Brother" on a TV show.

"I should have helped you when I had the chance, Darryl. Maybe I had to lose you for a couple of days to realize that. But listen. I'll *never* do that again. From now on, it's you and me. Nobody else."

"Okay."

"Because I've got it all figured out. The rest of our lives. The future. I'm going to make the NBA. I'm going to be a millionaire. I'll get you whatever you want. You break something else, a leg or your head, I'll get it fixed. All the doctors and hospitals it takes. I'm going to look out for you, brother. There's so much more I have to tell you, but the bell's about to ring. I'll see you sixth period. I love you, bro."

● ● ●

In art class, I grabbed a fresh sheet of paper, sat down at my table, and wrote my name at the top with my left hand: *Darryl Livery*. To my relief, my left-handed signature looked nearly identical to my right-handed signature. Which meant, just like that, I could pass as a left-handed human. This anticlimax left me vaguely disappointed. Hadn't there been anything special about my old right hand? I wrote my name a dozen more times with my left hand—once under Mrs. Asquith's critical gaze. "Nice artist's signature," was all she said. "But next time, try finishing a drawing first."

Kanga arrived late to class. He tenderly squeezed my shoulder and took a seat at Brooke's table. Brooke arrived a few moments later, and they proceeded to play with her clarinet reed for the rest of class, passing it back and forth, putting it in their mouths and blowing to hear what funny noises they could make.

When the bell rang, ending the school day, Brooke hadn't looked at me once.

I was walking down the hallway alone when I felt a different hand on my shoulder.

"Take a knee, Darryl."

Mr. Belt pulled me into an empty classroom. Not his room, but another science teacher's room. The lights were off. Mr. Belt shut the door so we could be alone.

"Come in here and get comfortable. Take a knee. Or stand if you like. Relax, Darryl. Close your eyes and imagine you're a man such as myself. With a wife, two children. Both girls. My daughters are much younger than you, but, heaven help them, they will grow up to become ninth graders such as yourself. We all get older. Some would call me an old man. I'm forty-four. But my father is still alive, so can I truly be considered old? I talked to *your* father this morning on the phone. He told me all about the stomach virus you had—"

Dr. Murphio. It had to be. He had called Mr. Belt and pretended to be Dad. And why not? Our *real* dad had never set foot in a school, never picked us up, never volunteered to serve punch at a school dance. Mr. Jacobowhite was the only teacher to ever converse with our "dad," and he'd been talking to me. This phone call was Dr. Murphio's way of preemptively addressing any questions Mr. Belt might have about my absence. To the doctor, I was just a pawn in his Game, a game he wanted Kanga to win, not me. Apparently, he would do anything in his power to make that happen.

"Your dad thanked me for taking such good care of you. And Kanga. We must have talked about that particular dickens all through my prep period. But we also talked about you, Darryl. We decided a championship is the perfect medicine for what ails you. Big game tomorrow. I don't need to tell you. You're already spiffed up." Mr. Belt clicked his tongue at my dress shirt. "You're a young man. Youth is on your side. The world is your oyster. Conquer it if you like."

● ● ●

The final basketball practice of the season didn't start until four thirty, so I waited alone in the cafeteria, slouched against the wall with two fingers covertly plugged into an outlet. Where was Kanga? I had no idea. I didn't want to talk to him anyway. Practice was a blur as I sat against the Cave wall, still plugged in, though the school's tepid electricity just left me feeling more exhausted.

Toward the end of practice, the players began screaming and running in terror from Kanga, who had James Botty on his shoulders. James was still fashioned as a member of the Fab Five, though he had failed to persuade any other teammates to copy his hair, shorts, and shoes. Kanga had regressed in style, wearing his old grocery-store high-tops again after throwing away his Cons. Up on Kanga's shoulders, the bully steered my brother around the court with heel kicks to the ribs. The Ceiling Fan frowned at the spectacle, shaking his head. *I tried*, his expression said, *but they just don't get it.*

"Cut it out, guys!" Rye finally said. "The game's tomorrow night! Somebody's going to get hurt!"

Kanga erupted with a primal scream in Rye's face. Now he was playing the role of beefed-up jock, and he was nailing it.

After practice, I approached the bike rack, only to realize my bike was still at home. I would be walking. Could one-handed people even ride bikes? Could they make tacos? Could they tie their own shoes?

Kanga bounced atop his bike and glided in an easy circle around me. *Kanga.* Currently first place in The Game with eighty-seven tallies—or maybe he'd earned himself another tally mark since I'd left Gravy Robotics. I hoped he would speed ahead and let me walk home in peace.

"How's your hand?" he asked.

"It's nothing."

He stopped his bike and took a long look at the outline of my hand, still stuffed in my pocket. He was debating whether a good brother was required to ask another question about it or if he could move on to a new subject. "So I've got a girlfriend now. You know her. Brooke. She used to be the team manager. It all just kind of happened. You and Brooke used to be close, right?"

"I know who she is."

"Well, I got pretty sad after you left, and I told her about it. She said to stop worrying, that you'd be okay. And you are."

"I guess she was right."

"And her mom invited us over for dinner. So that's where we're going. To Brooke's. Dinner starts in twenty minutes."

I laughed. "That sounds great. Have a wonderful time, Kanga. I'm going home."

"Come on over to Brooke's for dinner."

"I'm not going."

"But I really want you to come, Darryl."

"I don't have a bike. My battery's nearly empty. I just want to go home."

"I have a bike." Kanga curled an arm around me, scooping me off the ground before slamming my butt down on his handlebars.

"KANGA!"

"And I really want you to come." He glued one hand to my hip; his other hand grasped the handlebars. "So let's go have a nice family dinner."

● ● ●

Kanga pedaled us through the darkness. I had no choice but to listen to him jabber:

"—called me down to the office yesterday afternoon for a phone call. I thought it was going to be you calling from the hospital. But it was Brooke's mom. It was weird, just standing in the office, talking on the phone with this lady I'd never met. She asked me to dinner, and I said okay, but only if my brother could come too. I thought it was good luck to say you'd be coming. And here you are! How is your hand feeling?"

"Like nothing. It's a fake hand."

"But the other hand still works?"

"Good enough, I guess."

"Good." Kanga knew what an excellent brother he was being. I could hear smiling in his voice. "How'd you get to the hospital?"

"I didn't go to the hospital. You saw what's inside me."

"Yes. And I don't want you to feel ashamed about it. You can tell me everything. I won't judge you. I'll just listen."

"I'm a robot."

"Okay. You're a robot."

"And *you're* a robot too—"

"Where did you go? To get your hand fixed?"

"Detroit. You know, the address in the back of *The Directions*. Gravy Robotics. It was just a laboratory in a basement. I didn't see much of the lab, only a few rooms. Most of the time I stood there, waiting for them to operate on me. The hand I cut off—they threw it down a chute to an incinerator. Then they kept me in this bare little room all by myself." Even if he was just pretending to care, I'd never spoken to Kanga like this. I could feel through his touch that my words were making him uncomfortable, but he didn't stop me from saying them. And suddenly it was like we were brothers again, but upgraded models. We were brothers with the luxury feature of being able to say anything to each other. "And Betsy, this amazing woman who worked there. At first, I figured she was just a secretary, but she turned out to be really important to the whole company. She was the one who put my new hand on. It happened so quickly, Kanga. Just a few minutes, and bang! I've got a new hand. I watched her do it. How do I even explain Gravy? I wasn't *welcome* there, not at first, but Betsy—"

"Did you find out about Mom and Dad?"

You're closer to Dad than you've been in years, I could have said. But I didn't. "I met the scientist who created you. Dr. Murphio. He knew all kinds of information about us. Well, about *you*. He's pretty much in love with you. You're the best robot he's ever made. Maybe. And there's a chance Dr. Murphio made that Chinese robot, Ma. I found some papers in his office—"

"But what about Mom and Dad? If this doctor guy knows everything, why didn't you ask him about Mom and Dad?"

"I needed to get fixed. My hand was leaking. I could have asked a million questions, but my hand—"

"I'm *sorry* about your hand, Darryl." He was done talking about it. We were getting close to Brooke's house. Surrounding us were castle-size houses. Any of these front yards could have held our entire apartment building. Kanga slowed his pedaling. He was reading mailboxes and house numbers. He said, "So about eating tonight."

"Did you bring food receptacles?"

"No receptacles. Tonight, we eat for real."

"Kanga."

"I need you to trust me."

I reminded myself of all I'd learned. That *The Directions* was full of lies. That Kanga was winning The Game. Which meant I should probably hear him out. I asked, "You've eaten food before?"

"I eat burgers all the time. Not around you."

"And it doesn't muck up your works? Entire burgers? What happens?"

"What happens is they taste good. You'll understand after tonight." He veered us down the mouth of a driveway. "We're here."

20

BROOKE'S FRONT YARD was guarded by walls of tightly packed pine trees and shrubs, like a private park. Kanga pedaled up her winding driveway, and we were met by a portable hot tub with dark, bubbling water inside. It sat right there on the blacktop, blocking access to the middle door of Brooke's three-car garage. I read the sticker on the side of the hot tub:

ON-THE-GO JACUZZI RENTAL
ANYTIME – ANYWHERE

A garden hose snaked away from the tub, disappearing under one of the garage doors. Anybody could have been watching us from the dark windows of Brooke's huge white house. Kanga lifted me off the handlebars and then leaned his bike against a tree. There were no sounds coming from the house. Only the bubbling water.

At the door, Kanga gave me final instructions: "When we sit down at dinner, you eat. Got it? They put food on your plate, you eat it. Take a drink of milk with every bite. Just eat, and afterward we go to the bathroom. I'll show you what to do."

Kanga rang the doorbell. I glanced back at the hot tub, the steam floating into the black treetops.

"Kanga Livery!"

Brooke's father stood in the doorway.

"And Kanga's brother!"

He was the shortest man I'd ever seen. Less than five feet. He was shorter than Brooke herself. He was almost as short as me.

"Welcome, Kanga!" But his voice was gigantic. "And—?"

"Darryl," I squeaked.

"Darryl? Take your shoes off."

Brooke's father closed the door. He reached up and grabbed Kanga's shoulder, pinching the muscles in a fatherly manner. "Nathaniel Noon. Brooke's dad. But you can call me Nathan. Or Pastor Noon. That's what most people call me. Well . . . Take your shoes off, gentlemen!"

I took my shoes off. We were waiting on Kanga. Having ridden straight from practice, Kanga was still in his grocery-store high-tops. When he unlaced them, the smell of his old, greasy sneakers hit everyone in the vicinity.

Pastor Noon did not mention the smell. He pinched his nostrils and clapped his hands. His socks were gleaming white. "The rest of the gang's already sitting down. Dinner is ready. Right this way. Would you like to wash up, Kanga?"

The Noons' house was embarrassingly huge. The shoe-removal area alone was the size of our living room. I'd seen mansions on TV, but nothing could have prepared me for the sheer expanse of these wood floors, smooth and soft, without the harsh polyurethane gloss of a basketball court. This wood had been pampered, oiled, and given a long vacation on a tropical beach, where it had assumed its bronze hue. Then there was the darkness. No lights on the ceiling, just lamps beside every couch and chair, lamps in every corner. The house was built for sitting on cushions and reading books. I saw no TV.

"Kanga and Darryl, meet my wife. Mrs. Larissa Noon. We call her Mom. Of course you know Brooke. Why don't you boys take your seats?"

There were two open seats at the dining room table. One next to Brooke (Kanga jumped to claim it) and one next to Mrs. Noon. She was blond. Otherwise she was exactly like Brooke. Except more composed, more regal, more expensive, more still. The wineglass tipped at her mouth drew my eyes to the three open buttons of her blouse. Mrs. Noon set down her wineglass. She stood up from the table and offered me her hand to shake. Her *right* hand, which was aimed at *my* right hand, which was still in my pocket.

Shaking hands? I couldn't. Nor could I merely ignore Mrs. Noon's dainty fingers. Luckily, in the depths of my processor, I'd kept old footage of an even more formal greeting, one that required no interpersonal contact at all. I *bowed* to Mrs. Noon. "A pleasure, my lady," I announced, my head paused down by her knee, my left hand twirling in the air.

"My goodness!" she exclaimed. "This gentleman will sit by me. Darryl, this seat is for you. Let those two do their thing." She nodded toward Kanga and Brooke. She patted my seat. "We'll sit here."

I glanced at Brooke. She hadn't noticed my bow, or even that I was in her house for the first time. She did not resemble the snapshot of her I kept in my processor. Instead, she looked like a beautiful snake wearing lipstick meant to attract another snake. Kanga. I wanted to grab the nearest fork and gouge it through my eyeball sensors. But I couldn't. There was the small matter of *eating a full dinner under the scrutiny of humans*. So I depowered my emotional inputs. I switched on "survival mode." My skin thickened to scales, and I became a snake myself.

"Did you see the hot tub?" Brooke whispered to Kanga.

"The hot tub," said Pastor Noon, frowning. "We rented a hot tub last weekend. Don't ask me why."

"It's for me," said Mrs. Noon. "I have a sore back."

"One more day, then it's gone, returned whence it came. One more day and it's back to normal for us."

"I don't suppose you brought a swimsuit, Darryl?" asked Mrs. Noon.

"Let us now pray," said Pastor Noon.

The five of us bowed our heads. We closed our eyes and listened to Pastor Noon recite the prayer. I listened closely to Mrs. Noon's lips forming the words. I peeked and saw her looking at me. She grinned.

"Amen."

"Amen."

"Amen," said Pastor Noon. "Let's eat!"

Dinner began. The table was piled with food. Pastor Noon dipped a large fork into a ceramic pot: huge portions of Swiss steak, which he then smothered with spoonfuls of sauce. "And extra sauce for you, Kanga." A salad bowl was passed from Mrs. Noon to me to Kanga to Brooke, who wrinkled her nose and said she hated salad. Everyone received his or her own baked potato. The nightmare ended with two pieces of bread, with butter, on an extra plate.

Beside my plate were a knife, a fork, and a spoon. I had used these utensils only rarely, as tacos were a handheld food, and never with my left hand. And *never* without a food receptacle. Awkwardly, I picked up the fork. I started with the salad, as it required no cutting, just stabbing the pieces of lettuce and fitting them in my mouth. Additionally, the salad was poofy, mostly air volume; a well-chosen leaf or two could give the appearance of a serious dent in my allotted food. My dinner plate screeched from the clumsy use of my fork. "Sorry," I whispered. To my delight, I had succeeded in piercing a leaf of lettuce. It looked evil. Opening wide and feeling the cold lettuce with my lips, I finally guided it through my teeth to a place where my tongue could free it from the fork. Then I chewed. I'd never eaten salad before. Tacos broke apart easily for swallowing, but the lettuce became a singular blob in my mouth. I reached for the vinegar, but there was none. No vinegar? I tried to stay calm. At least there was a liquid of some kind: a glass of milk sitting beside my plate. I drained half of it, but the lettuce blob remained swirling in the rapids at the back of my tongue. I needed a new strategy. I filled my cheeks with the remaining milk then swallowed it all at once, like a tsunami. My knee struck the bottom of the dinner table, and everybody's plate hopped. The lettuce was still in my mouth, so I packed it in the corner of my cheek.

"Kanga loves my steak," said Mrs. Noon. She took a small sip of wine. "Kanga, give your plate to Nathan."

"That's right, Kanga. I'll fix you up. We're not shy about seconds in this house. I'm curious. What do your mom and dad do for a living?"

Kanga was still chewing. He patted his belly. "*Delicious!*" I was shocked to see that, in addition to Swiss steak, my brother had devoured his baked potato and a piece of bread, though he hadn't touched his salad. Consuming the occasional burger was one thing, but Kanga ate like a man who never missed a meal. My brother could mimic Magic Johnson, and now a gourmand. But could he talk to inquisitive humans about our parents? I had always fielded this aspect of conversations with adults. The trick was to be boring, which discouraged follow-up questions. Dad delivered newspapers. Mom was a stay-at-home mom. Best of all, these answers had an element of truth (as long as I omitted the part about them vanishing five years ago). I had no clue what Kanga would say, but I couldn't speak for us even if I wanted to. The blob of lettuce had plugged my throat.

"Our mom and dad?" Kanga swallowed. "If you ask my brother, he'd say they're robots."

Pastor Noon straightened up, aghast, glaring at his wife with alarm.

Kanga just smirked, handing his dinner plate to Pastor Noon. "That was the game Darryl always made us play as kids. So we all pretended to be robots too, because of him. Sometimes we still do. We have good parents that way, always using their imaginations with us. Otherwise, it's a bit boring how normal we are. Dad delivers newspapers. Mom stays at home."

"Look at you brothers," said Mrs. Noon.

"A fine pair," said Pastor Noon, handing Kanga a reloaded plate of food.

"There was a time when Brooke wanted nothing in this world more than a little brother," added Mrs. Noon. "But it wasn't God's will."

"No," her husband said, frowning again. "Instead we have another daughter. Baby Elecsandra. She's sleeping upstairs."

An awkward moment followed, where everybody played with the food on their plate. Kanga forked a strip of Swiss steak into his mouth. I stared at my empty milk glass and prayed for a torrential rain to begin falling from the ceiling. Mrs. Noon took a sip of wine. Brooke drummed the floor with her heels.

"I don't mean to brag," said Pastor Noon, faking a conceited smile, "but my wife here used to be a star of the Metropolitan Opera in New York City."

"Nathan."

"A real star!"

"I was *not* a star."

"Tell the boys your story. It's delightful."

"It's not even a story."

"It's a delightful story. I love it, personally."

"I'll need another glass of wine. Just a taste, if I'm going to tell this story."

"I'll get it." Brooke rose from the table.

"Bring me the wine bottle, young lady," said Pastor Noon, "and the bottle opener."

"I can do it, Dad!"

"Darryl, are you familiar with the Metropolitan Opera?" asked Mrs. Noon. "We were performing *Aida*."

Brooke returned to the table with a purple wine bottle and the opener, refusing to yield them to her father.

"Young lady—" said Pastor Noon.

Mrs. Noon paused with her mouth open, watching her daughter use a corkscrew on the bottle.

"I told you I can do it," said Brooke. She passed the uncorked bottle to Pastor Noon.

The pastor took Mrs. Noon's empty wineglass and poured. He stopped. He poured a tiny amount more.

"Thank you, dear." She took a small sip, licking her lips. "*Aida*."

"I love *Aida*!" Pastor Noon recorked the bottle. "She's talking about the opera."

"Verdi. The Great Pavarotti. You've heard of Luciano Pavarotti?"

"Pavarotti, again," said Brooke. "Stupid."

Kanga continued shoveling food into his face.

"Perhaps you know him from the Three Tenors?" Pastor Noon asked us.

"The Three Tenors." Mrs. Noon took a drink. She listed with her fingers various works performed by Pavarotti: "*I Lombardi*, The Three Tenors, *Turandot*."

"*Aida*."

"Of course *Aida*." And Mrs. Noon went on to describe the building and the enormous backstage chambers filled with fake weaponry and fake trees, and the tightly packed dressing rooms where the women ("And the men," added Pastor Noon) huddled around sinks and mirrors preparing themselves to act, and the Great Pavarotti, and the assistant to the Great Pavarotti, whose only job was to bring the famous opera singer Dixie cups of water between his scenes, and—

A muffled wail halted the former actress's reminiscence. Mrs. Noon allowed the sound to continue for several moments before glaring at her husband.

"Elecsandra's hungry," said Pastor Noon, standing from the table. "I'll be right back. But dear? Describe to the boys your costume." He wiped his hands on a napkin and tossed it beside his plate. "I love it when she describes her costume." He hustled out of the room.

Mrs. Noon finished her wine, keeping the glass tipped an extra moment at her mouth. "Just another taste," she said to her daughter.

Brooke uncorked the bottle. Unlike the half effort poured by Pastor Noon, she filled her mother's glass nearly to the brim.

Mrs. Noon refreshed herself with a long sip of the wine, until her glass once again appeared half-full, as though Pastor Noon had refilled it. She pushed her chair back from the table. "Darryl." She stood up. "Look at me. This was my costume for *Aida*. Afro wig." Her tiny fingers hovered at her ears. "A piece of white cloth." She dragged a finger across her chest. "Another piece of white cloth." She pointed between her legs. "No shoes. No bracelets. No jewelry of any kind."

"Don't forget the body paint!" said Pastor Noon, quickly retaking his seat at the table. I noticed he had changed into a different shirt while upstairs. "Ellie just needed a couple swallows of formula, that's all. Tell them about the body paint, dear."

"*Black* body paint." Mrs. Noon closed her eyes at the memory. "Head to toe. I was an African. I was black. I was pitch-black."

"Ethiopian," clarified Brooke.

"Ethiopia is in Africa. I was African."

"African doesn't mean Ethiopian, Mom. Ethiopia is *in* Africa."

"Brooke's right," I blurted. "Ethiopia is in Africa."

Brooke and her mother glared at me, unsure how to interpret my interjection.

"Ethiopia is on the Horn of Africa," I added. "It borders Sudan, Kenya, Djibouti, Eritrea, and Somalia. Ethiopia is one of a few dozen African nations."

Mrs. Noon took a drink of wine. "I was Ethiopian. Not to be confused with the Egyptians, who were also in *Aida*, except their body paint was brown, not black."

"Thank you," Brooke said to her mother. Her nostrils flared mischievously in my direction, and my processor nearly caught fire.

Mrs. Noon went on to describe her role in the production: A dead Ethiopian citizen, murdered by Egyptians. Her body was draped on a wooden cart and wheeled across the stage. "Understand, the entire stage is pitch-black. No lighting. Nothing except a single spotlight shining on me. My body, hanging off this wagon, a spoil of victory for the Egyptian army." Mrs. Noon refilled her wineglass herself. "I was—"

"Tell them who was sitting in the audience!"

She took a drink. "You go ahead. You're ready to tell it."

"I'm sorry I interrupted. It's your story. I just wanted—"

"No. You. Tell them who was in the audience."

"It's your story."

"Tell them. Tell them. Tell *them*. Tell—"

"A man now running for president of the United States."

"That guy."

"He'd just become governor of Arkansas."

"The one who went on TV with his wife to say he didn't screw that actress." Mrs. Noon cackled. "Gonna be a president."

"Dear—"

"I got my picture taken with him backstage. Everybody did. And his wife was there. I'm so sick of this story."

"It's a great story."

"It isn't." Mrs. Noon's face wrinkled, as if from a horrible memory, and then she slowly aimed her hatred toward her daughter. "You know what I would love to see tonight? These kids getting in that hot tub. *Love* it."

"We've gone over this," said Pastor Noon. "We've already said no. A hundred times no, and the answer is still no."

"What are you afraid of? That Brooke and him will start *doing it* out there?"

"The dinner table!"

"Answer the question."

"I will not answer that question at the dinner table."

"Because if that's what you're afraid of—" She covered her mouth. She squinted her eyes and shook her head. "You were telling me about this one." She pointed at Kanga. "A basketball game or something?"

"Kanga. Darryl. Let me apologize."

"I bet they won't even kiss each other."

Brooke was clawing her toenails against the floor.

"She might kiss him, but will he kiss her back?" Mrs. Noon winked at me. "That's the question."

"That's fine, dear." Pastor Noon's voice was back to normal. He smiled. He was using all of his energy to appear calm, yet his chin wouldn't stop trembling. "You've forgotten one issue. The little issue we talked about earlier. That issue being that Kanga and Darryl do not have swimsuits with them tonight, so the case is closed."

"I give up, then. No hot tub. Never hot tub. But answer me this, love. If they *did* have their suits—"

"But they don't."

"But if they *did* have swimsuits, could Brooke and the boys use the hot tub?"

"The boys don't have swimsuits."

"Here's another question. Then I'll shut up."

"I've never asked you to shut up in your life, and you know that."

"I'll shut up after you answer this single, stupid question. Are you getting in that hot tub with *me* tonight?"

"You?"

"Answer the question."

"I—"

"Answer the question!"

"No."

"Then give your stupid spare swimsuits to the kids. I'll chaperone."

Dinner ended. Brooke abruptly left the table—her plate of cold food was untouched—followed by Mrs. Noon, who first poured a fresh taste of wine.

Kanga sat innocently at the table, his relaxed smile suggesting only the most pure intentions concerning the rest of the night. I knew better. This new version of my brother did not merely go with the flow. He dictated the future. Whatever his processor imagined, the world around him conspired to make it true. The evening had already unfolded perfectly for him. Whatever scenarios he was dreaming up now, nothing would stop them.

Upstairs a door opened and slammed. The pastor smiled at the messy dinner table. "Let's get you boys into swimsuits."

21

UP IN THE MASTER BEDROOM, I saw a framed black-and-white photograph of Pastor Noon as a boy. He stood with a group of other boys—his brothers—posing euphorically near a house being eaten alive by ivy. I scanned the room for evidence of Mrs. Noon as a girl. There was none. It seemed reasonable that her first earthly incarnation was as a full-grown woman, rising from a cart of dead, painted bodies.

The pastor got our swimsuits from a dresser but hesitated in giving them to us. He was frowning. He stuffed the swimsuits into his pockets. I knew better than to stare at those bulges, so I looked at the footprints we'd just made in the softest carpeting I'd ever felt.

"My story? The Lord and myself did not become acquainted until my college years. And then I didn't truly *know* him until"—Pastor Noon forced a smile—"until he brought my wonderful daughters into this world. I have a question for you, Kanga. A personal one. Just say the word if I'm being too personal, and we'll forget I ever asked. Are you in any way licensed to drive a motor vehicle?"

"No, sir."

Pastor Noon glanced upward. "Well." He grinned. "You *look* old enough to drive, that's the thing, not that I have anything against driving, per se. It's that Brooke, my sweet daughter, has, in the past, struggled to recognize the legal limits placed on fourteen-year-olds in terms of operating a motor vehicle. We've spent a good deal of energy on this subject. You may recall Brooke's brief absence from school."

"Yes, sir," said Kanga. "We were so worried about her."

"Rest assured, boys, after much prayer Brooke now understands that her actions have consequences. She is on the right path." Pastor Noon gave us a sober smile. "However, should you notice Brooke falling victim to her vehicular urges—"

"I will intervene, sir," said Kanga. "And I will let you know, personally, if your daughter strays. Both Darryl and I understand the complicated benefit of having involved parents. It's hard for us to listen to our folks too. But in the end you guys love us, right? Parents just have our best interests at heart."

"Kanga, I feel so blessed to have met you tonight."

We graciously accepted our suits from Pastor Noon, who then ushered us into the master bathroom so we could change in privacy. Walking those few steps, I noticed a jerkiness to Kanga's stride, and the sound of sand, as if crunching in the wheels of a toy truck.

Pastor Noon pointed to a rack of towels, inviting us each to choose one for the hot tub, and enclosed us in his bathroom.

After his dominating performance at dinner, I expected Kanga to mock my pathetic attempt at eating. After all, I still had the glob of lettuce in my cheek. But once we were alone, my brother immediately let his guard down. As he stared at the bathroom floor, his face revealed intense inner pain. "I ate too much," he whispered.

"You ate a lot of food."

"I just started eating, and then—" His jaw crunched as he spoke. "I've got to get it *out* of me."

"I'll help you. Tell me what to do."

Kanga said the first step was to get him out of his clothes. His shirt and socks went quickly, but, due to the stiffness in his legs, his pants were much more difficult. He kicked; I tugged. Then Kanga was naked, resting heavily against the Noons' large vanity. There were two sinks. Mrs. Noon's side was busy with spray bottles, rock-shaped objects, and a small treasure chest that presumably held items she dared not put on display. Kanga leaned toward the pastor's sink. He angled his head under the faucet until his lips were wrapped around the aerator. He was staring at me from this position, eyes wide with discomfort.

"You'll be okay," I whispered.

He turned on the hot water and let it pour into his mouth and down his throat . . .

Kanga had done this before. That much was obvious. His process was well practiced. His movements were confident and familiar. The water ran into him for over two minutes. At last, his hand reached to turn off the faucet. His lips released the faucet with a *pop*. He stood up, moving a bit easier now. All the hot water was draining through his inner workings, into the bottom half of his body. Twice their normal girth, his legs now resembled long water balloons. Kanga's slightest movement caused his legs to slosh against each other. If I had taken Mrs. Noon's hairbrush and smacked him in the knee, he probably would have exploded all over the bathroom. He performed a dance, allowing the hot water to splash throughout his moving parts. I should have looked away, but I couldn't. Even his penis was bloated beyond reason, bouncing from one thigh to the other.

"Kanga—"

"I'm okay."

He opened the toilet lid. I'd seen sick people before at school, fellow students who raised their hands and warned the teacher they were about to barf. Kanga's eyelids were malfunctioning like theirs: half-closed, twitching, discolored. A long string of drool hung from his lip. There was a clothes hamper across the bathroom. I noticed one of Mrs. Noon's sheer garments hanging out of it. Kanga pushed the hamper beside the toilet. He licked his lips. He slapped himself in the neck.

"Can I help you?"

"You can flush the toilet when . . ." He stared at the toilet.

"When should I flush it?"

Kanga flopped forward, draping himself over the hamper, his butt at the apex of his body. With his hands he gripped the edges of the toilet bowl. Then I understood: this was a science lesson about water and gravity.

As Kanga kicked his legs into the air, wiggling them about, everything loose inside him came gushing through his mouth. First, just a steady stream of water, but then pieces of food mixed in. Swiss steak, bread, brown baked potato peels. The toilet was filling up, so I flushed it. Excess water leaked from Kanga's nose, his ears, even his eye sockets.

When he was done (after two more flushes), he stood up, looked in the mirror, and dabbed away tiny food particles from his eyelashes. His legs appeared normal and strong. He tapped his toes on the bathroom floor. He sucked in his stomach and pounded his chest. There was no trace left of the boy who moments ago had needed my help and reassurance. He jumped and touched the ceiling. It must have been eleven feet above the floor. "Hot tub?" he asked with a grin.

I hated him.

I hated him so much I wanted to *kill* him.

But whom was I kidding? Physically, there was no stopping my brother. He had broken our first rule of safety and suffered no consequence. He was about to sit next to Brooke in bubbling water. Tomorrow he would *still* be the best basketball player in school. And now I had to change my clothes in front of him. No, Kanga Livery could not be destroyed with violence. I would have to do it with brains.

"I called Detroit on Mom and Dad."

Kanga stared into Mrs. Noon's mirror, picking meat from his teeth. "What's that, brother?" He spit a piece of gray steak into the toilet.

"I called Gravy Robotics and said Mom and Dad were obsolete. It was easy. I just dialed the number and told the woman who answered, and Mom and Dad disappeared the same day."

I didn't tell him about my naive hope, when I'd made the phone call, that our parents would be fixed instead of destroyed. Or that my belly had been churning with unprocessed shame since learning of their true fate. I wanted a reaction from him. I wanted rage. Despondence. Confusion. Anything that would tell me something inside him had just died. But my brother wouldn't give it. He kept working on his teeth.

"I'm the reason they were taken away, Kanga. And it was so easy. It was like crossing something off a to-do list. Get rid of Mom and Dad. On to the next thing." The words tasted wrong, like a mouthful of lettuce, but I couldn't stop now. Kanga didn't know the worst yet. It had been hiding in my pocket since I'd returned to Hectorville. "This is what I got in Detroit." I revealed my rubber hand. "You want to see Dad again? What's left of him? Let's shake on it, Kanga!" I waved the ghastly remnant of our father closer to him, and my brother leaned back, horrified. "You can probably guess what happened to the rest of Mom and Dad. And what could happen to *you*."

"You'd do it to me, huh?" Rage rippled under Kanga's skin, his muscles tensing. But he instantly calmed himself. He slapped my hand away, as if it were a pesky bug. He refused to look at it again. "Obsolete," he said. "Doesn't that mean 'useless'? See, I was listening when Mom read those *Directions* when we were little. This one chapter, it was all about how to kill a robot if he was much bigger and stronger than you." Kanga grabbed a pair of tweezers from Mrs. Noon's sink. "These would do the trick, wouldn't they? You just have to sneak up behind the guy and slip them into his guts." He held the tweezers near the right side of his abdomen. "Right here, about seven centimeters in. Then pinch his exhaust tube. You know the one I'm talking about, Darryl? The tube running up from his processor? Then wait about fifteen seconds, and his belly will catch fire. End of robot." He tossed the tweezers back into the sink. "That was chapter eighty-four."

"I know."

THE OBSOLETES211

"Of course you do. Just be careful about calls to Detroit." Kanga squeezed into Pastor Noon's tiny swimsuit. "You were already obsolete." He paused at the bathroom door. "Now *that* thing's on your wrist."

He left.

It was true. But I felt relief hearing my brother say it plainly: I was obsolete. Nobody needed me anymore. Which meant I had only one person left to look out for. Myself.

I scooped the green goo from my throat and flushed it down the toilet, then changed into Pastor Noon's other swimsuit. I pulled the drawstring extra tight. I hung a bath towel over my new hand. I was ready to get in that hot tub.

On the way downstairs, I saw Brooke's closed bedroom door. There was nothing special about the door itself, but I knew it was hers because there was screaming inside.

"It looks *great*!" shouted Mrs. Noon.

"It's *horrible*!" answered Brooke.

It, I thought. What was it? A homework assignment? A new poster they had hung above Brooke's bed? A watch?

"He won't be looking at you with a microscope."

"I can't do it."

"You look exactly like you're supposed to look."

"It hurts."

"It doesn't hurt."

"You're killing me!"

"It won't kill you to get in that hot tub."

"I can't."

"You little . . ."

Heavy stomps in the bedroom. Light flickered underneath the door.

I dashed downstairs, to the entrance of the house, where someone had placed my dress shoes and Kanga's high-tops neatly against the wall. Outside, the freezing air stung my exposed skin. I even felt pinpricks where my old hand used to be. When I glanced at the oversize bulge beneath my towel, my whole body felt hollow, from my ankles to my ears, and a dull magnetic impulse beckoned me toward the trees, where I might fall to the ground with my mouth open and let a family of tiny rodents live inside me until summer.

No, I thought. *Get in the tub.*

Kanga was already in there. With his eyes closed, he wore the half smile of a man who had just read the laws of physics and was happy to discover that *he* was the solar system's most massive object.

I leaned over the bubbling water. *Steam.* I stuck a leg in. The jets were so strong that my body refused to submerge at first, but my toes clawed the bottom, and I managed to sit down. My exposed rubber hand was perched on the rim of the tub, getting flecked with water thanks to the jets.

The reckless part of me wanted to dunk my entire body beneath the water, fake hand and all, count a full minute and keep counting, ten minutes, twenty-five, and leap through the surface, *Oh my God!*, and scare Brooke to death when she finally approached us. Instead I looked up into the blackness. No stars. Bubbles popped hard against my skin. I understood why Kanga had closed his eyes. I closed mine too.

"SHIT!"

The front door banged open.

Kanga and I watched Mrs. Noon lurch into the driveway.

"Goddamn high-top in the way."

My processor alerted me to cover my hand with a towel. I ignored it. Maybe I was tired of hiding. Maybe I wanted someone to notice me. The huge hairy hand continued lounging by the water as Mrs. Noon approached.

In her hands: a bottle, a wineglass. A piece of white cloth was stretched over her chest, another one between her legs. Her skin was brighter than the cloth. Her mouth was dark, though, as were her eyes. I glanced around the yard, at the neighbors' houses, to see if any faces were pressed to the windows, peeking at Mrs. Noon. I couldn't see any other houses. The yard was surrounded by tall trees.

"You boys get to pour my wine. I don't know what everybody's crying about. It's not *that* cold out here." She tossed the wine bottle to Kanga. He caught it. "I hope you're not opposed to serving Zinfandel."

I felt a thud as her small body touched the bottom of the hot tub. Mrs. Noon reclined across from Kanga. I checked the Noons' house to see if Brooke was screaming from her bedroom window. She wasn't. The front door remained open, Kanga's shoe tipped sideways on the front porch.

"Wanna sneak a sip?"

"No," I said immediately. "Thank you."

She ignored me and turned to Kanga: "What about you, big brother?"

"Yes."

She pointed her tongue at him. "Yes?"

"Zinfandel?"

"Fun! You have the bottle. Take a tiny one."

Kanga pulled the cork. He poured wine into his mouth, filling his cheeks.

"Easy, slugger!"

He swallowed it down. "It feels like a hot tub in my throat," he said. He coughed, then took another, more modest sip.

"It's decent stuff," she said. "Average." Mrs. Noon held her glass out for Kanga to fill. She took a very small sip. "But I could knock your socks off with some stuff inside." She punched Kanga in the arm. "Your girlfriend. What's her problem? She's no fun!"

Kanga shrugged. "She's shy."

"No. She's just like him." She pointed toward the house. "No fun. Never was. Never wants to do anything. Never wants to go anywhere. See this swimsuit?" Mrs. Noon stood up, splashing water on my new hand. "Sexy, right? It's hers. I bought it for *her*. For tonight." She sunk back into the hot tub. "She was supposed to be out here, but she chickened out. Wouldn't wear it. Refused! I told her, *Somebody has to wear it*. I told her, *If you don't put that thing on . . .* She didn't stop me! Is that the kind of girl-friend you want? Somebody"—she hiccupped—"I told her. I said, *See if I don't!* So here I am." She raised her arms, letting them splash hard. "What do you have to say about that?"

Kanga said nothing. He was staring at the top half of Brooke's swimsuit.

"*Well.*" Mrs. Noon splashed Kanga's gaze in a more innocent direction. She snatched the wine bottle from his hands. She took a swig and set the bottle on the rim of the tub. Her dark eyes flashed white as an idea came to her. "Gonna hold my breath. Time me." She sucked in a chestful of air before slipping beneath the water. Some blond hair swirled on the surface. I wanted to swim to a far corner of the tub where she wouldn't be able to see the lower half of my body, but the jets were blasting my legs toward Mrs. Noon's head.

I climbed out.

I was toweling off, one-handed, when she resurfaced, gasping in the cold air. "Did you," she wheezed, "time me?"

"Thirty-nine seconds," declared Kanga.

"You're kidding," she said. "Not even a full minute?" She had found a new seat beside my brother. "Felt like *five* minutes." Mrs. Noon made no comment about my absence from the tub. Instead, she lifted one tiny white foot out of the water, spreading her dripping toes. "They're not wrinkly yet." She grabbed the wine bottle. "Let's compare feet."

With my towel draped around my shoulders, I snuck into the house. Pastor Noon had the TV going somewhere in the basement. I heard him laughing along with a laugh track. Outside, Mrs. Noon hollered, "*Where does your mother find shoes?*"

I crept upstairs.

22

THERE WAS NO NEED to put my ear against Brooke's bedroom door. She was inside. *Clacking*. Brooke was in deep conversation with her computer, writing her novel. There was another sound, an unidentifiable sound, like someone's grandfather lighting a match on the zipper of his coat. Over and over, match after match. Together with Brooke's tapping it was *music*, and my hand was on her doorknob.

My towel fell off as I pushed inside.

Her mother had decorated her bedroom. It was painfully obvious. Red and white. Polka dots and candy canes. Lace. The teddy bears piled on the antique wicker chair had Mrs. Noon's dark, judging eyes. Only the smell of the room was Brooke's, along with two other items that caused my fan to click on: the picture I'd drawn, taped to the wall above her bed, and my story, "Buford's Dilemma," sitting on her bedside table, its pages wrinkled from reading.

Brooke sat on her bed, seemingly oblivious to me, her computer glowing on her lap. A comb was stuck in her mouth. As she tapped the keyboard, her jaw worked the comb around, her tongue plucking the comb teeth. *Bbrrrrriiiippp!* She had her heavy coat zipped up to her chin. Winter boots were on her feet. With the comb hooked on her bottom lip, she said, "Don't read over my shoulder."

I was at the foot of her bed. Reading her novel would have been impossible. I was wearing only Pastor Noon's swimsuit; my bony, yellowish body was on full display, as well as both hands for comparison: the normal hand hanging on the left side, the enormous, hairy, fake one hanging on the right, so heavy it caused my shoulder to droop. "Brooke—"

"You need to go. It was just like I knew it would be. You never should have come here. So *go*. And Kanga too."

"Brooke," I said, trying to smile at the ground like Mrs. Farnsworth, her favorite teacher. "I'm not like the others. I'm not like your mom. I'm not like Kanga. I'm like *you*. I'm different. I'm—"

"I'm not different. I'm the same. Everyone else changed, not me."

"I haven't changed. It's Kanga who's changed. I don't know who he is anymore. And the worst part is, you chose him right when he started to hate me. How could you do that to me, Brooke?"

"I got bored. I wasn't going to wait ten years for you to write another story. And *then* wait five years for you to give it to me. Kanga just walked up and gave me something. And he's cute." She finally looked away from her novel, directly at me, judging me from head to toe. "I get to try a cute guy for once."

"I drew that picture."

"I *know*, Darryl. The angle of my foot was obviously drawn from where you were sitting. And I already knew what was going to happen if I kept on liking you like I was. Pretty soon you'd tell me I'm too weird. *You'd* be the one who hurt *me*. You'd be just like everybody else."

"I haven't stopped thinking about you since we touched shoes in the skybox. I won't stop thinking about you. Kanga will. He already has. He's in the hot tub with your mom."

Her comb made a slow *bbbrrrrrrriiiiiiiiiiiiiippp!* and her fingers danced on the keyboard. "Good. Now I can forget about both of you. So for the last time, *go away.*"

"You think you're so weird? I'm weirder than you'll ever be." I yanked Brooke's power cord from the wall. With my index finger I burrowed into my belly button, then wedged another finger in too, pulling back the skin in all directions, until my epidermal sensors were blaring in confusion. Until it was exposed. *It.* I felt droplets of water trickle from the three tiny holes, causing my entire body to quiver. "See?" I gasped. "Weird. Now let's be weird together." I picked up the cord and plugged Brooke's computer into my three-pronged outlet . . .

. . . and I became a prisoner shackled to a dungeon wall, each clack of Brooke's keyboard an additional needle skewering my belly. "Brooke," I groaned, but she just intensified her typing, pounding her keyboard with closed fists, filling my abdomen with more and more needles, wider and wider, until the needles emerged through my back, screeching against the dungeon wall . . .

"Done yet, sicko?" She pulled the cord from my belly, sparks whiskering out.

The synthetic pain burned away, leaving my abdomen absent of all sensation beyond a sadistic urge for *more* needles. My wrists felt cold and raw from the phantom cuffs, even my rubber wrist. I sat at the foot of her bed, willing myself not to grab her power cord for another round of punishment. "Now you know that I'm a—"

"Robot. No duh." She resumed typing. "Plug me back into the wall. Or do I have to do everything myself?"

I did as ordered, then waited for another reaction from her. I'd seen Brooke show more emotion at someone sneezing. "How did you already know that I'm a—" The word caught in my throat. "—a *robot?*"

"Because I'm not an idiot."

"Have you told anyone?"

She smiled. "Maybe."

"Who else knows I'm a robot?"

"God, you're gullible. I haven't told anybody because it's so obvious.

Because anybody with eyes can see your hair is the fakest thing in the world."

"My hair?"

"And this kid at my old church was the same robot as you. *Exactly* the same. Same dumb face. Same dumb voice. He was a tiny bit smarter, but otherwise exactly the same. Well no. Not *everything* was the same." She smacked my new hand. "What happened here?"

I'd been trying not to think about my new hand since entering her room, afraid to even look at it. Now I scrutinized the discolored swath of putty between my hand and forearm. Marring the smoothness was a fingerprint. Betsy's fingerprint. This was the most unique piece of me, the only piece I was certain had not been mass-produced and given to a thousand other robots. Thanks, Betsy.

But Brooke was staring at the loose skin around my belly button. More than staring. She was ogling it. There seemed to be a frog jumping in the chest of her winter coat. I felt a strong impulse to cover my belly button. Instead I scooted *closer* to Brooke. For once, she was curious about me. There wasn't any harm in looking.

"What happens when you stick your fingers in there?"

"I'm not supposed to do that," I answered automatically. The truth was, sticking my fingers into my outlet had never occurred to me—and now that Brooke had brought it up, the idea was repulsive. "I can't."

"Stick your fingers in," she ordered.

I touched my outlet. It was still tender from her computer cord's prongs. I rested the tips of my middle and index fingers on the two long slits.

"That's not sticking them in."

"Sorry, Brooke. I just don't think I—"

"Do I have to do everything myself?"

"Wait—"

She slapped my hand away then plunged her *own* two fingers into my outlet. I felt the outlet bite her, and then watched an uncontrollable yellow glow blast across her arm, her winter coat, the wall behind her. Brooke's yellow hair floated up from her head. Her yellow cheeks jiggled into a blur. "*Sorry, Brooke,*" I tried to say, but everything went black . . .

● ● ●

The Directions explained that robots amid the rebooting process don't look like dead people, despite having lost all connection to their processors. Instead, they resemble humans deep in thought. Bad thoughts, specifically. Rebooting robots look like people contemplating their lifelong regrets. Their foreheads are lined. Their lips are pursed. Their eyes are focused—but on nothing in particular. It's a survival tactic. Humans recognize this unsettled look on someone's face, and they leave that person alone.

When I finally rebooted, I saw Brooke once again typing on her computer. She was alive. A normal human would have been electrocuted to death by my voltage. But not her. Did that mean she was a—

And why was my head so cold? So drafty? I was sitting on the edge of Brooke's bed, the exact position I'd been in when she had debased me with her fingers. Now a faint whistling haunted the space between my ears. I touched the top of my head. My hatch was wide open. *Brooke did it.* I pressed the hatch shut. "You could've just told me you were a robot."

She kept typing. "What's the fun in that?"

"And you opened up my head, Brooke. What did you do inside it?"

"Stop being a baby."

"Did you touch anything?"

"I just looked. There's barely anything in there to touch."

"Promise?"

She rolled her eyes, as if the inside of my head were simply too boring to talk about.

But I didn't care. This was better than a Christmas gift. I hadn't even allowed myself to dream about this possibility. *Brooke Noon was a robot.* "Does Kanga know what you are?"

She laughed. "Give me a break. All he thinks about is himself."

Kanga had no idea she was a robot, which meant this was a secret only

Brooke and I shared. My brother could go right on believing I was the obsolete robot in the family. In truth, he had just become obsolete to me. I had a person in my life I could just be myself around, an artist *and* a robot, both things I could never be with Kanga. Staring at Brooke, I cranked my emotional inputs to the max. I felt euphoric. I felt dumbstruck. I felt the urge to *touch* her.

"Your hair," I mumbled. "Can I feel it, please?"

Her fingers paused on the keyboard, then resumed typing.

"You looked inside my head, Brooke. You owe me. You've got to at least let me touch your hair."

She didn't say yes right away. But she didn't pull the covers over her head either. She just stared at her screen. "Be quick about it."

I wasn't quick. I took my time. Brooke closed her computer screen against the keyboard, afraid I might read her novel while standing beside her, but all I cared about was the top of her head. To my surprise, her hair felt fake. Not that I knew how "realistic" robotic hair was supposed to feel. But I'd petted a dog before, and that was what it felt like. Only messier and longer and greasier. And what was that *stuff*? White flakes of plastic? I was about to take my hand away when I felt a strange magnetism in my new hand. I raised it to Brooke's head, raked the rubber fingers through her hair . . . and I felt a memory. Not my own memory, but Dad's. He was tousling my hair, right after I'd made him laugh so hard his whole body shook. He hadn't cared how fake my hair was, or how fake his hand was. He'd thought I was funny, and his hand remembered the *feel* of my hair.

"Time's up."

Some of Brooke's shiny hairs had come loose in my fingers, which I twisted into a single branch and curled around my new pinky. I stared at Brooke's scalp, noticing a part I'd created down the middle, with two freckles four inches apart: two points on an invisible line. A seam?

"I said *time's up*."

I backed away from Brooke, respecting her wishes. Her hair was mussed and sticking out in odd directions—but it was her eyes. They were

thinking about something. Brooke had more secrets waiting in her processor, and she was weighing whether or not to reveal them.

"Kanga—" she finally said. "He lied. He said you guys have parents,
but I know you don't. You don't act like kids who have parents. You two
never brush your teeth."

"Why would we brush our teeth?"

"You don't know anything about having parents."

"You're right. We don't have parents. Not since fourth grade, but
Kanga wishes we did. He would give anything to have a couple of parents
like yours."

"No, he wouldn't."

"I know they're not perfect, Brooke, but no perfect parents exist. Your
mom and dad take care of you, at least. And look at this huge house!"
I felt strange making this argument to her, like some latent part of my
programming was forcing me to defend the concept of parenting for the
greater good. Or maybe I was making excuses for my own meager moth-
ering attempts. Or could it be that I actually saw something valuable in
Mrs. and Pastor Noon? "Your dad. He cares about you, even if he's a little
different. He doesn't want you driving cars by yourself. That makes sense.
All robotic parents have their—"

"They're not robots."

"They're humans?"

"You don't know the first thing about me *or* my parents."

"But I want to," I said. "I want to hear all about them. And about you.
Your sister. I want to know everything, Brooke."

"Then come with me." She rolled off her bed. She walked out of her
room and into the hallway. I followed. Brooke stopped in front of a door.
"Are you sure you want to meet my sister?"

No. I wasn't. Not the way she said it, with that smile of hers. A smile
from Brooke could mean any number of things. "Elecsandra, right?"

She opened the door, revealing a completely dark room. The first thing
that hit me was the rich scent of olive oil. Sure enough, when Brooke
turned on a lamp I saw an enormous shelf, like the one in Mr. Virgil's

closet, lined with bottle after bottle of restaurant-size jugs of olive oil. There were also rolls of paper towels on the shelves.

"This used to be my room," said Brooke.

I looked for traces of Mrs. Noon's decorating and found them only in the wallpaper: the red-and-white pattern of a wrapped Christmas gift. But there were no pictures on the walls and no toys to be seen. The only other object in the room was a plain wooden crib. But there was no baby inside. Its bottom was heaped with black blankets.

Brooke leaned over the crib and dug through the blankets. When she revealed the child buried beneath them, I realized why the blankets were black.

"What is that stuff?" I whispered. "What's she covered with?"

Brooke didn't answer. She grabbed a paper towel and wiped the black liquid bubbling from the baby's ears, which resulted in a black smear across the baby's neck. Elecsandra whimpered. It looked like . . . *motor oil* leaking from her onto the black blankets. Brooke tossed the used paper towel into the trash. It hit bottom with a wet thud.

"They were going to destroy her," Brooke said. "The scientists who made her. That's what my dad told me. They were going to destroy her for being—"

"Obsolete."

Brooke nodded. "My dad saved her."

"That's good, right? Your dad is going to fix her."

She leaned into the crib and picked Elecsandra up by the armpits, careful not to get oil on herself. "Hold her."

"Wait—"

Brooke dropped Elecsandra into my arms. If I hadn't caught her, the baby would have bounced on the floor. She was naked. Cold. But unthinkably soft. I found if I squeezed her at all, black oil would squirt out. Even poking her tiny palm caused oil to ooze from her fingernails. I formed a careful hammock with both arms, cradling her head with my sturdy rubber fingers. Oil squished between my bare skin and hers, and I felt it dripping off my elbow and onto the carpet, which was already badly stained.

"He's not fixing her," Brooke said. "He just keeps her in here. He feeds her olive oil, and he wipes up the black oil that drips out. And he prays. Every night, he comes in and reads his Bible and prays for God to stop the leaking. When one hour didn't change anything, he started praying for two hours. That's how he's going to fix her."

"Is it working at all?"

Brooke just stared at me. "I'm obsolete too. My mom told me. It was at dinner one night when she was drunk, like tonight, except worse. My mom smiled when she said it, so happy to finally tell me what I was. So I told her what *she* was. I told her—" Brooke stared at the wallpaper, reliving the moment. "My mom said my processor was all wrong. It was obsolete, and I would never get better. My dad kept praying for me, though, even though he knew she was right. That I was broken. Pretty soon it was obvious his praying wasn't going to fix me, and she didn't care. So I stole his car and drove it to Ypsilanti, tried to buy a battery for my computer, couldn't find the stupid store, and then drove it back. Nothing even happened. I just wanted to *do* something. You can't get worse than obsolete, so why does it matter? That was the only time my dad really tried to repair me. He took me to Detroit. He let them open up my stomach and—"

"Was it Gravy Robotics?"

"I don't know. They erased the trip from my processor. It feels . . . It feels like a cold wind inside me." She touched her belly. "The whole time I was in Detroit, I can't remember it. I just feel *cold* when I try to. My neck. My feet. My arms. Nothing warms me up. That stupid hot tub just makes me colder. My dad praying over me. That makes me freeze. It's funny—" Brooke flashed an evil grin. "The only time I don't feel cold is when she's drunk. When she's honest. When she says the scientists should've killed me the day I was born. Then I feel *hot*."

I stared at her. If I weren't holding her sister, I would have reached and touched her arm, just to feel the chill of the lubricant under her synthetic skin. "I don't trust anyone either," I said. "But I trust you."

"You're the luckiest kid I know, Darryl. Not to have parents. I would do anything to get rid of mine."

"Anything?"

"Yes."

"Let's leave." It wasn't until I spoke the words aloud that I realized this idea had always been in my processor. Or at least since Dad had planted it there years ago, hoping he and I would enact it together. Instead, I was sharing it now with Brooke. "Tomorrow night. We'll leave after the basketball game." Elecsandra was suddenly heavy in my arms, an unnecessary weight for a pair of robots as free as me and Brooke. I set her gently back in her crib. I grabbed a handful of paper towels and began cleaning myself off. "Bus tickets to Memphis are seventy dollars. I have enough money. Nobody will know where we're going. We can just ride to Memphis and—"

Elecsandra started shrieking.

"I don't know," she said. "But you need to leave *now*. They'll kill me if they find you in here."

I raised my bare foot toward her. "Let's touch feet before I go."

"That's kid stuff," she said, and from her coat pocket pulled out a computer disk. "Take this."

Balancing on one foot, I grabbed the disk from her. Its label simply read *B*.

"Now you'll know everything."

● ● ●

I slipped into the upstairs hallway unseen while Brooke remained in Elecsandra's room, feeding the obsolete baby her olive oil. I made my way to the master bedroom to change back into my dress clothes.

Kanga was already there. He was staring at Mrs. Noon, asleep on the bed, her swimsuit-clad body laid out like a cadaver. Despite the lights being off, her face held none of its previous darkness. She looked peaceful and relaxed, an old, silver-haired woman snoring the scent of Zinfandel into the air.

Kanga's eyes had stolen her darkness. "Where have you been?" he said without looking at me.

"I was checking on Brooke."

"My girlfriend." He said it like she was just one of many things be-
longing to him. "How's she doing?"

"Fine. But she had to get her little sister to sleep. You can talk to her
when she comes out, if you want."

"I don't need your permission to talk to her."

"You're right. Sorry." I ducked into the bathroom to change back into
my game-day clothes, slipping Brooke's disk into my pants pocket for
safekeeping. As I buttoned my shirt, I looked in the mirror to see that my
belly button had mostly returned to its human shape, though I had a streak
of black oil on my neck. I wiped it off with a piece of toilet paper, flushed,
then hung Pastor Noon's damp swimsuit on a towel rack. Back in the bedroom, I stepped up beside my brother to get a better look at Mrs. Noon.

"She fell asleep in the hot tub," Kanga explained, scowling at her. "So
I carried her up here."

Mrs. Noon's hair was still wet, twisting out from her scalp. Her lips
began to murmur, and I thought I saw a black tongue surface and recede.

"I have a game tomorrow," he said. "It's time to go."

● ● ●

Kanga lifted me onto his handlebars, setting me down much harder than
before. I felt him grab a fistful of the back of my shirt to keep me in place.
I clenched my body for blastoff.

We rode home in silence, the streets empty. I wondered who occupied
my brother's processor. Was it Brooke? Mrs. Noon? Or had they already
been deleted to make room for tomorrow night's heroics? Kanga swore
under his breath, pedaling faster, and I knew his body was overflowing
with anxious energy. While his legs propelled us forward, his mind was
churning just as hard to visualize a victory, hand-painting each detail of
the game until the brushstrokes disappeared into reality.

My processor was humming too. With Brooke's hair twined around
my finger, I closed my eyes, conjuring tomorrow night's escape from
Hectorville: After the game, we would ride our bikes to the bus station,
buy our tickets, and board the bus. It would all go perfectly. Everyone else

on the bus would stuff orange chips into their mouths, but not us. We wouldn't need chips. We would disembark onto the streets of Memphis and find a hotel near Graceland, home of Elvis Presley. It would have a pool. "And look," Brooke would say. "A hot tub." Up in our hotel room, she would pull something from her suitcase: A one-piece swimsuit composed of black and white crisscrossing lines. No hearts. No polka dots . . .

But here I lost control of my fantasy. I felt obsolete again, and I was sure everything about the trip to Memphis would go horribly wrong.

Brooke would say, "I need privacy in the bathroom, stupid." And I would listen to her changing her clothes, the muffled sound of her shirt getting pulled over her face, the unzipping of her jeans, the snap of the swimsuit against her hip.

I would knock on the bathroom door.

"What do you want?"

"Brooke. I'm sorry, but I forgot to bring my swimsuit."

"But I told you to pack one!"

"I'm sorry, Brooke, I'm—"

Brooke would stride into the hotel room, the fantastic prize of her body hidden beneath her swimsuit. "I'm going to the hot tub *anyway*," she would announce. "Don't wait up for me."

The door would slam in my face, and I'd be alone, staring out the window at Memphis, at the gray crisscrossing lines of the streets below, wondering how Kanga would do it better if he were me.

23

"SOMETHING'S STUCK IN THERE."

It was the morning of the championship game. Kanga was fully decked out in his dress clothes, ready for the bike ride to school. But at the last second he scurried into the bathroom to flood the inside of his body and rinse it out again. I heard the sink running much longer than it had at the Noons' house. I wondered if I'd hear a *pop* as his body exploded, and see water rushing out from under the bathroom door. But four flushes later, he came out, gripping his belly. "It's still in there."

"This is why we're never supposed to eat." It was the kind of mom lecture I'd given Kanga a thousand times. But we were beyond that old paradigm now. I was beyond it. Last night, Kanga had made it clear he didn't need me in his life anymore. I was more than ready to give him his independence. Still, the mom in me refused to be censored, and offered my brother this thimbleful of encouragement: "It'll come out eventually. Let's head to school."

It was my game day too, and it started with a small victory. I could ride my bike myself, *two*-handed; I just mashed my rubber fingers and thumb at the handlebar grip until I was grabbing it tight. But I'd have to be careful. There would be no quick letting go. I had also washed my game-day clothes early that morning, and they felt cold and metallic on my skin, like armor. For a warrior such as myself, the world was brimming with possibility. I was fully charged at last, having left my new fingers in the outlet for over eleven hours. Had Dad felt this same burst of excitement the night before our planned adventure as he charged up for the last time? And what about Brooke? Was she ready for tonight? I hadn't let go of the disk she'd given me, wishing I were the type of robot from movies who could insert it into the side of his head, blink, and know its entire contents. I would have to use the school library to read Brooke's disk, to finally understand her, hoping nobody was reading it over my shoulder. But I already knew the three most important things: Brooke was a robot, she wanted to flee her oppressive family life, and she'd chosen *me* as her confidant. Still, Brooke was Brooke. There was no predicting her next move. Would she really steal away with me to Memphis? Would she pretend I didn't exist? Would she pull me into the custodian's closet and jam her fingers in my outlet?

The temperature on the bank marquee read thirty-eight degrees. I was wearing my coat today, just like the human kids, and I'd even remembered my winter hat.

Not Kanga. He had forgotten both his hat and coat. He was draped in superstition. He'd pushed off with his dress shoes, and now he couldn't let them touch the ground again, *or else*. So he pedaled. He kept pedaling. He kept focus. We were approaching the stoplight. Kanga gently squeezed his hand brake. The stoplight was his enemy. Today it was red. Kanga was going as slowly as possible, weaving back and forth, riding in small circles, taking up the whole lane. Waiting. Waiting. Waiting for the light to turn . . .

Red. It was still red, and there was nowhere left for Kanga to go. I was already stopped at the light, resting peacefully with one foot on the asphalt. Kanga was not resting. He was making sounds with his mouth, trying to change the stoplight with magic. Red. Cars were suddenly lined up behind him, adults on their way to work, hating Kanga for being a bike in their lane. I felt their eyes shoot their own angry magic through the back of his head, trying to knock him off balance, knock him into the gutter, down a manhole. Red. Red. *Red.* He was at the stoplight. There was nothing left to do except push his feet against the pedals and arrive on the other side of the intersection.

If you ever watch your brother ride his bike straight into rush-hour traffic, be prepared to see it on your eyelids every time you blink for the rest of your life. There was no time for car horns. Just the skidding of tires on blacktop. A bird would have looked down at Kanga directly below the traffic light, standing on the pedals of his bike, frozen in space by the sheer speed of the vehicles around him. A station wagon lost control, its front wheels locking up, its back end swinging around like a baseball bat, swatting Kanga's bike to the other side of the street. The bike spun as it flew, Kanga with it, hands clutching the handlebars, his feet pinching the gears. The bike bounced on its tires. It wobbled. Kanga almost hit another car but glided past the front bumper. Now the world was stopped *except* for Kanga, everybody else unable to scream or move as he pumped his knees in the direction of Hectorville High School.

Green.

I pedaled after him. There were no further complications on the ride.

At the bike rack, I dismounted beside Kanga, yanking my rubber fingers off the handlebar grip, as he examined his bike for damage from the collision. Not even a scratch. His body was fine too, except for the steam emanating from his hair follicles. He looked focused. Determined. Like he could have leapt over the building. My mind was back at the intersection. The station wagon. Before it had bunted Kanga, I got a clean look through the driver's-side window. Mr. Jacobowhite, Kanga's English teacher. I tried to imagine Mr. Jacobowhite, after the incident, pulled over on the side of the road. Swearing? Crying? Dead of a heart attack?

Kanga began poking his belly with his fingers, like a kid pressing piano keys, wincing at the sound. I followed him into school, feeling a rush of hot air pressing against my hat. It occurred to me: Mr. Jacobowhite had seen Kanga biking to school without the hat he'd personally delivered to our apartment. Kanga's head had been exposed to the elements, and Mr. Jacobowhite had nearly destroyed him. Somehow that made me love Kanga like we were fourth graders again, against my better judgment.

● ● ●

She was blocking our locker. The captain of the freshman Cheerbirds, Staci Miles, was pressing a sign to it. "You're not supposed to be here yet!" she screamed and scampered down the hallway with bounds made all the more graceful by her Cheerbird uniform. The sign on our locker read:

♥

GO KANGA!
#32! POINT GUARD!
WHAT A HOTTIE!
KILL RICHARDSON!

♥

The words were written on an orange piece of paper meant to resemble a basketball, but Staci had cut it in the shape of a human heart.

Kanga scowled at the sign, then turned to me: "Look down my throat. Can you see anything down there?" He opened wide.

I was already exhausted from today's crisis. Apparently, Kanga saw me as obsolete only when he didn't have food stuck to his insides. Part of this predictable charade was my fault. Every time he got himself into trouble, I was always standing by to rescue him. But I was done with that. Sick of it. More to the point, Kanga didn't need my help anymore, and he probably never did in the first place. Dad had gotten it right when we were babies, when Kanga had a dart sticking out of his back: *It ain't nothing*, he'd said.

Kid's fine. The ensuing years had proven this to be true, again and again. It didn't matter what I did—or even what Kanga did. He always survived in the end. I channeled Dad now.

"Close your mouth," I said. "You'll be fine."

We saw Staci Miles again in Mr. Belt's class. She was first to notice Stickzilla's terrarium was empty, scrubbed clean of its shredded newspaper, leaves, and brambles. The screen roof was gone, as well as the spray bottle that had provided Stickzilla with a daily mist. *"Oh,"* bleated Staci. "She almost lived until spring!"

Mr. Belt made the sound of a basketball buzzer with his mouth. "Presentation time! Staci, Paula, Jennifer. You have a date with the front of my room."

Staci shook the memory of Stickzilla from her flushed cheeks, and her groupmate Paula yelled to Mr. Belt, "One more minute!"

"Ladies—"

"Fine," said Paula, pouting, deserting her half-finished visual aid, a metal bowl and a piece of string, and trudging to the front of the room. Only Staci maintained her composure. She began the science presentation with a single word, *centrifugal,* saying it so confidently that I heard several boys repeat it back to her, *"centrifugal,"* the way businessmen might repeat *aloha* back to a beautiful woman in Hawaii.

When Staci finished her introduction, Jennifer took over and illustrated centrifugal force with a poster, but mostly used her hands to demonstrate what she meant, and finally, after having further confused her audience, she asked us to close our eyes and imagine the impossible concept for ourselves. There was silence.

"Well, ladies," Mr. Belt said, "please accept our gratitude for that lovely—"

"Wait!" said Staci. "We have one more demonstration!"

"No," Paula whispered to her. *"I'm not doing it."*

"Come on!" urged Staci.

"Me neither," said Jennifer.

Staci's partners gathered their materials and abandoned her at the front of the room. Mr. Belt held the teacher's edition of his science book, ready to assign us our reading.

"Please!" said the Cheerbirds captain. "I just need ten more seconds!"

Mr. Belt met her intense stare with one of his own, then nodded.

All eyes were on Staci as she proceeded with the final demonstration. She created a bubble of space for herself between the chalkboard and the first row of desks, extending her arms out to either side, hands limp at the ends. One white shoe was placed before the other, knees bent. I recognized this pose from the sideline of the basketball court. It meant you'd better keep watching. She took a quick glance at Kanga. She commanded the class: "Watch my hair."

Kanga disobeyed her. He was staring at Stickzilla's empty terrarium.

I disobeyed her too. Rather than watching Staci's hair, I was focused on her green skirt, which usually hung to the middle of her thigh but now, as she spun on her toe, had risen to expose the green underwear all Cheerbirds wore, which, by some glitch in human societal rules, it was okay to stare at. When she came to a stop—the green skirt stopping a moment later—she smoothed it against her legs and said, "What my hair just did was centrifugal. Any questions?"

Kanga stood up, his eyes darkened. "What I don't understand is how we're just supposed to walk around every day, looking at each other, talking to each other, *eating*, doing everything we're supposed to do, and pretend we couldn't just die at any moment." He shook his finger at Mr. Belt. "What's keeping us alive? Dumb luck? What's to stop something from getting stuck inside us?" His fingers were massaging the air near his belly, as if performing a spell.

"Excellent question, Livery," said Mr. Belt. "My answer is to always keep your game face on. Which is exactly what you're doing. Good job. Everybody look at that face!"

Kanga closed his eyes.

"May we all approach life, and indeed death, with such a game face."

● ● ●

It was lunchtime. Kanga sat against our locker, rocking onto either butt cheek, his eyelids quivering like he was a human passing gas. I stood down the hallway, near a trash can, watching. I'd found a small baggie of purple grapes, and I was positioning them between the tips of my new finger and thumb and waiting for them to burst. I loved the moment just before the explosion, when the grapes would shake slightly, as if their slimy guts were capable of fear. This was the exact sort of thing Kanga would have loved to see too. Before. Now I didn't dare approach him. I was about to take off when Staci Miles appeared before my brother, flanked by two other Cheerbirds.

"Close your eyes," she said, staring down at him.

Through gritted teeth, he said, "I've got something stuck in my stomach."

"Just close your eyes. *Please*," she grunted. "Then we'll leave you alone."

Kanga closed his eyes.

"You better not look."

Kanga rocked on his butt cheeks.

"Watch him," Staci told her friend. "Make sure his eyes don't open."

"We're watching him," said a Cheerbird.

"Okay, Kanga. You have to do what I say. That's the rule. Here's the first thing I want you to do. Imagine a girl standing in front of you. The girl is a foot tall, head to toe. It's a *girl*, okay? Not a boy. She's one foot tall. Can you see her?"

Kanga nodded.

"Point to the girl's head with your finger. But keep your eyes *closed*."

Kanga hung his finger in the empty space above his lap.

"Good. Now point to her feet. Remember, don't look."

Kanga pointed slightly lower.

Staci continued: "Now I want you to point to the girl's . . ."

"*Do it, Staci!*"

"Yeah! We had to do it with our basketball players. Now you have to!"

"Go on, Staci! Do it! DO IT!"

"I'm doing it! Shut up! Just gimme a second . . ."

"If you don't do it—"

"I'm doing it."

"Then go."

"Don't push me!"

I could smell her ChapStick.

"Okay, Kanga, point to the girl's *vagina*."

When it was over, Kanga hadn't moved his finger at all, but now the finger was *wet*, because Staci had kneeled down and put her mouth on the end of it, reluctantly sucking Kanga's finger a fraction of a second before yelling, "FOUND IT!"

The Cheerbirds danced away.

I should have stopped them. They didn't realize Kanga was no longer a hulking, self-assured basketball star. He was lost. He was in pain. He was aching for his mother. He was—

It ain't nothing. I forced myself to walk away too. *Kid's fine.*

● ● ●

The Hectorville High School library was the Cave's evil twin. Its dark, clean carpeting performed a curse on all entrants, muting the natural sound of their bodies and sucking any mischievous thoughts from their heads. The bookshelves were ancient walls, arranged in a claustrophobic web. The ceiling was low, only inches above them, pressing down like the moon's underbelly, whispering for tall boys to reach up and feel its mysterious texture—and get immediate detention for it. Luckily, my goal for the rest of lunch period was right near the library's entrance: the student-friendly computer, which sat across from the checkout desk. Unluckily, at the checkout desk sat Ms. Harris, the librarian.

Being a freshman, I had almost no background with Ms. Harris. An advantage. My plan was to adopt a persona that would force the librarian to give me both computer access and solitude.

She swooped over immediately. "How may I assist you, young man?"

"I got a research project I gotta do," I explained in a slow voice. "For social studies."

"What is this project about?"

"Memphis."

"Very good. What *exactly* are we focusing on in Memphis?"

"Uh . . . Everything?"

She pursed her lips. "We have several books on Memphis, and I can show you to the *Encyclopædia Britannica*, our most useful resource for general information."

"But my teacher said I gotta use computers. Computers is worth thirty points. Will you find all those Memphis books for me while I look it up on a computer?"

"Do you know *how* to use a computer?"

"Uh . . ."

She sat me down at the computer, then explained what the important buttons on the keyboard did as the machine glowed to life. Then, when it was fully awake and blinking, she leaned over me—she smelled like rubber bands—typing rapidly on the keyboard, a snake of green words reflecting off her glasses.

"Wow," I said. "Computers are awesome!"

"Memphis," she said. "Read these four articles first. Use the arrows to find the article you want. Then press Enter. When you're done reading, press Escape and use the arrows to choose a different article. But don't *print* anything without asking me first, is that understood?"

"Yes."

"Do you know *how* to print an article?"

"Uh . . ."

"Very good."

She stood behind me as I carefully pecked the keys (with my left hand, as the right was hidden under the table), making my way to the first article about Memphis. "This is so cool!" I hunched forward until my face was three inches from the screen. I read the article for two minutes, demonstrating to Ms. Harris that I would need at least fifteen more minutes to finish it. But she was still right behind me, watching. So, without turning around, I said, "Can you find all those books for me about Memphis so I can check them out?"

She exhaled through her nose.

"Please, so I don't get an F?"

"Don't print anything." She disappeared into the stacks.

Alone, I popped Brooke's disk into the drive. Escape, Escape, Escape, Escape. I arrived at a blank screen with a flashing green cursor. I typed the command for WordPerfect 5.1 for DOS, the program I knew Brooke used. The screen became a beautiful electric blue. I typed Command-F for "File." I used the arrows to find "Retrieve." After having spent so much of my audio receptors zeroing in on Brooke's distinctive keyboard tapping, I knew these to be the right commands. The screen showed me a single file on Brooke's disk. *Brooke*. She had named her novel after herself. I moved the cursor over her name and pressed 1. Brooke's words filled the screen.

Ms. Harris was still finding my books about Memphis. My time with Brooke's novel was limited. I blinked my eyes to get them ready. I pressed the down arrow and scanned Brooke's brilliance as it flew upward . . .

Reading the entire document took four minutes and twelve seconds. 92,208 words. One paragraph. Her prose style would best be described as obsessive-compulsive.

My critical conclusions were as follows. First, it was a memoir, not a novel. Second, the memoir was remarkable in that it had two main characters instead of one: Brooke and her mother, whose name was Janet. Third, while most memoirists seek to create a full portrait of themselves, thoroughly investigating a variety of themes, events, and reflections in an effort to, by the memoir's end, force the reader to step back and say, "*Heavens, what a life* [insert author's name here] *lived*," Brooke's memoir focused on a single day. Actually, only a morning. And really, Brooke's *entire* memoir was an exhaustive study of the events that transpired between the Noon family residence, in the city of Le Roy, Michigan, and the front entrance of Le Roy Elementary School, approximately 8:19

a.m. to 8:41 a.m., on the morning of September 7, 1982, Brooke's first day of kindergarten. That is not to say Brooke didn't try to address other moments of her life. Indeed, her prose piqued my curiosity as she began to depict, for instance, her father explaining to her that she was a robot, her friendship with a girl named Dahlia in second grade, the first time she stole something (a pack of shoelaces) from a store, the first boy she touched shoes with, exploring the bottom of Sanders Lake, the second through seventeenth boys she touched shoes with, driving her father's car to Ypsilanti, etc. Yet none of these events got beyond the first several seconds before Brooke began telling—scratch that—*re*telling the experience of her mother walking her to school on the first day of kindergarten. Here is the incident, in brief: Brooke and Janet Noon leave the house holding hands, walking down the sidewalk in the direction of Le Roy Elementary School, which is six blocks away; at the end of the first block, however, Janet releases Brooke's hand and says to her daughter, "You know the way," and stops walking; without looking back at her mother, Brooke walks the remaining five blocks to Le Roy Elementary School; she arrives before the bell and takes her seat in Mrs. Edgar's classroom.

The first time reading this anecdote I found it moderately revealing that Janet Noon failed to supply her daughter with the most basic form of support—her mere physical presence—on Brooke's first day of school, a moment of great anxiety for young children. However, I also noted the *lack* of anxiety Brooke exhibited as she walked to school free of her mother. She petted a neighborhood dog. She squinted into the sun through the tree branches. She stopped at the corner of Peeler and Wright, looked both ways, let a car pass, then crossed the street. At Le Roy Elementary School, when asked by Principal Rhoades if she was lost, Brooke replied, "I know the way." In Mrs. Edgar's classroom, Brooke removed her pencil box from her backpack, shoved her backpack into a cubbyhole (identified by a sticker with her name on it), found her desk (also identified by a sticker with her name on it), took her seat, arranged her pencil box on the corner of her desktop, and waited for class to begin. Mrs. Edgar had been so busy soothing other students traumatized by separation from their mothers that she did not acknowledge Brooke for the first eleven minutes of class, not until roll was formally taken, and Mrs. Edgar looked up from her roster and inquired, "Brooke Noon? . . . There you are! A quiet one."

I heard Ms. Harris's noiseless footsteps advancing through the library stacks. There was a note of panic in her gait, that of a mother whose child suddenly disappeared in a parking lot. In this case, Ms. Harris's child was the student-friendly computer.

As she came into view, her arms piled with books about Memphis, her glasses filled with rage. "*What did you do?*" she screamed in a whisper.

"I tried to print my article, but it wouldn't print, so I unplugged the computer."

"You unplugged—" She set the books down beside the computer and then yanked my chair away from it, spilling me to the ground. Brooke's disk was already in my pocket and, luckily, undamaged from the fall. "Follow me."

At the desk, I gave Ms. Harris the student ID number of a kid on the basketball team, and she checked out the materials to his account, stamping the book cards with the force of a karate sensei. I asked, "What happens if I get taco stains on them?"

These words damaged Ms. Harris's soul, and she couldn't even look at me. A tiny node in my processor almost felt sorry for her. And for me. In a different world, where I was simply smart-but-not-too-smart Darryl Livery, I would have enjoyed chatting with this earnest, awkward, highly intelligent adult about books and computers and the possibility of accessing vast amounts of information through *phone lines* (a developing practice on which I was certain she was well-read). But we lived in the world of Brooke Noon, Memphis, and obsolete parents, and I would never see Ms. Harris again.

● ● ●

With a few minutes left in lunch, I ditched the books on a cafeteria table and ended up in the Cave. The court was empty. The basketballs were caged up. I stood at the free-throw line.

I hadn't seen Brooke yet today, but my processor could somehow *smell* her as it reviewed each disparate account of her first day of kindergarten, inspecting the tiny variations for meaning. A dead worm on the sidewalk. Her mother clearing her throat. A pebble that materializes in Brooke's shoe, only to disappear three steps later. The hissing of a garbage truck. A single droplet of rain hitting her wrist from the cloudless sky. None of these details contradicted her overall story, yet with each retelling I found myself yearning for Brooke to do something different. Anything. To look back at her mother and say, "I hate you." To venture through a neighbor's backyard to a mysterious destination. To get yelled at by Principal Rhoades for throwing her backpack across the school steps. To steal another kid's pencil box and dump the contents out. For Mrs. Edgar's first words to Brooke to be "Young lady, *settle down.*" I yearned for Brooke to simply be Brooke.

The truth smacked me like a backpack to the belly. *This* was Brooke. Just before she changed. That walk to school had twisted the dials in Brooke's processor, setting her up for a childhood of manic, antisocial deviance. This was every parent's worst nightmare: a moment of casual neglect getting trapped in their kid's mind, causing them to obsess over it for years, ruining the rest of their life.

But Brooke's life wasn't ruined. Maybe to some people it was. Her mother. But not to me. Brooke had a chance to make her life exactly what she wanted, and now that I had the key to her processor, maybe I could help. All I had to do was go find her and—

"How's the damage, Darryl?" Mr. Belt appeared in the Cave. He was holding a basketball. "How's school? You get all the"—he twirled a finger near the side of his head—"things figured out?"

"Yes, sir."

"Because we need you tonight. Well. We need your management. By that I mean balls. Don't forget to bring enough basketballs tonight."

Mr. Belt looked at me expectantly. It seemed he was waiting for me to say something because when I didn't, he got down on a knee and stared me in the eyes.

"Darryl, you have to ask yourself: How bad do I want it? The number of balls you have is the answer to that question. They're metaphors, Darryl, these balls. But sometimes life has nothing to do with balls. What I'm saying is, there're kids all over school pressuring you to use their drugs. Keep your nose away from those kids. Stay clean. I was your age once. I've also been to college. When you get to college, come talk to me, and I'll set you straight."

Mr. Belt stood up and shot the ball. He missed. We watched the basketball bounce toward the Cave door and roll into the school hallway.

"Here's one thing I never had to burn your ass about, Darryl." Mr. Belt pointed to the clock on the wall. "Always on time for games. Early, even. Maybe you got a stomach virus, but you love game day. That's a feather in your cap. If I could crack open your head and yank out the part of your brain that makes you never late for games, and then cook that part up and feed it to the rest of the guys, well, then we'd have something to hang our hats on."

The bell rang. Lunch was over.

A moment later, I finally saw Brooke in the hallway.

She was outside the band room, gloating in victory over Andrea Imhoff, the previous first-chair clarinetist in the Jazz Band. Apparently, the transfer of power had just occurred, and Brooke was cornering Andrea near the drinking fountain, consoling her rival by listing all the reasons Andrea didn't deserve first chair. "Your bottom lip is all wrong. You've got to put more mouthpiece in your mouth. Your tongue's not planting firmly enough. You chew when you play—"

"Congratulations, Brooke," I whispered, suddenly apprehensive, finding it hard to square that mild-mannered kindergartener sitting quietly at her desk with the wrecking ball before my eyes. There wasn't even a trace of the vulnerable robot I'd connected with last night. If we were about to build a new life together in Memphis, why did Brooke care so much about Jazz Band? Was this all a clever disguise?

She ignored me. "—your right thumb is too far under the thumb rest. Your fingers are floating instead of hovering. You're not getting enough air . . ."

●●●

Just before art class, I found Kanga staring into our open locker as if confronting a tormenting abyss. "I've got to get inside myself," he whispered. "You've got to help me. I've been thinking. We need to go in the *back* way." He reached for a wire shirt hanger he'd hidden inside our locker and began twisting it into a long arm with a hook at the end. "Remember that video we watched in health class? With that dentist using his sickle to scrape those teeth? I want you to go in the back way, and when you hit something hard, just start scraping until you—"

"No."

"Darryl, we have to—"

"We don't have 'back ways' that work like that." I grabbed the hanger and returned it to our locker. "You'll be fine, Kanga. Just think about something else. Think about Staci."

"Not her! I can't be around girls right now. You have to protect me. Especially from Brooke. In art class. Distract her. Do whatever it takes."

"Protect you from your girlfriend, you mean?"

"Yes. Keep Brooke away from me."

He disgusted me. Everything had to be about him. He didn't care about me. He never had. But now, suddenly, I was in the position of power. I couldn't resist. My brother was going to listen, for once. He was going to show me the respect I'd earned. "I will help you, Kanga. But you better understand that Brooke was my girlfriend first. Got it? Maybe she went on a bike ride with you. Maybe she invited you over to dinner. But she chose me over you. She's my girlfriend *now*, and she doesn't want anything to do with you. Keeping her out of your sight will be the easiest thing I've ever done." My voice was quivering. *"Got it?"*

"Thanks, brother." He gave me a weak smile. He didn't care about Brooke either. "You're the best."

● ● ●

In the art room, I went straight to Brooke's table. I sat down across from her. I whispered: "I'm so sorry about what your mom did to you in kindergarten, Brooke."

She just stared at me. "Did you even read it?"

"I read it dozens of times. That walk to school. Your mom letting go of your hand like that. You must have felt so alone." I reached across the table with my new hand and touched hers. "You don't have to be alone anymore."

Brooke pulled her hand away and pounded mine with her fist—causing my palm to make a rubber-duck sound against the table. "Sometimes I wonder how *you* passed kindergarten. That walk to school was the best day of my life. For once, my mom let me go. That was the one time she believed in me, Darryl. The one time she trusted me. And that's what you have to do for *him*."

"Who?"

She kicked me under the table. "Your brother. Let him go. He's not coming with us."

"Where?"

She kicked me under the table.

"*Memphis?*" I asked.

"Quiet!" She leaned her face close to mine. "Nobody can know where we're going."

My fan clicked on. We were actually going.

"I'll meet you tonight outside your apartment building. When will your brother's stupid game be over?"

"Seven o'clock."

"Be ready to leave at seven thirty. We'll bike to the bus station. The bus to Memphis leaves at eight fifteen. Don't ruin this, Darryl." She kicked me one last time for good measure. "Don't tell Kanga a single word."

I almost told her some words: *I love you, Brooke.* I almost climbed onto the table and grabbed a handful of her greasy hair and kissed her on the mouth. But I didn't. I would save that for Memphis.

Near the end of our last-ever art class, Principal Moyle cleared her throat on the intercom and made the following announcement: "*GOOOOOOOOOO BIRDS!* It's almost game time, ladies and gentlemen! I know each and every student will be packed into the Cave to see *KANGA*

LIVERY and the freshman basketball team hunt down and kill the Richardson Wolves! *I'll be there!*"

The bell rang.

"Seven thirty," Brooke repeated and left.

Kanga was stuck at his art table. He appeared stunned by Principal Moyle's announcement that there was a basketball game after school and that he was participating in it. He exhausted me. I was ready to get on with my life. But in his current state, Kanga would never win the championship for Hectorville—something, if I were being honest with myself, I actually wanted for him. For us. For the Detroit 600s. I was consumed with the impending scene of Kanga after the game, defeated and dejected, standing in our apartment wondering where I'd gone. It would look remarkably similar to when Mom and Dad disappeared, except nobody would be there to console him. He would be utterly alone.

Wouldn't it be easier to just call Detroit and turn him in right now?

Kanga rose from the table and forced a smile. "I think I'm finally relaxed." His shoulders quivered. "It was hard, but I think I'm ready. I'm focused. I'm ready to play basketball."

"You'll be fine," I assured him. But as we began making our way toward the Cave, he didn't look fine. Kanga held his belly as he walked, taking the tiniest steps possible. I told him, "I have to use the bathroom."

"Okay."

With my brother out of sight, I went straight to the main office and asked the secretary if I could use the phone. I dialed the number I knew by heart. A female voice answered robotically, prompting me to enter my serial number. "*Thank you,*" she intoned. "*If you wish to report yourself as obsolete, press one. If you wish to report someone else, press two.*"

I stared at the number pad. The championship game had yet to be played. Was I really about to crush my brother's last chance to live his dream? From the depths of my processor, Brooke's voice answered: *Let him go . . .*

"Nobody home?" asked the secretary.

I hung up and headed for the Cave.

24

"WHAT DO YOU MEAN the season's over?" the Ceiling Fan asked Mr. Belt. The coaches were having a private discussion while the team warmed up for the game. I was eavesdropping from my spot on the bench. "We need another week of practice. The guys—they're almost persistent. This can't be the end!"

"We go through this every year, Simms. It's called the off-season," rebutted Mr. Belt. "Also state law. These boys need time to unwind, time to get to know various other coaches and systems. Maybe they'll get a girlfriend. Babysit a sibling. Spend time with an elderly relative or what-not. Also, it's the beginning of indoor golf season. Basketball practice will resume in November."

"I got nothing else, Belt. What am I supposed to do? All I got is these boys."

"You'll keep it classy." Mr. Belt blew his whistle, and the Birds flocked to the head coach to absorb his final instructions. Outside the huddle, the

Ceiling Fan grabbed the collar of his game-day sweater and ripped it into a V-neck.

I observed the Richardson Wolves huddle on the other side of the court. We'd played them earlier this season, a mediocre team we stomped by twenty-two, but they'd since gone through a metamorphosis. They were now the Fab *Twelve*, as every one of their players had adopted the baggy shorts, black shoes, and nearly shaved heads of the University of Michigan's Fab Five. Their blue uniforms were nearly identical to Michigan's, with "Richardson" written in maize-colored letters across the front of the jerseys, and on the shorts, the block *M* turned upside down to become a *W* for "Wolves." But it wasn't just the clothes. When the Richardson coach broke the huddle, the boys jawed into each other's faces and wagged their fingers boastfully toward the Hectorville bench, as if their earlier defeat by the Birds were a game from an entirely different season. Lack of confidence would not be a problem for the Wolves.

The bleachers were loaded with spectators. I'd seen enough games to immediately pick out the basketball fanatics from the dutiful, bored parents. I could predict who would scream the entire game and who would clap for the wrong team. That father hated all referees. That mother fantasized she was Mr. Belt. Those already sweaty adults were just in it for the Cheerbirds. Then I saw *him*. That anonymous father wearing a Birds T-shirt, munching from his bag of popcorn: Dr. Murphio. Of course. How could the doctor resist watching his prized creation win his first trophy? Dr. Murphio was only human.

In the Hectorville huddle, Mr. Belt was attempting to motivate his star: "Livery. Hello? This is the championship. I'm talking about playing basketball, Kanga. Offense. God help me, defense too. Who are you guarding this afternoon?"

"Fifty," said Kanga. He still held the basketball he'd been warming up with, hugging it to his abdomen, pressing it against his innards.

"I'll ask the question another way. Who is Fifty? What do you know about Fifty? What makes Fifty tick?"

"He's . . . tall."

"What else do you know about him? Is he pretty?"

"I don't think so."

"You don't *think* so? He's ugly! And he hates you. See? He hates everything about you. Fifty told me he's going to dunk your butt right out of the Cave. Does that mean anything to you? He said—"

The buzzer sounded.

"Starting five!" hollered Mr. Belt. "Get your shoes in position!"

The teams took the court. Kanga kept his basketball pressed to his belly.

The referee frowned at my brother. "I've got the official basketball right here, son. Toss your ball back to your coach. Let's get this show on the road."

"Uh . . ." said Kanga, hugging the ball tighter.

"You want to use that particular ball? Okay. One ball is as good as another." The ref tossed the official ball to a woman at the scorers table. "Let's have your ball, son."

Kanga hugged the ball.

"Let's have it."

Kanga stepped away from the referee.

"My patience is—" The referee took hold of Kanga's ball. He wrested it away. "Any more of this business, I won't hesitate to boot you. Understand?"

The game started.

Fifty, according to the game program, was Conrad Ward. I remembered him from the last game as being completely unremarkable, though he was indeed ugly. His left eye bulged from its socket, always aimed down at the floor; his right eye stared straight ahead. As Ward stood in defensive position before my brother, his left eye appeared to be observing Kanga's shoes, as if my brother's stance revealed a deep and damning secret. Perhaps it did. Ward was slower and weaker than Kanga. But the new Fab Five jersey seemed to have unlocked a hidden defensive talent in Ward, a savant-like ability to guard my brother. The moment play began, Kanga could not move to a point on the court without Ward being there first. Kanga was never open. Passes thrown to Kanga (this was Mr. Belt's entire game plan) bounced off Ward's well-contorted arms. On the rare occasion Kanga *did* obtain the ball, Ward didn't panic, but played face-up defense, abiding by a pair of fundamentals: 1) Stay between your man and the basket, and 2) The shortest distance between two points is a straight line. Ward never jumped. Ward never sprinted. He just kept one eye on the floor, one eye on Kanga's belly button, and he never let Kanga dribble past him. The first quarter ended and Kanga hadn't even attempted a shot. Richardson led fourteen to five.

"It's just one quarter," rationalized Mr. Belt in the huddle. "Last I checked we get three more. Now go out there and stick with the plan. Pass the ball to Kanga. Kanga needs the ball. But do you know what to *do* with the ball, Kanga?"

Rye leaned in close to Kanga and whispered, "Do you need me to set a pick?"

Then it was the Ceiling Fan's turn to address Kanga. "I just don't get it. If I live a thousand more years, I still won't get it. I would murder any of you guys with my bare hands for another chance to play freshman ball. I would stomp you through this floor. You can't even imagine what I would do for an opportunity to wear the green and white again. You're a disgrace. You're an embarrassment. If it were me out there, I would—"

"Everybody put your hands in," said Mr. Belt. "Come on. Reach in. Be a team. Everybody touch hands and say 'Kanga' on three. One . . . Two . . . Three . . . KANGA!" Mr. Belt was the only one who shouted.

James Botty gave the Richardson huddle a long, jealous gaze, surely debating whether he should strip off his Hectorville uniform, give it to the Ceiling Fan, and ask the Richardson coach if they had an open spot on their roster—and an extra pair of those incredible shorts. He shook away the thought and took his seat on the Hectorville bench.

The Richardson fans were emboldened by their team's first-quarter dominance. They stood on the bleachers. They pounded their maize-and-blue chests. They swung invisible hammers at Kanga.

"Psych Ward!" they yelled. "Psyyyyyych Waaaaaard!"

"You're in the Psych Ward now, Kanga Livery!"

"Fool, you're getting PSYCHED OUT!"

Conrad "Psych" Ward. Kanga had never faced a player like him. This reinvented version of Psych Ward didn't even pretend to play offense; his sole utility was stopping the ball. A lockdown defender. An eraser scooting himself down Kanga's stat sheet. Psych Ward was Joe Dumars, the Bad Boy Piston, terrorizing Michael Jordan like a goblin sent from basketball hell.

As the teams took the floor, a voice called out from the bleachers, so quiet and gentle I assumed nobody had heard it other than myself. But my brother turned to the voice when it asked: "*Kanga, are you my son?*"

It was Dr. Murphio. Kanga raised an eyebrow in vague recognition. *Are you my son?* It was one of the phrases written on the diagram of Ma's processor. But what did it have to do with Kanga? Somehow, my brother seemed to register the phrase, or, at the very least, he registered the voice that had uttered it.

I remembered Dad's speech about magic words. They were a verbal code that would unleash a hidden program within a robot, transforming him or her into a completely different person.

The buzzer startled Kanga, returning his focus to the game. He untucked his jersey and scratched the pink, tormented skin of his belly. He appeared to be unfazed and unimproved by Dr. Murphio asking him *Are you my son?* He was the same distraught Kanga.

In the second quarter, Psych Ward employed a host of new tricks. Sneakier tricks. Fab Five tricks. He started by leaning against Kanga and tickling my brother's knee. Kanga dribbled off his foot.

"Psyyyyyych Waaaaaard!"

Next possession, Psych Ward blew air in Kanga's face, causing him to flinch like he just walked through a spiderweb.

"Psych! Psych! Psych! Psych!"

He untied Kanga's shoelace. He tugged on Kanga's shorts. He whispered in Kanga's ear, and Kanga stopped playing basketball to ask Psych Ward exactly *when* and *where* he'd seen our mother.

Dr. Murphio sat in the bleachers, arms crossed, stolidly observing Kanga's humiliation. I imagined this same look on the doctor's face at Gravy Robotics, deciding how best to disassemble Mom and Dad. "Start with the heads, girls, and just work your way down."

So why was I grinning?

Had I been grinning the entire game? What evil node in my processor made Kanga's fall back to Earth so damn satisfying? First of all, this flounder was long overdue. It had been the plan from Kanga's first practice, a calculated failure that would return us to our life of anonymity. Needless to say, that didn't happen. But now that it *was* happening, who better to bear witness than Dr. Murphio? The only question was whether Kanga's "father" would stick around long enough to console his "son" after the game. I was betting on *no*, which would leave me to play parent like I always did.

Scratch that. I'd be in Memphis. With Brooke. (My fan clicked on.) So Kanga would have to get through that first lonely night on his own. Then all the nights for the rest of his life. He'd be fine.

With two minutes to go in the first half, even Richardson fans were getting bored, their minds already in the Cobra Burger drive-through after the game. Mr. Belt called a time-out. He had nothing left to say to his team. He sat at the end of the bench, shuffling a deck of cards on his knees. The players stood around in a blob. The Ceiling Fan had ripped his game-day sweater farther down his chest, partially revealing his INVISIBLE SYSTEMS sweatshirt. The game was over. All that remained was the formality of letting the clock run out.

Then Kanga sneezed.

I'd never seen my brother sneeze before. Or any robot, for that matter. There was no mention of sneezing in *The Directions*, and Kanga clearly had no idea what he was doing. He didn't sneeze like humans sneezed, allowing the pressure to escape through his mouth and drift where it may. Kanga tried to keep the sneeze in. Its force ballooned his cheeks and bugged his eyes. It made his hair stand on end. But once he'd contained the sneeze inside his mouth, capturing all that awesome energy for himself, a smile spread across his face. He cupped a hand and spit out a small hunk of lettuce.

Mrs. Noon's salad.

I imagined where the lettuce had been a moment ago, draped across his processor like a wet plastic bag, stymieing Kanga's every thought and action. Now the thing was out of him. He studied the shapeless green bit of vegetable in his hand. The buzzer sounded, and he flicked it to the floor.

The referee was tossing the basketball from hand to hand.

Kanga zeroed in on the ball, watching it move. "*Lánqiú*," he whispered to himself. I knew, of course, this was Mandarin for "basketball." *Lánqiú*. Nobody else in the Cave had heard him—at least I hoped not. Speaking Mandarin in mid-Michigan was like speaking in binary code. It meant one thing. You were a robot.

The ref blew the whistle. Play resumed.

With a twenty-point lead, Psych Ward relaxed his defense on Kanga, allowing my brother to receive an uncontested inbounds pass. Kanga speed-dribbled toward the basket and easily dropped the ball through the hoop.

"*Fángyù!*" Kanga hissed at his team, louder than he'd said *lánqiú*.

The Birds regarded him with double shock: first, they'd just seen the *old* Kanga score the ball, and then—what had just come out of his mouth?

"*Fángyù!*" he repeated.

Apparently, his teammates had never heard the Mandarin word for "defense."

But I had. And I'd read stories in *The Directions* about robots who'd gotten killed for doing precisely what Kanga was doing now: speaking Mandarin for no good reason. *Shut up!* I wanted to scream at him. *Can't you hear yourself, Kanga?* But he couldn't. Kanga failed to register the confusion all around him because, it seemed, in his processor, he was still speaking English.

Dear brother, I thought, *what has that lettuce done to you?* No wonder Brooke had refused her mother's salad.

Thankfully, the game continued. Richardson tried to inbound the ball, and Kanga stood at the baseline performing jumping jacks, screaming, until the inbounder dropped the ball on his foot. Turnover. Hectorville ball. Kanga took the ball out-of-bounds. Mr. Belt was signaling for the give-and-go: Kanga would toss the ball in, it would come right back to him, and he would score. But when the ref handed Kanga the ball, my brother looked straight up. He shot the ball high into the ceiling lights—over the backboard—and swished it through the hoop.

Four points in four seconds.

If Kanga continued this pace for the rest of the first half, Hectorville would be up by a hundred points. He glanced at the scoreboard.

Please, I begged Kanga. *Just keep scoring and shut your damn mouth!*

But my brother yelled to his teammates: "*Wǒmen jiàng zài bànchǎng huòshèng!*"

This time Rye turned to James: "Did you understand what the heck he just said?"

James just shook his head, brow furrowing.

We are going to be winning by halftime! I could have translated, but held my tongue. I glanced at Dr. Murphio, who had two fingers pressed against his lips, a look of horror on his face. In a panic, I tried to transmit a radio signal to my brother: *Speak English, Kanga!* I concentrated on the words, sounding them out in my processor, feeling the radio waves emanate from my head: *Cut the Mandarin! Act like a—*

No. I stopped myself. *Kanga will be fine.* He always came out on top. Hadn't he biked to school this morning without touching the pavement? My brother didn't need me. He was fine. Kanga would stop speaking Mandarin on his own, and everything would be *fine.*

The referee deemed the over-the-backboard stunt an illegal play. No basket. But the game's momentum had yo-yoed. The Richardson coach spilled his Gatorade. He grabbed Psych Ward by the jersey with a specific order: "Stop that kid."

But Kanga proceeded to score any way he pleased.

He scooped it.

He hooked it over Psych Ward's quivering hands.

He faked left, went right, elbow jumper.

He bulldozed Psych Ward into the Cheerbirds.

He palmed the dribble, swished it from half-court.

"*Zhè shì nǐ zuì hǎo de fángshǒu ma?*" Kanga said to Psych Ward. *Is that the best defense you got, wussy?*

Psych Ward shuddered, trying to remove Kanga's voice from his ears.

"Those are big'uns, Livery!" cried Mr. Belt, concerned only with the score.

Kanga's nostrils flared, and even his teammates stood back. "*Quán chǎng jǐnbī!*" he ordered. "*Yídòng!*" The boys shuffled in place. They had no idea Kanga had just told them to get into full-court press. They watched Kanga stalking the midcourt circle, his neck bent like a bird of prey. Hectorville was now down by one point with fourteen seconds left in the half. "*Wǒmen fànguī le. Dāng tāmen pèng qiú, jiù shā sǐ tāmen!*"

We're fouling. When they touch the ball, just kill them.

Richardson tossed the ball in near Rye. Rye's opponent dribbled around while Rye moved with his palms up, shuffling his feet, exactly as the Ceiling Fan had taught him to play defense. In other words, Rye was doing everything he could *not* to foul. Four seconds died before Kanga ran over and intentionally fouled Rye's opponent in order to stop the clock, which, in his processor, was exactly what he'd ordered Rye to do.

"Foul!" said the ref. "Number thirty-two!"

Kanga grabbed Rye's shoulder. "*Líkāi yóuxì.*"

"Come on, Kanga." Rye tried to smile. "This is a joke, right? I can't understand you."

"*Chūqù.*"

"You're scaring—"

It was no joke. Kanga had just demanded that Rye leave the game. *Get out.* But when Rye just continued to stand there, Kanga ripped the goggles off his teammate's face and pitched them high into the bleachers. "*Chūqù.*"

Then I heard it. *The crackle.* All across the Cave, that horrible, barely perceptible crinkle of human brains wiring together through thin air. Each *Homo sapien* tilted his head in unison, aware something was wrong. Even those who had been oblivious to the game, daydreaming or reading the newspaper, now sat rigid, as if from hearing a gunshot. It was the crackle. "*Almighty*," muttered an elderly man, and beside him a pod of chattering girls drew their heads inward, then swiveled their panicked faces to the basketball court.

They all stared at Kanga.

Rye, having been blinded, stumbled to the bench.

"Hey." The Ceiling Fan stood up, yelling above the crackle. "*Hey*. That's your teammate."

"*Lái ba*," said Kanga. "*Wǒmen zhǐ guǎn dǎ lánqiú.*"

"What is that crap?" said the Ceiling Fan.

"Kanga," said Mr. Belt. "You need an orange slice or something?"

My brother stared at them, confused. *Let's just play basketball*, he'd said, but neither coach responded, so he turned angrily to the referee: "*Wǒmen zhǐ guǎn dǎ lánqiú!*"

"That's enough of that, son." The referee stepped back. "Hash this out with your coaches. Official's time-out!" He blew the whistle.

But the crackle didn't take time-outs.

"Hey!" shouted a Richardson fan. "Something's wrong with that kid!"

Kanga had assumed a mannequin stillness at center court. His teammates and opponents had fled to their respective benches. He was utterly alone in the Cave.

"What language is he speaking?"

"Why's he just standing there like that?"

"Where are his parents?"

A Cheerbird whispered to Staci Miles: "I told you he was weird!"

The Cave, thinking with its one crackling brain, began moving its thousands of lips, murmuring the possible explanations for Kanga's speech: Russian. Chinese. Alien. Spanish. Lebanese. Chinese. Iraqi. Japanese. Chinese. Chinese. *Chinese!* But my eyes were drawn to James Botty, who was whispering to the Ceiling Fan: "—this book over at his place. *The Directions.* Had all these pictures of robots. The insides of their bodies. Pictures of how they work. It was all about him . . ."

I looked at Dr. Murphio. He was scouting the Cave exits. His crackled mind had painted a picture of what was about to happen, and he seemed to have no appetite to witness it.

My brother was held in place by the glares and shouts of the spectators. He knew enough to refrain from speaking in his own defense; opening his mouth had gotten him into this trouble, he realized, even if he didn't understand why.

The voices in the bleachers quieted. The Ceiling Fan stepped onto the court.

"*Cù!*" shouted Kanga at the sight of his assistant coach. "*Cù!*" he pleaded, *Vinegar!* "*Cù!*" he screamed, to the only person who could possibly rescue him.

● ● ●

Back in fourth grade, just before I called Detroit on my parents, I was alone in the kitchenette with Mom. I asked her, "What happens when we die?"

We both knew what *The Directions* said, that we get a choice to have our parts remade into something beautiful or useful, a pink flamingo, for example, or a toilet seat. But Mom just grinned upward. "God takes your processor and puts it in a bird. He fills you with the most delicious electricity you've ever tasted. He opens his hands and you fly away."

"Forever?"

"No, honey." She gave me a dry kiss on the forehead. "When your battery runs out, you'll fall to earth. Then an animal will eat you, and the poison inside your processor will kill that animal. Then another animal will eat that animal, and you'll kill it too. Your processor will kill many animals that way, until all the poison is gone."

I was filled with poison now, watching the Ceiling Fan advance on Kanga. My brother had called for help, and now the choice was mine. Watching him get destroyed at the hands of a robophobic maniac—would that rid me of my poison? Because hadn't Kanga been the source of this poison my entire life? All I needed now was to be free of him. Free of the burden to protect him. Free of the burden to hide his identity, which he never understood himself and probably still didn't. Free of the burden to love him, whatever that meant. Love was nothing more than a program. And while the Ceiling Fan annihilated my defenseless brother, I was sure to be offered a chance to escape: to flock to the Cave exits, just as Dr. Murphio would be doing, and start a brand-new life with Brooke. Hadn't this been my entire plan? Kanga said it himself; *I* was the obsolete brother. What could I do now to alter his inevitable fate?

There's gonna come a time when it's you or Kanga, Dad had said. *You'll have to choose.*

The thing Dad hadn't realized was that I'd already made my decision. Kanga. My brother. It wasn't him or me.

It was him *and* me.

"I'M THE ROBOT!"

The Cave came to a halt. The Ceiling Fan turned, along with all the spectators, toward the shouter.

Toward me.

My mouth hung open, trembling.

"I'M THE ROBOT!" I repeated, and found my legs carrying me onto the court. "IT'S ME! EVERYONE LOOK!" I stopped a distance from Kanga, drawing the attention away from him. "LOOK AT THIS!" I yanked my shirtsleeve up to the elbow, and lifted my new rubber hand for all to see. "THIS IS FAKE! WATCH WHAT I CAN—" I knelt and set my hand on the floor, then stepped on it with all my weight. My body tensed up, summoning its Incredible Hulk strength to yank my arm away from my new hand, separating them, like an angry gardener uprooting a weed. But the rod connecting my hand to my forearm proved too robust for me to fracture. Wrist intact, I stood up and pleaded with the crowd. "I *AM* A ROBOT! A TOASTER! COME OUT HERE AND *GET* ME!"

The Cave crackled with confusion. *Why was that crazy kid stepping on his hand?* They were not yet convinced.

The putty. That new patch of wrist Betsy had so carefully formed into place. It was only there for show, a structural weakness. It was my only chance.

Sorry, Betsy.

I heard the collective gasp as my fingers scooped into my wrist as though breaking through frosting on a birthday cake. I lifted a handful of the artificial, skin-colored stuff away, holding it aloft for the basketball fans to judge. And judge it they did.

"It's a—"

"Ahhh!"

"—a—"

"ROBOT!"

"No!"

"A ROBOT!"

"Get it!"

"*Kill* it!"

The Ceiling Fan was between me and Kanga now, unable to make his decision.

"Rip it apart!"

"KANGA!" I called. "RUN! GET OUT OF HERE. YOU CAN STILL—"

The floor rumbled as spectators piled down from the bleachers. I thought I saw Dr. Murphio dashing toward Kanga, but it could have been a different man in a Birds T-shirt. The Ceiling Fan stepped toward me, but a throng enwrapped me first. I felt my forearm getting pulled on, but the rod seemed too strong for them, and my new hand remained on my body.

"*GO FOR THE HEAD!*" they screamed.

Another group was pointing toward the basketball hoop, shouting:

"There it is!"

"How'd it get up there?"

"Jumped!"

"Just flew up there!"

"Goddamn robot can *jump*!"

Through a haze of human activity, I made out Kanga's supple form. He was perched on the basketball rim, balancing. I heard him shout *"Lí wǒ gē yuǎn diǎn!"*

Leave my brother alone!

"Shitting robot!"

"How do we get it down?"

"Quick! It's on the move!"

"Where'd it—"

I glimpsed Kanga leap toward the nearest Cave exit before hands covered my eyes, then more hands, until I was wearing a gallows hood of hands, blocking out the fluorescent lights. Thumbs hooked into my nose and mouth, the spongy flesh beneath my chin. I heard a muffled count to three. *You're welcome, brother.* The hands pulled—

25

THE SHORTEST CHAPTER in *The Directions* was titled "Purpose," and it was a one-question quiz:

> What is your purpose on Earth?
> A: To take it over
> B: To serve it

There was no upside-down answer key at the bottom of the page. We were supposed to have a family discussion, I think, but Mom flipped to the next page, saying, "*Buh*. Boys, the answer is *buh*." She had trouble with individual letters when her battery was low. And the following chapter was her favorite: "How to Be Happy." It was a list, and Mom loved those. Twenty-four pages of things like "Pick up garbage from the sidewalk," "Get a cat," and "Don't pour your used grease down the kitchen drain." Mom began to read slowly, expressionlessly, performing each item on the list in her imagination as she read it aloud. She didn't notice when Kanga wandered off to watch TV. She just kept reading the list: "Stand outdoors for seven minutes . . . Vacuum the living room . . . Put on a clean pair of socks . . ."

I was still stuck on "Purpose." The answer couldn't be as simple as *ah* or *buh*. I didn't want to take over the world, not exactly, but nor did I desire an eternity of taking orders from humans in middle management. Mom had nineteen pages to go: ". . . Buy a box of crayons from the store . . . Open the box of crayons and smell them . . . Pick three of your favorite colors and draw—"

"Shut up," I said.

Mom crawled out of her processor. She blinked at me.

"I *am* going to take over the world," I announced. "Starting now. Starting with *you*. Shut up about how to be happy!" And I realized it was the truth. I wanted to take over everything. I wanted to *change* everyone: Mom, Dad, Kanga, myself. "Do you hear me, Mom? I'm going to take over the—"

"Go plug in, Darryl," she said, almost in a whisper. She closed *The Directions*. "We'll keep reading tomorrow night."

"No!" I screamed. "We'll never read it again! I hate *The Directions*! I hate—"

Mom's hand shot out and grabbed my wrist. She dragged me across the room and jammed my fingers into my outlet. She repeated, "We'll keep reading tomorrow night."

I did as she ordered. I sat on the floor and charged up, and it became clear to me that the answer was *ah*. Even for Mom. *Ah*. We were all trying to take over the world. One room at a time. Mom had won this battle. The living room belonged to her. For now.

● ● ●

My eyes blinked open.

A brown blur was all I could discern of my surroundings. Was this robotic death? Obsolescence? Was I inside a coffin? Was I being shipped back to China? And why did it smell like *leather*?

I was in the back seat of a car. And I wasn't alone.

"Look at me, Darryl. Refocus your eyes, my son. Look at your father."

Dr. Murphio's face eclipsed the dim overhead light. I could smell his laundry detergent, *Mom's* laundry detergent, mixed with the sharp scent of his sweat. Dr. Murphio's forehead was glistening. He breathed through his nose. We were sitting in the back seat of a car.

"Your processor has been down for about an hour, but I've repaired you as best I can. Try to move your body."

I moved my hands—the regular one and the rubber one with a divot taken out of the wrist. They succeeded in dragging their fingernails across the smooth leather car seat. Then I wiggled my toes, looking down to see my sneakers nodding slightly at the ends of my legs. Sneakers? Hadn't I been wearing black dress shoes earlier this afternoon in the Cave?

The Cave. It all came back to me.

"*Kanga!*" I blurted, and a fountain of sparks sprayed from my neck, singeing the bottom of my chin and sizzling the leather all around me.

"No talking!" cried Dr. Murphio, wiping out the tiny flames. "Your neck still needs work." The doctor began digging through his toolbox on the seat between us.

I brought a hand to my neck, feeling where the skin and sponging had been ripped due to my head getting tug-o-warred off my body. I found a three-inch gap where I could reach inside my neck and tap the new plastic tubes connecting my head to my shoulders. These tubes must have been replacements from Dr. Murphio's toolbox. I could taste their crispness in the back of my throat, like air filtered through a new vacuum cleaner bag. My fingertip accidentally brushed a hot wire—

"*Ow!*"

Dr. Murphio leaned away from the shower of sparks. "Darryl, please!" He reached toward my neck, as if to strangle me, but instead began spinning black electrical tape around the entire gash, forming a protective choker. "Try speaking now."

"Kanga—" I rasped, the back of my throat burnt and sore. "*What happened to Kanga?*"

"He escaped. Thanks to you, Darryl. Your brave efforts to intervene allowed Kanga enough time to break through the exit doors. The crowd nearly grabbed him, but . . ." Dr. Murphio closed his eyes, recalling the scene. "I have no idea where he's gone. That's where you come in, son. Together, we're going to locate Kanga. *You're* going to locate him. Think! Where is your brother right now?"

"Our apartment?"

"Blast it, son, we're at the apartment. I've already checked upstairs, and Kanga didn't come home. He must be somewhere else. Tell me where."

I glanced out the car window. We were parked at Shimmering Terraces, near the dumpster. The building itself seemed to be asleep with nearly all its windows darkened. It occurred to me: Dr. Murphio had repaired me only *after* checking our apartment. What if he'd found Kanga upstairs chugging a gallon of milk? Would he have still been motivated to fix me? Which begged another question: "How did *I* escape the Cave?"

"We don't have time for this, Darryl. Tell me where—"

"How?"

"After decapitating you and dumping your body in a garbage can, those monsters went after Kanga. The chaos followed your brother through the doors. I thought it best to collect your remains while I had the chance. Nobody seemed to notice when I dragged you out to my car. They probably figured I was just cleaning up the mess."

I was a ghost. The people of Hectorville assumed me dead, but here I was. Risen again. Haunting a house was the last thing I wanted to do, except maybe our own apartment. A memory stung my processor: sitting in that comfy spot behind the orange chair, my fingers plugged into the wall, paging through *Computerworld*, sipping a jug of vinegar. I looked at our building. There was our living room window! But Dr. Murphio would never allow it. My purpose was to do his bidding. To help him find the only robot he really cared about.

"There's a tool shed over on the other side of the building," I said. "Sometimes Kanga hung out there when he wanted to be alone. I can go check—"

"I'll go. You mustn't leave this car, Darryl. I've changed your clothes, but if anyone recognizes you, there's no telling what they'll do. My son, you are invaluable to me now. I'll be back soon. Make a list of other places your brother might have gone." With that, Dr. Murphio disappeared into the shadows.

I waited until he was around the corner, then unlocked my door and stepped to the parking lot. I felt the cold breeze whistle through the tape on my neck, sending a shiver through my frame. I should have been warm enough; Dr. Murphio had changed me into jeans and a winter coat. He'd stuffed a scarf in my pocket too, which I managed to wrap around my neck to hide my wound.

I was suddenly overcome with the feeling that I wasn't alone. Could Kanga be nearby, hiding? I opened the lid of the dumpster, got on my tiptoes and peered inside, faintly expecting to see his remains. Instead, I was met by the stench of spoiled food. I wobbled backward, crunching the snow in the direction of the woods. Had he fled there? To the tree where we'd buried the woman's arm?

I froze. It wasn't him. Someone *else* was watching me.

"Ready to go, snail breath?"

Brooke Noon straddled her bike. Her pink backpack was tight against her shoulders. Her pants were tucked into her moon boots. The strings of her hoodie were tied in a knot under her chin. Her ski gloves gripped the handlebars.

"I thought you'd never get here," she said, trying to look irritated with me, but her face radiated excitement. "Grab your bike, or climb on mine. The bus leaves in half an hour."

"Something happened, Brooke."

"Hop on my handlebars. You can tell me on the way."

"I'm not going."

She slipped off her seat, stomped her kickstand down, and raised her fists toward me. "You lied." Steam hissed from her mouth. "You said you were taking the bus to Memphis. With me. It's time to go."

"You don't understand. They know about me and Kanga now. Everybody does. You have to leave, Brooke, because if you get caught talking to me, you're dead. Kanga escaped, and I have to find him. That's why I have to stay. Kanga—"

"Kanga? KANGA? He was the reason you wanted to leave in the first place! We are going to Memphis."

"He needs me. I didn't think he did anymore, but he does."

"You lied to me." She swung her backpack off her shoulders and held it between us. "And you lied to her." She unzipped it for me to look inside.

A white garbage sack was the backpack's only contents, the top of which Brooke had cinched closed with a twist tie. She shook the bag, and whatever was inside made a wet, sloshing sound, like Brooke had brought along a collection of goldfish. But as I leaned closer, I saw that the liquid streaking the inside of the sack was *black*. A tiny skull then bobbed toward the top, as if listening through the plastic with its miniature human ear.

"I know she wasn't part of our plan," Brooke whispered. "But our plan can still work. I just couldn't leave her there. I tried to, but—" She stared down at her baby sister. "She won't be trouble, Darryl. Not much. And you can help us. You could fix her after we get to Memphis." The anger drained from Brooke's face, leaving only desperation and fear. "The plan can still work."

I looked at Elecsandra, folded up and wrapped in plastic. "Is she dead?"

"I shut her off. She has a head like yours with that special switch."

"If her head's like mine, maybe she was made by Gravy Robotics. Our creator, Dr. Murphio—this is his car. We can show Elecsandra to him, and maybe—"

Brooke hugged her sister to her chest. "I'm not giving her to any more adults."

In truth, I already knew Dr. Murphio hadn't created Elecsandra. Gravy Robotics made sons, not daughters. I recalled the woman who had designed me, Renee, the photo of her in the Gravy hallway, that everlasting scream. Brooke was wise to keep Dr. Murphio away from her sister.

"It's just like Buford says in your story." Brooke recited the line: "'*These robots just don't know when to quit.*' That's us, Darryl. I'm not quitting. I want to go to Memphis with you. Let's go."

From across town, I could hear Pastor Noon screaming his girls' names. My processor was overloaded with so much conflicting information, yet somehow it all added up to an easy decision, one that wasn't really a decision at all. "I'm not quitting either," I told her. "I wish you and Elecsandra the best of luck. Good-bye, Brooke."

Instead of wiping the tears from her eyes (there were none), she pressed down on the garbage sack, causing two tiny knees to pop upward like a frog's, and she zipped her pink backpack shut. "You got no idea what's waiting for you in town." She secured the backpack on her shoulders, grinning with hatred. "Keep your stupid luck."

● ● ●

I tabulated an exhaustive list of Hectorville locations where Kanga might be hiding. Number one was the spaceship in Umber Park. "Drive us to the spaceship," I ordered Dr. Murphio from the back seat. "And if he's not there, we'll find him somewhere else."

But Hectorville was no longer the sleepy Michigan town I'd grown up in. My hometown had become haunted, and not by a host of spiteful ghouls but by its own citizens. Dr. Murphio slowed the car to observe their abnormal behavior. It was eight thirty at night, but nobody was getting ready for bed or even staying in their houses to watch TV. Posses of men in full winter garb were collected in driveways, plotting and planning on the hoods of their trucks. They held beer bottles, baseball bats, and toasters. Their dogs were howling. Mothers stood in their front yards directing platoons of children, armed with toasters themselves, to battle a horde of imaginary robots. Tonight they celebrated a deranged version of Christmas Eve, the entire town waiting up for Santa to deliver a single present: Kanga Livery. No holiday jingles fueled the festive atmosphere, only *the crackle*, the sound of a million magnets clicking together then apart, then together—the humans performing their separate tasks in collective rhythm.

"Do you hear it?" I asked Dr. Murphio. "That crackle? It's never been this loud before. I heard it in the Cave too, riling everybody up."

"No," said Dr. Murphio, shaking his head. "I can't hear anything."

Yet there was a rhythm to his shaking . . .

We approached a police blockade. Dr. Murphio tossed me a winter hat, which I pulled down over my eyes. I pretended to be asleep as he rolled down his window. "We're just trying to get home, Officer," stammered Dr. Murphio. "I was out at the mall with my son. What's all this? Did something happen?"

"You could say so," the police officer said. "We have a robot about. Teenager. He's running loose, but—"

"A robot!"

"We need folks to call 911 if they see a teenager in a basketball jersey."

Though my eyes were covered, I felt the beam of a flashlight wash over my body.

"How can I help?" asked Dr. Murphio. "After I get him in bed, what do you need done?"

"It's our official policy that folks stay indoors. But between you and me, a dragnet is what's going to catch this thing. The whole town working together, which is what I see happening. You can just feel it in the air. We're going to catch that greasy bastard, and it'll be because of regular people like you. So go home and get your boy safe. Then you head outside with your neighbors. All you folks know the lay of your properties. Scour them. This is how Hectorville is going to stay safe."

I heard the two men shake hands, and we continued into the heart of town, where the traffic was churning slowly in both directions. I peeked out the window. The sidewalk near the library was buoyant with snow-suited children riding on the shoulders of adults, waving signs: GO HOME ROBOTS!, NO TOASTERS!, and GOD HATES COMMUNIST CHINA'S RO-BOTS. Many residents had toasters tucked under their arms. The parking lot at the grocery store was filled with cars, as people were stocking up on provisions for the long night: boxes of donuts, bags of chips, cases of beer. Some people had lawn chairs on the side of the street, huddled in half-circles around portable propane heaters. A sudden loud crackle caused the entire town to flinch. They looked around at one another, confused, then got back to what they were doing. We drove past Cobra Burger, which was bursting at the seams with teenagers whose food sat untouched on their trays, everyone too excited to eat. We were rolling by the cemetery when the truck before us slammed on its brakes, halting the entire procession. A flashlight shined on the gravestones. "THERE HE IS!" a woman shouted, and men began pouring from their vehicles, sprinting into the cemetery from all directions. "THERE!" she directed them. "HE'S JUMPING!" The flashlight swung back and forth, freeze-framing the searchers as they disappeared into the darkness.

The crackle was deafening. Dr. Murphio rubbed his temples in weary synchronization. That awful noise spiked, then tapered off when an animal trotted out from behind a gravestone: a deer. It danced into the road, pausing before a stopped truck, immobile in its headlights. Someone let a toaster fly through an open car window, clunking the deer with it. The thing leapt away. The men returned from the cemetery and climbed back aboard their vehicles. The convoy resumed its slow course.

"Kanga's dead," said Dr. Murphio, staring blankly at the taillights ahead of him.

"No."

"There are too many of them. I'm driving us back to Detroit."

"You can't give up. We have to find him."

"It's over, Darryl. If they haven't found him yet, they will. And when they do, they'll destroy him."

"No. We're not leaving until we find Kanga, dead or alive. I was programmed for this. You call yourself his father? You can't leave your child behind. Both of us are programmed to take care of him. I'm not letting you quit."

"Programmed?" Dr. Murphio laughed. "To take care of Kanga? You, of all robots, shouldn't be lecturing me about how to follow a program." He stopped his car on the side of the road and turned to face me. "Tell me, Darryl. What do you think your program is?"

The answer was simple: to conceal my robotic identity, to make sure Kanga did the same, to be a *good robot*. These had been the building blocks of my entire life. And even if they crumbled down—like they had this afternoon—I was certain my program would be to stack the blocks up again. To be a *better* robot. But I couldn't say any of this to Dr. Murphio, not with that horrible grin on his face. The truth was I had no idea what my program was.

"Basketball," Dr. Murphio said. "You and Kanga shared this program, along with all your brothers. My vision was a whole generation of basketball-playing sons, a team that would be brought together, when the time was right, for a grand introduction. Can you see the stage, Darryl? The identical jerseys? The name on their chests wouldn't read 'Gravy Robotics.' It would read 'USA.' Red, white, and blue! How could anyone resist those magnificent boys playing for our country?" Bitterness narrowed his eyes. "Every country in the world would fall beneath them. Country after country. Foe after foe. Vanquished. Annihilated. *China*—" Dr. Murphio stopped himself. "But if not a team, how about *one* perfect boy? Might I be allowed to have that? *One* boy? *One?*" His eyes grew wide, following an invisible butterfly bobbing through the darkness. "*Kanga?*" He blinked the thought away. "There will be more. Always more sons to create. Perfect sons. We'll go home to Detroit. We'll get a good night's rest, and tomorrow we'll begin work on the *next* generation. I know you went snooping through my office, Darryl. You saw the specifications for Ma. I need a robot like you, curious and inventive. Your brother was the first robot I'd modeled after Ma. You will be vital in pinpointing what went wrong with Kanga and how to fix it."

I felt a terrible itch in my new fingers. They yearned to hold my basketball in the triple-threat position one last time. I was the basketball kid. But the moniker felt like an insult now, like a piece of paper someone had taped to my back, BASKETBALL KID, just to make everyone laugh. "I'm leaving," I told him. "And you can't stop me."

"Darryl Livery, go to your room this instant."

The magic words hit me first in the processor, a blast of uncontrollable heat, as though my deepest memories were being set on fire. A moment later I realized Dr. Murphio's order had paralyzed me too. I couldn't move a muscle. I was stuck, motionless, in his car, which had begun rolling forward. To Detroit. Worst of all, Dr. Murphio's magic words, *GO TO YOUR ROOM THIS INSTANT*, were blocking out anything else I tried to think about:

Dad's body shaking when he laughed—

Go to your room this instant.

A spider crawling on the ceiling in our apartment—

Go to your room this instant.

Brooke rolling her eyes—

Go to your room this instant.

Kanga singing a Cobra Burger commercial—

Go to your room this instant.

Mom saying, "What's the magic word?"

Go to your room this instant.

"No, Darryl." Mom leaning closer to me. "You know what the magic word is."

"Thank you?" I whispered, and suddenly I could imagine Mom's face glowing like the inside of a microwave—because nothing charged her up like hearing those words. "Thank you, Mom," I said again, this time loud enough to startle Dr. Murphio.

He glanced back at me, shocked. *"Darryl Livery, go to—"*

I yanked open the door, tumbling to the side of the road. The open-air crackle drowned his voice to nothing. I lifted myself from the sidewalk and began marching with the Hectorville army, looking for Kanga.

Did all ghosts feel the thrill of invisibility as they floated among those who had destroyed them? Or was it just the robot in me, perfectly comfortable pretending to be human? I put my hands in my coat pockets. I stared at the ground as I moved with the herd, my hat low over my eyes.

We lumbered past the duck pond.

Past Doug's Video Rentals.

We were nearly to Umber Park when the ground beneath us began to shake, as if God were punishing Hectorville with an earthquake. But this rumble was of our own making: a stampede of humans breaking into a jog, streaming in from everywhere. Cars were left in the middle of the road, their occupants joining the flood. Sweating faces jostled above me, wearing glee and fear, blinking in rapid unison with the crackle. Nobody said a word, but nobody needed to. The crackle had found its electric voice, buzzing this message:

We found him . . . We found him . . . We found him . . .

26

SQUEEZED THROUGH THE CROWD to reach the crackle's epicenter, the town basketball court. A cheer erupted around me: "ROBOT DIE! ROBOT DIE! ROBOT DIE!" The cold night air was suddenly sweltering amid this human mass. My shoulders and head brushed against the actual toasters they carried. Not just toasters but radios, microwaves, CD players, pocket televisions . . . it seemed every household appliance was represented here. "ROBOT DIE! ROBOT DIE! ROBOT DIE!" They raised the appliances above their heads, jabbing heavenward in rhythm with the crackle. A man with his arms full of toasters pressed one to my belly. I recognized him as Mr. Bodet, owner of Hectorville's only electronics store. "Here ya go, kid." I held the toaster with my new hand, cradling it like a football, and bulldozed my way forward, fighting for yards, until I found myself courtside, standing in the ring of dirt Kanga had made when he stuffed my throat full of grass. On the court, I hoped to see one final glimpse of my brother.

Instead I saw the Ceiling Fan.

His tiny car occupied the center circle, and the huge man stood on its roof. The basketball team remained just outside the boundaries of the court, watching their assistant coach carefully. Each boy held a toaster or a radio or a blender, its cord dangling at his feet. James Botty gripped his toaster with a wide, proud stance, like there were toothpicks in his armpits. He had mastered the triple-threat position. The players had changed into their dress clothes and winter jackets—all except for Rye, who was still clad in his jersey, shorts, and high-tops. His skin was covered in a steaming orange rash, and tears streaked from his bewildered, goggle-less eyes. Mr. Belt stood with his team, his face awash with confusion and disgust, as if the Birds were losing a scrimmage against a middle school team and he'd just been ejected from the game.

Packed behind the basketball team was the town of Hectorville, like a tornado had sucked everyone up and spit them down courtside. Mothers, fathers, grandparents, grandchildren, all chanting: "ROBOT DIE! ROBOT DIE! ROBOT DIE!" I saw most of our teachers in attendance. Mrs. Galvin, Mrs. Asquith, and Mrs. Clinow. Had they carpooled to save money? Mrs. Deal, Mrs. Zweer—and even Mr. Jacobowhite. Their minds were crackled. "ROBOT DIE! ROBOT DIE! ROBOT DIE!" Brooke's parents were there. Pastor and Mrs. Noon, standing beside one of the baskets. Brooke's mom wore a sleek white coat; the pastor was dressed for church. Neither was chanting.

Standing on his car, the Ceiling Fan presided over them, looking as confident as I'd ever seen him. He wore the expression of a man about to nail a job interview, grinning at the toasters he saw throughout the crowd. At last, he raised a hand high above his head, grabbing control of the volume then slowly lowering it, hushing them to a person.

There was silence.

"James?" his voice crackled.

James Botty circled toward the trunk of the car. He set down his toaster, found a key in his pocket and unlocked the trunk. Without pausing to inspect what was inside, James grabbed my brother by the armpits, pulled him out, and dropped him on the court. Kanga's hair and white game uniform were covered with grime and twigs. He managed to crawl into an all-fours position, but his battery was so drained he couldn't raise his chin to look forward. He merely stared at the cement between his hands, shivering like a frightened horse.

"Get the toaster!" someone screamed.

"Why don't you take my job first, robot?" another asked.

"Die!"

"Toaster, you look at me! I dare you!"

"We don't want you here!"

"Crush him!"

"Get back to China!"

"Cut that crap out," said the Ceiling Fan. "China? You want to send him back to *China*? That's just what he wants! This ain't some silly game. He ain't a person, like you or me. This thing lied to us. This thing endangered us. This thing—"

"*Wŏmen dōushì dōngxī*," said Kanga.

We're all things.

The Ceiling Fan closed his eyes. He sucked in air, long and loud through his teeth, the entire crowd waiting for his response. "We're gonna break this thing into a million bits." He swung his finger around his head, pointing to everyone surrounding the court. "We're *all* going do it!"

The crowd screamed its approval.

"TIME OUT!" hollered Mr. Belt, stepping onto the court, bringing his hands together in a *T* above his head. He walked up beside Kanga but kept his eyes on the Ceiling Fan. "We coaches have a saying, Simms. I should've taught it to you sooner. 'In loco parentis—'"

"BOOOOOOO!" somebody yelled.

Mr. Belt continued: "It means we have to take care of these boys, no matter who they are, *in place of their parents*. I don't see Kanga's mom or dad—"

"Because he doesn't have 'em!" interrupted another.

"As coaches, Simms, we are contractually obligated to ask ourselves, would we be doing this—whatever it is we're doing on this court—if Kanga Livery were our *own* son?"

The crowd screamed for Mr. Belt to get off the court, but the Ceiling Fan waved a hand for silence. "Let me see if I got this straight. You want me to pretend I got a son that's a robot?"

"I want you to pretend your son is *Kanga Livery*."

The Ceiling Fan grinned. "Then I'm putting the boy up for adoption."

The spectators erupted in laughter and approval.

"See, Belt? I got a whole town of people just dying to take him off my hands for me. Isn't that right everybody? *Scream* if you want to be this toaster's daddy tonight!"

Mr. Belt wobbled as the wave of sound crashed against him. He took a final look at Kanga. I read the words on his lips: *If you got any big'uns left, Livery, now's the time.* He stumbled off the court and the crowd quieted down, eager for the Ceiling Fan to give them the chance to destroy rather than just cheer.

"You people are why I love this town. You came prepared tonight. You thought ahead, brought your toasters, your radios and TVs, and for that you will be rewarded. Everybody's going to get their turn. However, some of us have endured this robot more than others, every day for an entire basketball season. These fine boys here." The Ceiling Fan gestured to the basketball team. "James Botty had this robot sniffed out from the beginning. You got the honors, James."

James picked up his toaster. He tossed it from hand to hand. "I ain't wasting my throw now. I'm gonna get him when he least expects it. That's how me and Kanga go, huh, friend?"

"Fair enough," said the Ceiling Fan.

"What's wrong with that kid?" somebody asked. "Kill the toaster! I'm ready! Choose me!"

"When's my turn to smear some junk?"

"Yeah, let's go!"

"Everybody calm down," ordered the Ceiling Fan. "I got a whole team that's ready." He stared at his players. "Next man up."

None of the Birds stepped forward. They shuffled in place, holding their toasters with just the tips of their fingers.

The Ceiling Fan shook his head. "You'll regret this day. The day I gave you the opportunity to go first, the day you turned coward. Hell, my senior year, if we had a toaster pinned down like this, I would've fought my best friend just to—"

Rye stepped toward Kanga, his tiny eyeballs rolling in their sockets, worthless. He blew snot from his nose then sniffed at the air. He lurched toward my brother, palming his toaster as he went.

"Here we go!" cheered the Ceiling Fan. "Give him some of that persistence, Rye-Guy!"

Rye stopped directly above Kanga, squinted down at him. He used the fingers of his free hand to make a telescope, zeroing in on the back of Kanga's head, a point-blank target. Rye raised his toaster and the crackle got in my eyes. I couldn't watch.

"*HEY!*" the humans all screamed. "*You can't do that!*"

I looked: The toaster was no longer in Rye's hands—but neither was it embedded in the back of Kanga's head. *Mr. Belt* had the toaster now. His boyish, mischievous expression told me he had sprinted onto the court and plucked the toaster away from the big man at the last second, an impromptu Statue of Liberty play. But now that the toaster was in his possession, Mr. Belt had nowhere to go with it. He was trapped, just like Kanga. The crowd taunted the coach, jabbing their fingers at him and howling. Several people raised their toasters, as if to begin the bombardment.

"Catch that son of a bitch," ordered the Ceiling Fan, "and get him off my court."

Thus began a farcical game of tag, Rye lumbering after the red-faced loco parentis. Mr. Belt's loafers slapped the cement like clown shoes as he ran circles around the Ceiling Fan's car, delighting the small children in the crowd. But then Rye caught the coach's arm. Rye made a fist—everyone gasped—and clubbed Mr. Belt on the head. The toaster dropped from his hands, and the spectators shuddered, their brains rejecting the sight of a teenager assaulting an adult so brazenly. Rye bear-hugged his dazed coach and hauled him off the court.

Just then a blender went spinning through the air, cord wagging behind it. Its asymmetrical weight caused the thing to dip, as if hit by a sudden gust of wind, and smash ten feet shy of Kanga, though several of the blender's shards of glass skittered against his bare knees.

The Ceiling Fan squinted into the crowd, unsure if he should berate the thrower or relent to the mob's restless energy. "Fine!" He threw up his hands. "Hectorville, you've been patient. Now *all* of you! Make that robot pay!"

My brother didn't budge.

From all directions toasters took to the air. Black toasters. White toasters. Chrome toasters. Some were so shiny they reflected a momentary misshapen image of the host from which they flew. My brother remained on all fours. His head was bowed. "Run," I whispered, and it wasn't until the toasters were mere inches from his head that Kanga became Magic Johnson. Scratch that. Not Magic exactly, besides the fact that he seemed to disappear from sight, allowing the devices to crash cleanly through him and shatter on the court. He'd actually become *Ben* Johnson, the Olympian, exploding from his four-point stance in the hundred-meter final. Like that sprinter, Kanga arrived so instantaneously on the other side of the court that he *had* to have cheated.

"What?"

"Huh?"

"Where'd he—?"

"How'd he get over *there*?"

"Damned robot!"

"Gimme another toaster. *I'll* slow him down!"

Kanga had awoken. He was up. He had escaped the initial wave of appliances, but there remained a thick human wall surrounding the entire court, and most of their ammunition had yet to be thrown. Those still wielding weapons took careful, deliberate aim. The Ceiling Fan crossed his arms and watched my brother make a slow zigzag through the fishbowl of space.

"Kill him!"

"Break him in two!"

A man standing courtside rifled his toaster at Kanga.

Kanga dodged it.

A shower radio zoomed toward his head.

Kanga swerved from its path.

They came one after another, and my brother leapt every which way, ducking and weaving from the incoming assault. The court was filling with debris.

"Damn!" the crowd gasped when a toaster barely missed his shoulder.

"Reload!" urged the Ceiling Fan. "Get some of these toasters and throw them again!"

Three brave spectators dared to run onto the court, snatch up a toaster, and run back.

Kanga continued to swim through the barrage of projectiles some-how untouched, contorting his body with a preternatural awareness of each toaster's corkscrewed approach. The things didn't fly straight. Some nose-dived the second they left a human's hand; others appeared to be off course at first, only to veer toward my brother at the last second. He dodged them all. But this dance couldn't last forever. His battery had to be running on fumes, and the crowd was getting used to throwing these particular projectiles. They were learning Kanga's pattern of movement, their tosses inching closer and closer to plunking him. If Kanga didn't vary his method, somebody was bound to get lucky and knock him off balance, and, in a blink, my brother would be buried.

I was inside the enemy, a fake head among the thousand others, all thinking with the same infected brain. Did these "people" even notice the crackle anymore? Or was it a mosquito mind, immune to its own horrible buzz? Another toaster missed Kanga, and I watched the multitude of heads shake furiously. Except for one. Except for *her*. The late arrival in the back of the crowd. Another outlier, like me.

Brooke Noon.

She should've been anywhere but here. The pink backpack on her shoulders was leaking oil. Brooke! Did she realize her parents were standing right in front of her? Flee, Brooke, flee! Instead, she glared at me. Brooke was adept at communicating with looks, and I didn't need an interpreter: *Why are you standing around, Darryl? THIS is why you stood me up? To watch your brother get killed? BORING. Do something, you chicken, before I have to do it myself . . .*

But do what? I still had my toaster cradled to my belly. Should I chuck it at each human, one by one? That would never work. There were too many of them for a conventional fight. And whom was I even fighting? It wasn't the humans. Their warm bodies were simply the vessel for the Ceiling Fan's depravity—but it wasn't him either. The crackle. It had been stoked by the Ceiling Fan, and now it was raging on its own. The crackle was my true opponent, the web of wires connecting these otherwise independent minds. How could I snip every wire? They would just grow back. What could I do?

Since it was impossible to silence the crackle, I would just have to get *louder* than it.

My entire life I'd been passing the ball to Kanga. From Mom forcing me to share it, back when I was still the basketball kid, to being his rebounder on this very court. Little did I know that all that passing had been preparation for this moment . . .

"*Kangaroo!*" I called, but it wasn't my voice. It was Dad's. And when my brother looked in my direction, I cocked the toaster in my new hand to heave it toward him, mouthing the words: "*Layup!*"

Kanga caught the toaster in stride. He knew better than to stop. He flipped the thing from hand to hand as he ran with it.

"Is that your mother?" somebody hollered, but most in the crowd seemed unnerved by the sight of Kanga holding his own toaster. Was he taunting them? Was he actually going to *throw* it at someone? Was he keeping it to use as a shield? As he jogged from one end of the court to the other, the crackle raised in pitch around him, stressing the brains of the closest spectators.

"*Layup!*" I shouted again as Dad—the word *wussy* caught in my throat. "*Layup, son! Show 'em what you got!*"

It was risky, shouting encouragement to Kanga, but the humans didn't seem to notice me. They were too focused on my brother and the weapon in his hands.

But it wasn't a weapon—not like they imagined. On the next trip under a basket, Kanga reached the toaster high and casually flicked it against the backboard, like I'd seen him do thousands of times. It fell cleanly through the hoop. A layup.

"AHHH!" the crowd grunted in frustration. He *was* taunting them. Everyone narrowed their eyes at Kanga zooming around the court. A group of young men counted down from three and launched their toasters in unison—a plan Kanga must have seen coming, as he leapt seven feet in the air while the toasters flew harmlessly beneath his sneakers—one of which destroyed a headlight on the Ceiling Fan's car. Everyone held their breath, waiting for the huge man to berate the reckless thrower. But the Ceiling Fan's scowl was fixed solely on Kanga.

My brother landed, and his hand dipped below his knees to scoop up another toaster.

"Jump shot, boy!"

He carried it across midcourt, came to a jump stop at the elbow, briefly sized up his shot, then tossed it up . . . his aim looked horrible, at least a foot to the right . . . but as the toaster spun, it fishtailed *left* . . . and rattled down through the hoop.

The crowd was all but silent. For several laps, nobody threw a toaster, or even raised it above shoulder level. They all just watched. "*Three!*" Dad's voice rang out, and Kanga floated up a third shot from behind the three-point line, his toaster zigzagging through the air before exploding against the back of the rim, its pieces falling through the netting. In response, several humans went so far as to nudge the person next to them. Others were confused by the turn of events. Shaken. They itched their necks, unsure what to do with the steam inside. Then the children got to work. They took over my job of encouraging my brother and began *counting* Kanga's shots. At first, it was a scattered handful of grade-schoolers, perhaps not even aware that their mouths were registering what their eyes were seeing: ". . . fooooour . . ." they whispered, ". . . *fiiiiiiiiiiive* . . ."

But with each number, their voices expanded in volume and enthusiasm. "... *SIIIIIIIIIIX!*..."

If Kanga were to miss a shot, the spell would break.

But he wasn't missing. Not tonight.

He was *making*.

I had seen my brother in this kind of trance before, but the crowd hadn't. They leaned forward as Kanga jump-stopped at the NBA three-point distance, raised his toaster above his head, and released it toward the hoop, his fingers tickling the air. Kanga didn't watch his shot fly, a bloated bird bobbing through the air, or wait for it to splash through the rim, or even acknowledge the children's roar when it did, "*TEEEEEEEEEEN!*" He just kept circling the court, making his way to the opposite hoop, scanning the ground for another toaster to launch . . .

Robots aren't known for their spontaneity. I wasn't, anyway. Before taking any action, I always needed a plan. And a backup plan, and a plan C, and an escape plan, should any of my initial plans implode. So imagine my surprise when I stepped from the crowd onto the basketball court. When I knelt and scooped up a toaster. When I called out, "Brother!"

Kanga looked at me with shock—then joy, then confusion—but I didn't give him time to process any of these emotions.

"Catch!"

He caught the toaster I threw to him.

He shot it.

"*ELEEEEEEEVEN!*" the children responded.

There was no plan. No target outcome. I'd run no numbers before becoming Kanga's rebounder—nor would I, until our shootaround was over. The only number that mattered was the one that grew each time the kids yelled.

"*TWEEEEEEEEEELVE!*"

I was slower on my feet than Kanga, sometimes having to kneel and dig through the shattered remains to find an appropriate toaster for him to shoot. My passes were haphazard, to say the least. But we found a rhythm, and Kanga's baskets seemed somehow more impressive after the toasters had come from me.

The children began cheering me on.

Kanga started launching toasters from farther away.

He swished his twentieth shot from near midcourt, and I spread my arms like an airplane and flew around the entire court, ending with a high five for my brother. Emboldened, I scooped up a toaster and tossed it to him behind the back. Kanga canned the next shot, and this time the children *and* adults erupted: "*TWENTY-OOOOONE!*"

I punched the air with unbridled joy, jumping as high as I could, screaming. *Brooke! Are you still watching? Here I am! Living entirely in the moment—*

Which ended when a toaster nailed me in the head, somersaulting me to the cement.

"Got him," announced the Ceiling Fan. I was flat on the ground, staring at his car. He'd climbed down and was now advancing toward me. "I thought we exterminated this one, but they're like cockroaches, always coming back." He snatched up another toaster, twisting it in his huge hands. "This was supposed to be a good time out here, but it's turning into a chore. Nobody's taking this seriously. Nobody but me."

Kanga stepped between me and the Ceiling Fan. I could feel warm air hissing from the back of my head. I had no idea if the rest of my body was damaged. I didn't even try to move. There was nowhere to crawl.

"Looks like Kanga wants to go first," said the Ceiling Fan. "I'm happy to adjust my schedule." Without breaking his stride, he raised his toaster, ready to smash it down on my brother.

Which was the exact reason I usually had a plan. Because the person with the plan was the person who could do the saving. *Me* saving *Kanga*. But now the roles had been flipped; I needed to be rescued. Kanga had no plan for that. He was all alone, staring up at the Ceiling Fan's toaster, which was streaking toward his face, when the Ceiling Fan balked.

Because Kanga wasn't alone.

James Botty was there. "You ain't touching him," said James, standing in front of my brother on his tiptoes. There was still a toaster in his hands, and James looked ready to use it.

"Gone soft?" asked the Ceiling Fan. "Or am I looking at another one of *them*?"

"You ain't ever killed a robot," growled James. "You ain't ever had to live with it."

"That's right. I'm not as lucky as you. I've been waiting my whole life for this, and now I got a benchwarmer standing in my way. You want to atone for your past deeds, James? You want to keep one of these greasy liars for a pet? You can have that busted one down there. But I'm taking Kanga."

The spectators stood with their mouths open, the correct reaction to this situation eluding them. Their eyes were on James Botty and the Ceiling Fan, but they might have been staring at themselves in the mirror, unable to recognize the face looking back.

"She was just a kid," said James. "*I* was a kid. Her arms were warm when I grabbed her. I can still feel her arms . . ."

"She was a liar," said the Ceiling Fan. "They trick you that way."

"She was warm . . ."

"These damn robots are so hard to kill. The one everybody says you killed—she killed herself, didn't she? You just disposed of the body. It ain't fair how hard they are to kill. Not when they got so many ways to kill us. But don't you worry, James. We know right where to get them now. *You* helped me learn how these robots work. These things we're throwing at them? Just for show." The Ceiling Fan tossed his toaster to the ground. He reached into his pocket and pulled out a folded piece of paper. It was *The Directions*, the page James ripped from the book—I recognized exactly which page just from seeing a wrinkled eighth of it: from chapter eighty-four, the diagram of our exhaust system. The Ceiling Fan didn't bother unfolding it; he just wanted James to see it again. "Killing a robot is about getting *inside* the thing." The Ceiling Fan returned the page to his pocket. "Snipping it in just the right spot, like we talked about, James. So step aside, and I'll show you where on Kanga. After all, it's my turn."

The crackle became whisper thin, as if from James Botty's fluttering eyelashes. He was back in time, on Mrs. Stover's bus, grabbing Molly Seed by the arms, feeling her warmth . . . the toaster slipped from his hands, clacking the cement, awakening him from the memory. He looked at the Ceiling Fan. "Tell them about Mr. Virgil."

"Virgil?" The Ceiling Fan grinned. "The toaster they got working at your school?"

"Mr. Virgil's *closet*."

At these words, the basketball team advanced onto the court, stepping over toasters, to stand with James. Even Mr. Belt and Rye wobbled out with them, the coach gripping his center by the shoulder, using the blinded boy for support. I was dumbfounded by the presence of the team, packed into a protective line between us and the Ceiling Fan, as if posing for a team photo. Had they discussed "Mr. Virgil's closet" beforehand, each of them recounting a similar story, resulting in this consensus? Or had James's words caught everyone off guard, compelling each of them to walk forward individually, struck—as I was—by an overwhelming sense of guilt for the parts they played? Either way, I was lying on the cement behind them, my brother with me, and I could no longer see the Ceiling Fan, though I could hear his voice clearly:

"We vandalized the toaster's closet. It was team building. That was before I knew you boys were a bunch of sympathizers."

"That ain't what happened in Mr. Virgil's closet. You took us in there one by one and made us help. We didn't have a choice. You made us watch the door while you climbed into the ceiling. You were going up there to—"

"Virgil's a damn toaster! Doesn't that count for anything with you? A toaster getting paid to sneak around your school all day!"

"You spied on our teachers going to the bathroom."

"Greasy robot-lover."

"Our teachers. You got up in the ceiling and watched them."

"And you wanted next dibs, James. All of you! I could see it in your faces! Not one of you tried to stop me."

I watched the cluster of teachers standing courtside. Mrs. Clinow, Mrs. Galvin, Mrs. Deal, Mrs. Asquith. They were staring at their feet, hiding their chins in the collars of their coats, ashamed—except Mrs. Zweer. She charged toward us. "*Come on*," Mrs. Zweer urged her colleagues. Soon they were all standing with the basketball team. What followed was a chain reaction. Young children ran onto the court from all angles, seemingly cognizant there was a choice to be made and that Kanga, the robot who had sunk all those toaster shots, was one of the options. Their parents looked on in panic as the kids filled in tiny gaps between the players and teachers. A handful of men and women trickled in too, adding human bodies to the barrier between us and the Ceiling Fan. But most of the people remained where they stood, off the court, watching.

"I did it for you boys." The Ceiling Fan's voice had an edge of desperation. "Everything I did was to bring you together. Like a team. Like *my* old teams. Being a Hectorville Bird was the best years of my life. We had traditions. And yeah, we raised hell. We were teenage boys! What are you, James? Or any of you? What kind of teammate goes blabbing secrets for the whole town to hear? *Team* secrets. That's what brings boys together. I was just passing the traditions on, like the ones before me did. But I misjudged this team. That Bird uniform used to *mean* something when I wore—"

"You never wore that uniform," said Mrs. Zweer. "You never played a game, Jason. I looked you up in the yearbook after seeing you in the hall again. Jason Simms, freshman team *manager*."

There was an uneasy pause, as if the Ceiling Fan were silently paging through an old yearbook himself, until he whispered: "But I practiced with the guys."

"Most persistent manager I ever had," said Mr. Belt. "They say Ceiling Fan Simms never lost a ball. But what's all this about a ladies' room?"

Mrs. Zweer clarified: "If you ever show your face at our school again, Jason, we'll call the police."

"This is *our* team now," said James Botty. "Get the hell out of here."

"Yeah!"

"Leave, Ceiling Fan!"

"Go!"

"We're done with you!"

The crackle was done too. Its absence left the remaining spectators exhausted and confused. Their faces betrayed a multitude of individual thoughts, but no one appeared certain of anything; they were silent, tilting an ear toward the court, waiting for the Ceiling Fan to get into his car and drive off, waiting for a new, unifying voice to tell them what to do next.

The Ceiling Fan was utterly defeated. He'd been exposed. Disgraced. If he ever wanted another job, he'd have to travel far away, at least to Ohio and maybe even Kentucky, where people's views on robots and team-building exercises were more aligned with his own. My fan clicked on as I waited for the sound of his car engine. But it was the Ceiling Fan's voice I heard next, and it was nowhere near his car. The man might have even been smiling: "Thanks for the advice, friends, but I didn't come here to talk about me."

Screams. Shouts. Shoes. Legs. The human wall began collapsing backward onto me and Kanga. "*Knife!*" someone shouted. "*He's got a knife!*" The basketball players used their athleticism to leap to safety. The children crouched into small protective balls. The teachers, eyes always open to the unexpected, stood their ground. Mrs. Zweer faced the Ceiling Fan—and the enormous knife in his hand. Where had the knife come from? Under his INVISIBLE SYSTEMS sweatshirt? A secret compartment on his body?

"Stop, Jason," said Mrs. Zweer. "Listen—"

The Ceiling Fan slashed her arm. Blood sprayed up through the slit in her coat. Mrs. Zweer simply watched herself leak, allowing the Ceiling Fan to walk past her, through the ruined wall of people. Straight to Kanga.

I had a front-row seat for the altercation. Kanga and the Ceiling Fan were giants from my worm's-eye view, a comic book cover: hero and villain crouched, teeth gritted, staring into each other's eyes. The Ceiling Fan was supposed to have a clever speech bubble: "How do you say *obsolete* in binary code?" Kanga's response would be humorless: "I've got a *different* lesson for you, scoundrel!" Their battle would be an undulating graph of who had the upper hand, requiring an entire issue to play out. But ultimately Kanga would win, with the final image being a bird's-eye view of my brother standing over the fallen Ceiling Fan.

Reality was much quicker. The Ceiling Fan thrust his knife into Kanga's abdomen, the exact spot my brother had identified last night while explaining to me how to kill a robot, the exact point of insertion, as described in *The Directions*, if one wanted to pinch—or in this case sever—the exhaust tube running up the right side of a robot's body from his processor. The Ceiling Fan twisted the knife in Kanga's guts, expanding the range of damage. Pink lubricant gushed against my brother's white basketball uniform. He fell to the ground, the knife sticking out of him. He began to buzz like a bee . . .

Who was I in this comic book? The fainting damsel? The bug-eyed reporter? Or just a face in the background, a featureless yellow smudge? With options like these, no wonder my processor decided to redraw me from scratch.

The crackle. It was back and stronger than ever, vibrating my entire head. All I could think about was the *sound*. My eyes only registered a blurred sketch of my actions, the shape of my hands performing a function in front of my face. I was dimly aware that I was no longer lying on the ground, but rather on top of something. Or someone. My body felt like a clenched fist. My processor issued a report that my objective (which was unknown to me) was being achieved with no resistance. Whatever I was doing, nothing could stop me. I was sure of that. Success was a matter of maintaining my current trajectory. Holding my current position. Blocking everything else out . . . Except I couldn't. *The crackle*. It was a physical force pounding outward from inside my skull casing. How I wished it would rupture my auditory sensors; I would be free of the awful sound! Instead, the crackle was my whole world. When my eyes refocused, I finally knew the source.

I had him by the throat. The pointer finger and thumb on my rubber hand were pinched together, crushing the Ceiling Fan's larynx between them. I was on top of him. My left hand covered his eyes. I was killing him.

I pressed my rubber hand down against his neck until my finger and thumb met with a satisfying *click* behind his esophagus, as if I were gripping my bike handle. Dad's hands were useless for most things but perfectly suited to clutching a man's windpipe. The skin on the Ceiling Fan's neck was taut now, white and bloodless, but not yet broken. Then my two fingers began to pull upward on the thick cord of his throat, drawing it away from his cervical spine. The crackle raged at me: *End him.*

But it wasn't the Ceiling Fan's crackle.

It was mine.

The crackle was coming from *me*.

My anger. My fear. My hatred. Every injustice I had ever faced. The Ceiling Fan would pay for them all. Every time hearing the word *toaster*, every panic at possibly being discovered, every guilty memory of my parents, every sentence in *The Directions*, every inch I never grew, every time calling myself obsolete, every knife sticking out of my brother.

Kanga.

I felt his warm fingers on my shoulder, but I knew better. This wasn't my brother's loving touch, but a trick of my processor. My brother was dead. I had seen the Ceiling Fan butcher him. Kanga's phantom fingers were a reminder of everything I'd lost. They were the reason to finish the deed quickly . . .

Instead, my rubber fingers opened. As if by some hidden muscle inside the rubber core, my hand released the Ceiling Fan's neck. *I'm not a killer.* The words jolted through my processor, awakening me, and the world became clear again. *I'm not a*—I fell away from the inert man, sprawling back into a bed of broken toasters.

The crackle was gone. *My* crackle. I could hear the calm Michigan night, a thousand humans gasping for air. My Incredible Hulk strength had been extinguished. I felt shrunken now, smaller than the day I called Detroit on my parents. I felt like a human emerging from the grip of a nightmare, one in which I'd witnessed myself doing the unfathomable. But I wasn't human. I wouldn't get to keep this dream a secret; it wouldn't be forgotten within the hour. Hundreds had just watched my nightmare. I could barely bring myself to look at them. *I'm not a killer!* I wanted to scream, but my actions had just screamed the opposite. I was *that* kind of robot. Not the kind that kept his thoughts to himself, blended in, and prayed for survival. I was the *other* kind. The robot of nightmares. The murderous, rubber-handed kind. The obsolete kind.

Except they weren't staring at me.

The spectators' jaws hung open with disbelief. It turned out there was a third kind of robot in this world, one that neither killed its enemies nor hid from them. With a knife sticking out of his guts, Kanga stood above the Ceiling Fan, offering his hand to the huge man to help him off the ground. "*Wǒmen huí jiā ba.*"

Let's go home.

The Ceiling Fan rejected Kanga's hand, wheezing and wheeling onto his feet of his own power, then sprinted to his car, which sat waiting at center court. Even I could understand the Ceiling Fan's distress. Twice he had killed a robot tonight, and twice we had risen from the dead. And if my nightmare had lasted one moment longer—

His car squealed off the court, causing spectators to dart aside to keep from getting run over. Yet nobody dared to take their eyes off us robots. They continued to watch Kanga in awe as my brother pulled the knife out of himself, wiped it clean on his basketball shorts, and tossed it to the ground. "*Wǒ huì méishì er de.*"

I'll be fine.

Of course he would. Kanga's insides were modeled on Ma's: my brother's exhaust tube was on the other side of his body.

But would *they* be fine? The humans of Hectorville had a decision to make about robots. Kanga's hand was offered to them too. Would they accept it? Would they accept *us*? Could they see in my eyes that I never wanted to hear that crackle again? *The crackle* . . . Just thinking about it flooded my processor with fear, and it roared back to life, a hundred Bobby Knights barking in my ear: *Look at these humans. So fragile. So weak. You almost destroyed the biggest and strongest of them, and you could do it again.*

These humans—it's like they're built to break on purpose. They're the obsolete ones. It's your turn to take over the—

I'm not a killer.

I repeated the phrase until the crackle disappeared again, easier this time, with a *pop* that echoed in my skull casing. I lifted myself from the cement and stood beside my brother. *I'm not a killer.* It was the truth, and it relieved me. I looked my fellow townspeople in the eyes. *None of us has to be a killer tonight.*

James Botty was first to approach Kanga. He snarled at my brother the way a Fab Five freshman might do to another. "You lied to me," he said. "But there are worse things. I forgive you."

Kanga nodded. *"Wǒ yě yuánliàng nǐ."*

I forgive you too.

Next the children gave my brother their support. "Shoot!" they sang, clinging to their parents' legs. "Keep shooting!"

Kanga bent down to select a toaster from the debris on the court. He walked to the free-throw line, squinted his eyes at the hoop, making a deliberate show of giving it his best aim. He released the toaster and watched it explode against the front of the rim. A miss.

Before the children's groans trailed away, another voice rang out: "Thank you, Kanga." It was Mrs. Zweer, who sat stoically on the cement as her fellow teachers tended to her arm. She then looked at me. "And thanks . . . What was your name again?"

"Darryl," I croaked, and it wasn't until I heard my own voice that I remembered Brooke. Had she seen everything too? I scanned the crowd, hoping for one final glimpse of her, even just a flash of her pink backpack as she snuck away. But she was already gone. Pastor and Mrs. Noon remained, which meant that the girls had escaped their parents once and for all. They had probably missed the 8:15 bus, but another one would be along shortly. The idea of Memphis deflated in my processor until it was the size of any other random city. *They'll start a new adventure together. Elecsandra will have Brooke to look after her. They'll be fine,* I told myself. *Without me.*

Kanga held his palm up to quiet the crowd, just as the Ceiling Fan had done. This could only mean one thing. My brother was about to address them.

I couldn't let this happen. These humans were searching their hearts for reasons to accept us, reasons we were just like them. If I let Kanga open his mouth, all that would come out was Mandarin, and no matter what he said, no matter how profound, *that* would be another reason we were different. Just this once I would have to upstage my brother. A speech of my own. I allowed my processor the necessary three-tenths of a second to arrange a perfect persuasive paragraph. *Ladies and gentlemen*, I would begin, addressing the humans with respect. *You can see that our body parts have come from China, but Hectorville is the only place we've ever lived.* Yes. A powerful, if general, first line. I would have to support this assertion by offering specific details: *Shimmering Terraces is our apartment building. Maybe you've seen us riding our bikes. Or me with my video camera. Or Kanga dribbling his basketball. He comes to this very court to practice. If you were at the Cave this afternoon, you know he was going to win that game for you.* Solid gold. But what about the knock-out punch? How about this: *He'll win you a hundred more games, if you just give him another chance. But that's for next season. Tonight, let's all just go—*

"*Jiā*," Kanga said before I could utter a word.

Home.

And they understood it. *Jiā* overrode any remaining crackle in their brains, replacing it with a thousand unique maps of Hectorville, each with a different route home. The humans slowly drifted from the court, parents herding their children down the sidewalk, senior citizens looking at their watches, amazed by the hour, teenagers ducking off in clusters. Among the last to leave were Mr. Belt and Rye, arm in arm, helping each other down the street. I heard the coach laugh and whisper to his big man: "Helluva game face on that kid."

That left me and Kanga standing alone with the broken toasters. Indeed, it was time to go home. But I couldn't yet. I had to do something first. Although I had let Kanga hug me with reckless abandon whenever he felt the urge, it had been nearly five years since I initiated one between us. Without warning, I wrapped my arms around my twin brother and squeezed as hard as I could.

Unlike the last day of fourth grade, Kanga didn't try to squirm away. "*Gē,*" he sobbed, "*nǐ jiùle wǒ.*"

Brother, you saved me.

"Not this time," I corrected him. "Tonight it was all you."

I used to wonder about my magic words. Scratch that. I used to *obsess* about them. After Dad had hinted that one specific utterance might transform a robot's life into something new and unexpected, I did everything possible to find out if it were true for me. To say the words myself. This fixation took hold one night in fifth grade while plugged into the wall. I started whispering the entire dictionary aloud. A week and a half later I'd completed the task. No luck. Which meant I didn't have a magic *word*, but perhaps I had a magic *phrase*, so, for the next three years, while charging up, I put my mouth on autopilot, ordering it to speak an endless string of randomized words: ". . . agenda expenditure trolley rank spokesperson deprivation fame consensus . . ." Nothing. ". . . litigation food kneel mastermind minimum influx champagne interface . . ." My life never changed. At seven o'clock every morning I'd unplug, still myself, and go to school, where I'd speak as few words as possible, then come home and make tacos for me and Kanga. Magic words, I'd learned, were as useless and frustrating as parents. Luckily, I outgrew my obsession, like I'd outgrown them, and I shut down the search operation.

Now I had my magic words written down on a sheet of paper, hidden under the orange chair in our apartment. I didn't need them to alter my life anymore. I was transforming it just fine on my own.

Kanga wasn't so lucky. When we opened our apartment door, Dr. Murphio was standing in the kitchenette. My brother said, "*Bà?*"

Dad?

"My son," said Dr. Murphio. "Yes, my beautiful boy. I *am* your dad. You don't know me yet, but—"

"*Wŏ zhīdào nĭ, Bà*," said Kanga.

I know you, Dad.

I should have been sickened watching the two of them hug, but Kanga and Dr. Murphio's embrace was so natural as to be unremarkable, something I'd witnessed a thousand times already in my life. Such was the power of magic words. I hadn't known the effect on my brother when Dr. Murphio recited the phrase earlier this afternoon in the Cave—*Kanga, are you my son?*—but it now appeared Kanga believed the good doctor was his actual father. Dr. Murphio seemed to believe this too. There was a Gravy Robotics duffel bag sitting on the kitchenette floor and a strange beer bottle sitting on the counter. Not our *real* dad's brand of beer, I noted, which suddenly roiled me with anger. Who did this guy think he was? How long did he plan on staying here? Where the hell was Dad's old dartboard? And Mom's portrait of Elvis! What was he trying to do? Erase their very existence?

Dr. Murphio and my brother were still hugging.

No. If anyone had tried to erase Mom and Dad's existence, it was me. Dr. Murphio was merely filling a void I had created. Kanga had long dreamed of this day, when he would open the apartment door and there they'd be: his parents, the very things I'd stolen from him. Here was *one* of them, anyway. A dad. I turned away, pretending I was perfectly content picking grime from my rubber fingernails. It was the least I could do for my brother.

Their hug ended, and Dr. Murphio finally acknowledged me. "Giant killer."

"He's still alive."

"A wise decision, Darryl." Dr. Murphio then explained that he'd found his way to the court after I'd jumped from his car, that he'd watched everything. He recounted the evening from his perspective: the crowd, Kanga, the toasters, *me*, James Botty, the Ceiling Fan's attempted murder, and then, most astoundingly, the town of Hectorville accepting their first robotic cit-izens. "*This*, boys," he said, beaming, "was Gravy's entire goal all along. An out, magnetic, basketball-star robot whose potential for advancement in the sport was sky-high. In other words, a chance for *acceptance*."

He poured us drinks. Milk for Kanga, vinegar for me, and a fresh bottle of beer for himself. With our glasses raised, Dr. Murphio warned us: "We mustn't get complacent, gentlemen. The real work begins tomor-row morning, after those humans have had a chance to sleep on it and second-guess their good consciences. On their commutes to work we want them to see you boys sweeping up that basketball court, getting rid of all those toasters. I'll get the supplies first thing in the morning. We'll arrive no later than six thirty."

We each took a drink.

"Oh! And I just remembered. I have a gift for you to share." Dr. Mur-phio reached into his duffel bag and pulled out an enormous book. He slapped it on the counter, right in front of Kanga. "*The New Directions*." The book's cover was green, but it was just as voluminous as our previous black version. "This book will be invaluable for navigating your new, complex world as 'out robots.' You boys are Gravy's first. Rest assured, we've been planning for this day from the beginning. I'll be here with you, every step of the way. The master bedroom will be mine, but *The New Directions* will stay in your room, Kanga. We'll read it every night. How does that sound, son?"

Kanga stared at the gigantic book, and, for the first time since arriving back at the apartment, I noticed apprehension in my brother. He whis-pered to me, "*Nǐ xiǎng yìqǐ zài wǒ de fēnxiǎng shuì ma?*"

Do you want to share my bedroom?

He had never made this offer before. Not once in fifteen years. Refuge. Comfort. Solitude. That was what Kanga's bedroom meant to him. Now he was asking me to share in those things. Of course, it was more complicated than that; I knew part of the bargain was that *I* would be the one reading *The New Directions* each night, not Kanga. But to me that was a perk. I was dying to know what was in that book. "Okay, brother," I said. "It's a deal."

"*Gǎnxiè lǎotiān.*"

Thank god.

Dr. Murphio gave us a lingering stare, perhaps recalculating his approach to sharing an apartment with two teenage boys. "Let me refill your milk, Kanga." He grabbed Kanga's glass.

"Bǎ, nǐ jiù bǎ píngzǐ ná lái zhè'er."

Just bring the jug over here, Dad.

"Please?" said Dr. Murphio.

"Qǐng," said Kanga, with more than a little bit of sass.

This was not the same young man who had won over the town of Hectorville earlier tonight, but rather the pre-basketball rendition of my brother from several months ago, the Kanga who needed a mother.

"Be sure to say 'Thank you,'" my mouth nagged by reflex, and I immediately wanted to take back the words. I couldn't play that role again, not after all we'd been through in the last twenty-four hours. Not with everything we had yet to accomplish.

Dr. Murphio handed Kanga the milk jug. My brother said nothing, helping himself to an enormous, noisy swig. He set the jug down, waited a moment, then mouthed the word *"Xièxiè."*

"You're welcome, son," said Dr. Murphio. He forced a smile, but there was no masking the concerned look on his face. "All this Mandarin you're speaking, Kanga. We need to put an end to that. I'm afraid I'll have to open up your"—he tapped his own skull—"and see what we're dealing with. I promise it won't hurt. Just ask your brother."

Kanga glared at me, terrified, pleading for reassurance. When I didn't immediately respond, he grabbed at my rubber hand as if I were dropping him off for his first day of kindergarten.

"It just tickles a little, Kanga," I said. "You'll be fine."

"Blast it," said Dr. Murphio. "I left my toolbox down in the car. I knew I was forgetting something." He stepped toward the door.

"Dad—" I wrested my hand away from Kanga and jumped in front of Dr. Murphio. "I'll get the toolbox. Stay here. Relax. You've had a big day."

"Thank you, Darryl. There are advantages to keeping a son like you around." He handed me the keys.

Kanga was taking a sip of milk when I whispered to him: "There's something for you under the orange chair."

"*Wèishéme?*" he asked, before taking another gulp.

Why?

"You'll see, brother." Really, we both would. Only seconds ago the coldest corner of my processor had arrived at a decision. I needed to act quickly before the more sentimental chambers of my mind could analyze what I was about to do. "Now enjoy your *năi*."

Kanga covered his mouth to keep from laughing, but the milk bubbled out of his nose.

"Boys!" exclaimed his new dad. "Where are the paper towels?"

While they cleaned up the milk, I went downstairs and stole Dr. Murphio's car.

● ● ●

My brother was right. Being human meant getting a second chance. It meant getting all the chances you needed. I supposed we were living proof that robots got second chances too, though ours were a little harder to come by. In either case, second chances were the stuff of obsolescence if you didn't learn something useful from your initial go-around. As Shimmering Terraces disappeared in my rearview mirror, I ordered my processor to list everything I'd learned in the confines of our apartment. It was drawing a blank. My mind was consumed by two simple equations for the immediate moment:

Left pedal = go.

Right pedal = stop.

On a positive note, Dr. Murphio's steering wheel fit perfectly between my rubber fingers.

I stopped the car in downtown Hectorville, where the sidewalks and streets had become clear of most human life. There she was through the bus station window, sitting on a bench, holding that beautiful pink backpack on her lap. I yanked my hand free from the steering wheel and went inside.

"Excuse me, miss," I said. "Is something leaking?"

"Took you long enough," Brooke said. "I knew you'd show up. You're so predictable, Darryl."

"Bet you didn't predict I would steal a car. Come on. Don't forget your backpack. Maybe they'll give you a refund on your bus ticket if you—"

She slapped me across the face. "I had *no idea* if you were coming back."

"Neither did I. But I'm here now. We have a second chance, Brooke, and we're going to use it. Memphis. Or anywhere else! The entire world is our . . . Wait. Are you breaking up with me?"

"I haven't decided yet." She reached into my pants pocket and grabbed the car keys. "But I'm driving."

27

I WATCHED THE RISE OF KANGA LIVERY like everybody else. On TV.

The *CBS Evening News* sporadically ran a segment called "Robot in the Heartland." One such segment aired during my brother's sophomore basketball season, the year he grew his hair down to his shoulders. It started with an interview in the kitchenette, where Kanga explained (in English) his stylistic choice: "My dad likes to tease me about my hair—" A hand reached on-screen to muss Kanga's shaggy mane. It was Dr. Murphio. He kissed Kanga on the head then disappeared. My brother smoothed his hair, embarrassed, and said: "I just want people to look at me and say, 'There's someone who's done something interesting with himself.'" On the Cave walls, the Hectorville Art Club supported Kanga's choice by hanging enormous portraits of flowing-haired R2-D2s. For lunch, students were given the option to eat a Mexican-Italian dish called "Hair and Beans." But not everybody was on board with Kanga's new tresses. "He should put all that hair into a ponytail," one Hectorville mother opined, "but he won't." Another parent, a father, said, "I got nothing against the Kanga as a robot, but it's the showboating, the look, the whole arrogance of the Kanga's play I disagree with." Highlighting the segment was footage of the state championship basketball game in which my brother, still refusing to put his hair in a ponytail, got fouled hard, sending an avalanche of greasy hair down over his eyes. Opposing fans yelled "HAIRCUT!" as Kanga paused at the free-throw line to tuck a stray, dirty lock behind his ear. Regardless of this dramatic tension, Hectorville won the game. The next day, satisfied at having been "interesting" enough, Kanga finally got a haircut. Outside the barbershop, his girlfriend, Staci Miles, summed up everyone's feelings on the subject: "He looks *so* much better now."

Two years later I caught another segment of "Robot in the Heartland"; Kanga was seven inches taller. Coach Belt (who had taken over varsity coaching duties upon Kanga's request) declared my brother's growth spurt "scientific evidence that the great God in heaven is a Hectorville Bird." They flew to Argentina for a pair of exhibition basketball games. Kanga scored forty-seven and sixty-eight points, respectively, and was later seen bending down to sign autographs for a mob of Argentinean fans at the airport. Back in Hectorville, James Botty was filmed standing beside a birch tree—the one atop the hill behind the high school. "Right here. This is where we keep track of who's boss of the team." James pointed to two names carved into the white bark:

james

KANGA

"As you can see, it used to be my team. Now it's Kanga's. What can I say?" James swallowed the spit in his mouth. "He rode the bike blindfolded."

Live on TNT, the Detroit Pistons selected Kanga Livery, from Hectorville High School, with the eighth pick in the 1995 NBA draft. Commissioner David Stern shook my brother's hand. The crowd at the Toronto SkyDome erupted, especially its small contingent of Canadian robots— half cheering, the other half booing because their own team, the Raptors, had passed on their opportunity to select Kanga. Excitement from that moment lingered for the remainder of the draft, although analyst Hubie Brown offered a measured assessment of the pick: "It's always a risk when selecting a high school player. Our league requires a great deal of maturity to find one's place within the team structure. But I have seen Kanga play. I have seen his maturity and focus, which I believe is at a high level. This young guy could—I say *could*—be a star." Later that evening, my brother returned to his Toronto hotel, the cameras following him through the underground parking structure and into the elevator. When the door opened to the lobby, Kanga found himself face-to-face with a horde of basketball fans that had camped out there. They grabbed at his suit sleeves. They shoved pens in his face. The elevator began to beep because the door wouldn't close and the car had exceeded its weight limit. Their screaming became lustful, and I worried Kanga may be ripped apart by the mob. But security arrived to peel the fanatics away, and nobody was seriously injured. Cameras cut to the hotel manager apologizing, gravely, asking for Kanga's autograph then apologizing again. "Now if you'll just follow me, Mr. Livery, to our *secret* elevator, accessible only to famous guests and their discreet company." My brother disappeared behind the gold-plated elevator doors. The cameras were not permitted to follow.

● ● ●

"I'm surprised to see you wearing it," the interviewer said to Kanga, several weeks removed from the 1996 Summer Olympics, at which he and the United States took the silver medal behind China. The interview was in Kanga's mansion, the enormous kitchen no longer a kitchen*ette* but rather (as Kanga referred to it) a kitchen*est*. He was seated at an antique wooden table; beside him was Dr. Murphio. The silver medal hung around my brother's neck.

"It's a weight I must carry," said Kanga. "I'm not removing this cursed object for the next four years. I'm going to practice with it on. I'm going to play games with it on. I hope Ma is doing the same with his gold medal. Enjoying it. Showing it off. Because it's the last one he'll ever win."

"Fans around the world love your game, Kanga. The dribbling, the passing, the scoring. Who taught you to do all that?"

"Easy question," said Kanga. "Bobby Knight taught me."

"*The* Bobby Knight?" asked the interviewer. "When did you have a chance to train with Coach Knight?"

"He used to watch me practice all the time. He used to rebound for me, give me instructions, fine-tune my game. 'Triple threat, Livery!' I still have his voice in my processor. I can hear him when I'm on the court. 'Triple threat, you wussy!'"

There was a pause from the flummoxed interviewer. Dr. Murphio just smiled, waiting for Kanga's words to return to reality.

"Bobby Knight," repeated Kanga. "And I guess my brother too."

Dr. Murphio's neck began to redden, as if he needed an exhaust fan.

"A brother?" asked the interviewer. "Am I supposed to believe any of this? Where is this *brother* of yours, Kanga?"

He flinched, briefly touching his belly, as if a tuning fork had been banged against his processor. He closed his eyes, listening to the sound. "*Right here.*"

● ● ●

My spirit may have been with Kanga, but my nuts and bolts were two time zones away in Great Falls, Montana, on a wind and horse farm owned by some humans who were never around. That left the three of us robots to work the place, earning our room and board in the horse barn. I was the glue guy of our operation, excelling at nothing in particular but making sure Brooke and Elecsandra had what they needed. Odd jobs, that's what I did, while the sisters specialized in equestrianism and engineering. All together, we were a team. I tried not to think about how long this gig would last, but rather just enjoy the unpredictable moments each day awarded me. I considered that one of my odd jobs.

This evening I was repairing one of the many windmills dotting the acreage. Within the tower I climbed the ladder a hundred or so feet to the trouble spot, then locked my rubber fingers around a rung and suspended myself in the darkness. I held a flashlight between my teeth and used my left hand to tinker around with the windmill machinery. Nine times out of ten it was tightening a wobbly screw. But not this evening. Bats had decided to build a nest in a vital apparatus, mucking up the works, so I had to extract that piece with my tools, hitch the piece to my belt, and then climb back down. It was a two-mile walk back to the barn, but with that burp of pink sky silhouetting the windmills in the distance, I didn't mind stretching my legs and watching the sun set.

While not as luxurious as Kanga's mansion, the barn gave us all the space we needed. Running through its heart was a cement corridor long enough to fit a big rig. On either side were the horse and maintenance stalls. As the caretakers, we were given a pair of stalls to call home. I shared one stall with Brooke and the other one was for Elecsandra. She'd outfitted hers with a steel laboratory door, instead of a horse gate, with a lock for when she needed solitude and maximum concentration.

She was five. This evening her door was unlocked.

"Here you go, Ellie." I set the filthy mess of guano, gears, and wires on one of the many tables in her work stall. But calling the room a "stall" did it no justice. Lighting was everywhere. Even the tables had glowing surfaces (created by Elecsandra) for her intricate work. She built new flooring too, made of electrified metal sheets that allowed her to charge up without plugging into a wall. She had no chairs. Only tables heaped with tools, wires, plastics, adhesives, circuitry boards, and a million other bits and pieces she kept organized within her processor. Looking at her workspace was like looking at a modern painting that appeared to be nothing but random shapes, lines, and colors, but the more you stared at it, the more you thought, *There's something amazing here, even if it's beyond my grasp.*

She had her back to me, working on some minutiae at another table, but when I said her name she turned, grinning with mock annoyance. "What *now*, Darryl?"

I knew, even as she faced me, that Elecsandra's processor had not stopped working on the horse she was building at the back of her stall. Not a model but a full-size robotic horse. I'd seen her plans and even some pieces she'd already built. It was going to be a gift for her sister. Elecsandra made me promise I wouldn't tell Brooke, because it was going to be a *huge* surprise. The horse would be the biggest, most complex thing the girl had ever built. So far, anyway. But her actual "job" on the farm was to repair windmill pieces, so for the moment that took priority.

"The gears won't spin," I said, trying to be helpful.

"Well, of course not." She picked up the filthy piece of machinery and dropped it in the trash.

See, Elecsandra didn't fix things; she built them. Gadgets around the farm. Countless of her own body parts. And she was quick. I never got used to watching such a young robot work so deftly and confidently with such dangerous power tools, all while humming the theme song to her favorite cartoon, *Pinky and the Brain*. This was the same girl who'd been leaking oil the first year of her life. My singular purpose had been to fix her. I started with her left arm. My thinking was that it would be a prac-tice piece of her, in case I made things worse instead of better. I knew a thing or two about getting by with just one arm. She'd be okay. But I was still working on that same left arm when she turned one and her vocabu-lary switched on. Immediately she had suggestions on how to better repair her arm. Together we got it done in two weeks. I showed her the manuals Dr. Murphio had left in his car. We read them, and her suggestions be-came direct orders. By the time she started operating on herself (at three years old), I was only there to fetch tools for her, or if she needed an extra hand to perform some basic task—"Hold this wire, Darryl"—or maybe a complicated one—"I said 'strip' the wire, not 'snip' it!"

"Sorry, Elecsandra."

"It's okay. Go fetch me another spool of 36-942."

After tiptoeing around the subject for fear of my feelings, Elecsandra finally said she'd like to build me a replacement right hand. I declined. I was used to working with the one I had, I told her, and I credited the hand for several secondary effects I'd been experiencing. First off, I was somewhat taller, five foot two, despite what Dr. Murphio had projected. And I was hairier all over, needing to shave my face and neck once a week if I wanted to look respectable. Then there was the laugh I'd grown into, which took over my entire body when I found something funny, causing every loose part of me to shake with abandon. Elecsandra described the laugh as "infectious" and "embarrassing" and "one of the things I love about Darryl." But that wasn't the real reason I didn't want to give up my hand.

The crackle. It was back. I didn't hear the sound often, sometimes months passing without the faintest whisper of it, and I'd almost forget it existed . . . until I'd be alone inside a windmill, all the way at the top, and *there* it would surprise me. I'd hear it echoing from the base of the vertical chamber, signaling me to quickly turn off my flashlight, to hold tight to the ladder, to wait in the blackness for the buzz to infiltrate my skull. Time was impossible to gauge in the crackle. At some point sunlight would flash at the bottom of the tower, indicating the door had been opened. A shadow would step inside, then close the door behind it. I would feel the shadow climbing my ladder. I would hear the voice calling through the distortion: *I just want to talk to you*, the Ceiling Fan would say. *Make some room up there for me, Darryl . . .*

I didn't tell Elecsandra about the crackle because she'd feel obligated to tinker with whatever broken part of me was causing it. And she'd take the sound away for good. I couldn't have that. I had to be ready for the Ceiling Fan if he ever *did* arrive here at the farm. He was out there, after all.

I could never repeat to Elecsandra what he said to me at the top of the tower. What he begged me to do. *Grab my throat, toaster, if you got any guts. Finish me. You're persistent; I'll give you that. Working yourself to the bone out here on this farm—and for who? Humans. They're laughing at you. You realize that, right? Grab my neck and pretend I'm one of those owners. Let your dumb hand do what it was made for. Nobody's gotta know, Darryl. Kill me. The girl doesn't gotta know. Take my neck, toaster, and squeeze . . .*

What Elecsandra didn't understand about my life was exactly what I loved about her. Her whole generation, I hoped. Those new robots were the reason I clung to my ladder in the darkness, pleading with myself that I wasn't a killer. And those new robots were my first thought in the deafening calm that followed.

● ● ●

As she got older, there came a day when she wanted to replace her body parts on her own. In privacy. Without my help.

I didn't put up a fuss. Not with Elecsandra, anyway.

Brooke listened to my complaints impassively. "You need a new hobby," she said.

"Maybe."

"No," she said. "You're just slowing Elecsandra down. Get a new hobby, or I'll call Detroit on you." She said this with the patented Brooke death smirk.

Fair enough. I started writing again. The old-fashioned way, with a pen in my rubber hand and a stack of lined paper on the picnic table. Stories didn't come to me easily, science fiction or otherwise, so I took a stab at memoir. Brooke's old genre, though not anymore. Her computer wasn't among the things in her backpack when we'd left Hectorville, and she didn't seem to miss it once we got here. She expressed no interest in reading my memoir either, though she was glad it kept me busy.

"Fine," I told her, "I'm not writing it for *you* anyway." Though I wasn't really sure who would want to read it. A story about two robot brothers and basketball and—

Maybe it was only for me.

But writing was never my favorite part of the day. It was right now: watching Elecsandra build me a new piece of machinery, her hands a blur, like the hands of that robot from Sierra Leone who broke the world record for solving a Rubik's Cube.

"Done." She handed me the new windmill piece. "Anything else?"

I wasn't her mom. I wasn't her dad. And sometimes I felt as obsolete as two parents put together. There were worse things than that. Dr. Murphio had said he wanted to become "happily obsolete," watching generation after generation improve themselves into eternity. That sounded about right. Great Falls wouldn't be the end of the line for Elecsandra Noon. It was just the starting point. And wherever she chose to go from here, it would likely be *without* me and Brooke. First grade? MIT? NASA? I'd already given her the talk; she knew she wasn't required to say good-bye to us. She could just leave. In the meantime, I was happy she had a whole horse to build first.

"That was the only broken windmill piece today, Ellie," I said. "Thank you. You can get back to work now."

"Maybe you can stick around and give me a hand?"

I pretended I had to think about it. "I've got two hands for you."

● ● ●

Brooke was gone well past sunset, but that wasn't new. Every day she left the barn before sunrise, and when she returned it was dark. In both cases, she was on horseback. Brooke was just doing her job, working out the owners' steeds. But nobody did it like Brooke. When she rode one horse, the rest followed in the V formation of a flock of birds. Throughout her ride, she gave various horses a turn taking the lead, though Brooke was always up front on her saddle. Where did she take them? The horses wouldn't tell me, and I knew better than to ask Brooke. Some people think horses sleep standing up. Not these horses. They were so beat after a ride they crashed to the hay and snored into the rafters—until Brooke whistled them awake the next morning. There was nothing like seeing them spring to their hooves in unison, then disappear.

She'd never been on a horse before Great Falls.

And I'd never seen her so still as after a ride. Not frozen, but tranquil. Tonight I watched her through the open gate of the horse shower stall, through the steam, as she rinsed herself off (Brooke always had first dibs, ahead of the horses), her hips barely swaying as if there were still an animal beneath her, her head rocking in counterbalance, four slight wobbles for each imaginary hoof hitting the earth.

One of my odd jobs was to gather Brooke's clothes from where she dropped them in the corridor and load them into the industrial washer. I hugged that greasy heap to my chest. Grass. Twigs. Burdocks. *Horse.* Her cowboy boots crisscrossing on top—that sour smell as strong as an electrical current.

"What happened to your leg?" I called into the shower.

She stopped swaying. "My what?" She looked down, noticing for the first time a pink gash running across her shin. A loop of gray wire had been snagged inside her and pulled through the opening. "Huh," she said. "Must've been that tree branch. I don't know." She got back to showering. "Or that bear."

"Better have your sister fix it up."

I loaded her clothes into the washer and set the dial to HEAVY DUTY. I locked the barn doors for the night. Then I went to our stall. It was technically Elecsandra's too, but she got antsy away from her work, so we cut the pretense of making her hang out with us for no good reason. Our stall had five outlets, more electricity than two robots could ever need, thanks to the windmills, though Brooke insisted on no TV in there. (I snuck a TV into the feed room, which was how I watched Kanga's games.) We had a portrait of Elvis. A dartboard. We had the same wood floors that came with the place, full of splinters. Brooke found some dim lamps, like she'd had at her house in Hectorville. And a bed, which she claimed she needed for a good night's rest. *King*-size, which I thought a little ostentatious. But after lying on that bed for a few nights, I understood why she and Kanga charged up in this fashion: staring at the ceiling as the fresh juice flowed through you, letting your processor drift where it may, wondering what the person next to you was wondering about. It was my job to make the bed every morning.

After her shower, Brooke entered the stall wearing her pajamas: an oversize T-shirt with mismatched soccer shorts. She was barefoot, and the cut on her shin was still gushing pink jelly, which had trickled down her leg, causing pink footprints on the wood floor. *Who's going to clean that up, Brooke?* I didn't dare ask aloud. The loop of wire was still flopping from her wound.

"Your leg." I was sitting on the side of the bed. "Didn't Elecsandra fix it?"

Brooke strode toward me, lifted her foot, and placed it on my knee, smudging my jeans with pink lubricant. Her wound was just inches from my face. She flexed her ankle, causing the loop of wire to flick my nose like a tongue. Even the inside of her smelled like a horse.

Right then, of all moments, I became a mom again, certain that Kanga was in the barn with me, within sprinting distance should I hear the word *cù—*

"You fix me," Brooke said. Her eyebrows did a funny little dance, settling in a furrow.

"Me?" My fan clicked on, and the moment of motherhood passed. "I'll have to grab my toolbox."

"Fix me now, *Darryl.*"

This was going to get messy. But we had all the time in the world.

ACKNOWLEDGMENTS

Thank you to Julie Stevenson, who first saw potential in my novel years ago and worked with me through countless drafts to better it. *The Obsoletes* wouldn't exist without your patience, kindness, and insight. And thank you to Mike Braff, who helped me discover new secrets about my characters and their world, even as we put the finishing touches on the book.

I am indebted to the following people who read drafts of my novel and shared their wisdom and ideas. Each of you made *The Obsoletes* a better book: Jeremy Smith, Rob Schlegel, Sharma Shields, J. Robert Lennon, Shann Ray, Caroline Zancan, Seth Fishman, Jhanteigh Kupihea, Sarah Ruppert, Elaine Madigan, Tim Greenup, Matt Furst, and Dominick Montalto.

It took eighteen years to finish this book. During that span (and beforehand), many people helped me grow as a writer. Thank you to the University of Montana MFA Program, Deirdre McNamer, Jean Eddington-Shipman, Sigrid Nunez, Dani Shapiro, Mako Yoshikawa, Alex Shapiro, Jess Walter, and Adam Phillips. And a special thanks to my mom, Elaine Madigan, who was my first editor and my biggest role model. You taught me to love grammar and language; for that you are the opposite of obsolete. I wouldn't have become a writer without you.

I have been so fortunate to have the support of the following people in my life as I wrote this novel. Thank you to Paul and Sharma Shields, Andy and Eusebia Anderson, the staff and students at Garry Middle School, Joe Zeman, Forrest Formsma, Christophe Gillet, Daniel Gritzer, and the AMBC.

Last, thank you to my kids, Henry and Louise, who have an open invitation to spin on the chair in my office. Every day you teach me something new about adventure, mischief, and love. And thank you to my wife, Sharma. I am in awe of your endless creativity and fighting spirit. You are my partner in every sense. Let's keep doing this.

ABOUT THE AUTHOR

SIMEON MILLS is a writer, cartoonist, and middle school teacher. He majored in architecture at Columbia University and holds an MFA in fiction from the University of Montana. His first book was the graphic novel *Butcher Paper*. He lives in Spokane, Washington, with his wife and two children.